WITH A PASSION PUT TO USE

WITH A PASSION PUT TO USE

An Eisenmenger and Flemming Forensic Mystery

Keith McCarthy

severn
House

This first world edition published 2008
in Great Britain and the USA by
SEVERN HOUSE PUBLISHERS LTD of
9–15 High Street, Sutton, Surrey, England, SM1 1DF.

British Library Cataloguing in Publication Data

McCarthy, Keith, 1960-
  With a passion put to use
  1. Eisenmenger, John (Fictitious character) - Fiction
  2. Flemming, Helena (Fictitious character) - Fiction
  3. Pathologists - England - Fiction 4. Detective and
  mystery stories
  I. Title
  823.9'2[F]

  ISBN-13: 978-0-7278-6639-4   (cased)

All Severn House titles are printed on acid-free paper.

Typeset by Palimpsest Book Production Ltd.,
Grangemouth, Stirlingshire, Scotland.
Printed and bound in Great Britain by
MPG Books Ltd., Bodmin, Cornwall.

'I love you.'
'And I love you.'
A kiss.
'I'd do anything for you. Anything at all.'

One

Helena Flemming watched John Eisenmenger leave that morning with a crushing burden of melancholy, born of an unholy liaison between guilt and dread. The guilt was because she knew that John did not want to return to ordinary diagnostic histopathology, to its drudgery and pedantry; the dread was for her baby.

It had all started so well. Her initial worries that John would greet the news of her pregnancy with dismay had proved unfounded; indeed, she had been hugely elated to discover that the prospect of fatherhood was something he viewed not just with optimistic trepidation, but with the nearest he ever came to excitement. The first ultrasound scan had been another milestone apparently passed successfully: the pictures of the strange shapes had seemed so simultaneously alien and abstract, and breathtakingly beautiful and poignant. The movements of her child had been the most affecting thing of all, hypnotic and thrilling. On the two-dimensional screen, she could for the first time see that within her was a life, that she was responsible for something that was beyond value.

Over the weeks, her excitement had grown with her confidence, and her fears had receded. She began to enjoy the experience of pregnancy, and saw that John was equally delighted. It seemed that she was emerging from the darkness of life with cancer, that there was life beyond the threat of death.

It seemed . . .

Just a spot of blood.

And then another.

After a week, she went to Audrey Ackerman, her general practitioner, who sent her at once to the antenatal clinic, where again she saw pictures of her baby, but this time with a feeling of nauseous despair.

Yet it was not what she had feared. Still there was movement, still the spectral silhouette of a tiny human being that moved, whose heart still pulsed. She still had a child.

The placenta was low, however. Afterwards John explained that sometimes the placenta did not move up as the womb grew to accommodate its cherished parasite.

It took her a long time to build up the courage to ask the question that of course she wanted to ask, that mentally had taken her by the throat and was squeezing the breath from her body.

'Will I lose the baby?'

And everyone she asked said no, she almost certainly would not.

But this was not enough. She did not want '*almost* certainly would not', she wanted pure, 100 per cent, unadulterated, untouched by human hand, '*certainly* would not'.

Just after which the spotting stopped. First one day, then a second, then the days stretched into a week and nothing . . .

She had been ordered by John to stay at home and forget about work, despite the fact that their fiscal affairs were beginning to become yellowed around the edges, but she was on the upswing of the pendulum of her emotions and she accordingly decided to return to the office, with John reluctantly agreeing.

Which lasted two days.

She was reading through the papers on a case of alleged assisted suicide when, quite suddenly, she began to bleed, and bleed heavily. Her first reaction was terror, but anger soon supervened. She had done nothing strenuous – hadn't rearranged the office furniture, or ridden a bucking bronco in the lunch hour – so why was this happening?

Back to the antenatal clinic, back to the ultrasound scanner, back to the feeling of free-falling anxiety; back eventually, though, to the relief. Still there was a living, moving baby inside her, still she was a mother. They admitted her and forced her to rest in bed for nearly a week. The bleeding stopped after thirty-six hours but they refused to allow her to get up. A second scan was undertaken and still she was more than just a woman, still she was gestating.

When John had found this locum job at St Christopher's, a

medium-sized hospital on the outskirts of the small market town of Donnington, about 10 kilometres from the city, they had rented a small house in the town centre not far from the market square, so he would not have to commute and she would at least have different walls to stare at. She was barred from physical exertion of any kind and ordered to rest as much as possible, with only occasional walks for exercise, while John became yet again an NHS drudge in order to pay the bills. Thus far, it had largely worked: there was still some spotting but no overt bleeding. She was having weekly scans and had even grown slightly more used to the fear of what they might reveal.

It was scant comfort.

She often reflected on how stupid she had been to assume that pregnancy would be a time of unadulterated joy.

Two

A dam Dreifus did not hear his wife, Ruth, enter the room. 'Adam?'

Still he did not react, remaining completely motionless with his back to her. For a moment, she thought some medical catastrophe had occurred, that he had suffered some sort of seizure as he sat in his chair at his desk in the study, going through some paperwork.

Of course, it would be paperwork to do with the clinic, his obsession, his raison d'être.

'Adam?' This repetition was in a more urgent, strident tone.

He looked around. He was pale to the point of greyness; she remembered that her father had looked like that as he had lain in the chapel at the funeral home. She had thought at the time that he had been badly embalmed, and perhaps he had been.

She saw that Adam perceived her – at least the eyes turned to her – but she could see also that he took in little.

She came further into the room. 'Are you all right, Adam?'

He nodded, but it was so slow and so distracted it failed

to convince. If anything, it suggested that a mental malady was allied to the physical one.

'Has something happened?'

When he dropped his gaze to the royal blue pile of the carpet and kept it there, she came forward. Her intention was to go to him, to comfort him in what was clearly a state of shock, but this elicited immediate action from him. He stood up, still grey, still clearly in some sort of fugue state, but just sufficiently in contact with reality to say, 'Nothing. Nothing at all.'

That was a lie. Of course it was a lie. He looked as if he had just been given a one-way ticket to the crematorium, so whatever it was, it was hardly going to be 'nothing'.

But a lie about what? It could – it ought – to have been a white lie, a pallid thing that was as much a part of polite conversation as 'please' and 'bless you'. Only she had reasons for believing otherwise.

They had been married for twenty-seven years and she had thought until recently that she knew or suspected all of his secrets, but now she was beginning to wonder otherwise. He had changed, had become even more withdrawn from her, and all attempts to find out what was happening in his life met with denial of the situation.

Something was going on. And she had a strong suspicion that she knew exactly what it was . . .

He held out his hands, smiled a somewhat ghastly smile and said, 'It was just a dizzy turn.'

'You'd better sit down again, then.'

'Not here. Perhaps in the sitting room.'

They walked out of the study together, he allowing himself to be led by her. She noticed that his slight limp, the result of a childhood accident, was accentuated. When he was ensconced in the sitting room, she fetched him a drink of iced water, saying, 'You're working too hard, Adam. You can't keep it up. You can't do a full-time job in general practice and run the clinic.'

'I've got to.'

That was what he always said. *I've got to.* As if without the clinic he was nothing, a thing without existence.

In some ways she had always admired him for his dedication. It had always seemed to her to be a small positive from the catastrophe that was the death of Annabelle: devastation turned to devotion, grief to hope.

But she saw increasingly that it was eroding him, too. The long hours, the constant battle for funding, the failure to find success, all were eating into him. Once she had pointed out to him that, whether he found his particular grail or not, he could still count his life a success; at least, she had said, he had tried. The look he had given her had been enough to tell her that not only did he not agree, he despised her for such weak, cowardly talk. He was in a fight, she realized then, but whether he could ever win or not did not matter. It was the struggle that mattered, the struggle that formed the boundaries of his world. Without it, he would be forced to stare into oblivion and perhaps be absorbed by it.

'Why don't we take a holiday? We haven't been away together for nearly four years.'

But he was not listening. His colour had returned, or at least a pale caste of it, but his eyes had lost the look of normality and had regained a distraction that she found disturbing.

'Adam?'

This time he came back to her quickly, even tried to reassure, although he failed. 'Sorry . . . went off again there. I'll be all right in a tick.'

'What about a holiday? A cruise, perhaps. Do you remember our honeymoon?'

They had spent two weeks on a Caribbean cruise.

He smiled. 'How could I forget?' He patted her hand and said then, 'Maybe in a few weeks.' A smile forced its way to the surface. 'I've got to put that mirror up, first.'

She laughed at that, because it was a standing joke between them. He had been promising to put the antique mirror up in the sitting room for over a year.

'You're still beautiful, Ruth.'

She smiled, partly because she liked to hear his compliments, partly because she wanted to hear them and partly because she still needed to hear them.

When he had promised to rest for a while, she left him and returned to the kitchen. On the way she sneaked into the study to see what he had been looking at when she had found him so peculiarly absent.

She did not understand business, and she certainly did not understand the workings and machinations of Atopia, Adam's beloved clinic. She saw that he had been looking at what appeared to be accounts, but they meant nothing to her. On one of them, the one he had been holding as he had had his funny turn, she saw the name Anita Delorme.

Adam was dreadfully tired, but was it just because of too much work? Was it something a little more tawdry, a little more athletic?

She turned away and went to her handbag, where she had a scrap of paper on which was a name. She had picked it out of the Yellow Pages. She had no idea how good he was or how much he charged, but she had finally discovered one important thing.

She was desperate.

Perhaps this man – the private investigator – could help her. Perhaps he could tell her whether she still had a marriage.

Three

'If you have any problems, just ask me.'

Eisenmenger smiled and said politely, 'Thank you.'

'I know how daunting it can be, starting work in a new department.'

'I'm sure.'

'A microscope that's new to you, procedures that are unfamiliar, a strange laboratory. I appreciate that you may need someone to help you find your feet.'

'Fine.'

'You're on for autopsies today. Are you happy to do them?'

Eisenmenger's smile was beginning to feel slightly limp, wilted by the strain. Would the man never stop patronising him? 'More or less,' he said, keeping the sarcasm to an undertone. Not that Arnold Throckmorton was the kind of man to notice such adornment, not even if he'd been given a script with a clear stage direction. Eisenmenger even thought he saw a look of disbelief on the chubby face as the slightly protuberant ears took in the reply.

'Tomorrow you'll be doing the cut-up. It's often quite large. Do you think you'll be able to cope?'

Eisenmenger did not trust himself to speak.

'Don't hesitate to ask if you have a problem with any of the cases,' Arnold continued blithely. 'We have some quite complex cases here, you know. We do major ovarian and endometrial cancer operations. Colorectal, too.'

'If I run into difficulty at any stage, you'll be the first to know.'

Arnold evidently decided to give him the benefit of the doubt, although it was done with much reluctance. A nod and then, 'Welcome to St Christopher's.'

He left. Eisenmenger took a deep breath and wondered if he could stand the next three months in such company. At least, he reasoned, he was not alone with Dr Arnold Throckmorton: he had two more colleagues, Doctors Barry Schwartz and Chloe Branham. He had yet to meet them, but he could not believe they would prove as obnoxious as their head of department.

He looked around the office; it was cramped and depressingly gloomy. That he had spent half his working life in such offices did little to leaven his feeling of deep despair. He had hoped this was behind him – that his future would be spent working for himself, picking and choosing the work he did – but it had turned out otherwise.

He went to the window. It wasn't frosted but might just as well have been. The light rays that came through were only the strongest that had started out from the sun and even they had been weakened and diffused by the experience of battling their way through the grime. He had to practically press his nose against the glass to make out the outside world, and what he saw hardly made it worth the chilled, hard discomfort. The greyness of an ugly concrete building not 5 metres away, the sky a dull slit above, the street a dark strip three stories below. There was no sign that humanity still existed in the world he beheld beyond the glass.

'Oh, well,' he whispered, turning away to sit down at the bench on which an ancient microscope resided. It was gunmetal grey and cold to the touch, styled in a way that would have looked futuristic in the sixties and seventies when it was young. When he moved the objective lenses around with his hand, he felt a grating sensation from dust and glass particles that had taken up residence within its workings, and when he switched on the power there was a brief moment of illumination before a slight brightening and then darkness. The bulb had blown.

'You know, I don't think either of us should be here,' he murmured, sitting back with a sigh.

Four

I n the previous few weeks, Lambert had been uncharacteristically subdued, giving Beverley some relief from the usual low-level aggression he spread around her like an artillery bombardment designed to soften the enemy up and make them wish they were dead. Although this respite was not unwelcome, it gave her at the same time cause for concern, because she had read enough history to know that when the guns fell silent, an assault was on its way.

In retrospect, she had to admire his strategy. She had never before associated the habitually malevolent Chief Inspector Lambert with subtlety, and perhaps therefore she had underestimated him. Because she had expected the usual full-frontal assault, the realization that he had used psychology came as a shock sharp enough to leave her winded. Even as she came to appreciate the full scale of her reversal, she could admire the game play.

Detective Sergeant Larry Grover.

Lambert had introduced Beverley's new junior colleague with all of his customary peremptoriness; an effective cover, lulling Beverley into a completely erroneous sense of normality.

'Inspector Wharton, this is DS Grover. He's going to be helping you out.'

Larry Grover had stepped forward as Lambert stood aside. Beverley had stood up because a senior officer was in her office and she was always as respectful as she could possibly be to people she wished would curl up and die. She was immediately glad that she had, because when she saw DS Grover she knew she had a fight on her hands.

He was not quite as tall as Beverley, although he had wide shoulders and an upright posture. His hair was deep black and cropped short; his face was a paradoxical mix of humility and arrogance. In his blue eyes there was a look that she would not expect to see in a junior new to the station, one that lacked the usual nervousness, humility and desire to please. She was nonplussed, but not for long.

She held out her hand. 'Welcome.'

It was taken but without enthusiasm, as if he wondered where it had been or what particular pile of shit Beverley had been clawing her way through, and it was dropped after the briefest of clutches. He managed not to look at his palm to check for contamination but Beverley could see the desire so to do. 'Thanks.'

Lambert said, 'I'll leave you to get acquainted.' To Beverley in particular he said, 'Make sure DS Grover is made to feel at home.'

Beverley's gaze lingered on the door as it was shut. When she turned to her new junior colleague, she presented a façade that was neutral but that was also as welcoming as an electrified fence. 'That's your desk.'

She indicated the desk that had been untenanted for some weeks now. Despite this, it was not unoccupied, since Beverley had used it as a temporary storage depot, building small, untidy ziggurats of files. Grover frowned, looked briefly towards his new boss, then walked uncertainly to his new abode. 'What shall I do with these?'

'The floor.'

'Shouldn't they be filed?' He indicated the four filing cabinets behind the desk.

'Those don't live there.' Beverley did not understand why he should believe they did. 'Those are case files. They've come from Records in the basement.'

Grover nodded.

The question had been odd, not one she would have expected from a reasonably experienced DS, even if he were new to the station.

'Where have you come from?'

'Shropshire. Telford.'

He might just as well have said the moon for all it meant to Beverley.

'And how long have you been a Detective Sergeant?'

He stopped suddenly in his labours, his eyes as they beheld his new boss suggesting something that might have been embarrassment, or that might have been a challenge.

'Officially, three weeks.'

'What?' Beverley was so startled she did not realize she had spoken until she heard the word slip past her ears.

'Three weeks.'

Beverley hesitated, then nodded slowly, her eyes refusing to shift from her new helpmeet, as the ramifications of this titbit of information percolated through her neuronal pathways. She asked in measured tones, 'And before that? How long were you a DC?'

'Ten years . . . '

She made no reply to this, as she was wondering why he sounded guilty, and he found himself forced to add, ' . . . in Scenes of Crime.'

'SOCO?' Beverley did not bother to hide the incredulity, unless it was beneath a fine lacquer of contempt.

Grover nodded.

'And you decided to transfer?'

'I wasn't getting much satisfaction from it.'

Beverley took this datum and added it to the growing store of information that was suddenly appearing behind her eyes.

'So in terms of experience as a detective, you've got, precisely . . . three weeks?'

'Not even that, really. Until Friday I was still working as a SOCO, waiting for a posting.'

Beverley opened her mouth but could dredge up no words to meet the situation. Grover said then with some defiance, 'I passed the promotion board with a commendation.'

She saw it all, now. Beverley had been given the equivalent of a toddler. He was, in summary, a handicap, shackles around her ankles and wrists. Beverley's efficiency would be reduced; she might even fail in a case, perhaps fatally.

She sighed. 'Fan-fucking-tastic.'

Grover's reaction to this was immediate. 'There's no need for language like that.'

Appreciating that perhaps this babe in arms had claws, Beverley replied, 'Isn't there?'

'There's never a need for profanity.'

'Why not? What's wrong with it?' Beverley genuinely could not see the problem.

Grover hesitated before answering, 'I just don't like swearing.'

Beverley snorted. 'If you don't like swearing, what are you doing in the police? Or don't they swear in Shropshire?'

'They understood. Toned it down when I was around.'

'Nice of them.'

Grover's mouth curved down at the corners; he was apparently for the first time embarrassed. Beverley enquired, 'Anything else I should know about you?'

'Not especially.'

'Are you married?'

'No.'

'Girlfriend?'

'No.'

'Boyfriend?'

He coloured. He actually coloured. 'No!'

Which Beverley found interesting. She smiled and nodded and for the moment asked no more questions. Grover resumed his transfer of files from the desk to the floor. Only when he had finished did Beverley ask, 'What did Lambert say about me?'

'What do you mean?' His eyes were large, certainly large enough for wariness and not a little alarm to be seen behind them.

'He gave you a little biographical detail on me. He always does.'

Beverley enjoyed his discomfort and was quite sorry when it ended, except that instead of the prevarication and dishonesty she had expected, she was given what appeared to be a verbatim account of what he had been told.

'He said you were a whore.'

This short but undeniably expressive description of her, with its biblical overtones, left Beverley slightly stunned and, in consequence, she was beaten to her turn in the dialogue by Grover.

'He also said you cut corners and that you were not a little corrupt. Oh, and that you were a nymphomaniac.'

In an attempt to introduce some levity, Beverley asked, 'Isn't that the same as a whore?'

This was the point at which she began to discover that Grover was not cursed with a sense of humour. 'Not at all. A nymphomaniac has a psychological illness, whereas a whore has merely subordinated her moral framework to her need or desire for money or other advantage.' Grover, somewhat belatedly discovering a sense of propriety, added, ' . . . Sir.'

Beverley leaned forward, forearms flat on the desk, the back of her left hand on the palm of her right. 'Thank you for that, Grover. I must admit I wasn't expecting to receive the truth in such a straightforward manner, but at least I know where I stand.'

Grover opened his mouth, exposing teeth that were both plentiful and dazzling, but before he could proceed with the business of speech, Beverley continued, 'Now, I'll tell you my side of things. I think Lambert's a stuck-up, stupid bigot. I think my superior officer couldn't find his backside with both hands in the dark. I think that I don't much care what Chief Inspector Lambert thinks.'

It was patent that Beverley's new detective sergeant held great respect for their boss. 'I'm not sure you should be saying things like that about a chief inspector.'

Beverley laughed. 'Aren't you? I am.'

Grover seemed to have decided against shock and was heading into outrage. 'Chief Inspector Lambert . . . '

Beverley stood up abruptly, tired of this subordinate and his straight-laced certainties, not least because they had been given to him by a man whom Beverley considered to be a waste of genetic material. 'Look, Detective Sergeant Grover, did you defend *me* to Lambert when he assassinated *my* character?'

Grover hesitated, which meant that Beverley already knew the answer when she was told in a low tone, 'No, I didn't.'

Beverley greeted this with grim satisfaction. 'I thought not.'

'I . . . '

'And *I* . . . ' interrupted Beverley, 'don't give a shit what you've got to say. You're *my* DS, not his. You're going to be working with *me*, not him.'

'There's no need . . . '

Beverley could hardly believe what she was hearing. 'No need? No need to swear, you mean?'

Grover's eyes were wide, his mouth rapidly resembling them, but Beverley was not particularly interested in his answers. She was a detective and she had a mystery in front of her that she wanted to solve. 'What the bloody hell are you, Grover?' In truth she was now swearing just to provoke him. 'You're a copper who doesn't swear, and you clearly have an arse as tight as a nun's twat. What's going on? Is there a new branch of the police? Uniformed, CID, Special Branch and now the Prick Platoon?'

Grover was staring at her as if he were in an alley unexpectedly confronted by a mugger. There were several moments during which Beverley was half-convinced he was going to lash out at her, that she had pushed him too far. It would not have been the first time she had pushed someone – a suspect, a rival, even a colleague – beyond the point of normal response.

Yet Grover did not oblige. After a minute, maybe more, he clawed back his composure and said in a calm, almost condescending tone, 'I know you're deliberately trying to provoke me, but I won't react. You may despise me, but that doesn't make you anything worth emulating.'

Beverley shook her head tiredly. 'I don't despise you, I just don't understand you.' She thought a while, then tried again. 'You do drink, don't you?'

'Occasionally.' This was offered so cautiously that Beverley had no confidence she was in for a string of boozy nights out with him.

Into Beverley's despair, Grover added in a low tone, 'I believe.'

'Believe? Believe what?'

Possibilities floated through Beverley's mind: pictures of leprechauns, flying saucers and Elvis dressed as a burger chef bobbed up before her eyes, even as she knew the dreadful truth.

Grover confirmed her fears. 'I believe in the one, true Lord.'

Grover, having established a bridgehead, advanced, stopped and then stood on top of a soapbox. 'Police work and Christianity aren't exclusive. The police are a force for good in the world. We battle evil, just as Jesus did, just as his disciples taught that we should.'

Beverley, perhaps to her credit, had never thought of herself as a 'force for good', in either her dreams or her actions. She was more of the opinion that she was marginally better than the opposition, and not only was that good enough but it was also extremely useful. Grover, though, had found his place in the text and was delivering the sermon with gusto.

'Without us, society would collapse, the forces of evil would run rampant, the innocent . . . '

Beverley said loudly, 'OK. You've convinced me.'

Grover, disappointed that his proselytizing had been interrupted and unconvinced by Beverley's offhand attitude, was not for giving up. 'Have you ever considered . . . ?'

'Don't even think about it,' was the advice he received, which ended matters.

There was silence for some time after that, while Grover rearranged his new desk and Beverley harboured dark thoughts. She now understood the enormity of the blow that Lambert had dealt her.

Five

Clive was an unlikely source of happiness to anyone. He was short and slightly swarthy, with hair that was unnaturally shiny. He wore a grey moustache and was permanently chewing. with a sour expression on his face, as if he could not quite believe that he was masticating putty and not gum.

To Eisenmenger, though, this unprepossessing, not to say slightly repellent, sight was the first good thing he had seen at St Christopher's.

'Clive!'

'Hello, Doc. Small world, ain't it? How's tricks?'

He was smiling as only Clive could: mostly right-sided and decorated with eyes that held something of the cynical about them. He had opened the door to the mortuary in answer to Eisenmenger's ring and now stood aside.

As he walked through, Eisenmenger said, 'I didn't know you were here.'

'Yeah. Two years now.'

He led Eisenmenger through a short hallway into a window-less office on the left.

'Tea?'

Clive seemed to have an insatiable need for the stuff. Eisenmenger wondered if the lining of his intestines resembled the insides of an unwashed teapot, and if without a constant supply he would crumble into dry, tea-less dust.

'Why not?'

The office was long and without natural light. A desk at one end held the inevitable computer, and there were two easy chairs along one wall, and a table with a kettle and tea-making equipment at the other end. While Clive made a brew, Eisenmenger sat in one of the easy chairs. Over the desk there was a calendar on the wall that Eisenmenger knew he should not be staring at.

'You don't take sugar, do you, Doc?'

Eisenmenger caught Clive's knowing smirk as he unglued his eyes from the soft-looking, curvy flesh and swung his head around to say, 'No, thanks.'

Eisenmenger took a gulp from the mug Clive handed him, and found that it was exactly as he remembered Clive's tea – hot, wet and tasting strangely of paint stripper. Or, perhaps more likely, embalming fluid.

He asked, 'So how does Dr Throckmorton compare with Professor Russell?'

Clive laughed. His was a deep, throaty chuckle, one that Eisenmenger had seen have a curious effect on those possessed of a double portion of X chromosomes. 'Well, he's not a complete and utter shit,' he said.

'That's a relief.'

'Mind you, he's crap at autopsies.'

'In what way?'

Clive scowled. 'Everyone dies of heart disease round here.'

'Oh, I see. One of those.'

Clive nodded sagely. 'And he reckons to complete the PM in ten minutes.'

Eisenmenger, who had performed probably 3,000 autopsies in his career, normally took at least thirty minutes and, if the case was complex, often closer to an hour. Suspicious deaths could see him in the dissection room for six or more. 'Cut and thrust?'

'Yeah. He's got a thing against slicing the brain, too. I usually end up doing it.'

Almost all aspects of the work of a pathologist were open to external assessment; the only exception was in the mortuary where no one but the technician saw what went on.

'What about the coroner?'

'What about him? The coroner's taken in just like most other people. He thinks that when Dr Throckmorton farts the fairies get up and dance.'

'Oh, dear.'

'I've given up with him. I do my job and let him get on with it. I wouldn't mind but in the past I've tried to help him and what thanks did I get from Gee-gee? Sweet fucking Fanny Adam. He just takes the credit.'

'Gee-gee?'

Clive finished his tea, apparently oblivious to the strange flavours within it that were making Eisenmenger fear for his stomach lining. 'He thinks he's God's gift to pathology. G.G., see?'

Clive gave everyone nicknames. Eisenmenger knew that his own was Doctor Death.

'What about his colleagues?'

'Chloe's all right. A bit of a weed, but nice enough. I call her 'Sweet Pea', because I reckon a good hard frost would kill her. Barry's winding down to his retirement at the end of the year. Mind you, I reckon Peter Rabbit's been winding down for most of his career. Just wants a quiet life. That's why Gee-gee can lord it over everybody, because there's no one to stand up to him.'

It sounded to Eisenmenger like a department from hell and he was immensely relieved that he would be in it for only a few months.

'So what have we got today?'

'Only one. A collapse. Nothing special.' He handed Eisenmenger a typed sheet that had been sent by the Coroner's Office.

Edward Ernest Melnick, aged 56 years. Found dead by his wife when she awoke yesterday morning. Had been out the night before. Was known to be a heavy drinker. Mrs Melnick called an ambulance but resuscitation was not attempted. There are no suspicious circumstances.

There never were. Eisenmenger had once read a coroner's report in which a man had been found with a stab wound in the back and it had concluded with the frankly incredible statement that there were no suspicious circumstances. In fairness, after several hours of hard work and much ratiocination, Eisenmenger had eventually concluded that the wound *could* have been self-inflicted and, since the deceased was known to be suicidal and psychotic, and since he was found in a room locked from the inside, no one else had been sought in connection with the death. Yet that anyone could have concluded that there were 'no suspicious circumstances' a bare six hours after the incident was something Eisenmenger would never be able to comprehend.

'Shouldn't take us long.'

'That's what I thought. Do you want to check the body before I open it up? Then you can get changed.'

Eisenmenger stood up. 'Fine.'

Janet Lennox was in the garden when she heard the front door slam shut, caught by the wind. A few moments later she heard the deep, almost thunderous growl of Donald's ridiculous car starting up. She held the secateurs in her hand, the dead head of a rose between their curved blades, as if she were deliberately toying with it prior to execution, sadistically teasing it, making it wait for its end. As the sound of the car faded into the distance, the dying bloom's tenure on this mortal realm was abruptly ended with a swift snip. There was something unnecessarily aggressive about the act.

The sun, previously bright, had gone behind a tall bank of grey and white cloud and the temperature around her had dropped; dropped inside her as well.

Where was he going?

She had given up asking about his movements many years before. Donald had always thought he could lie and lie effectively, but he could not. She was able to detect at once his deception and it was now too hard to disguise her own disappointment, too painful to act along with him.

She could even guess who it was. That girl who worked

for Adam Dreifus, she was sure. She had seen Donald's face when he had first seen her at the practice party the Christmas before last. It was an expression with which she was all too familiar. Was it three or four times now that he had indulged himself in this way?

She smiled, but it was not an expression of anything other than self-pity.

She had loved him once and she knew he had loved her, but she was experienced enough in life to know that love was not a static thing. It was born, grew, grew old and then died.

Hers, she knew, had lain mouldering in the grave for many years now.

Six

E isenmenger sat in front of the dictation machine after the autopsy and wondered what Edward Melnick had been like in life. He could only reflect that, if he had been as diffi-cult and irritating as he was proving in death, Eisenmenger was immensely glad not to have known him.

Even as these words danced a small samba around the back of his thoughts, he sought to quash them. It was the wrong attitude. He should enjoy the challenge, welcome the oppor-tunity to escape from the tedium of yet another humdrum corpse. Just because the cause of death did not leap out at him immediately, it did not mean catastrophe was looming.

It was his experience of recent events that was causing him to be pessimistic. Helena's troubles were taking their toll on him as much as they were on her. Just as he could see the strain around her eyes, in the movements of her hands, the thin line of her lips even as she slept, so he could feel it within himself, pinning him down, tightening his muscles, weighing down on every thought, every idea, every smile.

Come on, now. Just do what you've always done.

The main cause of his frustration was that he had been

expecting this to be quick and easy, a pleasant introduction back into routine autopsy work, and this expectation had proved ill-founded. Edward Melnick had been a heavy drinker and more often than not the internal organs of heavy drinkers proffered abundant reasons for which their owner should have failed to maintain a tight grip on this woe-filled world: oesophagitis, gastritis, cirrhosis, portal hypertension, lobar pneumonia, pancreatitis, tumours of the upper gastrointestinal tract . . . The list was long and varied and spectacularly lethal. Moreover, even if one of these was unaccountably missing from the entrails that Eisenmenger carefully disinterred and then sliced and diced, almost always the effects of the asso-ciated habits of heavy drinkers – smoking, poor diet, lack of exercise – were there to make sure the patient displayed on the dissection table had a good reason for being there.

Almost always, but not inevitably.

As was the case today.

He found no evidence of an infection, nor had Melnick had a significant bleed into the gut; the pancreas had not raised a protest by exploding its enzymes all over the abdominal cavity and the liver had courageously withstood the effects of a prodi-gious ethanol intake. There was no cancer and no significant lung or heart disease.

It happened, though, Eisenmenger told himself. Sudden death occurred in heavy drinkers, a fleeting visitation from the Man in Black that left few clues for the eager young pathologist. It even had a name, because as in black magic, so in science, and to name it was to gain power over it. *Sudden Unexplained Death in Chronic Alcoholism – SUDCA.* Which was exactly the equivalent of naming lights in the sky *UFOs,* thereby appearing to make the unexplained something under-stood, while doing nothing of the sort.

SUDCA was a diagnosis of exclusion, the only positive finding being fatty change to the liver, of which Edward Melnick was possessed, albeit to a small degree. In order even to contemplate writing it on a death certificate there had to be no other apparent cause of death. Eisenmenger would have to take extensive samples of the organs to look at under the microscope and thus confirm the naked eye appearances, and he would also have to undertake full toxicological analysis of blood and urine.

He called out to Clive. 'Full tox, please, Clive.'

Clive looked up from his labours as he sewed the scalp back over the skull of their patient; a skull that now contained not grey matter but cotton wool. 'You're joking!'

'Sorry.'

'You don't know why he died?'

Eisenmenger shook his head.

'He smells of booze,' Clive pointed out.

Which was true but, alas, of insufficient scientific rigour to allow Eisenmenger to deduce the cause of death. Death from acute alcohol poisoning did occur but was rare in heavy drinkers and would most certainly require accurate biochemical measurement of the level of ethanol in the blood. Eisenmenger felt it unlikely that Clive's nasal apparatus was sufficiently quality-controlled to satisfy the coroner.

'Nevertheless . . . '

Clive returned to his sewing, exuding consternation and discontent in approximately equal measures, while Eisenmenger returned to the organs. They were still arrayed on the dissection board, cut open and arranged in slices, and he began to dissect out small pieces for histological examination. 'I'll need a pot of formalin.'

This was produced without comment.

Having put the tissue samples into the pot, and while Clive began to massage the limbs in order to persuade recalcitrant blood to seep from its dark hiding places within them, Eisenmenger dictated his report on to tape before turning to the phone. He would have to ring the Coroner's Office and he wondered how this call would be received.

As it turned out, badly.

It started well, in that the voice who answered the phone was female and, when he introduced himself, welcoming. 'Oh, yes. Dr Throckmorton said you'd be helping us out over the next few months. I'm Jean Grentz, one of the coroner's officers.'

Which was nice.

She asked then, 'Have you rung up to give the cause of death on Mr Melnick?'

'Yes, and no.'

'Oh?' Her tone informed him that she did not quite follow.

'I'm going to have to do further investigations, I'm afraid. I'll need full toxicology and I'll have to look at some histology.'

There was a pause. It was a pause that he could imagine was filled with subvocalization on the part of Jean Grentz. Then, 'So when will you have some idea of what he died of?'

'I can get the histology done by tomorrow but the toxicology isn't really up to me, is it? If you can pick it up this afternoon, I suppose a few days?'

'But what do I tell the relatives? What about the coroner?'

'Tell them that at present it's unascertained.'

More subvocalization, then she made a grab for a lifeline she thought she saw in the conceptual undergrowth. 'But it will be natural, won't it?'

Eisenmenger did a bit of subvocalization of his own. He had come across this attitude in coroner's officers on the odd occasion before. They seemed to view his job as limited to finding a natural cause of death, regardless of what might really have happened. 'If I knew that, I wouldn't need to do the investigations, would I?'

He heard the beginnings of panic in her next words. 'But this means I'll have to open an inquest.'

'And it would be quite useful if you could make some enquiries, get me a little more information. Such as the precise circumstances of how he died, medical reports, that kind of thing.'

There was a long pause, at the end of which he was beginning to fear she might have come over all faint. He was actually about to speak when she opined, 'I'm not sure what the coroner is going to say about this, Dr Eisenmenger. He's not used to this kind of thing.'

Not used to what? Eisenmenger was unclear on the point and made his own enquiries for clarification.

'Well, this uncertainty,' she explained. 'Dr Throckmorton and the others always give him a definite answer there and then. It saves time.'

'I see.'

'And money.'

'Of course. Very commendable.'

'So, you see . . . '

He remained polite, although he felt like being otherwise as he interrupted her. 'I'd still like the toxicology and histology reports before I give a cause of death.'

She agreed because she had to, but he felt fairly certain he had not started well in his temporary career at St Christopher's University Hospital.

Seven

Helena had always been an intensely private person, a near obsession made worse by the tragedies of her past. For nearly nine years since those terrible events she had known deep within her soul that the world was an evil place, and that the only safe way to live was to be separate from it. Yet her enforced rest placed her deeply within a quandary. Dr Ackerman had told her that a short walk every now and then would not harm the baby – would probably help – but she did not wish to go out. She was happy in her own womb. She was finding, however, that not to do so was slowly increasing her insanity. She had heard of cabin fever and had assumed it was an urban – more properly perhaps, a rural – myth, but she now discovered there was truth at its heart.

She had to get out.

There was a small park nearby. It was fairly well-tended, with the grass kept short and the beds weeded. There was a shallow pond with a fountain at its centre, and paths curving away into more secluded areas where occasional park benches rested in the shade.

Getting there, though, was not easy for her. It seemed to her that she had been ill for a long time now – first breast cancer, then a pregnancy that was teetering on the jagged edge of miscarriage – and this had preyed upon her, making her feel vulnerable almost to the point of rawness. As she walked the short distance to the park, she felt like a hermit crab far from her shell and she started to feel dislocated, divorced from all that was around, even from the memories that defined her. She seemed only to be living her life in a weirdly extenuated way, as if existence were being stretched and all the flavour removed; as if she were a ghost of herself, haunting the places around her.

For all the medical diagnoses she had been given over the past few years, there was in her heart a fear that she was fundamentally diseased, in some way *wrong*. Why did she have to develop cancer at such a young age? And why couldn't she have a straightforward pregnancy? Why did it have to be complicated, on the edge of disaster? Was she tainted, perhaps genetically misprogrammed?

She had mentioned these fears to John and he had pointed out gently that there was nothing that connected breast cancer and a low-lying placenta. She knew he was right, but that didn't stop her wondering if in some way she was cursed, if the lack of a rational explanation for these problems coming one after the other meant only that there was an irrational one.

The happiness of her childhood had not just been lost, it had been macerated in front of her, slaughtered as savagely as her parents. The reverberations of that event seemed still to be sounding through her life, affecting every part of her existence, even now. She still felt bitter when she saw the happiness that others derived from family life; even the presence of John in her life had not been able entirely to blunt her anger.

She came out of her thoughts and found herself in the park, walking past tended flowerbeds and the moss-specked granite fountain. The morning sun felt good on her skin, the air might even have been as fresh as she thought it to be. A woman pushing a double buggy was coming towards her. She looked worried and tired, the buggy heavy with shopping bags hung from the handles. The children, no older than two, were asleep; they were dressed identically, even down to shoes that were tiny and made of navy blue, shiny leather.

Twins.

Helena stopped and just watched as the woman walked past her, uninterested in her presence.

There was a sudden and painful twinge of sorrow behind Helena's eyes as she realized that she would give anything – and she meant, literally, anything – to be in that woman's position, to have her reasons for being tired and worried, rather than the ones she had at present.

Despite herself she began to cry, then hated herself for being so weak and showing her feelings in public. Hurriedly she walked to a nearby bench, sat down and pulled a handkerchief from her sleeve.

And she began to bleed.

That same morning Eisenmenger was confronted by a depressingly obese pile of pots beside the cut-up bench. These varied in size from small through to enormous; the smaller ones were transparent, the larger ones of white plastic. One was so large – the size of a small toddler – it could not be accommodated on the bench and thus sat on the floor, as if in disgrace.

'Oh, God.'

Sitting at a computer opposite was a girl of about twenty-five or thirty with bobbed hair of grey highlights and, Eisenmenger soon discovered, the broadest of Birmingham accents. When Eisenmenger uttered his supplication to his creator, she turned and said commiseratingly, 'It's quite a pile, isn't it?'

'Is it always this bad?'

'On Tuesdays.'

He sighed. It had not escaped his attention that the rota for the month ahead had him down for cut-up every Tuesday; it was part of the locum's burden. 'When do you want me to start?'

She looked at the clock on the wall in front of her. 'It'll take me at least an hour to book these in. Shall we start at ten, after I've had coffee?'

Which suited Eisenmenger. Before he returned to his office, he found the laboratory chief and requested that the histology from Melnick's post-mortem be hurried through to him. This caused some amusement.

'Oh, yes. The post-mortem.' Derek Zoon's tone was mocking. Large and tall and coming to the end of his career, he wore glasses on a cord around his neck and bright blue braces that curved over his rotund chest and abdomen, splaying apart slightly at the most protuberant point, like lines of longitude on a planetoid.

'Is there a problem?'

There was a shake of the head that might have suggested there was not; everything else about him, however, whispered that there was. 'We'll try.'

Eisenmenger recognized the phenotype. There was constant, low-level hostility between the technical and medical staff in many labs and it was usually the lab chief who was the point of focus for this. Frequently, lab chiefs saw themselves as the real heads of the laboratories, with the medical staff a sort of irritating encumbrance: dilettantes who were possibly necessary but nonetheless to be put in their place at every possible opportunity.

'Can you do more than just try? It is rather important.'

'We have 200 blocks to cut and stain today, doctor. They're important, too.'

Not strictly true, as they both knew well. There would be some which were urgent, the diagnosis required as soon as possible, but the majority would be routine – warts and skin tags and biopsies of normal tissue done as part of defensive medicine – and therefore not necessarily to be reported that day.

'I believe the council give the department a not inconsiderable sum for the coroner's work.'

Zoon frowned. 'So?'

'So, I think that on the odd occasion when circumstances demand it, this department should place some priority on any work generated by the coronial practice.'

Zoon hesitated, still frowning. Eisenmenger could almost see the debate going on behind the eyes. Should he slap this incomer down? Or should he acquiesce before the stakes were raised?

After a moment's hesitation, he said, 'I'll see what I can do.' And with that he turned and stalked back to his office.

Back in his office, Eisenmenger began to authorize reports on the computer, a task that was never enjoyable and always boring. It was bad enough when the computer system was familiar, was made synergistically worse by a strange one. Even the straightforward reports took him two or three frustrating minutes. He found the whole process somehow paradigmatic of his situation.

He had nearly finished when Arnold Throckmorton found him, entering the room quite abruptly and without knocking.

'Come in,' murmured Eisenmenger, words that were wasted because Dr Throckmorton was clearly not a man who ever found it necessary to listen.

'Ah, John.' This was uttered as if he could not suppress his astonishment at finding Eisenmenger not only in his room, but actually working. 'Can I have a word?' This was purely rhetorical, for he continued before Eisenmenger had even parted his lips. 'I've had a call from the Coroner's Office.'

Eisenmenger discovered only resignation within himself. 'Oh, yes?'

Dr Throckmorton sat himself down with a sigh in a chair at what was nominally Eisenmenger's desk. 'You've upset them.'

Eisenmenger felt strangely elated. 'How?'

'The case yesterday . . . you didn't give them a cause of death.'

Eisenmenger orchestrated his facial muscles into what he thought was quite an authentic frown of consternation, even retracting his head slightly as he did so. 'And?'

'You should have done.' Dr Throckmorton sounded as if he could not quite believe that he had had to say this.

'Should I?'

Throckmorton leaned forward confidentially. He was almost close enough to touch Eisenmenger on the knee and there was a ghastly moment in which this scenario blossomed into garish possibility in Eisenmenger's head. 'We don't usually do toxicology except in road traffic accidents and when we know there's been an overdose.'

'But surely there are cases where you haven't got a convincing natural cause?'

This was apparently a novel concept to Eisenmenger's head of department. 'Not really.'

Eisenmenger felt a wave of melancholy wash through him. 'Never?' This was just to ensure that he had heard correctly, although he knew he had.

'No.' This was compounded a second later by a statement that left Eisenmenger feeling winded. 'There's always something that might have killed them.'

Fighting the urge to blaspheme, Eisenmenger said as blandly as he could, 'There's always something that *might* have killed them, but that doesn't mean it necessarily did.'

Arnold Throckmorton laughed as if he had just heard a joke. 'My friend, how many times have you had to make a judgement call? A body with a little bit of narrowing of the coronary arteries, perhaps a touch of early pneumonia? You must have been faced with that situation on many occasions. Did you ask for all these investigations every time?'

'It would depend how much narrowing of the arteries there was, or how much consolidation of the lungs there was. Also it would depend on the age of the deceased.'

Eisenmenger could see that he might have been speaking a language unknown to Dr Throckmorton. 'But this is surely absurd. We all know the dead man did not die unnaturally.'

It was a sentiment with which Eisenmenger could not agree. He did not necessarily believe that Edward had been the victim of homicide, but he felt strongly – passionately – that it was his task to prove the negative, and that he must never make assumptions unsupported by evidence. He saw, though, that he and his newfound colleague occupied, if not different universes, certainly very different parts of the same one. Accordingly, he chose not to continue the combat but instead pointed out, 'I don't quite see how you've become involved. If I do an autopsy for the coroner, it's purely between me and him.'

Arnold Throckmorton's face bore a podgy and perpetual smile that stretched the faintly pockmarked skin of his cheeks into twin bulges, thereby forcing his eyes into retreat. Only the thick frames of his glasses gave any accentuation to the upper part of his face.

'John, John . . . ' For some reason this repetition of his first name irritated Eisenmenger, perhaps because it had not a small amount of tired arrogance about it. 'You are new here, you do not understand how things work. We and the coroner are used to each other . . . '

'Don't rock the boat?'

Throckmorton shrugged. 'Why look for trouble that doesn't exist?'

'In order to make absolutely sure that it doesn't. If there's nothing there, then all well and good.'

'But this man, Melnick. He died of heart disease. It's obvious.'

Eisenmenger had always found restraint the best way to tackle outrage, but Dr Arnold Throckmorton was testing his adherence to this maxim to the full.

'Is it? Not to me.'

For the first time Eisenmenger saw that he had penetrated the other's complacency, that Throckmorton was becoming annoyed. 'Look, I know you've done some forensic work . . . '

Throckmorton left this sentence halfway through to fend for itself and, as far as Eisenmenger was concerned, it did not do well on its own.

'A tad,' Eisenmenger conceded. He did not bother to keep the irony out of his voice, but he could have rolled it up and hit the overweight and overweening pathologist on the head with it and there would have been no more reaction.

'Coronial work's different. We're just here so that something can be put on the death certificate.'

Eisenmenger had almost to practise superhuman control in order to say as calmly as he could, 'Nevertheless, I want toxicology done on the blood samples I took. It's my case and that is what is going to happen.'

Dr Throckmorton just stared at him for a second or two, then shook his head. He got up slowly as if he had been sitting there long enough to ossify his joints. Just before he set sail for the door, he said sadly, 'My friend, I fear that unless you change your attitude you will soon come to regret it.'

Eisenmenger raised his eyebrows and smiled. Despite his outwardly calm external aspect he was roiling inside as he replied, 'I'd rather regret doing the toxicology than regret not doing it.'

Throckmorton did not look happy, but did not continue the debate. The look on his face was one of angry impotence as he grunted and left the room.

Eight

Helena stood up, panic a thing as real as the ground over which she hurried, as the anxiety that had ruled her life for the past few weeks. She had to get back – to home in the first instance, to a doctor if, as she feared it might be, necessary.

She began to walk, not really aware of where she was going and as she did so she felt for her mobile phone, thinking only to call John, thinking as well that she should not be so dependent on someone, and thinking way, way back in her mind that she was being an idiot again . . .

'I'll have that.'

Just a boy, not even particularly menacing. Neither his appearance nor the tone of his voice suggested violence but, nonetheless, she knew at once that he was quite capable of it. He was a good 15 – perhaps 17 – centimetres taller than her, and wearing a fleece and a beanie; ginger hair, she remembered afterwards.

Stupidly she opened her mouth to explain that she wasn't well, as if he would care about that. 'I'm . . . '

He reached out for the phone and instinctively she clutched at it harder, even pulled it back towards herself. She saw the anger flare in his mouth as much as his eyes, a crimson emotion that seemed to her to be childish, the kind of thing she had seen in small children deprived of sweets or crisps.

She had wandered into a relatively secluded part of the park, where the path led through thick hydrangea bushes overhung by magnolia trees. There was no one in sight.

No one, therefore, to see him shove her hard so she stumbled backwards, tripping over the slightly raised kerb of the path and falling partly into a bush and then to the damp grass. No one to see him bend over her, grab the phone and stand up.

No one to see him look briefly at the phone, nod once in satisfaction at his prize, look again at Helena, then kick her hard in the stomach.

The cut-up did not prove as formidable as it had first appeared. Although the hospital's surgeons were clearly busy people, they were not required to perform particularly complex operations. St Christopher's was not a cancer centre and therefore only the most basic of oncological surgery was done, supplemented by the usual emergency fare. Although to the patients the operative procedures were still significant, this meant the pathologists had a relatively easy task. A hysterectomy for a tumour might require forty-five minutes to dissect, but one for fibroids could be done in fifteen. The time was made to pass even more quickly by the biomedical scientist who assisted him, for she proved to be a lively and pleasant companion who had few illusions concerning Dr Throckmorton, or her chief. He learned much about the department, some of which he had already surmised and a lot of which was new to him.

Having popped down to the small hospital shop to buy some overpriced and under-filled prawn sandwiches, he went back to his room to start reporting some small surgical biopsy specimens. The knock on the door was timid, almost a brush with the knuckles rather than a sharp contact, and Eisenmenger was not completely sure that it was anything more than a wind-driven rattle. He said tentatively, 'Yes? Come in.'

Even then there was a pause before his invitation produced results, and the door only swung open hesitantly. The face peering around the woodwork was that of a female who wore large wire-rimmed glasses on a face that at first sight appeared to be no more than twelve summers old.

'Dr Eisenmenger?'

He admitted this with a grave nod of the head.

The owner of the head advanced into the room. He saw now a small woman, petite to the point of emaciation and pale with it, nervous and almost avian. Her attire was untidy and might have come from a charity shop, but only one that was less than fastidious in its product selection – an upmarket one would have rejected it.

'Sorry to bother you. I'm Chloe Branham.'

Pathologists, he knew from experience, were a curious collection, a set of objects whose only common attribute was their eccentricity, their peculiarity. He had met tall ones, short ones, morbidly obese ones and near-skeletal ones; pathologists who were clinically insane and those who were laid back to the point of brainstem death. He should not have been surprised by anything, but Chloe managed this feat.

'Oh, yes,' he said. 'Of course.' He stood up, hand out. She walked towards him and took it, or rather, he took hers, and found it a thing of fragility. Eisenmenger wanted it to be a beauteous fragility but discovered that it was only a pathetic one.

In a voice that, if not piping, was certainly in a register that resembled more the piccolo then the bassoon, she offered, 'I know you're still settling in, but I wondered if you would be able to help me with a case I'm looking at for a meeting.'

She held out a cardboard slide tray.

He took it and opened the flaps to reveal three glass slides. She said, 'It's from the cervix of a sixty-year-old woman.'

As he sat at the microscope and put the first piece of glass on its stage she said, 'I hope you don't mind.'

'Not at all.'

She was shifting her weight from one tiny foot to the other, a motion that was distracting. Eisenmenger could not stop himself from comparing her to a sparrow.

He wondered why she was showing it to him. He had diagnosed it after the first slide – a small-cell carcinoma of the cervix. It was unusual, but quite characteristic, although he personally would have done confirmatory stains.

He turned to Chloe and gave her his opinion. For a second there was what appeared to be shock, as if the concept that she might be right was out of the question, but then she exhaled with such vigour that for a moment he feared she might collapse completely, deflated to a deformed shell. 'Good,' she managed to say in the middle of this. 'That's what I thought.'

'You seem relieved.'

She came forward to pick up the slide tray. 'It's nice to get these difficult cases right.'

'There's no immunohistochemistry, though.'

'I'll get it done after the meeting.'

She was in the process of taking the slides when he asked, 'What was the original diagnosis?'

She stopped abruptly. 'Oh.'

He waited while poor Chloe did a fine display of fluster-ment and finally said, 'Lymphoma.'

'Really? That's a brave diagnosis without further tests.'

She nodded and was heading for the door when he enquired, 'Who made it?'

'Arnold.' She decorated her reply with a brief and embar-rassed smile as if grassing up a fellow criminal.

'Will you tell him ?'

'Oh, no. I don't think so.'

'Why not?'

'There's no need to make a fuss, is there?'

A twitched grin and suddenly the air in the office was soaked in embarrassment, her pleasure at making the correct diagnosis as far away as salvation. The phone's sudden, petu-lant trill – demanding attention as incessantly and implacably as any toddler – was a relief to both of them. As Eisenmenger reached across to answer it, she took the opportunity to escape, as eager to leave as if he were a ticking bomb.

'How odd,' murmured Eisenmenger, then turned his attention to the caller. It was Clive, telling him that the samples from Melnick's post-mortem had just been picked up by one of the coroner's officers. They would be at the toxicology lab by the evening. The results would follow in about another three days.

As he put the phone down, his thoughts returned to Chloe. He had met two of his medical colleagues and was yet to find a normal one. He could not wait to meet the third.

Nine

Helena knew from the look on the young girl's face that this was *bad*. Not bad as in *not good,* but bad as in *catastrophic*. And there was really only one type of catastrophe when it came to early pregnancy.

Miscarriage.

The young man who had done this to her was just the kind of lad she defended on a daily basis, that she forever sought to see the best in. He did not know what he had done, of course, and probably never would. No righteous revenge for her – these days there hardly ever was for such a petty crime.

Petty? He has killed my child.

Life seemed to be a succession of setbacks, each one different if not worse than the last. Was she destined never to find relief? Happiness, she appreciated, was not part of the human condition – it was a transient emotion, one that could not and should not last – but surely she deserved some contentment? She felt as if she had never rested properly since the tragedy of her parents and the even greater loss of her stepbrother, Jeremy.

Wearily she asked, 'Is it bad news?'

But the girl was only an ultrasonographer who was, according to her name badge, blessed with the name of Stephanie Babcock. Her job bore a fine title but it signified, as far as she was concerned, nothing. Her smile was spoiled by the eyes, the confidence of her mouth negated by the uncertainty of her gaze. 'I wouldn't say that. The doctor will discuss the results with you.'

The gel on her belly was cold, and it was a cold she had come to hate. She could imagine that under other – completely contrary – circumstances she might have learned to relish the wet chillness of it, the sensation of the probe as it slithered over her skin, pressing and massaging. The beginnings of a discolouration were making themselves apparent where she had been kicked, and the pressure of the ultrasound probe exacerbated the ache within her, making her fearful of the damage that might have been done.

Helena rubbed her skin clean with the tissues Stephanie handed her. It hurt her to raise her head from the couch. She could feel that she was bleeding freely, and that soon she would need a fresh sanitary towel. She was then left alone, with Stephanie murmuring, 'Dr Ramirez will be in in a moment.' It was a neutral tone that failed to convince.

So Helena had to lie there, examining a ceiling that was in no fit state to be seen while the sounds of a hospital – faint but intrusive calls, an annoying humming, footsteps carrying occasional voices past the door – vied for her attention with the smells of things that she couldn't quite, and didn't want to, recognize.

Dr Ramirez was Mediterranean and short, dark of hair and eye. She had hair that was swept back tightly away from her forehead, and teeth that Helena noticed were pearls of whiteness, almost translucent, certainly luminescent. She had a green cardboard folder in her hand and as she came in, she asked, 'Miss Flemming?'

'Yes.'

'I'm the on-call obstetrician.'

Things were looking up. At least she was not the on-call podiatrist. As Helena nodded, Dr Ramirez opened the folder and continued while looking at it, 'The casualty doctor has asked me to see you.'

A sharp twinge of pain, almost as if something under tension

had snapped within her, caused Helena to gasp. This provoked
a glance from Dr Ramirez but no more. What was in the folder
proved more interesting than anything Helena might have to
say about matters.

Eventually, presumably having supped from the well of
knowledge to her satisfaction, Dr Ramirez surfaced and found
enough enthusiasm to turn to her patient. 'I'll need to do an
examination.'

'You don't say.'

Dr Ramirez, for reasons either of culture or of arrogance,
failed to see the joke. 'Yes, I do. I will send in the nurse to
help you prepare.'

And so the nurse helped Helena prepare, after which Dr
Ramirez returned, wearing on her right hand a disposable plastic
glove. She dipped her fingers into a pot of lubricant and holding
these up, she said to Helena, 'I will be as gentle as I can.'

Helena knew what that meant from experience that was
bitter to the point of acrid. As the lubricated fingers pushed
inside her, and as Dr Ramirez pushed down with her left hand
on to her abdomen, Helena's tension increased.

It was only released by the sudden, spearing pain that
seemed to stake her to a cross.

Perhaps the weight of years of NHS servitude had taken their
toll on Barry Schwartz; certainly, he appeared to be weighed
down by something. There was about his eyes a sense of
detached sadness and about his mouth an impression of
distressed melancholy.

'I heard you were coming to help us.' This was a statement
of what he had heard, not an expression of joy or even interest.
'Settling in?'

'More or less.'

'You know where to get coffee, don't you?'

'Yes, thanks.'

'And sandwiches? Or perhaps you prefer a hot meal?'

'I got something from the hospital shop.'

'Oh, yes.' He sounded dismissive. 'You can get sandwiches
and rolls there, or you can get them in the staff restaurant –
one-third discount – but they're a bit unprepossessing. There's
a small sandwich shop not far from the hospital, though, that
has a good selection.'

'I'll bear that in mind.' Eisenmenger wondered whence this obsession with comestibles came.

'Good.' He nodded gravely. 'Well, I'll leave you to get on. If you have any questions, just ask.'

Despite this invitation he showed surprise when Eisenmenger took him up on it. 'How old is Dr Throckmorton?'

'Oh. Sixty-two, I think.'

'Thinking of retiring?'

Barry Schwartz smiled. 'Aren't we all?'

Eisenmenger's next question was less than tactful. 'Is he any good?'

Dr Schwartz's miniscule hesitation told Eisenmenger far more than the effusive affirmation of complete confidence that followed.

'Still, it must be difficult sometimes, working in such a small department with just the three of you.'

Which acted as quite an effective brake on Barry Schwartz's momentum. A pause, something of fluster, something of embarrassment. 'Well . . . '

'Chloe's quite inexperienced . . . ' He put this in as a prompt.

'Yes . . . yes, she is.'

'And Arnold's . . . ?'

He let that linger, hanging like a lure, one that concealed a barb.

Just a frisson before the lure was skilfully refused. 'Arnold's very busy. Head of department.'

And Eisenmenger nodded at once and made it quite plain that he knew exactly what Schwartz meant, that head of department was a tremendously onerous position, that it was entirely understandable that such duties might take their toll on other aspects of his work.

Except, it wasn't.

Schwartz left. Eisenmenger shook his head and smiled to himself. It was not his problem. He could simply stay out of it while he was working there and leave them to sort it out for themselves.

For the tenth time that morning the phone began to ring and it was with some exasperation that he picked it up, expecting something trivial and work-related.

'John Eisenmenger.'

He listened for a few minutes, jerked from complacency by the slightly accented voice of Dr Ramirez, on-call obstetrician.

Ten

'I 'll be there right away.'
As Eisenmenger put down – dropped – the phone, he wanted to get out of the department at once but there were too many years of professionalism hammered into him, too strong an exoskeleton of responsibility, for him just to run off without keeping others informed. He went looking for his head of department.

Not in his room.

In fact nobody was anywhere. Even Barry Schwartz had somehow completely vanished in less than ten minutes. It was as if they were holding a secret meeting, perhaps to discuss their new, temporary colleague.

He looked in the laboratory, then in the secretaries' office. He thought about the mortuary, but decided to leave that to last because he considered it the least likely place to find them. Then he hit upon the library. This was euphemistically named because it was just a room with books and journals on shelves on the walls and a table in the middle, with a dirty window through which could be faintly seen an even dirtier brick wall.

He entered without knocking. Why should he not have done? It was a common area, after all.

Thus he came across Dr Throckmorton and Chloe, she standing, he sitting by her side at the table. She was holding a sheet of paper, he was writing something.

He might have been taking dictation.

It was entirely innocent.

No reason at all why his abrupt appearance should prove in any way embarrassing.

Accordingly, he could not explain the atmosphere in which he found himself: one that was turgid and warm, yet that had about it a degree of tension that almost made the elastic around the tops of his socks snap.

'Oh . . . '

Dr Throckmorton smiled. There was a patina of perspiration on his forehead and cheeks but that was, as far as Eisenmenger could see, an ever-present characteristic, one that presumably defied the flannel and the towel. Chloe, on the other hand, was alarmed. Not that she did not seem to be perpetually close to this state, but Eisenmenger felt that here she had ascended to another level.

Dr Throckmorton asked, 'Yes, John?'

Eisenmenger pushed the questions back from his lips and explained, 'My partner's been admitted to hospital . . . I've got to go, I'm afraid.'

'Oh, dear.' There was a sound of concern about this remark, one that to Eisenmenger's ear sounded completely false. Chloe, Eisenmenger noted, took the opportunity to move slightly away from her head of department. 'Has she been admitted here?'

'Yes, to the obstetrics ward.'

'Well, you must go, John. We shall cope.'

Chloe nodded encouragement mutely and perhaps a little too timidly.

'I'll be back as soon as I can,' Eisenmenger said.

'Of course, of course.'

Eisenmenger hurried away and, despite his worries, a significant part of his brain was occupied with speculating what, if anything, he had just interrupted.

'There's a blood clot behind the placenta.'

Helena's voice was almost singsong, yet tired and soft. She couldn't stop her eyes from watering, and didn't particularly care.

Eisenmenger held her hand as she lay in the bed. It hurt him that she was looking away from him, and had barely glanced at him since he had arrived.

'I know.'

'There's nothing they can do. Either it'll stop bleeding or it won't.'

He squeezed her hand.

'If it doesn't . . . ' she said, then stopped because there was no need to continue.

After a long while he said, 'We can try again.'

But he saw that it was no comfort to look ahead, that her thoughts were incapable of moving anywhere other than the immediate past. She was close to losing a child, something that was irreplaceable. It was not like having a dog run over and rushing out to the pet shop the next day.

She might not even have heard him.

'It's stopped hurting,' she whispered.

'That's good.'

A long time passed before she asked, 'Is it?'

He had no answer.

Eleven

When it came, the end was a thing of soft anticlimax, as if to lose a life were a thing of no consequence. For Helena this only increased the despair, for she felt as if she were being mocked, as if something were saying to her that the demise of her baby was not even worth marking with pain, or some great effort, or any sort of cataclysm. As it was, there was just a gradual diminution in the cramps as the blood flow increased, as she lay in her bed and held John's hand.

Neither of them spoke. Neither had anything to say.

Neither of them could even think of what could be said that was not trite or irrelevant, or that was in any way of comfort or use.

Eisenmenger stayed with her until the early hours of the morning, until Helena seemed to be asleep and the hospital was noisy in the subdued way that hospitals are at night. Helena had been given analgesia and a light sedative and he felt reasonably confident that she would not wake until the morning. He asked the nurses to let him know if there were any problems and, from their pool of light around the desk in the midst of the darkened ward, they promised they would.

Then he left the ward.

And Helena's tears began in earnest.

Twelve

'When you've quite finished, Inspector.'

It was a voice she knew so well yet that did not, to her ear, grow more honeyed with familiarity.

She turned away from the image back to Charles Sydenham, forensic pathologist extraordinaire. Their relationship had matured beyond the point that she felt it necessary to follow any of the normal social conventions, to pretend politeness; matured beyond the point, indeed, that it was in any way fit for consumption.

'Yes?'

He sighed a sigh of magnificent proportions. 'I need the space you're standing in.' He indicated that she should move so he could approach the corpse from the other side.

Corpse.

The word seemed inappropriate, seemed to imply a completeness that this particular piece of deadness did not possess.

For a start, the top half of the head was no longer intact. It had been ruptured by a sort of jagged red wasteland of tatteredness, a volcanic hole erupting from the back as if something had been born in the cranium and decided to leave the family home. The face deceived. She was no longer in any way beautiful – and it was entirely possible that she had once been so – because the blast had broken the facial bones, forcing them outwards slightly and causing a distortion that nature had not intended.

She was sitting at a kitchen table in a small but exquisitely fitted kitchen. She wore a business suit that looked to be expensive and was certainly neat. A shotgun lay to her left on the stone floor.

Beverley moved, then asked, 'Haven't you got anything for me yet, Charles?'

'Only facts, dear girl. Only facts.'

She smiled but only to hide irritation. Sydenham stood up from his crouching position and seemed to believe that everyone in the room had been waiting for some form of soliloquy. Sydenham was good at soliloquizing and never missed an opportunity. 'Facts are the nails with which we construct the case, Inspector. And that is a metaphor for life. Without facts, the whole of civilization would fall apart.'

And without bullshit, I suspect so would you.

The three forensics officers in the room worked on assiduously, but the Scenes of Crime officer continued to stare at Sydenham long after politeness should have suggested that he look aside, his expression suggesting that he had seen a fair number of dickheads in his time but that here he had encountered something from the hall of fame.

As if to press his claim that he was head, shoulders and, indeed, *glans penis* above everyone else in the room, Sydenham took this attention as interest and addressed his next remarks to Scenes of Crime. 'Take your job, for instance.' Scenes of Crime had often wished someone would, but remained taciturn on the subject. 'It is your sole purpose in life to pin down the truth, to enshrine facts into something permanent, because without that foundation, the whole criminal justice system would collapse as surely as a skyscraper built on a marsh.'

Scenes of Crime, who had no idea, and no interest in, what Sydenham was talking about, and who was also seriously worried that he had caught herpes off a recent acquaintance of his, said only with a grimace, 'Yeah.'

Sydenham would almost certainly have continued his fascinating soliloquy – was even taking in another breath as fuel – had Scenes of Crime not turned then to Beverley and said, 'I've finished here.'

'When can I have the photos?'

'A couple of hours?'

'No more,' she advised.

He left without another glance at Sydenham, just as Grover came into the room, and Beverley could not suppress a scowl.

*   *   *

'Helena?'

The visit started like this and ended, an hour later, in exactly the same way. She was in a side room with a faint background smell composed of air freshener, disinfectant and laundry. It was clearly intended to be pleasant and uplifting, but managed merely to be sickly sweet to the point of emesis. It was warm, too: an asphyxiating warmth that formed a kind of unhealthy sheen on Eisenmenger's skin. Such emotion was not helped by his subconscious, which whispered inaudibly but tellingly about the staphylococci that lurked on the hands of everyone, the pseudomonas in the hand-wash and the clostridium in the corners.

He began to wonder how anyone could get better in such a place. Certainly, Helena did not seem inclined to.

She had barely reacted to his arrival and had followed this lack of acknowledgement with a lack of everything else. She spent the entire time staring, though not at him and not at anything he could see. He suspected he would never be able to see it.

It was not the most enthralling hour he had ever experienced. Indeed, as he made attempt after attempt to engage her, each one failing even to cause a single muscle's reaction, he found irritation rising inside him; rising and excoriating him from within. He wanted so much to communicate with her, and he loved her so much, that her superficially obstinate refusal to respond to him was correspondingly intense and correspondingly corrosive.

She had managed a semblance of animation only when she had made her statement to the police regarding the assault, although she had been unable to provide them with much that was of use to them. Red-haired teenager, an expensive but otherwise unremarkable mobile phone, no witnesses. They didn't laugh, but that was only out of courtesy. They had left and she had been well aware that their assurances that they would do what they could were nothing more than politenesses, that the crime of the murder of her child would remain forever unsolved.

She had sunk back after that.

Now he left her – with a kiss that, had she not proffered her cheek with the slightest of movements, he might have supposed she had not noticed – and as he did so he could not discard the feeling that once again he had wasted sixty minutes of both her time and his, that she was completely enfolded

by grief. It did not take a postgraduate qualification in psych-
iatry to discern that this was more than a passing reaction to
the miscarriage. He saw a total collapse, a complete loss of
functioning. It was as if her whole psyche had shifted,
becoming misplaced and disarranged, so that it was now
centred upon the negative, upon despair.

He stopped at the nurses' station and waited to attract the
attention of the efficient-looking staff nurse who sat there. It
turned out she was so busy being efficient that she effected
to fail to notice him for over five minutes, during which time
he became well acquainted with the slightly frayed Alice band
on the top of her head. When she did stop what she was doing
– filling out endless sheets of paperwork, presumably as part
of her personal effort to keep the NHS bureaucratic ocean
topped up – she seemed surprised that anyone should wish to
communicate with a member of staff.

'You want to speak to one of the team?' she repeated. It
was not quite an incredulous tone, but it was one that suggested
he was a radical thinker on the subject.

'Please.'

She looked at her fob watch. 'I'm not sure . . . '

'If you could try.'

A small hesitation, then she relented. 'All right.'

She looked up the bleep number in the nursing Cardex,
then tapped out numbers on the telephone: first two, then a
pause, then seven, then another pause before she put the
handset down again.

She returned to her paperwork and he could only assume
she did not have enough glances left to throw one to him.

The phone rang.

'Are you able to come to the ward, Dr Robinson? Helena
Flemming's partner is here and would like to talk to you.'

She listened, then replaced the receiver. 'He'll be along
shortly.'

Eisenmenger thanked her politely – she was already engrossed
again in the return for paperclips or whatever it was – and moved
away to examine the noticeboard, where he was told about the
summer ball, the importance of hand washing, how to contact
the Patient Advice and Liaison Service and the opening hours
of the chapel.

Dr Robinson appeared. He looked tired but managed a smile

as they shook hands. Eisenmenger wondered how many staphylococci and clostridia had just moved home. They went into a small office off the main part of the ward.

'Sorry to bother you.'

'No problem. You're worried about Helena's affect, I suspect.'

'It's not good, is it?'

'No. We're getting a formal psychiatric assessment tomorrow, but I'll be surprised if that doesn't evaluate her as severely depressed.'

Eisenmenger nodded morosely. 'And if it does?'

He hesitated. 'There is some *good* news,' he ventured.

'What's that?'

'We have at St Christopher's a consultant who's taken a special interest in obstetric psychiatric problems, Dr Cowper. He has a special inpatient unit about a mile from the hospital. He's the one who's coming to look at Helena tomorrow. She couldn't be in better hands.'

'You think she'll need inpatient treatment?'

Dr Robinson backed off a little and began with, 'I'm no expert.' Having performed this neat little piece of repositioning, he went on, 'But I think she may. At least for a week or two.'

'What does he use? Drugs?'

'Only light tranquillisers, where needed. Nothing heavy. It's mostly psychotherapy. Cognitive therapy, that kind of thing.'

Eisenmenger's experience of such units was old but not good. As a medical student, he had spent some time in such a unit dealing with eating disorders. During his stay, there had been one attempted suicide and a member of staff had been assaulted with a dinner fork by a vicar's daughter. He tried to draw solace from Dr Robinson's kindly intentioned words.

Dr Robinson asked, 'Is there anything else I can do?'

Eisenmenger shook his head and thanked him.

Before Eisenmenger left he looked in again on Helena. She had not changed her position one millimetre.

Thirteen

In the few days since Grover had arrived in her professional life, Beverley had come to appreciate that her new sergeant possessed an almost superhuman degree of doggedness. In other circumstances, she would have been delighted to find a colleague who was neither lazy, nor slobbish, nor inclined to give up at the first setback, but in Grover she found these attributes to be distinctly concerning. She *wanted* Grover to realize that he was not fit for the life of a police detective, that whatever place moral imperialism had in the world, it was not accompanying Inspector Beverley Wharton as she tried to rebuild her career.

She had initially hoped that a scene such as this would help, that it would make him think again about his obviously romantic notions of the detective's life, but she had been quickly disappointed. His time in Scenes of Crime had made such sights relatively routine to him. She had hoped to see him vomiting in the corner, but instead had to hide her disappointment.

He had not thus far, however, proved himself a particularly useful addition to the ranks of the detective elite, having spent much of the last few hours either wandering around aimlessly, or standing self-consciously in the corner. She had ignored him until now and saw no reason why she should not continue with a successful strategy.

She asked Sydenham, 'So what facts have you got?'

'Single blast from a double-barrelled shotgun, apparently at zero range . . . '

'Apparently?'

He halted abruptly, as if he had just hit an unexpected bump in what had appeared to be a smooth-surfaced road and, as drivers are apt to be, he was not best pleased. 'These are preliminary findings, Inspector. There are some burn marks on what is left of the mucosa of the hard palate which are indicative, but until I find the wadding, I can't be certain.'

'Wadding?' This from Grover. He had on his face a look of interest, but then he didn't know Sydenham, and he had an as yet untapped pool of the stuff. Sydenham was clearly fed up with being unable to run smoothly through his didacticism. 'Yes, wadding,' he said, with some petulance.

Beverley explained tiredly to Grover, 'At the base of a shotgun cartridge there is a plug of paper or felt that separates the shot from the powder, called the wadding. It's expelled with the same force as the pellets, although it doesn't go nearly as far. If it's in what's left of the brain, then that strongly suggests point blank range.'

Sydenham said, with a hint of sourness, 'Bravo, Inspector. I've managed to teach you something.'

To which the best answer was no answer.

He continued in a tone that might just have been described as 'huffy', 'There are no other injuries apparent on the body although, as you know, we will have to await a full postmortem to be certain.'

'So she did it herself?' She knew the answer, in retrospect had only asked the question because it would aggravate him.

'Did I say that?'

Beverley sighed. 'Not exactly . . . '

'No. I did not.' Having discovered that Sergeant Grover was an unblooded member of his audience, Sydenham homed in on him as his stooge. 'I hope you, my dear Sergeant, will quickly learn that pathologists are good – and I am very good – but they are not the easy answer. We give you gold, but you're the ones who have to work it into the jewellery.'

Beverley was pleased to see that already Sydenham was working his black magic on her sergeant, that Grover was looking at him as if he could not quite believe what was confronting him.

Grover was saved from comment by having to move for a forensics officer and Beverley took the opportunity to ask, 'Anything else we should know?'

She realized at once this question was a mistake, that she had just exposed her neck to an adversary who would exhibit no mercy.

'My dear Beverley, if I were to begin at this very instant

to detail alphabetically all the things you do not know that
you should, I would probably be on my deathbed before I had
even got through the As.'

Grover's mouth did not exactly drop open, but the look in
his eyes told the story equally well.

Sydenham, rather charmingly deluding himself that he had
impressed Grover, decided to turn his back on the audience
and resume his tender loving care for his patient.

'Well? Is there?' Beverley had raised her eyebrows and her
mouth was slightly pinched as she asked this, but she did not
allow this to sound in the question.

'Not at the moment.' This was thrown over his shoulder,
with more than a hint of disdain about the words.

Beverley smiled at his back. It was a smile that no one
would have wanted to see. She walked from the room.

Eisenmenger eagerly opened the toxicology report that had
just arrived on the samples taken from Edward Melnick's
body, but the words, far from clarifying the situation, only
served to confuse it. Eisenmenger had been fully expecting
a negative result, that this particular case would be one of
those unsatisfactory ones where there was no single, natural
disease process that could be clearly identified as responsible,
where Death had been more subtle and had spread his toxin
more diffusely, through several channels. The reality, though,
was altogether different.

The post-mortem blood samples contained ethanol at a
concentration of 357 milligrams per 100 millilitres.

Which was interesting, but not of itself necessarily significant.
It was a very high level and, in the system of an inexperienced
drinker, might have been high enough to induce death by ethanol
poisoning, but Edward Melnick had not been a callow youth
unused to the ways of Bacchus. Eisenmenger had known of cases
where gentlemen such as Mr Melnick had managed to remain
upstanding even carrying concentrations of ethanol in excess of
550 mgs per 100 mls.

So he had been drunk, but not lethally so.

Yet there was a second positive result in the dense, tech-
nocratic verbiage that passed for a toxicology report. Edward
Melnick's post-mortem blood had also contained Metformin,
a drug commonly used in the treatment of diabetes. Not in

fatal concentration, though; indeed, the report suggested that it was within the range of values normally associated with therapeutic usage.

Eisenmenger read these words and frowned and, having frowned, he sighed and stared out of the window at the grey wall that passed for a horizon.

There was a knock on the door, then there was a pause and then, because Eisenmenger did not answer, did not even *hear* this evidence of interruption, the door was tentatively opened. Chloe's face appeared in the gap thus created, bearing an expression of trepidation. It was closely akin to her normal expression, just with an amplification of consternation.

'John? Am I disturbing you?'

He came to, turning around as he registered surprise. 'Oh, Chloe . . . No, not at all.'

Which was, of course, a fabrication, but one, he hoped, to be judged in the grand scheme of things as motivated by nothing more than kindness.

'I was just wondering if your partner is all right. I heard . . . '

Yet what she had heard was apparently beyond her vocal apparatus, for here her voice faded as if there had been an interruption to the power supply.

As he wondered not *what* she had heard, but *how*, he said, 'She's fine, thanks, Chloe. She's lost the baby, though.'

And Chloe's look of shock was, he knew at once, genuine. Indeed, there was a moment when he feared she would be overcome by this snippet of news, this simple sentence of five words, for her eyes closed and she seemed even to sway slightly.

She recovered though, and came into the room. 'Oh, I'm so sorry . . . So very, very sorry . . . '

She put her hand on his and he felt how tiny and warm it was: the hand of a small mammal, one that lived on its nerves, forever fearing predators.

'Thank you,' he said, feeling touched by her emotion. A voice in his head questioned why he should be so more affected by the grief of another than by his own grief; why the reflection should be brighter than the real thing.

'I've never . . . '

'No . . . '

'But I can appreciate how she must feel,' she hastened to add, presumably to reassure him of her femininity.

'Thanks.'

'If there's anything I can do . . . '

He repeated his expression of gratitude. She was turning to go as he said, 'Perhaps you can help me with this toxicology report?'

He handed it to her and there was silence as she read it. He saw in her face total concentration.

'Was he a heavy drinker?'

'Oh, yes.'

'So I wouldn't be too bothered by the alcohol level.'

'No.'

'So it's a negative report: a natural death.'

'What about the Metformin?'

'It's not at a lethal level.'

He twitched a smile. 'No,' he agreed. 'No, it's not.'

'Well, then.' She handed the report back. 'A natural death.'

'Except for one curious fact,' he murmured.

'What's that?'

'He hadn't been prescribed Metformin. Why should he have been? He wasn't diabetic.'

Fourteen

There was no sign of a break-in. The house had been secure and her handbag had contained close to £200 in cash, as well as several credit cards. No evidence at all to suggest that robbery had played a part in this death.

The house was neat and tidy, almost suspiciously so. Beverley had trouble with people who were too fastidious in their housekeeping arrangements, who were happy only with straight lines and empty spaces in their world. Something inside her insisted that such people had to be hiding something, if not directly by imposing order on a disordered universe, then indirectly, by concealing from the world their true selves, their real personalities.

The house was large, too. Four bedrooms, detached, in a good neighbourhood, in an up-and-coming town. Even quite small houses in Donnington were becoming distressingly expensive and Anita Delorme's abode could by no effort of the imagination be described as 'small'. The garden was wide and long and spacious, and also neat; the decking outside the French windows looked new and there was a conspicuous and brazen gas barbecue tucked away under a sort of purpose-built shelter to one side of it.

Grover came in and stood just beside the open door, looking sheepish. With uncharacteristic compassion, she acknowledged his existence.

'Do we know what she did?'

Grover said, 'Not yet.'

She judged from what she had seen that it had been a very good job. 'Find out.'

As Grover was leaving the room, Beverley asked, 'She lived alone?'

'So the neighbour said – the one who alerted us.'

So there were no children, nothing obvious to hole the finances below the Plimsoll line, so perhaps it was not suspicious that she spent her money on a nice house.

Grover disappeared to ask more of the neighbours and Beverley began to open drawers and cupboards in the back sitting room, looking for details of the life just ended; details that would, she hoped, colour an accurate portrait of this dead woman.

Anita Delorme.

Had she been attractive? The thing in the kitchen could have had supermodel looks or the kind of face to frighten small children as far as one could now judge, and there were no photographs to help her decide between these choices. The only two present were of an elderly couple, one black and white and obviously years old, the other colour and clearly slightly more recent, but both of the same people.

The parents.

Another task to relish. *I'm sorry to bother you, but I'm afraid I have some bad news . . .*

How many times had she had to do that? It was never

going to be good, never even going to get the smallest bit better.

In a wooden bureau – Beverley suspected that it was antique – she found a chequebook, the last filled-out stub dated three days before. It had been for a takeaway pizza meal. Had she eaten it alone? Other stubs told of nothing more exotic than hairdressing, supermarket shopping and milk bills paid.

A very self-contained young woman.

Nothing to indicate a reason for biting the end of a shotgun while fiddling with the trigger.

Nor was there anything to suggest that she had ever owned a firearm. The area was suburban and Beverley guessed there would be more chance of finding an illegal immigrant working as an au pair than of finding a gun.

So, perhaps she belonged to some sort of gun club?

She turned away from the bureau and looked again around the room. The books on the shelves were mostly paperbacks, mostly tattered; so she read a lot – why shouldn't she? She had no family to distract her. There was a goodly proportion of classics, old and modern, as well as a reasonable reference collection and some coffee table books on fashion. Nothing on gardening and nothing on shooting, though.

Sydenham came into the room, looking pleased with himself, as ever.

'I've finished here.'

'Anything else you can tell me?'

'Unless someone took a club hammer to her skull first, I think I can confidently say that it was the shotgun what done it.' The mocking use of poor grammar was Sydenham's idea of a joke.

'But who wielded it?'

Sydenham snorted, his face assuming an expression of exasperation. His face had only a limited repertoire: it could only change from supercilious condescension to exasperation, anger and contempt, and then only for short periods. 'How the bloody hell should I know, Inspector? What do you think they employ you for?'

'But surely you've got some idea?'

Contempt switched on as exasperation faded out. '*When* I've done the autopsy, I *might* be able to tell you if she *could* have held the gun herself, but that's all I'll be able to tell you.

And, until then, you'll just have to get off your pretty little bottom and ask a few questions yourself. Even if she could have held it and pulled the trigger, that doesn't mean she did.'

Beverley seriously considered telling him what she thought of him – what most of her colleagues, male and female, thought of him – but said nothing. She could not afford to antagonize people, not in her position. She would never find herself capable of describing Sydenham as a friend, but she had enough enemies already to be going on with.

She put on a tight smile as she said, 'I'll see what I can do.'

And this apparent capitulation, this victory over her, seemed to cheer him, as if his ego enjoyed winning the spat, demonstrating his superiority. As he left the room, his demeanour was distinctly bouncy and he was whistling something from Gilbert and Sullivan in a faint discord.

Having given her consent to the removal of the body by the undertakers, she left the room to the forensics team and went upstairs. As she walked through the house, impressions crowded in on her, as they had done ever since she had first entered the house.

Nice carpets . . . recently decorated throughout . . . elegance . . . easy sophistication . . .

This, she knew, had been a woman who had had a good life.

So why did you do it, Anita?

Unless, you didn't . . .

The bathroom contained nothing that helped. Amidst the unguents and lotions, the creams and the mousses, she found no suspicious powders, no brightly coloured pills in plain white envelopes, none of the paraphernalia that might suggest a more esoteric aspect of Anita Delorme's life. Two of the bedrooms were clean, tidy and made up, but clearly unused, ready for guests. The third was the one that Anita had slept in, the fourth a study. On the bedside cabinet was a book, opened and presumably half-read. It was a Booker Prize winner, the kind of thing that Beverley occasionally felt the urge to read, then invariably felt the need to throw away after she had wasted fifty pages of her life on it. Beneath it was a nearly completed newspaper crossword, beside it were a box of tissues and a DAB radio/alarm clock. In the drawer were some contraceptive pills, two pens and an iPod. Three glossy women's magazines on a rug at the side of the bed were the only concession to untidiness. The large, dark wood wardrobe was packed with clothing, most of it expensive, some of it with designer labels. Beverley admired her taste, and wondered if she would have liked or hated Anita Delorme, deciding probably the latter. In the matching chest of drawers she discovered an impressive cashmere collection and the kind of pricey lingerie that she had long coveted.

She closed the drawers, straightened up and looked around the room. Everywhere she went she found an ordered life, one that in many ways she envied, and nowhere did she discover a reason for Anita Delorme to have exploded the contents of her head all around the kitchen.

As she was going into the study, Grover returned. 'According to Mr and Mrs Perkin, she was very nice and very personable. Always ready to help out with feeding their cats when they went on holiday, that kind of thing.'

'Any boyfriends?'

'Not that they know about.'

'Any recent illnesses?'

Grover had thought he was doing well until that moment. 'Oh . . . I didn't ask.'

Beverley wasn't surprised, would in fact have been astonished if he had. 'They got on with her well?'

'Absolutely.'

'So, as far as they're concerned, she was the perfect neighbour.'

'Pretty much. No bad vibes at all.'

'Shocked that this should have happened?'

'Absolutely.'

'Right. Now go to the other side and ask the same questions. Then go over the road and ask the people in the houses opposite. Ask them the same questions each time.'

'OK.' There was a hint of hesitation and Beverley waited for the question she knew was coming her way. 'Why?'

'Because the more viewpoints we get, the more we can see what might have been true rather than what the Perkins thought was true. Did everyone think she was the perfect person? Is there someone around here who wondered about her lifestyle?'

Grover nodded. He had been making notes as Beverley

explained her thinking, the perfect student. As he left the room, Beverley watched him go, unable to fool herself that she wasn't very depressed.

She turned back to the echoes of Anita Delorme's life. She still didn't know enough about her, still felt that she was looking at a reflective surface below which the grain of the life was hidden. She had hopes of the study, though. The study intrigued her.

Why would she have one, for a start? Was she a closet author, spending her nights toiling away over the last, great novel, the epochal work that would crown Western civilization, making all other efforts worthless? Perhaps she had been undertaking an Open University course, degree following degree in a fever of academic achievement.

Neither of these seemed to accord with the vague impressions that Beverley had of Ms Anita Delorme.

It was not a large room, but then it did not need to be. No more than a box room in which was a small, neat desk, a leather chair and shelves on the wall. On the desk was a sleek, relatively new computer, complete with colour laser printer, scanner and large, flat panel monitor. On the shelves were box files, ring binders and books.

Beverley sat at the desk and regarded the expensive computer.

Bank statements – where were they? Beverley could not believe that such a tidy person would not have them safely secured and ordered somewhere. She looked through the box files, scanning the titles written on them in black marker pen, and quickly found plenty of other things, mostly neatly filed in folders or envelopes, including a will – everything to the NSPCC – as well as some recent utility bills, documents relating to a car (Mercedes SLX, which made Beverley wonder again just what Ms Delorme's job might have been), and some stuff about private health care insurance.

She nearly missed the file because it was on the floor and open, the spine therefore obscuring its label.

Open and empty.

This whole business was becoming odder and odder with every passing minute.

Had they been stolen, perhaps . . . ?

She looked around the room again, and noticed a pile of

papers that she had previously overlooked because it was partially hidden by a copy of yesterday's *Daily Telegraph*. There they were, her much longed-for bank statements. Her mood rose, now she would perhaps see . . .

Except that they shed no light at all. Indeed they were boring. Salary went in – about two thousand a month – and payments went out: food, utility bills, the odd car bill. Nothing extraordinary, and no overdraft.

But perhaps that was the point.

How had Anita paid for all those luxuries great and small that she had left behind? Beverley went back two years and found no record that the car had been bought, no holidays taken, no antiques purchased. Even the computer in front of her did not exist, at least according to the bank.

Had she been going through the statements in the hour before her death? Had something in them – something that at present eluded Beverley – formed her decision to take her own life?

What about credit cards?

Beverley was suddenly sure this would be the answer. It had been a possibility right from the off. Anita had bought her world of special things on tick and, Beverley guessed, the ticking had stopped.

She thought to find evidence for her hypothesis in a file labelled 'CC', which, although it contained statements from three credit card companies, failed to support her contention. Anita had dedicatedly paid off her bills every month. The disappointment of this was only partially alleviated when she spotted that the next file along was labelled 'Social'. It was in here that she found at last a photograph of Anita Delorme.

A woman laughing, carefree, being pushed on a swing; the person pushing her unknown, the person taking the photograph equally anonymous. She had a wide mouth; happy, bright eyes and a slightly plump but nevertheless attractive figure.

Not stunning, but not hideous, either.

Certainly she could imagine that Anita Delorme would have proved interesting to men of a certain age, of a certain way of thinking.

She put the photograph in her pocket and returned to the bank statements. Apparently Anita had been employed by a company called Atopia, based at Benhall Grange. The name meant nothing to Beverley. Given the present-day trend of businesses adopting rather bizarre names, it might indicate anything from a milliner's to an insurance company. Putting the bank statements back in their file for a later, more detailed, perusal, she closed the lid, then had another look around the study. When nothing else came to her attention, she stood up with the box file under her arm and descended the stairs.

With Sydenham gone, the body was now in the care of the forensics team. Two undertakers had arrived and were having a smoke in the front garden, while three bystanders watched from the pavement under the eye of a uniformed constable who stood just outside the garden gate. The front door to a house opposite opened and Grover was revealed, an elderly woman seeing him out. The woman's demeanour suggested that she was suffering from logorrhoea: Beverley could see her mouth moving continuously even when Grover had his back to her and was stepping on to the paving stones of the path. Beverley smiled to herself. Neighbours fell into two classes – those who hated the idea of the police invading their cosy suburban world and those who fed on the feeling of excitement.

She probably gets Agatha Christie and Colin Dexter books from the library every week and reads them until she falls asleep in her chair.

Grover came hurrying over the road to her. 'I didn't think I'd ever get away.'

'Let me guess. She's always had her suspicions?'

Grover was astonished. 'How did you know?'

'She's of a type.'

'She seemed very nice.'

'Look, Grover. We don't want nice and we don't want "suspicions". Maybe in Shropshire nice is what the police like when they go talking to witnesses, and maybe they just *love* people who have always suspected their neighbours were homicidal maniacs or running a brothel, but around here that kind of thing doesn't rate too highly. I want someone who can tell the same story two times in a row and who isn't obsessed with immigrants, young people or how sitcoms aren't as funny as they used to be.'

Her sergeant did what he was good at: he did indignation. 'That's not fair!'

Beverley cut short the debate by asking, 'What's her story?'

Disgruntled, Grover explained, 'She says Anita Delorme has had a regular male visitor for some time.'

Beverley could have imagined the witness using just such a term. 'Regular male visitor', the words enunciated using just enough acidic disapproval to sour any creaminess that might be induced in the listener's mind, to abort romantic notions of young lovers with a world of happiness before them. 'Regular male visitor' placed the relationship firmly in the territory of prostitutes and seedy affairs.

'Description?'

'Not much, I'm afraid.'

Once again, their witness was showing her expected form. 'What does that mean?'

'Middle-aged, about medium height. Dark-haired and medium build.'

A description that in theory potentially described half the male population of the country, but in reality described none of it. 'Was he taller than her, same height, or shorter?'

Grover's eyes sparked distress. 'I didn't ask.'

Another lesson to be learned. Beverley said as patiently as she could, 'Never ask them how tall someone is, always give them a point of comparison. I don't know how tall you are, but I know you're shorter than me by about 3 centimetres. This isn't a job interview. If you just ask them open questions, they'll give you open answers.'

'Right.'

'Same with the age, the hair, everything.'

'OK.'

Short breath, then, 'When was the last time she saw this miracle of mediocrity?'

'About a week ago.'

'When did she first notice him?'

'I'm not entirely sure.'

'How often was Anita seeing him?'

But once again Grover had to admit a deficiency in his interview technique. 'I'm not sure.'

He added, 'But she remembers the car very clearly.'

'And?'

'It was a Jaguar, Mark 2. British racing green. She remembers it because her late husband used to have one just like it.

In fact, she even checked the registration to see if it was the same.'

'Was it?'

'No.'

'Does she remember what the registration was?' Beverley asked this knowing the answer.

'No.' Grover said this tentatively, as if he were afraid that Beverley would find this incredible, that he would be instructed to take a rubber cosh to the witness until a confession was obtained.

Grover had done enough. It was not much, but it might be something they could use. Beverley's anger was returned to store.

'OK. Go back to her and try to get a halfway decent description of the car's driver.'

Grover's show of relief was almost pathetic. As he turned and walked away on his errand, Beverley watched him and tried not to scream.

Fifteen

'Helena Flemming?'

Time was turgid, no longer a flowing stream but a viscous and stifling substance that held Helena in aspic and trapped her pain inside her to torment her for as long as it wanted to.

'Yes.' She stated the affirmative, gave it no curiosity. She did not even turn her head from the window through which she had been staring. The glass reflected ghosts of her and of her visitor but Helena was without interest in the tall, patrician woman who could be made out standing beside her chair. Neither was she interested in the panorama of the hospital grounds beyond these spectres, in the weak sunshine that had followed the earlier rain.

'My name's Harriet Worringer. I was wondering if you had time for a chat . . . ?'

Helena had time enough for eternity, but she did not have the time to 'chat'. She did not want to 'chat', just as she did not want to talk, or gossip, or discuss, or debate. She wanted nothing, except perhaps an end.

She remained silent.

'I could come back later . . . ' Harriet said.

Helena's eyes were familiar with the grounds outside her window, the window in her room, the one that formed the backdrop for her melancholy, but it was not the landscape through which she moved. That was a far more threatening one, one where she was prey, where she had nothing with which to fight back and could only survive by remaining un-detected. Movement was the key. She had read somewhere, or perhaps seen on some television programme, that the vast majority of predators relied on movement to detect their prey. To remain firmly entrenched in the background without venturing into the foreground was the best strategy for survival in any hostile environment.

'Would you mind if I sat down anyway?'

The thing that stalked Helena, though, was a subtle and therefore deadly pursuer. It struck when the day seemed at its brightest and the surroundings seemed at their most innocuous, when the shadows seemed far away. She knew it well, though, which was an advantage; she had met it first when her entire family had died within the space of two months.

Familiarity most certainly had not bred contempt.

Something far more corrosive had been born: despair.

'You may not believe it, but I think I know something of what you're going through. I lost my only granddaughter, Annabelle, when she was just nine.'

Helena did not react.

'And before I had my daughter, I had four miscarriages.'

Miscarriage. Helena pondered this term with supreme idle-ness, struck by its implications. It sounded almost pejorative, as if blame were being apportioned, as if the mother were a miscarrier and therefore had made a mistake and dropped something and, in doing so, broken it.

As if gifted with clairvoyance, the old woman went on, 'I hate that term. It's a euphemism that's become as offensive as the original word. But, of course, to say, I *aborted . . .* '

There was a pause and it was in this that Helena discovered

a small miracle: the voice had caught her attention. 'No. *I* didn't abort anything. I was as much the victim as the poor things that died; after all, each time a part of me died as well.'

Helena looked across at her visitor for the first time. She saw no reaction to this movement, perceived only an elderly woman looking into the sadness of her past, one who was as immersed in it as much as Helena was in hers.

'The first one was the worst. For three months I waded through something that I'd never known before. "Hell on earth", I suppose, would be a fair way to describe what I experienced.'

Someone nodded and Helena discovered somewhat belatedly that it was her own head moving; yet still this apparently pleasant, older woman did not seem to be looking at her or even to be intellectually present in the room with her.

'In those days, grief was a private thing, not to be shared with anyone. Even my husband didn't know how much I was suffering to be honest, though, I didn't allow him to know (that was the way then) – and therefore he couldn't help me. One shouldn't complain, of course. Things were so much simpler, yet so much harsher, then.

'It faded, though. They say that time is a great healer, but it's not time that does the healing, it's oneself. There comes a moment when one must awake from the blackness and realize that hope has not died. Hope never dies, you know.'

She turned at this and looked directly into Helena's eyes. Above a small smile there was grief in her eyes, grief that advertised itself by a gentle but bright shimmering. 'No normal human being loses hope. Without hope we are mad . . . and you are not mad, Helena. Far from it. You are probably the sanest person you know.'

Slowly, Helena whispered, 'I don't feel like it.'

'You've lost your child. To the doctors, it was just another medical problem; an "IUD", they call it – intrauterine death – but it was infinitely more than three initials to you. To the father it was a sadness, but one that can be surmounted; after all, he has abundant seed to spread around and he had no great investment in the process. Yet to you, it was everything.

'The loss of a limb is traumatic because one has in one's head an idea of what one should look like and that image persists even after amputation. Reality and imagination conflict. Losing a child is like that. Within perhaps days of learning you're pregnant, the idea is imprinted on your very being that your baby is a part of you. You're hard-wired to think like that, you cannot help yourself.

'You haven't lost a baby, Helena. You haven't lost something that is separate, you've had a part of your being removed, a part that had become as integral to you as the legs on which you walk, the hands with which you wipe away your tears.'

Helena knew about the myth of the Sirens, knew that their calls were beyond human refusal, and even as a voice told her this woman was deliberately enticing her out of her exile, she could not help but listen.

'That's exactly how I feel,' she admitted in a whisper.

A small but eager nod. 'Yes, and that's how I felt, all those years ago . . . but . . . ' And here her face folded into one of sorrow and one, too, of trepidation. 'I have to be honest with you, Helena.'

'About what?'

A sigh. 'It doesn't go away. Not ever.'

Helena dropped her gaze. In a low voice she murmured, 'I know that.'

'But of course you do. I knew you would.'

Helena was lost again, the memories of her dead parents and stepbrother a vision too intense to ignore, and into this her visitor said softly, 'I still wonder about my children, the ones I never knew, the ones who were not to be given the chance.' As if by some sort of mesmerism, Helena found herself again listening to the words. 'What would they have been like? Would they have been fair-haired or dark? Would they have been tall or short? Was I never to have sons or more daughters?'

A gentle laugh, but even as Helena heard it she saw the tears in the eyes above it, realized how rheumy they were.

'But listen to me! You don't want to hear the foolish ramblings of an old woman. You have cares enough of your own.'

Helena said at once, 'No . . . I do.'

'You're sure?'

Helena's nod was the first step on the journey back.

Sixteen

It was late in the afternoon as Beverley looked through the photographs that the Scenes of Crime officer had taken of the Delorme death. She sat at her desk as she did so and tried to ignore Grover, who sat opposite as he typed up the statements that had been taken from the neighbours. She glanced up at her sergeant. Lambert had struck a mighty blow against her and despite the pain she could not but admire him for it. Making a career in the force was hard enough for an attractive woman, but giving her someone like Grover as an assistant was like tying her to a millstone and leaving her to tread water for a few weeks. It would have been hard enough if it had merely been someone who was green to the point of gangrene, but to have someone who seemed more suited to a seminary and who thought of his immediate superior as some sort of succubus was beyond toleration.

Much as she wanted to do otherwise, however, she had to cope.

And overall, she did not consider that she had made too bad a start on the case, even with a handicap that was equivalent to chopping the fingers off a flautist. It appeared that Atopia was some sort of medical clinic near the river, about 15 kilometres away. It had been open for sixteen years, and was owned and run by one Dr Adam Dreifus. Checks on Anita Delorme had found no criminal convictions, no file notes concerning possible national security violations and no speeding offences, although apparently she had had a penchant for parking where she shouldn't, accumulating no fewer than thirteen tickets in the past five years.

And, intriguingly, although she did not have a gun licence, she had applied for one.

'So what do you think, Grover?' Her question was as much

to find out if he *was* thinking, rather than the specifics of the process.

'I'm sorry?'

'I said, "What do you think?"'

He looked lost, Beverley decided – not alarmed that he did not know what was being asked – just adrift. She was on the point of providing her sergeant with his third and final chance to answer (and doing so in a voice that would not have hidden her opinion of Grover's fitness for the plain-clothes branch) when, 'Oh, you mean the killing?'

Beverley showed her surprise, did so by the smooth movement of her eyebrows. 'Do you think it was murder?'

Grover was a thing of simple beliefs: things were right or wrong, people were saints or sinners, Anita Delorme must have been murdered.

'It must have been.' Beverley found she could at least admire the confidence, and decided that it was the kind of confidence that had provided the world with the charge of the Light Brigade.

'Why?'

She had noticed before that this innocuous little word of three letters, this interrogative that did not even require a tongue to pronounce, was a thing of great destruction. It sounded weak, insipid, not worthy of notice and so was invariably missed, and in that lay its power.

'Women don't kill themselves violently.'

'Don't they?'

A shake of the head. 'No. That's what men do. Women choose less messy ways – tablets, perhaps a hosepipe on the exhaust, maybe even hanging.'

'Been reading up, have you?'

'A bit.' This sheepishly.

Beverley said nothing and returned to the photographs. Grover asked his superior's coiffure, 'Don't you?'

She looked up at Grover. 'Don't I what?'

'Think it was murder.'

A smile. Not just any smile, but a lazy one, one that spoke of secret knowledge. 'I don't know.'

'But you must do.'

Beverley's fuse had always been short but, where Grover was concerned, it was dangerously so. There was just no time to run once it had been lit. 'I don't *must* do anything, Sergeant.'

He coloured. 'No, Sir.'

'Until we speak to her general practitioner – have you found out who it was, by the way?'

'We've found nothing in her house, so we're going through the Primary Care Trust.'

'Well, until we speak to her GP, we don't know for instance if she had a history of depression. For all we know she was discharged from St Christopher's two days ago having swallowed three hundred aspirin and half a bottle of kettle descaler.'

At which Grover's expression was so deflated that it actually pierced Beverley's armour, and after a slightly awkward pause she asked in a gentler tone, 'Have you any other reason for your theory?'

Grover considered, then asked simply, 'What reason might she have to commit suicide?'

Beverley shrugged. 'Any number.'

'Well she was single, so by definition it wasn't marital problems . . .'

'At least, not in *her* marriage,' interrupted Beverley, which rather made Grover pause.

'What does that mean?'

'Just because she wasn't married didn't mean she wasn't having relationship problems. This chap with the Jag. Maybe he was married . . .'

Grover could not see that this would be a problem. 'But surely, that would be *his* problem, not hers.'

Momentarily, Beverley was back in just such a situation, remembering all too clearly how much the problem of whether her lover would leave his wife had agonized her.

'Yes,' she sighed. 'Of course, you're right.'

Grover pressed onwards, victory a sweet scent in his nose that turned his head and warped his judgement. 'And she clearly had no financial problems.'

Beverley almost laughed. 'Yes . . . you're absolutely right,' she agreed brightly. 'No financial problems at all.'

For a moment Grover was misdirected into a land where he got things right, then he appreciated that there was a subtext to Beverley's agreement. 'Is there something I'm missing?'

'Look, Grover. I understand that in the universe you inhabit,

everyone and everything can be fitted into boxes – they're
either criminals or honest people, saved or damned, redheads,
blondes or brunettes – but in the real world, the world I have
to wade through, it's not that simple. Sometimes saints sin,
and sometimes sinners do the right thing. Even I do the right
thing sometimes.'

'I know that,' protested Grover, to all appearances oblivious of the implied insult. 'I'm not as naive as you seem to
believe.'

'No? Then why do you assume that just because someone's
not short of money, they don't have money problems?'

'Well . . . '

'Hasn't it occurred to you that she had really a rather good
lifestyle considering the salary she was on?'

'Thirty thousand's not bad. It can go a long way, especially
if you're single, like she was.'

Beverley shook her head. 'No.' This was not a debating
point, this was an assertion of reality, but Grover missed the
signpost.

'If she'd been careful . . . '

'No.' It stopped him, made him think, but even then Grover
did not, to Beverley's eye, demonstrate a particularly gracious
acceptance of what he was being told. 'She had too much
money.'

'She didn't have much in the bank . . . '

Beverley pursed her lips, told herself that Grover had a lot
to learn, fought back the thought that the universe would not
live long enough to teach it all to him. 'Look, take my word
for it, she had more money than she knew what to do with.
She didn't have a lot in the bank because she was smart,
because she bought goods and services with cash rather than
draw attention to herself with the odd hundred thousand mouldering away in the vaults of some crappy little building society
somewhere.'

'But that's not a reason to kill yourself . . . '

'Isn't it? Maybe she was being blackmailed.'

'Blackmailed? What about?'

'About the way she was able to afford so much. About how
she was financing her lifestyle.'

There was then a pause for consideration. 'Perhaps it's also
a reason for murdering her.'

'Perhaps.' Before Grover could lay claim to some sort of victory, Beverley added, 'All I want you to do is to keep your mind at least partially open. Don't close it to anything.'

And maybe it was in this spirit that Grover said after a short pause, 'I suppose we've got no evidence that she was doing anything illegal. Perhaps she was independently wealthy; perhaps that's how she managed to afford all those luxuries.'

'Independently wealthy, you say?'

'It's possible.'

Beverley felt severely depressed. In which particular field, she wondered, had they grown Grover?

'Independently wealthy . . . as in Lady Fotheringay-Phipps? You think that Anita Delorme is perhaps fifty-fourth in line to the throne and that she lives incognito amongst the peasants for her own reasons?'

The sarcasm penetrated. 'I still say it's possible.'

'Grover, it's possible but improbable. I deal in what is both possible *and* probable.'

'You also said not to close my mind to anything.'

'Well, open your mind to this. She didn't have an overdraft and she had no significant credit card debts. After tax, she earned two thousand pounds per month yet her bank statements suggest that she wasn't saving any of it. If we assume for the time being that she wasn't the heir to a few hundred billion, where did she get the money for the holidays, the car, the expensive clothes and, I suspect, a lot of other things we don't yet know about?'

Grover actually opened his mouth, but his superior had not finished. 'Isn't it odd how she suddenly became independently wealthy only a short time ago?'

Which surprised him because he had not picked up on this. 'Did she?'

Beverley nodded, enjoying the moment. 'So what does that tell you?'

He tried, but could only shrug. She said, 'I don't know either. So let's find out. First you're going to find out if she had any loans we don't know about. Then you're going to check her credit rating. Then you're going to find out where she bought her car and her more expensive items of clothing, and you're going to find out how she paid for them.'

Grover's eyes widened appreciably at this itinerary, but

Beverley hadn't finished. 'Meanwhile, you're going to be finding Anita Delorme's next of kin. I want to know the woman who turned into that mess in the kitchen. And at the same time, I want to know where she got that gun. She didn't have a licence, so that means either she stole it or she was given it by someone else, or her killer brought it with them. I want to know which of those is the truth.'

If her sergeant thought to raise a revolt at this list of demands, he had at least learned in the past couple of days not to proceed with the venture. 'Yes, Sir.'

Beverley stood up.

'But first, we're going to pay a visit to Benhall Grange.'

Seventeen

B enhall Grange was a mock-Regency house on a hillside that overlooked Donnington and, more importantly perhaps, could clearly be seen from almost every vantage point in that fair town. It had started life as the home of George Hayward, who made his millions in the canal boom of the nineteenth century; money that his son then lost in the twentieth century because he saw the wonderful opportunities that intercontinental travel by airship offered. Andrew Hayward had been the last of the line, living in the Grange as it slowly decayed into senescence while he consumed the remains of his family's fortune, having a liking for vintage French wines, truffles and rare first editions. He died in 1985 after falling off his library ladder, leaving the house in his will to Atopia. He had done so because he had suffered from a life-long allergy to book leather, a considerable handicap given his hobby and one that Atopia had apparently helped him with. The chairman of Atopia was Adam Dreifus, a local general practitioner.

As Beverley and Grover drove down the gently curving driveway, the sight of the whitewashed, two-storey house set at the centre of a wide circle of gravel was striking to behold.

The thunderous sky from which rain fell upon them provided a suitably dramatic backdrop.

'There's money here,' remarked Beverley as they joined about half a dozen other cars parked at the perimeter of the circle in front of the house.

Grover said, 'Private medicine.' He said it in a tone that suggested censure.

'You don't approve?'

Grover shrugged. 'Why should the rich have better health care than the poor?'

'Why should they have better cars, bigger houses, whiter teeth? They do. End of story.'

Grover was clearly unimpressed with this reasoning, but did not reply, which suited Beverley just fine.

The front door was black, and shiny enough to pluck her eyebrows by. A large brass knob in the middle of it was too big to be grasped by one hand and a plaque to the right told them that they had come to the right place, as if during the trip down from the road they might have forgotten the large sign at the top of the drive.

'Do we knock?' asked Grover. 'Wait for the footman to answer the door?'

Beverley pushed the door and it opened smoothly. She said to Grover, 'Before you come in, I suggest you wipe your feet and scrape off all the prejudices.'

The entrance hall was two stories tall but narrow. Plants that might have been aspidistra were positioned in alcoves, the walls were painted duck egg blue and the floor was a chequer work of stone tiles on which their feet made harsh staccato noises that were blurred by faint but immediate echoes. About 20 metres in was a staircase that wound around the far wall beneath a window that must have been 6 metres high and that illuminated the whole space with a preternatural glow. On the left was a reception desk behind which sat a pretty young woman of Asian extraction, on the right were comfortable Regency-style armchairs around a low table. Two of these were occupied by a middle-aged woman and a teenage girl. The woman looked at the newcomers with a trace of interest, whereas the teenage girl's expression suggested that she would have stopped looking bored only if a rock star or Premiership footballer had come in.

She was staring intently at her mobile phone, presumably texting.

The pretty young girl of Asian extraction – called, according to her name badge, Daksha – looked at them expectantly. Grover obliged.

'This is Detective Inspector Wharton, I'm Detective Sergeant Grover. We'd like to talk to Dr Dreifus.'

The middle-aged woman's interest increased at this announcement. The teenage girl, lagging slightly behind, flicked a glance at them, then returned to her phone.

Daksha frowned and hesitated. 'I'm not sure that he's in yet.'

'But he is expected?'

'Oh, yes. Soon.' She glanced at the woman and girl. 'Definitely soon.'

Grover looked at Wharton, who was just debating her next move when the front door opened again and in came a man with longish, curly hair, a smart metal briefcase and a slight limp. He also had a look of irritation on his face.

Ignoring them completely in a preoccupied sweep through the hallway in which they were standing, he could be heard muttering to himself.

'Dr Dreifus?'

He stopped, the irritation deepening into anger. 'What is it?' This was almost petulant. He had a sharply pointed nose and a five o'clock shadow that Beverley suspected was permanent. He was handsome, although in the way that conventionally was called 'unconventional'.

But there was more to it than that. He exuded something. She could not name it but she could sense it, an instinctual thing. His looks were a small part of it, almost an irrelevance. He was magnetic because of what he was, because of the way he warped the space around him.

He's an important man and he knows it.

Daksha said helpfully, 'The police are here for you.' The audience, now totally engaged, turned their attention to the good doctor who, upon hearing this news, shifted gears from petulant all the way down to wary.

'Police?'

Beverley stepped forward, regulation smile upon her face: not friendly, just not menacing. 'May we have a word, Dr Dreifus?'

'Well . . . '

'It's quite important.'

The audience, now swollen to three by Daksha, felt a rising tension. Dr Dreifus, in a break with theatrical tradition, decided to involve them. 'Jemima, here, has an appointment.'

Jemima looked at them belligerently while her mother nodded slightly.

'I'm sure Jemima won't mind. We'll be as quick as possible.'

He still did not look very happy, an emotion which was clearly shared by Jemima's mater, but Beverley had adopted a voice that had behind it a great deal of determination, much as a glacier has no intention of stopping until it, and it alone, decides to.

Dreifus had clearly seen a glacier before.

He said to Jemima's mother, 'I'm terribly sorry, Mrs Huxley, but you can see the position I'm in.'

Whether Mrs Huxley did see his position was moot, since her facial expression could only be interpreted as unhappy. She said frostily, 'We've haven't got long. Jemima's got ballet.'

Which surprised Beverley, since Jemima's resemblance to a prima ballerina was, to say the least, well-camouflaged by fat.

'Of course, of course. We won't be long.' Dreifus said this with such certainty that Beverley almost felt convinced by it

He turned back to them. 'This way,' he said curtly.

Eighteen

'I hope this isn't going to take long. I have an extremely busy schedule this evening.'

'A lot of patients to see?'

'And after that administration. This is a very complex organization to run.'

'How come?'

'We don't just see patients, there's also a great deal of

research done here. The fees from the patients pay for that research.'

She saw that Grover was looking slightly less severe, presumably mollified by this admission of good works. She asked, 'So what are you researching into?'

'Allergy. More specifically, hypersensitivity.'

Grover surprised them both by asking, 'Anaphylaxis?'

Dreifus turned to him. 'That's right, amongst other things. You know something about it?'

But Grover only shook his head, looking slightly alarmed at being thus examined and mumbling, 'Not really.'

Back to Beverley and perhaps slightly disappointed, Dreifus said, 'It is an area that is woefully underfunded in this country. Cancer, yes; heart disease, yes; but most forms of disease affecting the immune system, no. Not "sexy", the funding bodies tell me.' He sneered the word as if it were excrement he had stepped into.

'Even so, this is all very opulent . . . '

'Absolutely, but necessarily so. When one is paying such high fees, one expects a certain standard of care, and in that standard a degree of opulence is mandatory.'

Grover's disdain was returning, rushing in like a rip tide. Before Beverley could stop him he said, 'It's not right, though, is it? That these people should receive a higher standard of care than others . . . ?'

Dreifus had clearly heard these sentiments from other mouths, at other times, for his attitude was anything but defensive. 'I think you're being unnecessarily polemical. I am a general practitioner during the day, working here only in my spare time, and this is a non-profit enterprise. "These people", as you call them, subsidize the research, nothing more. The research is very much for the good of all, irrespective of the ability to pay.'

Before Grover could respond, Beverley interjected hurriedly, 'The research lab is here as well, is it?'

Dreifus nodded, but instead of reinforcing this with vocal affirmation, he asked, 'Look, this is all very interesting, but you are holding up my consultation. If this is all you've come about, I'm afraid I must insist that we terminate the discussion now.'

Beverley gave the impression that she was completely

uninterested in what he might or might not want. 'You surely can't run it all on your own? You must have some sort of help in managing the place.'

'Yes . . . yes, I do.'

Beverley sensed a subtle change in the atmosphere and wondered if Grover noticed it as well.

'Anita Delorme.'

That Beverley should utter this name unnerved Dreifus, as if she had uttered some sort of incantatory spell, attempted to conjure djinns.

'Yes.'

Beverley leaned forward and said with utmost seriousness, 'Then I'm afraid you have a problem. Anita Delorme was found this morning without the back of her head and quite a lot of her brains decorating her kitchen.'

She knew from experience that simulation of surprise was a very difficult thing to achieve and she was well used to judging it. Dreifus passed the audition. He looked as if someone had crept up behind him and, finding his sensitive little place, had jabbed a stiletto in.

'Oh, my God!' This whispered and sustained, his face first frozen into surprise, then horror.

But she wondered then, momentarily, if there was also something else.

She said, 'I take it you weren't expecting her to come in today.'

'What?' He was having trouble focusing. She looked across at her sergeant and saw the familiar look of distaste, but this time it was fixed upon her. Gamely ignoring this unspoken rebuke at her insensitivity, she said to Dreifus, 'You don't seem to have missed her, so I assume it was her day off, or something.'

Slowly he pulled himself out of a deep reverie. 'She'd asked for yesterday and today off.'

'Did she say why?'

'No.' He had to concentrate to answer this.

'What were her duties?'

But the reverie was proving a strong and determined opponent, and he was again some way away from the conversation. She was just about to repeat the question when he asked abruptly, 'You're saying she committed suicide?'

'I'm saying she's dead. I don't know who was responsible.'
'Murder?'
'We haven't excluded that possibility.'
'But who would murder her? And why?'
'We don't know that it was murder. We just don't know that it wasn't.'
'But she wouldn't have killed herself. Why would she do that?'
'That's what I'd like to know.'

A frown had formed on his forehead and it was deepening rapidly, like a threatening meteorological depression. 'No,' he decided at last, 'She couldn't have killed herself . . . not like *that*.' As if this were a rather impolite way to die, something done only by artisans and other lower orders.

'How *would* she have done it?' As soon as Beverley asked this, she regretted it. Dreifus flushed angrily. 'Anita was a bright, attractive and very talented young lady. She had everything to live for.'

But Beverley had heard such assurances many times before and was long past putting any value upon them. She nodded understandingly, though, before passing on. 'Could I ask what salary you paid her?'

'What's that got to do with anything?'
'I don't know, but I'd still like you to tell me.'

A sigh. 'Thirty thousand pounds per annum, give or take.'

This correlated with the sums going into Anita's bank account but, nevertheless, she said in a surprised tone, 'Really? That's quite a lot.'

'She had a very responsible job. This clinic has an annual turnover of nearly a million pounds.'

'All from private medicine?'
'We have various fund-raising events throughout the year.'
'And Anita Delorme handled the accounts?'
'That's right.'
'Alone?'

He looked hard at her. 'The accounts are handled in accordance with strict procedures.'

'And you had absolute confidence in her?'
'Yes.'

Beverley considered this. There was something about the reply she didn't like and she wondered if he had just lied to her. A look across to Grover told her that he was at least doing his job and making assiduous notes. Back to Dreifus she asked, 'Did you know much about her private life?'

A shrug. 'Not really.'

He's hiding something.

'Know anything about boyfriends or her family?'

'Nothing.'

Oh, yes. You're hiding something.

'But you must have seen her CV?'

'Yes.'

His manner had become clipped, almost staccato.

'Can I, then?'

Unaccountably she saw surprise, as if this request had come via his blind spot, as if it did not follow at all that she should want to see something like Anita's CV. 'Oh . . . yes, I suppose so.'

He got up and went to a filing cabinet. It took him quite a while, but he eventually succeeded in finding the CV. He brought it back to Beverley. She flicked through it, noting that it was professionally done and that it was impressive. First class degree in accountancy from the London School of Economics, MBA from Surrey, jobs working for Oxfam and Cancer Research UK. She wondered how much of it was make-believe, and handed it to Grover for safekeeping.

'She had a very good lifestyle,' she commented.

Dreifus played a good, solid forward defensive. 'Did she?'

'Oh, yes. The car, of course, you know about, but there were also the holidays, the clothing, the visits to expensive health resorts . . . '

She saw that she had caught his interest but his next question belied it. 'What has this to do with me?'

'I don't see how she could have lived like that, even on what you paid her.'

There was *definitely* something he did not like about what she was implying. 'I really can't comment,' was all he said.

'No?'

'No.'

She looked at him, intrigued. *What do you know that you don't want us to know, Dr Dreifus?*

Abruptly, she said, 'We'll need to look through her office.'

He responded quickly. 'I don't know if that's going to be possible.'

'Really? Why not?'

'There's confidential information in there.'

But Beverley could see no force in this argument. 'Surely not patient data? What would Anita Delorme have access to medical notes for?'

'Confidential *financial* information.'

'Really? But aren't you a charity?'

'Yes.'

'So all your accounts are a matter of public record.'

'Well, I suppose . . . '

'So what's the problem?'

A slight pause during which Dr Dreifus looked as if he were giving birth to an egg with sharp corners, then, 'Very well.' He stood up, almost launching himself from the chair. 'It's just down the corridor.'

He marched out of the office, seemingly not bothered about whether they were in his slipstream or not. Two doors down and he stopped and felt in his pocket for a key, with which he gained entrance to the office beyond.

They followed him in. Beverley looked around at an office that was tidy and neat, just as Anita Delorme's home had been. Three filing cabinets, ring binders on shelves, cardboard files in piles in an open-fronted cupboard, a computer with its attendants in front of a window, nothing out of place. A wall-planner beside the doorway, a cactus on the windowsill.

She turned to Dreifus. 'I don't want to detain you.'

'But . . . '

'Your patient is waiting.'

The reminder had its effect. 'Yes . . . well . . . ' He thought deeply, then financial considerations won him over. 'I'll be back as soon as I can.'

She called after him just before he left the room, 'What car do you drive?'

He looked surprised as he answered, 'An Audi. An Audi A6. Why?'

'No reason.'

Nineteen

Eisenmenger returned to the house through driving rain that was a perfect reflection of his mood. He had just spent two hours with Helena; two hours in which he had suffered anguished frustration at her apparent lack of interest in anything. No topic of conversation had found any connection with her and the only answers he had managed to elicit had been both monotoned and monosyllabic, noises made just to get him to leave her alone rather than to impart information or to make some form of emotional contact. He had looked for signs of improvement, at first eagerly, then desperately, but had seen little. He had talked later with the charge nurse who had expressed optimism, but Eisenmenger was enough of a cynic to suspect that he had heard platitude rather than realism. It had been suggested that he should take the opportunity to talk to Helena's key worker who would be around the next day – it would help her understand Helena and her illness. Eisenmenger seriously doubted it would be of much value, but felt strongly that he would do anything to help Helena's recovery.

So he was now back in their temporary home, ready-prepared lasagne for one sitting in the microwave, the prospect of another evening alone before him.

He missed Helena worse than he had ever thought he would, more than he had ever thought he would miss *anyone*. He had known in his life only three women really well. His wife, Deborah, had been the first, and Maria the second; both of these had seemed to be 'true' loves and, perhaps at the time they had been. Time had taught him well, though, that few truths were eternal and that all things decayed, it was just that they decayed at different rates. The 'truth' of his love for Maria had lasted only a short time, that of his love for his wife somewhat longer. He had believed that what he felt for Helena would last for aeons, still fervently hoped that it would.

Helena, he knew well, was resilient, but even her spirit had bent before this final blast from fate. He could only hope that it had not broken, could only stand by and be ready to help whenever and wherever required. He did not admit to anyone how hard he found his role in this, for really there was no one to whom he felt he could talk. Without Helena, he felt he had little. Even his work – his traditional refuge in times of crisis – was tedious and bland: merely a production line of routine reporting and risk reduction. He wondered how his colleagues could face the day each morning knowing that this was their lot for the rest of their working lives.

The only vaguely flickering brightness in the gloomy prospect was the case of Edward Melnick, who had died somewhat unexpectedly and in a way as yet unexplained. It was a mystery and Eisenmenger hoped to turn that mystery into a sanctuary from the bleakness in his life. Accordingly, he had brought the file home and, after his peculiarly tasteless supper, he sat down on the sofa and began to reread the papers.

Not all deaths are explicable. This was one of the rules – one of the limitations – of morbid anatomy. It had to be born in mind at all times, but there was a continual pressure on all pathologists to overcome this boundary. Relatives, coroners, clinicians all refused to accept that occasionally people dropped dead (or perhaps faded away) without a single obvious cause. It was, in a way, a tribute to pathology that people could not believe that occasionally it failed, that once in a while no clues were found.

The instance of Edward Melnick was not quite like that, though. Had the toxicology come back as negative, then he would have been happier, would not have felt something exciting him, something causing him to feel as he often felt during the investigation of a suspicious death.

But this wasn't suspicious, was it?

So what if Melnick had therapeutic levels of an anti-hypoglycaemic drug in his blood? That wouldn't have killed him. By definition, therapeutic levels were not dangerous.

At least, not dangerous unless he had had an allergy to it, which was one possibility.

However, there had been no signs of anaphylaxis, the

catastrophic allergic reaction that could lead to sudden death. Eisenmenger was happy that there had been no facial congestion, no blueing of the lips and tongue, no swelling of the back of the throat. He had not taken the blood samples that would have proven the case, but he was satisfied that this was an extremely unlikely possibility.

So how did the drug kill him?

He knew only that Metformin was a drug that lowered blood sugar and that was therefore used in diabetes. Could it, he wondered, lower blood sugar in a normal person to a catastrophic extent? He had an old copy of the *British National Formulary* – the bible for all those prescribing drugs – somewhere in his belongings. It took him some minutes, but he located it eventually.

And he discovered thereby the cause of death.

Metformin in normal dosage did not lower blood sugar to a catastrophic extent in a non-diabetic person . . . unless that person had consumed a large amount of alcohol.

At least he had a mode of death. Edward Melnick had got very drunk and then somehow he had taken a couple of Metformin tablets. They had interacted with the alcohol as he slept, lowering his blood sugar to the point of coma, and he had died.

Which was brilliant. His only problem now was to explain how the drug came to be in Melnick's blood. Metformin was not available over the counter, nor could it be purchased at will from a supermarket.

He turned to the reports that the Coroner's Office had supplied.

It was clear from the rather terse note that accompanied them – *Reports as requested* – that he was still not their favourite person, but he overcame his disappointment by imbibing a large mouthful of Pouilly-Fumé and moving manfully on.

There were three reports – one from the Edward Melnick's wife, Rose; one from the landlord of The Eagle public house; and one from Melnick's general practitioner. None of them was what he might have called 'weighty' (the longest was two pages), but he hoped there would be quality even without the quantity.

Mrs Melnick had had the privilege of being the spouse of

Edward Melnick for twelve years. It was a second marriage for both of them. The statement did not say whether her first had been a happy affair but it appeared that her second had not been a thing of unending and unsurpassed joy. Indeed, it seemed that their partnership had been characterized by a cold war that erupted on regular intervals into spectacular fire-fights. Mr Melnick had been violent and selfish, a heavy drinker. According to Mrs Melnick, he had been capable of small-minded viciousness, such as the time he had stolen her savings and lost them all on a bet on the Cheltenham Gold Cup, and the time he had deliberately hidden her tablets after an especially violent altercation.

She had last seen him alive at six o'clock in the evening when she had cooked sausages and chips for him. He had then gone to The Eagle where, as far as she was aware, he had passed the evening. She had not heard him return home, for they slept in separate rooms. She was not bothered when he did not appear the next morning – he rarely rose before eleven – but when he missed lunch she went to his room to wake him and found him fully clothed, lying on the bed. He was quite cold.

The statement from the publican held no surprises. Edward Melnick had been a 'regular', by which it appeared that he spent every evening and a fair number of afternoons in the pub, where he was regarded as a 'good bloke' who stood his round when asked and who would do anything for anyone (unless, apparently, he had married them). On the night he died, he had consumed his regular six pints (with two whisky chasers) and then tottered off home. There had been no un-toward incidents, nothing to distinguish that night from any of a thousand others.

The general practitioner was Adam Dreifus. Eisenmenger knew him slightly, and had not warmed to him. He reported concern at the heavy alcohol consumption but Edward Melnick had refused help, had refused to accept that it was a problem. There were also several other minor medical complaints – diverticular disease, an ingrowing toenail, gout – but nothing that seemed to Eisenmenger to be significant in his death. There was no mention of diabetes.

He put the reports down, his mind completely blank.

Time for more wine, he decided. That would improve the situation.

He was beginning to get a headache and knew the alcohol was not helping, but did not care. Some paracetamol was the answer. He got up and went to the kitchen, unsure of where they were. Helena had a faintly annoying habit of hiding things like medicines and plasters at the backs of drawers and cupboards and his brain seemed incapable of retaining the knowledge of their precise whereabouts. He knew also that his method of locating the tablets would result in accusations that he was behaving like a burglar, leaving a trail of disorganization and disruption in his wake.

That is, if life had been normal . . .

This unexpected and uninvited reminder that Helena was not with him, was sick in a very real way, brought him low, but it did not last.

Tablets.

Edward Melnick might not have been diabetic, but what about his wife?

Her statement said that he had once deliberately deprived her of her tablets. Tablets for what?

Twenty

As the door closed, Beverley said quietly, 'Don't hurry back.'

Grover said, 'He couldn't wait, could he? Money to be made, I suppose. Mustn't upset Lady Muckamuck.'

Beverley didn't reply. The rain was slashing at the windows, rattling the glass in the frames. Grover continued his diatribe. 'I bet he wouldn't have hurried off like that if it had been an NHS patient waiting in the foyer.'

'At least he's raising money for charitable work.'

'Private medicine is morally wrong.'

'Indefensible?'

Grover looked at her. 'Pretty much.'

Beverley was beginning to find her sergeant's over-simplistic view of the world irritating but she wanted to poke around in Anita Delorme's office before Dreifus returned to oversee affairs. She forewent a debate, instead curtly directing Grover to the filing cabinets while she addressed herself to the files that were piled on the desk.

'And hurry,' she advised.

Neither of them spoke for ten minutes, until Grover gave up trying to seem experienced and asked, 'What are we looking for?'

'The accounts of this place.'

'Why?'

Beverley was having trouble opening a desk drawer and had started looking for a key. 'Because Anita Delorme had too much money.'

'You can't believe she was stealing from this place?'

Genuinely surprised, Beverley looked up at him. 'Why not?'

'Because someone would have known.'

'You think so? Why?'

'Because there are checks and because I'm sure Dr Dreifus would have noticed.'

'I think he's running this place on a shoestring and just managing to keep going only by the skin of his teeth. I bet you she's been given total freedom when it comes to balancing the books as long as they appear to balance.'

'But if she's taking money, then they wouldn't balance, would they?'

'No, but they might *appear* to balance, especially to an untrained eye. She had a degree in accountancy, don't forget. Do you think Dreifus has either the experience or the time to keep close tabs on her? I bet she was given absolute trust. She had a good CV and she was reasonably pretty; like the fool that every man is, he thought that was a sign of an honest heart.'

Grover radiated his lack of support for this hypothesis but said nothing. Beverley found herself with an inexplicable urge to convert her sergeant to her view of matters. 'Don't forget, Dreifus isn't only trying to run this place, he's also a full-time general practitioner. In that situation he'd have to delegate and then hope that he finds the right person to delegate to. Perhaps he chose wrong in this case.'

Grover nodded but it conveyed a diplomatic agreement, one with the intention of ending the discussion, rather than true acquiescence to the cause that Beverley was espousing. He then said, 'It must be hard work to run a place this.'

Beverley saw a chance to tweak her junior's tail and failed to resist temptation. 'I'm sure he only does it because of his dedication to his patients.'

Grover appeared astonished at this display of naiveté. 'If he's dedicated to anything, it's money,' he said firmly.

Beverley shrugged. She did not really care. 'Whatever. It's not his motives regarding this place that I'm interested in at the moment.'

They continued searching for a while longer, after which Grover asked, 'Do you think it's possible that Dreifus was her lover?'

Beverley did not look up. She had come across a box file marked Office Upgrades. It was filled with receipts for computer equipment. In the past year, several tens of thousands of pounds had been spent. 'Well, apparently he doesn't drive a green Jaguar,' she said. She put the file to one side so they could take it away with them for some closer perusal later. 'But that doesn't mean he isn't *one* of her lovers.'

Grover looked up at her. 'She's got more than one?' he asked. The incredulity was almost comical.

Beverley's head stayed down, her eyes remaining on the search. She was trying not to laugh and could not reply at once. The sudden opening of the door saved her from betraying her amusement. They both looked up to see a middle-aged woman standing there. She was dressed in a dark blue nurse's uniform, replete with fob watch. She was tall and thin and probably had a good figure, although it was difficult to tell because of the uniform. Her face, though, was attractive: her lips were full, her mouth wide and her eyes kindly, while her ash grey hair was tied back in a ponytail.

'Oh!'

They both straightened up. Before they could speak, she continued, 'I heard someone in here . . . I wondered who it was.' Her voice was soft, one that had received an education and listened to it.

Grover showed her his warrant card. 'Police.'

'Oh!' she said again as her eyes widened. She showed the flexibility of the English language by uttering the same vowel sound in a completely different manner, thus conveying a new meaning.

Grover began, 'If you wouldn't mind . . . '

But Beverley interrupted him. 'Do you know Anita Delorme?'

'Of course.'

'Well?'

'We're just colleagues, but we get on OK.'

'Do you ever see her outside of work?'

'Not really.'

Beverley was firing questions off, hoping to pre-empt for as long as possible the inevitable enquiry as to why they wanted to know. For the same reason she was using the present tense, as if even as they spoke Anita Delorme was happily doing what she always did in the evening.

'What do you know of her personal life?'

The defence against curiosity failed and she didn't reply. 'What's going on? Is Anita all right? Has something happened?'

Beverley was matter of fact. 'She's dead.'

Once more the eyes widened, once more the vowel sound, this time conveying a third meaning. For an instant she might have been about to faint. Certainly there was horror – or well-simulated horror – at this news. 'Oh. Oh, my God.'

'We need some background.'

She was oblivious. Their needs were not for the moment important. 'Poor Anita.'

Grover stepped in. 'Could we have your name?'

She responded to the change in voice. 'Charlotte Pelger.'

'And you're a nurse here?'

She nodded.

'For how long?'

'Three years.'

Beverley did not want to be impressed by Grover but she had to admit he had made progress. She took over. 'What was she like?'

'What do you mean?'

'Was she a happy person?'

'Very. Always jolly.'

'And recently? Still happy?'

She hesitated. 'Well, she'd been a bit down, I think.'

'Do you know why?'

She shook her head, then shrugged. 'Sorry.'

'She was attractive, I think.'

She picked up on the past tense. 'What's happened?' This in a querulous, almost frightened tone.

Beverley saw no reason to spare this health professional, one who was only a colleague of the deceased, many of the details. 'A shotgun blast to the head.'

This time, Charlotte Pelger did look unwell: her eyelids fluttered and the eyes began to roll upwards. Grover stepped forward and took her shoulders, guiding her to a chair. Over his shoulder, he asked, 'Did you have to?'

Beverley shrugged, refusing to betray the whiff of shame she felt at her own callousness. Charlotte continued with her own part, muttering to herself, 'Oh, my God. How horrible.'

'Just take a few deep breaths,' advised Grover.

It took a few minutes, but she eventually recovered. There were now tears in her eyes and she had to dab at her nose with a handkerchief. Beverley saw someone who embodied caring not just as a profession, but also as a personal quality. She wondered how the nurse managed to do her job.

'I'm sorry to have shocked you,' she offered. 'But we have to find out as much as we can about Anita.'

'Of course.'

Beverley leaned against the side of the desk at right angles to her. She said gently, 'She fitted in well?'

'Absolutely.'

'Everyone liked her?'

Charlotte nodded.

Without a pause, Beverley asked, 'How much?'

The nurse looked across at her, surprised. 'What do you mean?'

'Was she seeing anyone who worked here?'

'A man, you mean?'

Beverley explained patiently, 'Was she more than just friendly with anyone?'

At first, Charlotte Pelger seemed about to succumb to self-imposed ignorance, but then she became possessed by a spirit of intrigue. 'Well, it's funny you should say that . . . '

But it wasn't funny – not to Beverley or Grover, anyway. 'Why?'

'Because I think she *was* seeing someone. She tried to keep it quiet, but it was fairly obvious.'

Grover got to the trigger first. 'Who?'

She looked delighted to be asked. 'Donald Lennox.'

'Who's he?'

'A colleague of Dr Dreifus.'

'He works here?'

'No. At Water Lane Surgery. That's where Dr Dreifus works during the day.'

'What car does he drive?'

She appeared surprised by the question but answered nonetheless. 'A green Jaguar. One of the classic types.'

Grover was delighted with himself until, with her eyebrows arched and forming a perfect mathematical figure, Beverley enquired of her sergeant, 'Anything else you'd like to know?'

Grover spotted the sarcasm – could hardly ignore it – and accordingly shook his head. Beverley dismissed him with perfectly realized but silent contempt. Of their witness, she asked, 'What about next of kin? Did Anita ever mention any relatives?'

'Her father. She used to visit him quite often, I think.'

'Did she mention his name? Or where he lived?'

'A nursing home, I believe.'

'She didn't say where?'

If she had, it had been forgotten.

At which point, Dreifus returned.

He might have looked flustered, he might have looked annoyed, or he might have looked both. Certainly he did not look especially upset that he had just heard about the tragic death of a colleague.

'What the hell do you think you're doing?'

Nurse Pelger at once appeared guilty, Grover surprised and Beverley noticeably unhappy. It was the latter who spoke.

'Didn't I make it plain? We're trying to discover how Anita Delorme came by her death.'

'I know that, but what is Nurse Pelger doing here?'

Why was he so worried?

'She has kindly consented to help us.'

It was an obvious answer yet it seemed to surprise him. 'Well, of course . . . '

Beverley abandoned him and turned to his employee. 'Thank you for your help.'

Charlotte Pelger stood up at this, radiating delight that she was being allowed to leave and shame that she had been caught out by the boss. Without further speech, she hurried from the room.

Dreifus turned his attention to the office.

'What's going on here?'

'We're gathering evidence in a potential murder enquiry.'

He pointed at the files on the floor. 'What are you doing with those?'

'We'll need to take a lot of this away with us.'

'But you can't take the accounts. We're due to be audited by the Charity Commission.'

'We won't need them for long. You can have them back in a few days, along with the computers.'

Dreifus could not believe what he was hearing. 'What?'

'We'll need to look at the hard disks.'

'What the hell has this got to do with Anita's death?'

Beverley was quite honest, quite matter of fact. 'Probably nothing . . . but I won't know for sure until I've looked.'

'But you're paralysing the operation by taking all this.'

'I'd have thought it was pretty much paralysed already, what with your one and only manager having lost most of the top of her head.'

Dreifus adopted a look of disgust at her callousness but she had won the argument. 'Yes . . . well, you'd better not have them longer than two days.'

She was able to assure him, without any evidence whatsoever, that she would not.

Twenty-One

'**M**r Delorme is having a nap.'

'I'm sure, but I have to speak to him.'

'Why?'

Of all the tasks in Beverly's life, this was the worst. She wanted to take a deep breath and get it over with, come away

as soon as possible and get on with things that were less
harrowing, less cruel. She did not need people standing in her
way, asking her stupid questions about things that were none
of their business. She leaned across the desk, noticing idly
that there was a photograph on it of a pretty black girl of
about nineteen. 'Look, love. Perhaps you missed it on the
warrant card, but I'm a detective inspector and I want to talk
to Frank Delorme. Why I want to talk to him is his business,
not yours.'

It had been relatively easy to find Anita Delorme's father.
An unusual surname and a search of the Social Security data-
base had found him in one of three nursing homes dotted in
the countryside around Donnington. 'Anita Delorme' was the
name down as Frank Delorme's next of kin, the address that
of their dead woman.

The nurse in charge of Guiting Lane Residential Care Home
had kissed goodbye to both fifty and her sense of humour
some years ago; it was doubtful if anyone had called her 'love'
in the past twenty years. Beverley watched with growing
interest as her rather pudgy features contracted in anger to
produce a visage that was considerably smaller and harder
than it had been. Where, Beverley wondered, was she tucking
the fat?

Her uniform was spotless, a badge of perfection. The room
was small and without natural light. The only evidence that
they were still in the normal, human universe was the rumble
of heavy traffic that seeped in from the main road outside the
home. Beverley decided that she would go mad if she were
forced to spend long hours in there, and speculated that perhaps
it went some way to explaining the nurse's attitude.

In something of a reptilian hiss, the nurse said, 'I beg to
differ! Mr Delorme is a very sick man.'

Beverley betrayed no sign that she was intimidated, because
she wasn't. The thought that she should have given this task
to Grover danced playfully around inside her head as she
asked, 'What's wrong with him?'

'Parkinson's disease and dementia. Severe dementia.'

Which actually changed matters. She asked then, 'How bad
is he? Does he remember his daughter?'

'Sometimes. His condition is very variable.'

'Is there a wife?'

'No. She died three years ago.'

'No other relatives?'

'None.'

Beverley decided that a change of tactics was called for in view of this information. She lowered her voice and said in a confidential tone, 'His daughter is dead.'

The nurse's face relaxed and the fat returned as magically as it had gone. 'Oh, my Lord ... ' She looked genuinely distraught. 'How?'

'A gun injury.' Anticipating the question, she added, 'We need to exclude any chance that it wasn't self-inflicted.'

The nurse nodded. 'Of course.'

'Will this news mean anything to Mr Delorme?'

The nurse was definite. 'No. Even if he appreciated the significance of what you said to him, he would soon forget.'

She asked, 'Could I see him? I mean, just see him?'

'Of course.' The nurse stood, their earlier antagonism forgotten. She led Beverley into the main hall, then through to the back of the house past the kitchens, where there was a brightly painted conservatory that ran along the whole rear of the house. The garden was wide but short, mainly lawn bordered by flowerbeds.

There were seven people in the conservatory, four of whom were watching a television at the far end. Two elderly ladies were sitting side by side and chatting quietly, their faces smiling. Beverley felt a weight of depression come upon her as she guessed their talk was of the past, would never now be of the future. The seventh figure was a small, crooked old man who dozed in a tall-backed chair, his mouth open, his bald head spotted with scabs. Beverley saw in him a sickening caricature of the man in the photographs in Anita Delorme's house. He had dribbled and even in his sleep he was trembling slightly.

'This is Frank Delorme.' The nurse spoke quietly but not as quietly as she would have done had he been a younger, fitter man.

Beverley asked, 'Did his daughter visit him often?'

'About once a month. She was fairly good . . . not like some of them.'

'Alone?'

'Almost always.'

'She sometimes came with someone? Do you know who? Was it a man?'

The nurse frowned, disapproving of Beverley's slightly hectoring tone. 'Yes, it was a man. She didn't introduce him. Except . . . I think she once called him Donald.'

'How many times did she come with him?'

'Four, maybe five times.'

'Could he have been another relative?'

The nurse shook her head. 'Oh, no. I don't think so.'

There was something about her tone that prompted Beverley to ask, 'Why are you so sure?'

'They were holding hands as they left and I saw them embrace and kiss. It was not the kind of kiss you'd give to a relation, no matter how close.'

Beverley looked again at the recumbent old man before her. His breathing was heavy, almost rattling.

'When will you tell him?'

The nurse frowned. 'I don't know,' she admitted, then added, 'Maybe I won't.'

Which surprised Beverley. It seemed intolerably cruel to keep this old man in ignorance. 'But, surely . . . '

The nurse smiled sourly. She was used to such an ill-informed reaction. 'For most of the time, he won't remember the news anyway. And maybe, every so often, it will come back to him briefly and then he'll be distraught and uncontrollable. Is that what you want?'

Beverley looked back down at him. 'Maybe not,' she murmured.

'Believe me, it's far kinder to leave him with the idea that she's going to come back to visit him sometime soon. Time means very little to him now. He'll be quite happy to hang on to that belief for ever, not realizing that he's stuck in the same moment, day in, day out.'

Although she did not like this deception, Beverley accepted it without further comment. As she gazed down on the noisily sleeping old man, she reflected on the nurse's use of the word, 'happy'.

It was not a word she could find anywhere in the scene before her.

Twenty-Two

There was an air of inevitability about their discovery that the shotgun had been licensed to Dr Donald Lennox. As a matter of routine, his name was put through various databases, but nothing else of interest was found, except that Anita Delorme was a registered patient at Water Lane Surgery, but on the list of the third doctor in the partnership, Lynette Parker.

'Cosy,' remarked Beverley.

'There's more,' Grover admitted. He said this grudgingly.

'Go on.'

'I've checked with the car dealer where she bought the car, and with the health resort. She paid in cash, every time.'

'Well, well.'

'And her CV was dodgy.'

'How do you mean, "dodgy"?'

'It wasn't a first class degree from the LSE. It was upper second and from Warwickshire. Also, the MBA was a correspondence course from the Open University.'

'No disgrace in either of those,' she said ruminatively.

'But not exactly distinguished, either.'

'What about previous jobs?'

'She had worked for both Oxfam and CRUK, but not in quite the exalted positions she claimed.'

'So, all in all, Anita Delorme was a construction, designed to impress.'

'And she was crooked, through and through.'

Once again, Beverley was struck by Grover's absolutism, found it uncomfortable.

He asked, 'Isn't it time we spoke with Dr Lennox?'

Beverley looked at her watch and saw that it was just after ten o'clock. She decided that she did, indeed, need to see a doctor.

*   *   *

Water Lane Surgery was new, purpose-built and soulless, a factory for health. It was overlooked by St Jude's, the parish church of Donnington, and was, conveniently perhaps, right next to the graveyard. There were parking spaces for perhaps twenty cars, of which six were reserved for the surgery staff. In one of these, beside a battered red Mini, was the haughty green Jaguar. Beverley and Grover went in through the main door, past the glass front of a dispensary on their right, at which stood an elderly woman dressed in a faded green woollen coat and with hair that had fallen out in tufts, exposing shiny pink scalp. She was not happy, talking in a relentless and immediately wearing screech. The woman behind the glass was past middle age and appeared to be a match for her foe. There was a look on her face that suggested hard implacability.

Beverley and Grover ignored this potential breach of the peace and approached the reception, which consisted of a another glazed hatch behind which they could see a computer terminal on a bench. Beyond that was an office in which two ladies of a certain age sat and gave the impression of working assiduously. They were dressed in identical blouses of blue with fine red flowers. For a moment, Beverley found herself with nothing in her head apart from the word *hideous*.

She rang the bell that was supposed to summon attention. Behind her was a large waiting room, along one wall of which were wooden chairs. About half of these were occupied by patients who had nothing to do except stare at the newcomers as they had probably stared at every newcomer for the past twenty minutes. Most of these were old and some, even Beverley could see, were ill.

The sound of the bell came to Beverley's ears at once but, strangely, took its time on the journey to the auditory organs of the surgery staff. Only after half a minute did one of them respond, and even then she did not actually look across at the hatch but broke away from her labours with a gaze that was fixed upon the floor and an expression that suggested she was absolutely certain that this was not in her job description.

'Can I help you?' She had mislaid her smile although she tried to do something with her voice to elevate it above bored irritation.

Beverley showed her identity card and said merely, 'I'd like to talk to Dr Lennox, please.'

The woman was plump and well hidden by make-up. She stared first at the card and then at Beverley, and then the card again, as if she were at passport control and Beverley did not quite match her photograph.

'He's in the middle of surgery,' she volunteered at last.

'I'm sure. I'd still like to see him.'

'But I can't disturb him at the moment.'

Grover looked around. The audience was small but it had become rapidly attentive. With an eerie degree of perspicacity they had detected something of greater interest than the public health posters on the walls around them, something with the air of a drama.

Beverley had met someone who had the air of an immoveable object but knew that she had the measure of it. It always gave her pleasure to take on people like this, people who had been given a small castle to defend and who enjoyed pissing on those outside the walls.

'If you tell him it's about the death of Anita Delorme, I'm fairly certain you'll find him eminently disturbable.'

A faint look that melded disbelief and uncertainty decorated the features of this estimable lady. 'Well . . . '

'Something of which I am *completely* certain is that he won't thank you for not informing him of our presence here.'

The relaxed confidence with which Beverley gave this advice worked. The phone was picked up and a button depressed. 'Dr Lennox? Sorry to bother you in the middle of a consultation but I have some police officers here and they say they need to talk to you.'

A pause.

'They say it's about someone called . . .'

But she had mislaid the name and Beverley had to supply it again in response to an entreating look from the receptionist.

She said into the receiver, ' . . . Delorme. Anita Delorme . . . '

She listened for a moment, then put the phone down. 'He says he'll be out in a minute.'

And a minute it was. From the far end of the room a door was opened and there came first an old man who was walking slowly with a Zimmer frame, then a tall, fair-haired man of perhaps forty, who had a small, tight mouth bracketed by deep creases. He hurried to overtake the elderly man, making a direct course for Beverley and Grover. The audience watched without knowledge of the details but with full understanding of the emotional nuances. They were used to seeing their doctors calm, unhurried and in command, but Dr Lennox was emanating small but distinct signs that he was none of these things. It was like seeing a vicar drunk, and just as entertaining.

Without waiting for introductions, Dr Lennox enquired, 'Could you come this way?'

And he was off, rushing back on the return journey without pause for refreshment, assuming they would follow.

Which, of course, they did.

Behind them, the phone in the receptionists' office rang for the fifty-third time that morning.

Twenty-Three

There was something about the act of phoning a general medical practice that touched a fundamental fear in Eisenmenger. He could not believe that it was learned fear. He was convinced that, along with the fear of heights, it was programmed into him, something that the millennia had taught him to run from instinctively.

'Watcr Lane Surgery.'

He was unaware, of course, that this was the same lady who not thirty seconds before had confronted Beverley Wharton.

'Could I speak to Dr Dreifus?' he enquired. Such a question, he knew, would be as a cattle prod to this no doubt respectable woman's posterior.

All doctors' receptionists spoke in the same voice, with the same tone – the one that was supposed to send subliminal messages that the caller was not wanted, that he or she was ringing at a most inopportune time. Were they trained to do this? He found it hard to accept that people were born with such impatient condescension already dripping from their vocal cords.

She did not disappoint.

'Oh, no,' she said at once. She did not quite laugh but it was there, at the edge of her refusal: hysterical laughter, as if such an idea could come only from the realms of madness. Patients were never allowed to speak to their doctors on the phone. Medical people had far more important things to do than actually speak to the people they were charged with treating.

But Eisenmenger had not, in fact, finished. 'My name's John Eisenmenger. Doctor John Eisenmenger.'

He did not overly labour the emphasis, but at the same time he did not brush over it, and it had the desired effect.

'Oh . . . ' He had found a small but fatal weakness in her defence. 'Doctor Eisenmenger?' she enquired, just to make sure; faintly, he fancied.

'I'm a consultant pathologist . . . at the hospital.'

He was not a cruel man but he found himself enjoying the agony he was inflicting. It was the single most important function of the doctor's receptionist to prevent unauthorized access to her employer, to ensure that everyone was directed through the proper channels – that is, that they were given an eight-minute slot for which they would turn up ten minutes early and actually get into the presence of the doctor twenty-five minutes late. He had effectively removed her primary reason for existence and he knew this was possibly the worst thing that can happen to any organism.

Nevertheless he was remorseless in his attack. 'Is Dr Dreifus available?'

She was game, he was forced to admit, for she attempted to rally.

'Is it about a patient?'

Not that it mattered. If a doctor wished to speak to another about a patient, his new sports car or the number of boils on his left buttock, a mere receptionist could not interfere.

'Yes.'

'Oh . . . ' He did not hear her intake of breath – the dying swan's last song – but he could imagine it. 'I think he's in his room. I'll just see if it's convenient.'

He waited patiently. In his mind he licked his finger and chalked up an imaginary point.

'Yes?'

His victory became a thing of the past as he faced a fresh battle. This voice was gruff – not that of a happy bunny, more one of an angry bear.

'Dr Dreifus?'

'Yes.' These were not replies designed to offer friendship, they were more like tin-tacks thrown out of the back of a retreating car, designed to deter those who came after it.

'It's John Eisenmenger, from histopathology at St Christopher's.'

'Oh, yes. You're working as a locum, aren't you?'

Well, yes, he was. Eisenmenger discovered to his shock that his dislike of Dreifus was mutual. Worse, Dreifus seemed to think that locums were second class, a social grouping of a lower caste than normal medics. He said, 'For a few months.' Before Dr Dreifus could express any more contempt, he hurried on, 'I performed the autopsy on Edward Melnick.'

Eisenmenger was impressed, for Dreifus took less than a second to locate the deceased patient in his memory bank. 'Oh, yes. I wrote a report for the coroner.'

'That's right.'

'What about it?'

'When Mr Melnick died, I found that he had some Metformin in his blood.'

'Metformin?'

'That's right. I was wondering if he was diabetic. You don't mention it in your report, but I just wanted to check . . . '

'If I didn't mention it, then I'm sure he wasn't.'

'Do you think you could just check . . . ?'

There was a pause, then, 'Very well. If you insist.'

'Thanks.'

There came to Eisenmenger the sound of a keyboard. It was not a delicate pitter-patter of fingers dancing over the keys, more of digits attacking individual letters and battering them into submission. It was obvious that Dr Dreifus was neither happy nor an expert typist.

'No, he wasn't,' he announced at last.

'Oh . . . well, that's odd, isn't it?'

'Is it?'

'How did he get hold of the drug?'

Dreifus seemed to think that this interview had gone on for long enough. 'Was the Metformin at overdose levels?'

'No, but . . . '

'Well, what relevance is it? If he didn't die of an overdose of Metformin, why are you so concerned about it?'

'Because I think he took the Metformin while he was drunk, and that resulted in a catastrophic hypoglycaemic attack.'

'Really. What is this to me?'

'It's very odd, don't you think? That he should have taken a drug he was not being prescribed.'

Dreifus made it plain that however odd it might be to John Eisenmenger, to Dr Adam Dreifus it was a waste of time. 'Not particularly,' he decided. 'Now, unless there is something else you wish to discuss?'

The door was closing inexorably but Eisenmenger thrust his foot in the gap and his lips to the crack that remained. 'Is his wife a patient of yours?'

'What relevance is that?'

'Is she diabetic? Is she on Metformin? If so, it might explain how he managed to get hold of it.'

'Yes, I suppose it might.'

'Is she, then?'

A beat, nothing more, before he got his reply. 'I'm sorry, Dr Eisenmenger. You know as well as I do that I really can't comment.'

Eisenmenger had heard more sorrow in the voice of the announcer at a railway station.

Twenty-Four

In another room, Beverley sat in the patient's chair, with Grover in the one adjacent, the one intended for the worried parent. The room was cramped and had also to contain an examination couch, a small handbasin and a desk. Because of this, Beverley and Lennox were almost touching knees and, as he sat down, she saw him pilfer a glance at her legs. He asked, 'What can I do for you?'

She had to admire this external display of nonchalance, although she judged that this did not mirror accurately what was happening within. Certainly the alacrity with which he had rushed out to greet them suggested a man who had concerns.

'As I said to the receptionist, we're here about Anita Delorme.'

His face became at once suitably grave. 'Ah, yes. Very sad.'

Grover was in Beverley's visual field and she could see quite easily that this answer disgruntled her sergeant. 'I understand you knew Miss Delorme.'

He nodded. 'We were friends.'

'Friends?'

'That's right.' He smiled reassuringly, dropped his eyes back to her legs and then brought them up to her face, inevitably passing her breasts along the way.

'Nothing more?'

The eyebrows were hoisted to suggest surprise at the implication. 'Goodness, no.'

'How long have you known her?'

He had to concentrate to get the figure right. 'I suppose about a year.'

'And you met her how?'

'Gosh . . . let me think . . .' He thought. 'I think it must have been Adam who introduced us.'

'Adam Dreifus?'

'That's right.'

'Where was that?'

'The practice Christmas party. I think that year it was held at the Manor Hotel.'

He was apparently having to concentrate to recall each detail, but it was clear to Beverley that they were all lined up in his head, that he had herded them together beforehand, fully prepared for this interview.

She asked, 'How did you find out she was dead?'

'Adam told me.'

She noted that he was relaxing, believing he was over the worst, that he had read his lines well and done justice to his material, and, noting this, she said, 'The gun that killed her was yours.'

But of course he would have predicted that this point would be made. When he dropped his head and his tone became guilt-edged, she saw only artifice and disliked him for it. 'I guessed as much,' he said.

She had trouble keeping the sarcasm from her voice. 'Would you care to explain how that came about?'

If he caught her tone he ignored it. 'I introduced Anita to shooting. I'm a member of a local clay-shooting club. I used to take her along sometimes. She showed some skill at it, too.'

'And . . . what? One day, she just asked you for a gun and you said, "Sure. Take any one you want."'

'She'd joined the club. She had yet to buy a gun for herself, so I said she could use one of mine until she got one.'

'Which club is this?'

'Apperley.'

Beverley glanced across at Grover to emphasize that she expected him to check all this. Grover met her gaze but whether or not he understood, Beverley could not say. Turning back to Lennox, she said, 'You do realize that what you did was illegal?'

He tried a smile, which was a mistake as far as Beverley was concerned. 'Yes, technically . . . '

'Yes, definitely, Dr Lennox. It is against the law to lend a gun to another individual. Anita Delorme had no gun licence . . . '

'She had applied.'

'She had yet to receive one, though. Perhaps she would have been turned down.'

'That was hardly likely to happen.'

'You know as well as I do that that's no excuse.'

Lennox did not reply, but his face suggested that she was just being pedantic.

'Do you know where she kept the gun?'

'In the loft. She was very careful about hiding it.'

'And the ammunition?'

'Same place.'

She allowed no pause before switching lanes quite abruptly and saying, 'You have a nice car, Dr Lennox.'

He betrayed some surprise. 'Thank you.'

'It's quite memorable, a classic car like that.'

He was not stupid and she had guessed he would pick up an inference, but he impressed her with the speed and depth of his grasp of the situation. He paused, his face clouded and then he sighed. 'Oh.'

'Especially if one of Anita's neighbours used to own one.'

He hesitated, and she could see he was unsure of what she was getting at.

'She recognized it.'

He gave a quick nod. 'I see.'

She said – not asked, but said – 'You were her lover.'

With pursed lips and in a soft voice, he admitted, 'Yes.'

'Were you still her lover at the time of her death?'

The nod again.

'How often did you see her?'

He had become tense and fidgety: no longer a man hiding behind manufactured defences but exposed and all too obviously vulnerable. 'Weekly, sometimes more.'

'Always at her house?'

'Occasionally we got away to a hotel or something, but, yes, usually at her house.'

'Did you love her?'

He reacted to that one. 'What does that mean?'

'Well, you haven't exactly expressed overwhelming remorse, have you?'

He was angered by this, as she had known he would be, as she had hoped he would be. Eyes suddenly blazing from a face suffused with blood, he demanded, 'How dare you?'

'It's a reasonable question, Dr Lennox. Not every relationship is founded on love. People have affairs for all sorts of reasons.'

'Well, the reason for mine was strong mutual attraction, I assure you.'

'Yet you do not show it.'

Clearly exasperated, he retorted, 'Don't be stupid, Inspector. I could hardly go around in widower's weeds, wailing and gnashing my teeth, could I?'

She did not choose to argue the point, instead asking another question that she knew would make him uncomfortable. 'You have a wife, don't you?'

'Yes.'

'Do you love *her*?'

'Yes ... '

'Does she know about your affair with Anita Delorme?'

'Now, look here ... '

From which Beverley concluded that she did not. 'Do you make a habit of having affairs, Dr Lennox?'

He stood up, obviously forgetting his desire for discretion. 'That is outrageous! What does that have to do with anything?'

Beverley looked up at his face, her own impassive. As if he had not spoken or reacted in any way, she enquired, 'Anita had a very good lifestyle, didn't she?'

He was already calming. He sat slowly back down and said in a more level tone, 'I suppose so.'

'I know so. Holidays, cars, investments. The best of everything for Anita.'

'She enjoyed life,' he assented with a small nod.

'Were you giving her any money?'

'Well, I used to pay for dinner, and the hotel bills.'

'But you did not give her lump sums, or large gifts, like a car?'

He was adamant that he did not.

'When did you last see her alive?'

There was hesitation. 'Two days ago.'

The day she died. Beverley wondered why he was suddenly cagey. 'What time? And what were you doing, and where?'

'I left her at about seven. We had met in Furrier's Wood.'

She waited for him to expand on this. Various ideas passed through her mind involving long walks, gathering wild flowers and bird watching, but she suspected the truth would be rather more carnal.

He looked fixedly at her, making it a contest – one that he lost, as he demanded, 'Well?'

'What were you doing in Furrier's Wood?'

'Is that relevant?'

It was amusing, this prevarication; he struck her as an incompetent magician refusing to accept that the audience could see how the tricks were done. 'Don't be coy, Dr Lennox. Did you make love?'

He breathed sharply in, made out that he was about to protest vehemently, then collapsed and, with a curt nod, admitted the truth of this.

'Did you have any kind of disagreement on that last afternoon?'

'No.' He said this defensively.

'You didn't row?'

'No.'

'When was the last time you had a row?'

A frown appeared on his forehead, but it was the product of annoyance rather than concentration. 'I don't remember. I'm not sure we ever had one.'

Grover had been busy scribbling a transcript of the interview but he looked up at this declaration of perfection.

'Never?' enquired Beverley.

'I don't think so.'

Beverley pursed her lips, seeing that his eye caught the movement and that he knew this was a predator on the lookout for another kill. She said with a touch of disbelief, 'She was quite happy in the role of mistress? She didn't want to formalize the relationship?'

'We never discussed it.'

She allowed silence to do the questioning and, as ever, it proved a trusty helpmeet. He offered, 'She was quite happy being single.'

Beverley heard cynicism in her own thoughts as she asked, 'And you? Are you quite happy being married?'

A grimace attended Lennox's affirmation of this assertion; she wondered why.

Beverley had been the mistress too many times to believe any of this. There came a time in every affair when the question was raised by one party or the other. Usually sooner rather than later, either the adulterer or the mistress would wonder about the future, about whether there was more to existence than varying the restaurant, varying the bed and varying the position.

She made play of deep consideration of his reply. 'Can I just run through this? You and Anita Delorme had this perfect relationship in which you met regularly to acquaint each other with your bodily parts, having the occasional expensive meal in between, and never once did either of you think six weeks, six months, six years into the future?'

He actually smiled, which he might have thought was clever but struck Beverley as merely arrogant. 'That's right. We both understood what the situation was.'

Even Grover, who by definition believed in the virgin birth and assorted miracles, and was probably in two minds about Father Christmas and the tooth fairy, showed by the expression on his face that he thought this unlikely. His height increased in a motion that in a snake would have been described as *uncoiling* and he said distinctly, 'Oh, come on.'

It was the fate of the junior police officer in interrogations to be treated as a piece of furniture and it was not in most people's experience to have such items issue sarcastic remarks. Accordingly, Lennox appeared surprised by this interjection. Surprised and irritated. He glanced briefly across at Grover, but his remarks were addressed to Beverley. 'I had nothing to do with Anita's death, Inspector. Nothing at all.'

'Did she give you any clue that she might be contemplating some sort of self-harm?'

Even this question he found to contain a germ of offence. 'Of course she didn't! Don't you think I would have done something if I'd had any inkling that she was thinking of suicide?'

'I'm sure you would have done, but perhaps at the time you didn't appreciate the significance of some remark which now, in retrospect . . . ?'

'Nothing. Nothing at all.'

She found the vehemence curiously unreassuring.

'Had she been down of late?'

'No.'

'Not distracted or distant?'

'Not at all.'

Beverley took each of these negatives without comment, but she did not in any way accept them as representing reality. Donald Lennox struck her as the kind of man who would have been unlikely to notice if his lover had tattooed a suicide note across her abdomen and, even if he had, would have carried on fornicating anyway.

'So all this is a mystery to you.'

He nodded. A look of concern and consternation passed across his face like a warm, wet squall on a late summer's day. 'It's absolutely terrible,' he said, the accompanying non-verbal communication completely negating any import the words might have been intended to convey.

'When you left Anita at Furrier's Wood, where did you go then?'

'Home.'

'And who was there?'

'Just my wife.'

'Do you have a key to Anita Delorme's house?'

'No.'

'No? Are you sure of that?'

'Why would I want one? If I went there, it was with her.'

It was plausible. She asked, 'Your wife's name is what?' There was no obvious inflexion in her voice, but quite miraculously she seemed somehow to breathe significance into this uxorial reference.

'Janet.'

Another pause, of exactly the same duration, before Beverley asked, 'And could she confirm your statement?'

He laughed, an explosive release of tension, or perhaps hope. 'Are you joking?'

'No.' She kept this plain, almost perplexed.

Another laugh. The last had been bitter, this was concentrated acid. 'You can't say anything to her. I've been having an affair, for God's sake!'

Beverley considered this, then turned to Grover. 'Tell me, Grover. In your reading of the various criminal law reforms of recent years, has any reference been made to placing the interests of philanderers before those of victims of suspicious deaths and their relatives?'

Grover played along nicely. 'I can't remember anything, Inspector.'

Turning back to Lennox, Beverley explained, 'Neither I nor my sergeant can recall the precise legal reference on which you base your protest.'

Lennox was becoming very flustered and this brought with it anger. 'I didn't do anything . . . '

'So you say, Dr Lennox. Unfortunately, I have to check that.'

'But . . . '

'You have offered your wife as the only person who can corroborate your story. Unless you can give me another person's name, I'm afraid I have no choice.'

'OK,' he said after a moment's struggle with the implications of what she had said. 'But can it wait until I've had a chance to talk to her first?'

Beverley had not thought that she looked like something that had dropped out of her mother's womb the night before, but this question implied otherwise. Shaking her head sadly, she pointed out, 'I really don't think that would be a good idea. I want to listen to what she has to say, not what you want her to say.'

He looked increasingly panicked and was becoming visibly agitated. 'You don't understand. My wife doesn't deserve to be dragged into this.'

Beverley stood up. 'You dragged her into this, not me.' But having pointed out his culpability, she relented. 'We'll be as tactful as we can, Dr Lennox. I can't guarantee she won't find things out you wish she hadn't, but we won't draw diagrams for her.'

He failed to look reassured.

As they walked back out through the waiting room, they were again the object of intense curiosity. The row at the dispensary was still going on.

'An unhappy customer,' remarked Beverley.

Lennox's mind had been off elsewhere, presumably rehearsing what he was going to say to his spouse when he got home. He looked up and said, 'Oh . . . don't worry. Jeanette will cope.'

Lennox collected his next patient, leaving them with scarcely a backward glance.

Grover could hardly contain himself.

'Did you see him?' he demanded.

'Yes, I saw him.'

'He didn't care about her. To him, she was just some sort of . . . ' But the words were not there, presumably because Grover's stock of sex-related phrases was limited. Beverley helped out. 'Sex toy?'

Grover pounced on this. 'Exactly. He had no feelings for her at all.'

Beverley had known plenty of lovers like Lennox – too many, in actual fact – and she could only agree with this sentiment. 'No, he didn't.'

They had reached the car. Beverley was left waiting for Grover to unlock it as she was treated to yet another diatribe.

'That's absolutely despicable. Men like him make me so angry. He is making a mockery of love, of God's gifts . . . '

'Do you think you could let me get in the car?'

Grover pressed the button but that did not prevent him from developing his theme. 'What he has been doing is disgusting. What about his wife? What about the vows he made on his wedding day?'

Beverley ran out of patience. 'Enough, Grover! I appreciate that your delicate sensibilities have been badly bruised, but we're here to investigate a sudden death, not study to become a priest.'

Grover started the car and began to reverse out of the parking space. Only when they were on the road did he respond. 'It occurs to me that someone who can treat another human being like that is quite capable of murder.'

Beverley did not bother to hide her contempt. 'Everyone's capable of murder, Grover. Every single one of us walks on the path towards damnation but for circumstance.'

'No, I can't accept that, Sir. There are some people who are inherently evil, and some who are good.'

'And most are just poor bastards who make the wrong decision in the wrong place at the wrong time. Make the right decision and maybe you're a hero, maybe you're still a nobody; make the wrong one and you're most certainly doomed.'

Grover was emphatic, his head shaking vehemently. 'I can't accept that. Donald Lennox is a parasite. He's got no conscience about what he does. Just as he used Anita Delorme for sex when it suited him, he'd quite easily discard her when she became a nuisance.'

Beverley had had too many arguments with her own conscience to relish another with this Jesuitical bigot. After a long pause, in which Grover drove steadily and safely through the traffic, she said only, 'I'm not sure you should assume that this was a one-way relationship. I rather suspect that Donald Lennox gave just as much as he took.'

Grover did not understand what she was talking about. He had the last word, though.

'That man will burn in hell.'

Beverley said nothing, but as they drove away she wondered how hot would be the fires in her own afterlife.

Twenty-Five

It was easy for Eisenmenger to find Edward Melnick's wife because he had been given the address in the information supplied for the original post-mortem examination. He would normally have asked the Coroner's Office to undertake such a task, but on this occasion he felt that it would be the easier, wiser and more instructive course to do the job himself. This decision he began to regret, though, as a journey he began in optimism ended in something tinted less in a rosy hue and more in one of battleship grey.

Chez Melnick was a flat on the eighth floor of a forty-year-old tower block. The lift worked but served also as a public convenience and art studio; there were soggy-looking items in the corners that caused faint shudders to manipulate Eisenmenger's frame as the lift ascended. This ascent was performed in a hesitant, slightly alarming manner and with an accompaniment of gloomy clanks and ghostly sighs from all around his little cage, as if the shades of the night were playing mind games with him. When it arrived at its destination, there was a slight bounce that served to remind him that he was suspended by a thin metal cable in a straight-sided shaft with nothing but death waiting 25 metres beneath him. There then followed a pause, a thing of expectancy on the part of Eisenmenger for, not unnaturally, he had assumed that having taken the trouble to lift him to the eighth floor, the elevator might at least allow him a glimpse of his destination.

The lights flickered.

'Oh, great,' he sighed.

He pressed the button that claimed mutely but persistently that it would open the doors, feeling that it was cold and slightly damp. A muffled whirr made itself known from somewhere but he could not have placed great precision on the location of its source; it might have been from the Other Side, an attempt at communication, the details of which had been lost during the long voyage to normal space.

He pressed the button again, harder this time, and for longer. Nothing.

Then, just as he was debating in an abstracted, academic sort of way whether it would be better to plunge to his end quickly or to have to die slowly of starvation surrounded by a variety of bodily secretions and excretions (not all of which would be his own), the doors began to open.

It was slow and it was painful, and he didn't wait for it to be completed, stepping hurriedly through the gap as soon as he could, certain that at any moment he would hear the electric snap of cables and the screeching of metal as his temporary prison fell to destruction.

It did not, of course. Probably this ritual was repeated a hundred times a day and formed part of the weave of normal existence for those who inhabited the tower block. He stood still in the grotty corridor that was decorated as indecorously as the lift. The smell in his nostrils was one of damp, dust and desolation; it was a post-industrial smell, one that could not have reached anything other than a modern nose.

He moved forward, searching for flat numbers. His target was 817 and it took several minutes to find the right corridor. It was along a balcony that looked out on to a cityscape of patchy grass, scattered tower blocks, football pitches and industrial estates. He could see innumerable cars, some parked, some abandoned, some moving between places unknown to him on errands he could only guess at.

All the doors were the same and, although in theory all were readily identifiable from the black-on-silver adhesive numbers stuck to the doorframes, in actuality many of these were missing. It took a good deal of deduction to find the right flat. He rang the bell and waited. He heard a siren brought from the distance on a wind which, up here, was blustery and strong. A pigeon fluttered to a landing on the rail about 20 metres away. It was joined quickly by another one, and a ritual of approach and retreat, pecking and shaking of wings was played out as Eisenmenger waited.

Perhaps she was out.

There had once been glass in a narrow strip of window to

the left of the door but that was now gone and the window was boarded, and so visitors could not tell if anyone was coming in response to the doorbell. He had actually begun walking away, resolved to return to earth by the use of his own legs, when the first sounds of life within the flat made themselves known. These took the form of bolts being drawn back, chains being freed and keys entering locks and being turned. By the time the preparations for the door to be opened had actually been completed, Eisenmenger was back in his starting position, a reassuring smile fixed across his features.

The face that peered out at him looked untouched by grief, although it had an appearance that told Eisenmenger it had been touched by a great many other things. Thinning, once-dyed hair, swept tightly back; puffy flesh around the eyes; large mole to the left of a sagging lower lip. He saw nicotine stains around the chipped crimson nail polish.

'Yes?' This was snapped.

'Mrs Melnick?'

'Who are you?'

He took this as affirmation that he was addressing the correct person. 'My name's John Eisenmenger.'

'And who might you be?'

'I'm a doctor.'

'I don't need a doctor.'

Rose Melnick was not the most handsome of womankind. Clive, when faced with women such as she on his slab, was wont to proclaim that 'she hit every branch as she fell out of the ugly tree'.

'I'm glad to hear it, Mrs Melnick. I'm actually here about your husband.'

'What about him? He's dead.'

If there was pain behind this statement, it slipped past Eisenmenger without him noticing. 'I know he is. I did the post-mortem.'

At last he made an impact. She was short and crouched, her face consisting of slightly overhanging folds of flesh in between which suspicious eyes peeped and a suspicious mouth pursed its lips at him. His announcement made the eyes widen, the mouth dilate. 'Post-mortem?'

'That's right. I was wondering if I could have a word with you.'

Suspicion returned. 'Why?'

He knew that to show hesitation would be to fail and there-fore he said confidently, 'To talk about why he died.'

She snorted. 'I know why he died. He drank himself to death.'

'I'm not so sure about that.'

'No? Well, I am. He was drinking himself to death the day I met him and he never stopped, not once.'

'It may have a played a part, Mrs Melnick – it may have played a big part – but there's more. There must be.'

'Why?' This demand was made in a voice that was perfectly poised between commanding and querulous.

'Because I hear what you say, Mrs Melnick, but that alone doesn't explain why he died then, on that particular day and no other.'

She frowned, had heard something in his voice that touched her, it seemed. He could guess that it was sincerity; perhaps she had memories of it from a fonder time.

'How can I help?'

'I'd like to talk to you, Mrs Melnick. Find out the details of what happened on the day your husband died.'

'The coroner's already done that.'

'I know, but there are things I need to check up on that I don't think they'll have thought to ask about.'

Still she hesitated.

He produced from his pocket a half-bottle of whisky. 'Perhaps over a toddy?'

The outburst of welcome that blossomed on Mrs Melnick's less-than-enticing visage was almost worth the cost of the spirit. 'Why not?' she asked.

And so, Eisenmenger was allowed entry to the domicile in which Edward Melnick had died.

He found it an uncomfortable experience, due partly to a motley collection of furniture that had long ago passed pension-able age and was well on the way to senescence, and partly to the unpleasant suspicion that soon dawned upon him that neither Mrs Melnick nor her living quarters had been exposed to the pleasures of ablution for some time.

She enjoyed the whisky, though. If Mr Melnick had managed to outdo his wife when it came to consuming alcohol, Eisenmenger could scarcely imagine how prodigious he must have been. Nearly half the bottle had gone within ten minutes, and Eisenmenger's small portion sat untouched before him.

He shifted his weight because there was a spring that wanted to probe him intimately. There were antimacassars everywhere he looked and he wondered idly if Edward Melnick had been partial to Macassar on his hair; from the state of them, he strongly suspected that he had been. He asked, 'How are you coping, Mrs Melnick?'

She looked up at him, startled. This enquiry seemed to have found her absent without leave, swimming in the warmth of the whisky. 'Fine,' she decided. 'Fine.' Then, 'Why shouldn't I be?'

'All this must have come as a shock . . . '

She examined him as if she suspected ridicule. 'I told you. He was a boozer. I knew it would come to this sooner or later.'

'But even so . . . '

She had suspicious eyes, forever slit-like. He could see that a less careworn and slimmer Mrs Melnick might have proved an attractive proposition to a man of a certain age and a certain type. She said over her glass, 'I'd known Ted for thirty years before we married. We went to secondary school together. We used to smoke fags on the way home and share records. Then he got a motorbike and we used to go for rides in the country together.'

She stopped, sipping her drink. Eisenmenger held an internal debate and decided on silence as the best prompt.

'Even then he was a drinker, but still a gentleman. He joined the police and I met Andy at work. We drifted apart, although I kept a soft spot for him.'

She had become less harsh, less aggressive, perhaps because of the liquor, perhaps because her abrasiveness had been a front behind which she had been hiding her grief. He asked, 'How did you meet again?'

'Andy became sick. For a long time the doctors didn't know what was wrong with him, of course. He was losing weight and had this horrible cough. Eventually they said he had cancer. They called it a long name, but it didn't make any difference, he was still a goner.

'It was while I was visiting Andy in hospital just before he died that I came across Ted again. He was visiting a mate. We got talking, remembering old times, like you do. I didn't have a chance to think any more of it because a few days later Andy died.'

She paused and Eisenmenger felt compelled to say into this gap, 'I'm sorry.'

She nodded brief gratitude and he saw tears in her eyes. 'He was a good man, was Andy. Not clever, if you know what I mean, but kind and willing.' Her weeping came through in her voice, catching at the back of the words. There was more than a hint of over-sentimentalized mawkishness about her now.

Another drink of whisky, this one bigger. Eisenmenger helped her to a refill. He picked up his own glass but it failed to find its way to his lips.

'Ted came to the funeral. He hadn't known Andy and I was touched. After that, we got to seeing each other now and again, at first just for the odd drink, then a visit to the races, then he took me to a show in London.'

Another application of whisky to lubricate the clockwork of memory and sentiment.

'Before long, it was like old times.'

'He was still a policeman?'

'Close to retirement, but yes, still in the force. He'd had a short marriage – even had a son – but it didn't work out.'

'He was still drinking heavily?'

She paused with the glass on a return journey to her face. For a moment he wondered if he had inadvertently broken the link between them, if she would realize that perhaps he had reasons other than interest and humanity in listening to her slightly pickled reminiscences. Then she seemed to lose the reason for pausing – why on earth would she want to stop sipping the whisky? – and the glass continued on its way to its tryst with her mandibular apparatus.

'Oh, yes,' she said, unconscious of the irony.

'When did you marry?'

''Bout two years after Andy had passed over. He wanted to do it sooner but I told him it wouldn't be proper.'

It was a point in the conversation that was potentially tricky but Eisenmenger could not leave things just yet. He allowed himself the smallest taste of the whisky – at which she nodded, as if he had passed a small test – before asking, 'When did things start to go wrong?'

A pause, and not just a pause, but a pause and a frown. For a moment he thought he had spoiled things, that she would not allow him through those particular rooms in her memory, that these apartments were not for pushy strangers who bought their way in with whisky, hoping to plunder valueless but precious ornaments. He waited, expecting to be told to depart in a fruity way, suspecting that Mrs Melnick had a temper of her own, one that was modelled on her late husband's template.

He was spared, however. When she spoke again it was in a tone that was anything but angry or affronted. Indeed, he heard tears at the back of her tongue, and it was obvious that she and her husband had once had something good, that her everyday attitude was as much to keep herself from pain as to demonstrate to an audience that she could cope.

''Bout three years ago.'

Another application of her own special tonic, then, 'He'd been retired for three years and had started up a little business of his own. He'd had such high hopes, but it hadn't gone well. It was the failure of the business that hurt him – his pride couldn't cope. Whenever he had a client, he wasn't too bad, but whenever business was bad he'd start drinking the stuff as if he'd got a bet on the amount he could down.'

'What was the business?'

'Private detective.'

Although he was surprised, Eisenmenger did not display this. Why should an ex-policeman not become a private detective? It was a traditional, if slightly hackneyed, route for those retiring from the constabulary.

'And things were bad when he died?'

She might have been about to confirm his deduction but she suddenly stopped, a thoughtful look on her bleared features. In a voice that suggested to Eisenmenger that she was thinking through this for the first time, she said, 'No, they weren't actually.'

She sounded confused.

'Really?'

'Well, he had a case. For Ted, that was good.'

'But he was still drinking heavily?'

'Worse than he'd been for a long time. We barely spoke.'

'Was there something else that could have been stressing him? Causing him to drink?'

'Not that he told me.'

'What about debts? Did he have debts?'

She laughed. A more accurate description might have been 'cackled'. There was a bronchial underpinning to the sound that suggested that secretions deep within her chest were being stirred sluggishly. 'Don't be stupid,' she was saying. 'Of course he had debts.'

'So you can't think of any reason why he might have been drinking more heavily?'

She shook her head. The whisky was nearing its end and she was looking at the bottle on the table with some concern. Her eyes darted up to Eisenmenger's face, perhaps seeking evidence that he had brought another bottle, that he was some sort of whisky dispenser on legs.

Eisenmenger, though, was interested only in the last few days of Edward Melnick's existence on this plane.

'Tell me what happened on the day before he died.'

She spoke, but it was slow and her interest seemed to be centred on the whisky. 'How do you mean?'

Finding that open questioning was not working, Eisenmenger changed tactics. 'What time did he get up?'

Her mouth was open slightly and she gave the impression of extreme thirst, as if her mind and body had forgotten the taste of scotch.

He repeated the question.

She came back to him, closed her mouth, focused her eyes. ' . . . About eleven . . . Yes, about eleven.'

'Was that the time he normally got up?'

'If he'd been out drinking.'

'He had breakfast?'

'I did him a fry-up. He liked his fry-ups, did Ted.'

'And then what did he do?'

'He went out.'

'What time did he get back?'

'Just in time for tea. Six, it was. He rarely missed.' Her whole attitude was now one of fond reminiscence, casting light on an aspect of the marriage that had hitherto remained in shadow. 'Sausage and chips was his favourite.'

Edward Melnick's diet appeared to have contained enough saturated fats to block a main drain, let alone a coronary artery or three but, strangely, Eisenmenger had seen with his own eyes that he had not suffered from severe ischaemic heart disease.

'He went to the pub after that?'

She nodded, but her thoughts were clearly on the last time she had seen him alive.

'He wasn't on any medication, was he?'

She failed to understand the question. 'What do you mean?'

'Did he take tablets regularly for anything?'

'No.'

'He didn't have a headache, or any other reason to take paracetamol, or aspirin, or anything like that?'

'Why?'

'Did he?'

She paused. On her face was a look that from one angle might have represented an effort of memory, from another might have been calculation. 'No. He said nothing about a headache.'

'Are you diabetic, Mrs Melnick?'

She was affronted. What was it to him? 'You what?'

'Do you have sugar diabetes? Do you take tablets for it?'

'Why?' There was something of outrage, something of wariness in this enquiry.

He adopted a calming, doctorial tone. 'If you do, it might explain how he died.'

She was suspicious. 'I don't see how that comes into it. He drank himself to death.'

'But why did he die on *that* day? Why not on the day before or the day after? Why isn't he still alive now, still eating your fry-ups and going down to The Eagle?'

He made her cry and had known that he would. He felt awkward, as though he had behaved unethically, but it worked. As her tears turned rapidly to maudlin blubbing, he went on, 'You do take tablets for diabetes, don't you?'

A nod. He suddenly felt guilty about plying her with whisky, rationalizing his action by telling himself that she had not had enough to put her in danger of the same fate as her husband. 'Is it at all possible that he got hold of some?'

Before she spoke she produced a crumpled and less-than-pristine handkerchief from the recesses of the left sleeve of her lilac blouse. A trumpeting blow of her nose and then, 'I keep all the tablets in the kitchen cupboard . . . I suppose he could have done.'

Was she lying? There was something about her attitude, about the pause especially, that he did not like, but whether it was guilt or fear was something he could not assess. She had sounded almost artful in the middle of the sentence.

And then she asked, 'Did he take some of mine, then? Is that what killed him?' For a moment she seemed to compound the impression of culpability, but then he saw another side to the question. She had a fear of medications that was not uncommon in a lay person. Medicines were dangerous things. One false step and they turned away from a path to health towards a lethal minefield. He said noncommittally, 'I don't know. Possibly.'

For a short while she was silent, the whisky, if not forgotten, then certainly not the only object in the foreground; suddenly, though, she was horrified. Her eyes opened, breath entered her body and she exclaimed, 'He'd just been to see the doctor!'

'What about?'

She was thinking hard and did not immediately respond. He could see that through the whisky she was seeing things she had not noticed before. 'He had gout, you see . . . '

'He'd had an attack, had he?'

On her face was a frown, but it was not one of disapproval. 'No . . . he just said he needed more tablets.'

'Was he given more tablets?'

'I think so.'

'Can I see them?'

She was hesitant but then reluctantly agreed. She stood up with some difficulty, then made her way out of the room. She moved as if she were making her way along a ship's deck in a force eight wind.

He heard her slamming her way through cupboards in the kitchen for a while, then she returned with a white paper bag in her hand, folded over at the top. She handed it to Eisenmenger and when he opened it, he found inside it a box of Etoricoxib tablets, an anti-inflammatory drug which was commonly prescribed for gout. A printed label had been stuck on it, on which were Edward Melnick's name and address, followed by the injunction to take one tablet per day as required.

Everything was as it should be.

Eisenmenger wrestled with his disappointment and tried to counter it by asking, 'Which doctor did he see?'

'Dr Dreifus. He always saw Dr Dreifus. He's a lovely doctor, is Dr Dreifus. Always very considerate. The whole practice is. Always a kind word. One of them even gave me some bereavement leaflets, called round personal. There wasn't enough they could do . . . '

The events of the last few weeks, until now held at bay by her anger with her husband for dying, made an impression at last and she began to sink into gloom. He watched her, trying to imagine what she was going through.

Quite abruptly she looked up at him, catching his scrutiny but not registering it. 'I *know* what happened about the tablets!' she said before he could speak again. 'They didn't have them in when he first got the prescription. He didn't get them until the next day. The day he . . . '

She stopped, suddenly alarmed, or frightened, or perhaps overcome by remorse. 'That last day,' she said in a low voice, after a second.

It seemed she had found bereavement at last.

Twenty-Six

Janet Lennox thought her visitors were Jehovah's Witnesses.

A man and a woman, one standing slightly to the front, both neatly dressed. The woman was red-haired and had a thin face with high cheekbones and bright eyes that seemed to Janet Lennox to be full of black, brown, golden and yellow flecks. The man was younger and had an attitude of subservience. His face was rounder, his hair black and cropped short, his eyes pale blue; they held uncertainty in a way that was completely missing from the other one's gaze.

'Mrs Janet Lennox?'

'I'm not interested, thank you.'

She had begun to shut the door even though she was already thinking it was odd that they had known her name.

With a soft but determined thump the door met resistance.

She pulled it back and was on the point of remonstrance when she was presented with an opened plastic wallet; on one side was a picture of some sort of crest and on the other were some printed words and a small photograph. She had never seen a warrant card in real life before and could not immediately name it, although she knew at once what it signified.

Her mind presented her with a smorgasbord of reactions and she was thus rendered for a moment speechless. She felt surprise, she felt shock, she felt curiosity, she felt outrage, and, as if all these were not enough to fill her up, she felt certainty.

Certainty that this was to do with Donald.

From somewhere she found some consternation and injected this into her facial muscles.

'What?'

It was a fine display. Had Beverley not passed many years beyond the cynicism event horizon, she might have been drawn into the deep creases of the frown that had appeared on the forehead of Janet Lennox, might have been affected by them.

'Police, Mrs Lennox. Can we come in? We need to have a chat.'

'Why?'

'Because we're the police and we need to have a chat.'

'But what about?'

Beverley had not started out with high hopes that she would like Mrs Lennox and had not, in truth, invested much effort in trying, a decision that she was now silently applauding as the height of prudence. 'Mrs Lennox, does it matter? Are you really going to deny us entry so that we are forced to discuss delicate matters on your doorstep where anyone can hear?'

It was actually very unlikely that anyone except birds, beasts and birch trees was going to hear anything, since the house was at the end of a longish drive and surrounded by dense forest. Mrs Lennox, however, clearly feared that eavesdroppers followed the police around listening for gossip they could sell to the neighbours; she accordingly yielded, albeit without a trace of grace.

It turned out that Mrs Lennox was so dedicated to the care of her home and its furnishings that she did not care to risk them being touched by the likes of constabulary lackeys and they were ushered through the house into the conservatory, where the only things they could spoil were cane furniture and a few cacti. She also apparently regarded the social pleasantries to be dispensable, as they were not offered refreshments and no sooner had they seated themselves than she demanded, 'Well?'

'We're looking into a death.'

'A death? What has that got to do with me?' As if death would not dare to set its dirty foot in the environs of someone such as she.

'Probably nothing. The person in question was called Anita Delorme. Have you heard the name before?'

'No.' She expressed extreme outrage at the question.

'She worked at Benhall Grange.'

For the first time, Jane Lennox ventured from her lofty retreat of disdain. 'Adam's clinic?'

'Dr Dreifus. That's right.'

Mrs Lennox was discovering that outrage was incompatible with curiosity. A small skirmish thus ensued in which nosiness, as it so often does, proved the stronger. 'How did she die?'

'A gunshot.'

'Oh, dear.' Which, Beverley decided, was about as extreme a reaction as Mrs Lennox ever proffered.

'The problem is, we can't be sure if it was suicide or murder.'

'Good grief!' She was either astonished at their incompetence or intrigued at their situation. Beverley rather suspected the former.

At this point Beverley moved into delicate territory. Her promise to Donald Lennox notwithstanding, she needed facts. 'We need to exclude your husband from the investigation.'

'Donald?'

Beverley nodded. 'He knew Anita, and we need to know where he was on the night she died.'

'Donald?'

Ignoring the repetition, Beverley asked, 'She died some time during the evening of the twenty-second. What time did he come home that night?'

But the witness had questions of her own. 'What do you mean, "He knew Anita"?'

Beverley was aware that Grover was staring at her, his mouth slightly open as if transfixed. 'My understanding is that your husband had met Anita Delorme socially. We are excluding everyone who knew Anita Delorme. Now, could you tell me when your husband returned home on the twenty-second?'

Grover frowned but said nothing. Mrs Lennox was likewise frowning but for different reasons. She was either delving deep into her memory or making a few calculations.

'Mrs Lennox?'

'Well . . . I don't know.'

'Please, try, Mrs Lennox.'

But more seconds passed.

'What time does he normally come home?'

'Well, it depends.'

'Roughly.'

'Unless it's his half-day, I suppose about seven, seven-thirty.'

'So, what about the twenty-second? It wasn't long ago, you know.'

'No . . . '

'Please, Mrs Lennox.'

And eventually, she pronounced. 'The normal time.' A pause, then, 'Yes. I'm fairly sure it was about seven, maybe just after.'

'No later?'

'No. Certainly not.' She appeared to reach the end of her answer, but then surprised them by adding, 'Yes, it was definitely seven.'

It was Beverley's turn to spread a bit of silence, after which she asked wearily, 'There's no possibility at all that you are mistaken?'

'None whatsoever.'

Of course there wasn't. People like Janet Lennox were bastions against anything as human as uncertainty.

It was a conviction that only wealth could buy.

'Fine.' Beverley stood up. 'We'll be asking you for a formal statement in due course.'

They were shown out, although there was a slight feeling that they were being hurried out, and at last Grover could explode. 'What are you doing?'

They were halfway down the drive and Beverley needed a rest anyway. 'I beg your pardon?'

'She's lying.'

'You think so?'

'It's obvious.'

Beverley was only able to raise her eyes to heaven, cry softly but beseechingly, 'Jesus Christ,' and continue her way back to the car.

As Grover got in, Beverley said, 'I *know* she's lying, Grover. You think I don't know when someone like Janet Lennox tells me porkies?'

'Then why didn't you challenge her?'

'Because it would have done no good. The Janet Lennoxes of this world are tougher than anything else the criminal justice system has to deal with.'

Twenty-Seven

D onald Lennox expected a row when he returned home that evening, but he found the atmosphere to be surprisingly normal. At seven-thirty he was a little later than usual – he had seen no point in rushing home – and he found Janet in the sitting room reading the newspaper. She looked up not with sorrow, not with anger, not even with reproach; she looked up with a smile. True it was not the best of smiles – it did not spread far beyond the vermillion borders of her lips, and her eyes held something that suggested it was not entirely indicative of her heart's true feelings – but it gave Lennox something to work with.

'Hello,' he ventured. He put a covering of exhaustion on the greeting, an attempt to evoke some sympathy.

'Hello, dear,' she said. Again, he could detect nothing untoward in her tone. With a feeling of relief he came to her and placed a light kiss on her upturned cheek. 'Has it been a tough day?' she said.

He straightened up. 'Aren't they all?'

The smile had not changed; it might have been a facial deformity. He noticed this but dared not ask. He enquired, 'Drink?'

'Some vermouth would be nice.'

He escaped with some gratitude into the kitchen where the spirits were kept, stopping en route to take off his jacket and loosen his tie. He had just prepared a whisky and soda for himself and poured a vermouth over ice for Janet, when she came in. 'What's for supper?' he asked, as he handed her the drink.

'Salmon.'

'Excellent. Have I got time for a shower?'

'It'll be at least half an hour.'

He left her putting some potatoes on to boil, feeling chirpier than he had for several hours. He was beginning to believe that perhaps the police had yet to call on his wife, and he therefore fancied that he would have a chance to prepare the ground. True, Janet did not seem to be quite her usual self, but he could not believe it concerned Anita Delorme. After all, the other times they had found themselves in an equivalent position, she had reacted in a far more incendiary manner . . .

His insouciance, however, did not last. As the evening wore on, and as Janet's strange demeanour obstinately refused to transmute into normality, he found the strain becoming intolerable; how, he wondered, to broach the subject? It was when the salmon, peas and boiled potatoes had been consumed, the cheese and biscuits attacked, a bottle of white wine deceased, that he girded his loins and decided the time had arrived.

'Janet?'

She was dabbing her mouth with her cloth napkin in the fastidious way that she always did when he said this. 'Yes, Donald?'

He hesitated, unsure how to proceed, but was helped by his beloved. 'Let me guess,' she said. 'You want to talk to me about Anita Delorme.'

There was then a silence, one in which they gazed at each other, he open-mouthed, she with such venom it was a wonder he did not shrivel and so die. The napkin was still hiding the lower part of her face, a pose that might have suggested modesty. When the napkin came down, the smile of the earlier evening had gone and its substitute was a vicious, feral thing.

'Well, is it about Anita Delorme?' she demanded, and really wanted an answer, because she said again, 'Is it?'

He sighed and said, 'Janet, look . . . '

'I've had the police here today.' Before he could find something to say to this that would be placatory, something that would be suitable, and not inflammatory, and preferably not incriminating, she went on, 'But then you know that, don't you?'

'A colleague died. A shotgun was involved. The police aren't sure if it was murder . . . '

'A colleague?'

'Yes.

'They said you knew her "socially",' she pointed out.

'Well, I suppose . . . '

'So was she a "colleague" or a "friend"?'

'Just a colleague. They're asking everyone who worked with her.'

The shake of her head was slight but quite definite. 'She worked at the Grange, Donald.'

He said nothing for a moment before, 'She had contacts at the surgery . . . '

Even he didn't think that he sounded very convincing. Janet Lennox might just as well have been listening to the weather forecast. When she spoke, it was with complete certainty in her words. 'No, she didn't, Donald. She was your lover.'

'No, Janet. That's completely wrong.'

'Please, Donald, don't.' This was a plea, the kind that someone with a machine gun makes to someone who's annoying them. 'She died after working hours. They wanted to know what time you got home in the evening.'

'Yes, I know . . . '

'She was your lover.'

He held his breath, before whispering eventually, 'It was nothing more than a little fling.' He hung his head.

She did not want to cry. She kept back the moisture that brimmed over her eyelids by sheer force of will. 'You swine!'

He looked up at her. He was handsome but, unfortunately for her, he knew it. 'Janet, it was nothing . . . '

'It never is.'

'No, really . . . '

'How many times is this?'

'It meant absolutely nothing to me.'

'Four, I think.' The pause was perfectly timed. 'At least,

four that I know about.' Another of the same, before, 'How many other lovers have there been?'

'None. I swear.'

'So she *was* your lover?'

'I didn't mean that . . . '

She stood up abruptly; so abruptly that the chair wasn't expecting it and toppled over backwards in surprise. 'Stop fucking lying, Donald!'

Janet never swore. *Never.* On the last three occasions, she had screamed at him, she had lashed out at him, but she had not sworn. Janet was an upper-class English woman, and consequently so inhibited that her corsets could have contained a nuclear explosion.

'Janet!'

'I lied for you, Donald. I told them you weren't late that night. Please, don't tell me now that I did it for nothing.' It was a plea, but one that held a sharp blade.

He breathed in deeply and slowly before saying, 'OK, OK.'

She waited. She knew what was coming but she wanted to hear the words, hear the contrition.

'I got friendly with her . . . ' he began.

'Oh, for God's sake.'

'Honestly, Janet. It was a few drinks on a couple of occasions, the odd meal . . . '

'The odd bout of fornication?'

He would not look at her but the word, although low, was quite audible. 'Yes.'

She stared at the top of his head, at the developing tonsure, for a long time, her mind running through the other three occasions. A drug rep, one of the senior managers at the local Primary Care Trust, a GP trainee. All of them half his age and, more importantly, half hers. 'Why were you late?'

He looked up at her. 'What do you mean?'

'The night the police asked about, the night she died. Why were you late? Had you seen her?'

He searched her face, perhaps for a suggestion that he could deceive her. Apparently, he saw none. He nodded. 'Yes. In the afternoon.'

She breathed in through pinched nostrils, every cell of her body radiating disgust and contempt. 'I won't ask what you were doing.'

'Do you really want to know?'

'No, Donald. Not in the least. I have no desire whatsoever to discuss with you the details of your rutting habits with any trollop who comes into range, but I do want to know if you had anything at all to do with her death.'

'Of course I didn't!'

'So if you left her in the afternoon, where were you that evening?'

When he spoke, his voice was low and steady. 'I went to a pub and sat there for a couple of hours, staring at a shandy. I kept wondering what I was doing and why I was doing it. I kept telling myself that I must be mad. I was going to end it, Janet. Honestly, I was. I'd even told Anita that it couldn't go on.'

'Are you telling me the truth?'

The tone of his reply was forceful. 'Yes.'

'You had nothing at all to do with her death?'

'No!' Then, 'I love you, Janet. I always have.'

If he had hoped her anger would collapse as he said this, he was quickly disabused. She strode from the room without a further word. He stared after her, his face unemotional and unmoving, until he said tiredly, 'Fucking great.'

Twenty-Eight

'How have you been, Helena?'

Helena was in her customary position, seated in front of the window, her attention on the world outside. It was the perfect illustration of alienation, of an outsider looking inwards to a world that was separate. She turned her head slowly, as if fearful that any movement that was too sudden might cause injury.

'Helena? Remember me? It's Harriet.'

Helena's expression was at first a frown, then the merest whisper of recognition. She did not speak, however.

'Do you mind if I talk to you some more?'

There was not even a shrug in response to this question, an absence of reaction that was vibrantly assertive of uninterest. Harriet sat down on the bed, betraying no sign that she was in the slightest part discommoded by Helena's blankness. She noted a cup of tea on the cabinet beside the bed; the surface was partially covered by a thin, contracted skin and there were wisps of milkiness in the greyness that made it look unappetizing.

'I've been reading up about you. I hope you don't mind.' Helena did not appear to be bothered by this news, however, and said nothing.

'You've had a lot of tragedy in your life, haven't you?' Helena glanced across at her.

'Am I right in saying that you've got no remaining blood relatives?'

Helena shook her head.

'Only your partner who is close to you?'

A nod. It was slow and slight, but it was a nod.

'He's worried about you, you know.'

A pause, but then Helena acknowledged that yes, John Eisenmenger was most probably worried about her.

'You're not alone, then.' Helena's expression was fixed, even as she agreed without apparent enthusiasm that she was not alone.

Harriet explained, 'I just have my daughter and her husband now.' Helena neither said nor did anything. 'No one else who is either close or even just a relative. Without them, I would be completely alone.'

Perhaps Helena did not see where this was heading; certainly she gave no external indication of comprehension. 'I've come to rely on them. My greatest nightmare is that one day, when I need one of them, they might not be there.'

At which Helena's eyes widened slightly. Harriet paused, then asked gently. 'Is that what worries you? That one day John might not be there when you need him?'

Helena was looking at her now with a novel intensity. Her eyes did not leave the old woman's face even as she began to nod, and remained nodding for many seconds. Making no sign at how satisfied she was that she had managed to engage Helena in the conversation, and had done so with relative ease compared with previous occasions, Harriet said, 'But he will be.'

A frown. 'Will he?'

'Yes, of course he will. He loves you.'

Helena did not react or, more accurately, she did not *appear* to react. She just stared at Harriet for some seconds until Harriet began to believe that she was somehow paralysed. Then she noticed Helena's eyes beginning to widen and to moisten. Suddenly Helena was crying, and through this she said, 'So did Mummy and Daddy. So did Jeremy. So did . . . '

She broke down completely.

'So did who?'

But Helena could not reply and Harriet had to guess. 'Baby?' she asked acutely. 'Did Baby love you?'

And Helena nodded as she wept.

Harriet let the tears flow, waiting patiently for Helena to recover. Forlornly, Helena said at last, 'They all loved me, and now they're gone. Love's not enough.'

Forlornly, but Harriet thought there were undertones of anger in the words.

'It's not the whole answer, but it's a prerequisite. Without love, there's nothing.'

'Oh, yes?' Helena was scornful and Harriet felt unexpressed delight to hear it. 'I don't think there's anything even with it.'

'That's a bit unfair on John.'

Helena frowned. 'Why?'

'You're denying his love.'

'I'm not doing anything of the sort. He loves me. I've never said any different.'

'But you're also saying that it doesn't mean anything to you.'

Helena paused, seeming almost puzzled, as if she had never thought of it like that. 'Yes, it does,' she decided.

'Then show him. Show him his love isn't wasted on you, because that's basically what you were implying just now.'

Helena opened her mouth to argue, stopped, shook her head. Quite without warning she began to cry again. When she spoke, the despair was back. 'I *know* he loves me, and I love him . . . ' She stopped, then, 'But it's not sufficient, don't you see? Everyone around me leaves eventually, one way or another.'

And beyond that Harriet could get no more that day. Helena returned to her well of depression and eventually Harriet left her after talking for some time *to* her and no longer *with* her. But she was satisfied. It had been brief but for the first time she had elicited responses that resembled normality. She had seen anger, too, and that was important, for it had been anger that was not directed inwards. For the first time, she felt certain that she could pull Helena through this.

Twenty-Nine

B everley was reading Charles Sydenham's final report and wondering where Grover was. She was irritated by his absence and aware that it was unfair of her to be so. There was a principle here, after all. Subordinates were not autonomous entities allowed to indulge in freethinking, no matter how capable they might consider themselves of such acts.

Sydenham's report was not alleviating her mood. He put the time of death at anywhere between seven and midnight, and it was as he had at first intimated: in theory Anita Delorme could have done the deed herself and, such as it was, the evidence certainly suggested that the blast had been at short range and into the roof of the mouth. Did that mean that murder was out of the question?

No, it did not.

She could easily imagine a sequence of events in which murder resulted in a picture such as the one that had met her eyes in Anita Delorme's kitchen.

In almost every instance, suicide was suicide and murder was murder and no one, not even Grover, would waste a second considering otherwise. Suicide usually screamed out to be recognized as such, not so much because they left a note (more often than not, they did not), but because there was nothing, not even so much as a whiff, to suggest rottenness. No one would have sufficient motive to hasten the departure of the deceased, there would be nothing odd about the circumstances, there would be nothing in the life of the victim that sounded the alarm.

Murder, too, was almost always obvious. Short of signing their names in the blood of the corpse, most killers went out of their way to make it easy for the sleuth to catch them. The motive was usually radioactively bright, the opportunity confined to a single individual, the means covered in fingerprints.

Anita Delorme's death fell exactly on the dividing line. In the scales of decision, it balanced perfectly.

It would have been devilishly hard with an experienced, non-goofy sergeant to assist her, but with Grover . . .

At which thought, the object of her despair entered the office. He nodded at Beverley and then shut the door.

'Where the fuck have you been?' She had noticed that she was swearing more now that Grover had taken against it.

Grover, though, was too excited to do his usual haughty reprimand concerning profanity. He went to the chair in front of her desk and sat down. 'Picking up the report on the finances of Atopia.'

'And?'

'Atopia's practically bankrupt.'

'Is it now?'

He handed the file over. 'It's been bumping along the bottom for a good few years but, according to this, this year it's really taken a dive.'

'Do we know why?'

Grover nodded portentously. 'The income's about the same but the outgoings have gone haywire.'

'On anything in particular?'

'The accounts suggest that it's due mainly to their spending on office and computer equipment. New computers, new printers, a fortune on printer accessories, stuff like that.'

'Is it real?'

Grover smiled grimly and shook his head. 'The receipts for a lot of this stuff are from a company called Pax Supplies. They're registered to an address in Norwich.'

'Who are the company officers?'

'It's a one-man outfit.'

It was obvious that Grover was enjoying drawing this out, that he had learned something of huge significance. Beverley was getting tired of the game, though. 'Just tell me, Grover.'

'Frank Delorme.'

Her irritation forgotten, Beverley smiled – something that was a rare sight for Grover. 'How very interesting. How very interesting indeed.'

'I thought you'd like that piece of news.' Grover hesitated, then said, 'It looks as if you might have been right.'

It was reluctant but it was an admission, albeit a qualified one. 'Might have been? I was bang on the button. She's been ripping Dreifus off.'

'But that would mean she'd have to be doing it with the help of her father, wouldn't it?'

'Her father's demented and she's got power of attorney. She just collects the cash and spends it while he dribbles his life away in a nursing home.'

Grover frowned at Beverley's flippancy. Perhaps because of her disapproval, he opted to minimize the importance of this discovery. 'I'm not sure that it's relevant, though.'

'Aren't you? I am.'

'How does it tie up with her relationship with Lennox? Was he involved in the fraud?'

'Possibly, but I doubt it.'

'Then I don't see that it adds much. OK, so you were right and she was syphoning money out of Atopia and into her own pockets, but if it doesn't implicate Lennox, then so what?'

'Grover, if you're going to make any sort of career as a detective, try not to dress up assumptions as facts. *If* Lennox is a killer, then perhaps this new aspect is irrelevant, but only *if*.'

'But it was his shotgun . . . '

Lord, please help me not to kill him.

The irony that she was turning to God in a time of need did not escape her.

Thirty

'I'm sorry to bother you, Dr Eisenmenger.'
He could not place the voice for a second, then realized with surprise that it was one of the coroner's officers. Of course he hadn't recognized it – the tone had fooled him. Normally, they spoke to him as if contempt lay a semitone or two beneath the words, adding resonance and timbres of irritation. On this occasion, however, there was an unmistakeable air of deference.

'What is it?'

'Something's come to light. It's probably nothing . . . '

'In connection with what?'

'The Melnick case.'

Eisenmenger leaned back in his chair. He was at once both interested and enjoying himself; he thought he could smell the sweet scent of a pie made of humble that was about to be served to him. 'What about it?'

'We spoke to Edward Melnick's son, Alfred. He's a son by his first marriage.'

'What did he have to say?'

'Well . . . he accused his stepmother of killing his father.'

For all Eisenmenger's suspicions about the death, murder had been well down the list. 'Does he say why she might want to do this?'

'Apparently, there's some sort of insurance policy. A natural death would bring her quite a few thousand pounds. He didn't know how much, but he said his father told him of its existence.'

'And did they get on? The stepson and Rose Melnick, I mean?'

'He didn't say so directly, but I got the impression there was no love lost.'

'So it might be just malicious gossip, mightn't it?'

'Almost certainly . . . '

Eisenmenger heard hope. The last thing the Coroner's Office needed was the Melnick case turned into a forensic examination. He had to ask himself if he did, either. 'What do we know about Alfred Melnick?'

'He's a delivery man. Married with three children.'

'So he's probably short of money.'

'Very much so, I'd say.'

'And the police were satisfied, right? I mean, there's nothing you're not telling me about the circumstances of the death, is there?'

'Nothing.'

Eisenmenger thought a little more. 'So it probably is just malicious gossip. I don't know for certain yet how he died, but I would put murder fairly low down on the list.'

'Oh, good.'

He didn't hear the sigh but the gratitude was a fair substitute.

He felt content for all of thirty seconds after he had put the phone down.

Rose Melnick's story had been slightly odd, hadn't it? Her attitude had been just a touch worrying, too. Nothing concrete, certainly not enough foundation on which to build any kind of an edifice designed to last, just slightly perturbing.

That was it.

Not enough to disturb, but enough to perturb.

He wondered what he should do. Various possibilities occurred to him, amongst which were to phone the Coroner's Office back and get them to bring the police in, and phone the police himself.

Neither held much attraction. After all, supposing he was really just making a prat of himself?

What, then, to do?

Beverley Wharton.

She was the obvious person to talk to. He could do so unofficially, without fear of ridicule or, at least, that the ridicule would go any further.

It was so logical.

So why did he feel so guilty?

Harriet was very aware of how important it was to get Helena out of her room and the rut that it represented, but it was not until her fourth visit that she succeeded. Her first suggestion – the large common room where many of the women spent at least part of the day in conversation – was quickly vetoed. In the end, they settled on one of the rooms that was usually used for group therapy sessions.

'Why don't you want to socialize, Helena? You eat in your room, and you never go into the lounge. It might do you some good to talk to others who've been through the same experience as you have.'

'Might it?' Helena sounded unconvinced. She was fiddling with a shred of material that was hanging off the chair on which she sat. Harriet saw this – saw that the tatter had become a proxy for a comfort blanket.

'It would prove to you that you're not alone. A bit of company might help a lot in making you see things in their proper perspective.'

Helena smiled but it was a secret thing, one that came from a joke only she could know. She said, after some consideration, 'When you've suffered an injury – had your face scarred – the last thing you want is to be put before a mirror.'

'Is that what you think? That you've been scarred?'

Helena was surprised. 'Yes, of course.'

'But what happened to you wasn't your fault. No blame attaches.'

'So what? Only consequences matter. Only the effects. The boy who kicked me when he stole my phone isn't living with any sequelae. He has no scars and he is untouched. He has no blame.'

'So why do you have to have it?'

'There's always blame. You can't wish it away. If the boy doesn't have it, then I must.'

'Not everything is someone's fault.'

Helena stopped fiddling and stared directly into the older woman's eyes. 'Yes, it is,' she proclaimed flatly.

'No such thing as an accident?'

'Look hard enough and someone will have made a mistake, not done what they should have done, put the wrong thing in a box, taken too much of something else.'

Harriet wondered where that came from.

'Just because the boy who attacked you doesn't feel guilt,

it doesn't mean he is guiltless. Certainly he is as far as God is concerned, and as far as the law is concerned.'

Helena shook her head. 'The law is an artificial construct designed only to make society function. Justice extends only as far as pleasing as many of the people as possible. It's mob rule with a wig and gown on.'

Harriet observed, 'That was quite a speech. One of yours?'

'John's. He used to say things like that to annoy me.'

'But now you agree with it, perhaps.'

'I would allow that there's no such thing as natural or complete justice, yes.'

Harriet saw that Helena had begun to fiddle with her comforter again and decided that perhaps this was interesting. She suggested, 'Tell me about John.'

Helena's fingers stopped for a second, then continued in a manner that was, if anything, more frenetic. 'When I first met John, he used to irritate me so much.'

'Really? Why?'

'Because he was so calm, so serene, so bloody self-assured.'

'Why should that be a problem? Surely better that than jumpy or capricious or neurotic.'

'But it can also be infuriating. Nothing ever fazes him. Everything's a puzzle to be solved and, boy, does he enjoy solving puzzles.'

'He's a cold fish, then.'

Helena was quick to shake her head. 'No, I wouldn't say that. Just . . . English.'

Harriet laughed. 'Oh, dear! That bad.'

She was rewarded with a small smile. 'He can be very affectionate, very caring . . . he *is* very caring, all of the time, but he doesn't choose to show it.'

'And that bothers you . . . ?'

But Helena apparently did not feel that this was the basis of her aggravation with John Eisenmenger. 'Now I come to think about it, I don't think it docs, really. I'm not sure I could cope with a man who was soppy, over the top . . . '

Harriet could not resist pointing out, 'Which is very English of *you.*'

Another small smile. 'I suppose it is.'

'And it doesn't explain why you found him so irritating at first.'

But Helena could find no explanation, despite trying to analyse her feelings for Eisenmenger, and it was left to Harriet to suggest after a few moments, 'Perhaps he was too like you.'

Helena's reaction was interesting, for she jumped, almost as if physically prodded. Harriet's first thought was that this was outrage, but she quickly realized it was actually incomprehension. 'What?'

'You seem to me to be like that as well. Calm, self-assured, contained . . . '

'My God! Do I? Let me tell you, I don't feel it. Far from it . . . ' Helena lapsed into silence, perhaps brooding on her present state, and Harriet said quickly, 'But what about before you lost your baby? Were you perhaps like it then?'

She watched as Helena's first, unthinking reaction was going to be another denial, before a second and more considered opinion fought through. 'Maybe . . . '

'Sometimes our annoyance springs from seeing our own traits in those around us.'

Helena laughed delightedly. 'I must tell him! He'll be mortified to learn that he's just the same as me.'

'Why would that mortify him?'

'Because he prides himself on tranquillity and rationality.'

'You're a lawyer. You're surely rational.'

Which observation caused Helena to pause. 'I was once,' she said slowly. 'Now, I'm not sure.'

'And maybe it's not so good to be purely rational. Emotions are important things, too, you know, as long as they don't rule us.'

'Is that what I'm doing?'

'To a certain extent.'

Helena considered this, but if Harriet had hoped that insight would lead to redemption, she was disappointed. With a slow, sad nod, Helena said, 'You're right, of course. I'm so pathetic, aren't I?'

'Not at all.'

'No? Look at you. Look at what you've been through. You're not letting your emotions crush you into nothing.'

'What happened to me happened a long time ago.'

'But you're so . . . so balanced about it.'

Harriet shrugged. 'Perhaps I appear so.'

'It's obvious that you are.'

She shook her head. 'You don't know me, Helena.'

'Tell me, then. Tell me about yourself.'

Harriet hesitated, aware of the danger of becoming too close to the client – of the client becoming too close to the counsellor – but she wanted to build on the progress she felt she was making. 'It's very boring.'

'Let me be the judge of that.'

'Well, I'm sixty-eight years old. I was born in Donnington and lived here most of my life. I have a degree in clinical psychology from Aberdeen. I have worked here, at the unit, for nearly a year, having previously worked at St Benjamin's.'

'You mentioned your family. Tell me about them.' At Harriet's hesitation, Helena added, 'If you want to.'

A smile. 'I was married to Derek for thirty-nine years. He was a doctor, here in Donnington. We had one child, a daughter. The miscarriages you know about.'

'And your daughter is married?'

'Yes. Very happily. She met him when he came to work at Derek's practice.'

Helena felt she had gone as far as she could, but Harriet continued anyway, her tone now suggesting that she was recalling events as much for her own benefit as for her listener's. 'It hasn't been easy for them. When they lost their daughter, I thought it would destroy their marriage, but it didn't. I think it strengthened them. Ruth threw herself into charity work and Adam started his clinic.'

'Clinic?'

'When he's not being a family doctor, he runs a clinic at Benhall Grange. Researches into allergies. He wants to make sure that what happened to Annabelle never happens to anyone else.'

'You must be very proud.'

Harriet took a moment to answer, as if she had never considered the proposition before. 'Yes,' she decided. 'I suppose I am.'

Thirty-One

Beverley had suggested they meet at a bar over a drink, but Eisenmenger had a head that was old enough and wise enough to opt for somewhere without alcohol to cloud his judgement. He was all too aware of Beverley's power to entrance and enslave. Accordingly, they were sitting in the Blue Waters Cafe in the hospital, drinking coffee and surrounded by a mix of patients, relatives and hospital staff.

It had, he felt, been a wise choice. Beverley had not proved immune to ageing but was using it to her advantage, and she had only become more interesting because of it. Given such a prospect, what did the odd extra crease here and there matter? She was, as always, well manicured, subtly coiffured and assured in every movement.

She had seemed genuinely pleased to be with him again, as well.

Yet he also knew very well that she was as accomplished at deception as she was at seduction.

'It's lovely to see you, John, but I very much fear that this is not for pleasure.' She was sipping the black coffee he had bought for her, fingers long and unbent so that the cream-coloured mug was held only by fingertips. She had appraised him as efficiently as he had her, perhaps more so.

In response he said, 'Not entirely.' She guessed he was too much of a gentleman to shut the door completely.

And therein lies your downfall.

She was certain that, had she wished, she could have made him hers. She sometimes dreamed of doing so, not only for her own pleasure but, just as importantly, for the displeasure of Helena. She did not like Helena – thought her stuck-up, cold – and Helena did not like her; in fact, had a pathological hatred of her. Completely irrational, of course. When Beverley had investigated the murder of Helena's parents, it had seemed obvious at the time that Jeremy, Helena's stepbrother, was the guilty party. It wasn't her fault that he had committed suicide while in custody . . .

'So, what business do we have to discuss?'

Reluctantly, he explained what he had discovered about the death of Edward Melnick. Reluctantly, because now that he was at this point, he was all too aware that this was a construct made up as much of suspicion and imagination as fact and experience. It was a delicate gossamer web, barely seen except by the dewdrops of his own paranoias.

She listened without changing her expression of concentration. She kept her eyes on his face, never left it. It was an intensity of scrutiny that might have embarrassed him had he not known her well.

When he finished, she continued this scrutiny until, 'This has to be a waste of my time.'

He was not surprised, he even smiled. He had half hoped this was what she would say, thus absolving him of his suspicions and therefore responsibilities.

'A known drunk comes home one night and accidentally takes his wife's medication, then dies. There is nothing to suggest that she somehow forced or tricked him into taking it, and the only motive you can find comes from the son who reckons she killed him for some sort of pathetic insurance policy.'

'Don't forget he was treating her badly.'

She shook her head. 'I don't like two motives, John. It smacks of desperation. You don't accumulate reasons to murder someone like collecting points on a reward card. Either she knocked him off because he was a drunken bully who deserved it, or she did it for the money.'

'The son seems convinced she murdered him.'

She smiled. 'Her stepson,' was all she said, but he understood. Stepchildren were not infrequently ill-disposed to their new parents.

He sighed, but it was light-hearted. 'Ah, well. I just thought I'd mention it. I knew that I was just being silly.'

She nodded as if that had crossed her mind as well, but then said, 'I'll look into it.'

'What?'

She had finished the coffee some time before, but only now did she put the cup on the saucer. 'I'll look into it.'

'But . . . '

'It's an idiotic, fanciful idea, but it's *your* idea, John. Anyone else and I'd have got up and I'd be on my way back to the station by now, but you have a knack of sniffing things out. You're like a dog scenting something the rest of us are just not equipped to detect. You're probably wrong but, if not, I don't want to miss it.'

He was not particularly happy with the concept that he was Beverley's faithful hound on the trail of crime, but he let it pass. Indeed, he tried to argue her out of it.

'But you've just said the motives aren't strong.'

'No, they're not, but they're not inconsequential, either. Haven't you heard? Domestic violence is no longer taken lightly by the police.'

'When I spoke to her, I would have said that she still loved him. Underneath all the pretence, she seemed genuinely knocked back by the blow.'

It was getting close to lunchtime and the cafe was filling up. The smells of toasted sandwiches and hot soup were becoming apparent, making Eisenmenger feel hungry.

'Genuinely knocked back or just remorseful for what she'd done? Anyway, most wives who kill their husbands still love them.'

'But we're not talking about a spur of the moment thing, are we?' he pointed out. 'If she murdered him, she planned it.'

'Still doesn't mean it wasn't related to her domestic situation.'

'And if she murdered him, she chose a very, very sophisticated way to do it . . .'

She heard the ellipsis. 'Meaning what?'

'I would have judged her to be a carving knife in the gizzard type. Give him what for and damn the consequences.'

She shook her head, then put her hand out to touch his. He felt warmth and softness and something close to a sexual thrill. 'Let me be the judge of that, John, dear.'

Thirty-Two

'I am starting to become extremely irritated with your constant attention, Inspector.'

'I'm very sorry to hear that, Dr Dreifus . . . '

'I mean what, precisely, do you think you are investigating?'

Beverley did not mind Dreifus and his outrage. She was used to the picture before her: that of a middle-aged, successful and important (not to say self-important) man using indignation as both a shield and a weapon.

They were once more in Dreifus's office at Atopia. She noted that he was drawn, attenuated to the point of transparency; under his eyes were bags that were not only dark but that seemed to pull at his eyes and, although he had clearly been making an attempt at shaving, he had either been doing so in the dark or on a roller coaster.

'A death that I cannot be sure was not murder.'

'I appreciate that the police have their own – peculiar – way of doing these things . . . ' He added such emphasis on the word *peculiar* that the second syllable became practically an accusation on its own, before he continued, ' . . . but surely it would be less inefficient to determine that single basic fact before wasting resources on unnecessary investigation . . . '

She was about to respond, but Dreifus had more to say and was determined to say it. The sarcasm was not so much laid on with a trowel as poured over her using a wide-bore hose, ' . . . in the course of which, innocent citizens are subjected to long and tedious interviews which keep them from their work, and which begin to amount to harassment.'

Beverley had always held the tenet that accusations of harassment were the last refuge of the guilty, and she was starting to suspect that Dreifus was guilty of something, even if wasn't the death of Anita Delorme.

She waited for a second to ensure she would have a clear

run at the goal before saying calmly, 'Nevertheless, Sir, *I* am the one in charge of the case and *I* will conduct it as *I* see fit.'

He clearly didn't like this, but contented himself with a brisk, 'Well, get it over with, then,' before retreating into sulky silence.

She made sure that Grover, who had been seated beside her without saying anything, was poised with the pen before asking, 'I need to determine your whereabouts on the evening Anita died. That would be eight days ago.'

He could not resist remarking, 'I know when it was,' as a prelude to a sigh which presumably indicated he was fishing in his memory for an answer. After a short while he said, 'I came straight here after surgery. I suppose I would have got here about seven-thirty.'

'When did you leave the clinic?'

'Just after nine-thirty.'

'Would there be anyone here who could corroborate that?'

'Well, my last appointment was scheduled for eight-thirty, but I doubt that I actually got around to seeing whomever it was until closer to eight forty-five – I never do. Daksha Singh leaves at eight-thirty, Charlotte Pelger at nine, the research staff at any time between six and nine, depending on what they're working on; one of them might have seen me leave.'

'Who would have seen you arrive here?'

'Daksha. The girl on reception here.'

'What did you do when you first got here?'

'More often than not I start seeing patients straight away.'

'I assume we can check that?'

He made a show of great forbearance as he said in a steady voice, 'Yes, you can. There will be records of whom I saw when and, if that's not enough for you, I'm sure Nurse Pelger will be able verify what I say.'

Beverley smiled as she might at a small child reluctant to stop playing on the swings and come home. 'And what did you do after you'd seen your last patient?'

He was becoming exasperated, which told Beverley he was becoming worried about something. She speculated whether it was because he was a guilty man nearing a lie or an innocent one nearing a hole in his memory.

'I don't know . . . Almost certainly it was something to

do with management. Running this place takes up a lot of time.'

'Did anyone see you?'

'Normally, Anita would probably have seen me, at least for the first part of that time, but, as we know, she wasn't here . . . '

'You don't have a secretary?'

He did not.

'Did you make or receive any phone calls?'

He was not sure, but he thought not. Beverley said, 'Never mind, Dr Dreifus. We can check the phone records.'

A nod.

Her next question was not strictly relevant to his alibi for the death of Anita Delorme. 'Dr Dreifus, during the course of our investigation, it has come to light that this clinic is in serious financial trouble . . . '

He reacted to that. Oh, boy, did he react to that.

'What? What?'

'Our analysis of your records shows us that you are nearly bankrupt . . . '

'Rubbish!' Just to make sure that everyone understood, he then elaborated on this. 'That is absolute rubbish.'

'Really?'

Suddenly he was flushed, excited, almost spray-painted with perspiration. What was more, he hesitated before explaining, 'We're not as healthy as we might be, but that doesn't mean we're *bankrupt.*'

But Beverley had more. 'We also believe that Anita Delorme was systematically defrauding the clinic, to the tune of several tens of thousands of pounds.'

She was watching for his reaction and saw a man who might have just sat down on a piece of electrified barbed wire. 'What on earth are you talking about?'

She repeated her accusation, although she was fairly confident that he had heard every word of it the first time.

'Defrauding *me*?' He emphasized the first of these two words, as if by a subtle alteration of the way he pronounced it, he could come closer to comprehension.

'You didn't know?' She had not needed to ask this. If Adam Dreifus was not in near-terminal shock, then she was a piece of pineapple on a cocktail stick. In any case, he did not answer.

She suspected he was incapable of answering.

When she next spoke, she used the same tone she used when she had to speak to bereaved parents. 'I can see that you didn't.'

But he still did not seem to hear.

She waited five beats before asking, in exactly the same voice, 'Did you know that your colleague, Donald Lennox, was having an affair with her?'

He might have been fighting the effects of a drug. From staring at the surface of the desk, he looked up at her and then tried to concentrate before nodding. 'Yes,' he admitted.

'Did you ever have an affair with her?'

Which startled him awake quite effectively. In a steady, strong voice he said, 'No.'

And she believed him.

Thirty-Three

While she returned to the station, Beverley left Grover at the clinic taking statements from Daksha Singh and Charlotte Pelger, and asking amongst the scientific staff if they could add anything to what they knew of Anita Delorme, and if they could corroborate Dreifus's story. She took this opportunity to look into Edward Melnick. She made routine searches of various databases, including Revenue and Customs, Social Security and Criminal Records. She also looked into the record of his service with the police force and discovered that Melnick had had an interesting disciplinary record, including several instances of violence against suspects and, towards the end of his career, an inconclusive investigation for corruption. She suspected that his departure not long after this had not been coincidental. Otherwise, apart from a poor credit record and, one year before, a conviction and ban for drink-driving (fined but not imprisoned), his was an entirely blameless life, at least as far as officialdom went.

Rose Melnick barely existed, accept as a voracious user of
social services. She certainly had yet to bother the law enforce-
ment authorities.

The background thus sketched out, she decided then to talk
to the widow herself, aware that her own instincts regarding
the guilt or innocence of suspects were good but far from
infallible. She rang the number she had gleaned from the files,
but was only successful some three hours and four attempts
later.

'Mrs Melnick?'

'Yes?'

'My name is Beverley Wharton. I'm a police inspector.'

Mrs Melnick reacted badly to this announcement. 'Police?'

'I was wondering if I could come and have a chat with
you.'

'What about?'

'I want to clear up a few matters regarding your late
husband.'

'What matters?'

Beverley didn't hear. 'When would be convenient? Tonight?
Say an hour's time?'

'I don't know . . . '

'Half past seven, then. I'll see you then. Make sure you're
in, Mrs Melnick.'

Beverley cut the connection, a small smile demonstrating
her satisfaction.

Melnick's widow had been exactly as she had expected, as
John Eisenmenger had led her to believe. Suspicious, recalcitrant, unintelligent but cunning; none of these meant that
she was guilty of despatching her husband to the afterlife but
they did suggest that a little digging might well bring to public
attention some indiscretions, perhaps major ones.

Grover returned ten minutes later. He had been unable to
verify the precise time that Dreifus had left.

'What now?'

'His wife. Let's see what time she says he got home.'

Grover made a sour face. 'She'll probably lie through
perfectly capped teeth, just like Janet Lennox.'

Thirty-Four

Beverley could see that Grover was finding life amongst the monied classes something of a trial. His face as they drove up to Dreifus's house bore a look that many a martyr's had probably born in times long gone when they were being burned at the stake: it melded extreme pain and extreme superiority.

'Are you all right?' she asked of him as they came to a halt in front of the house. Her voice failed to carry sympathy.

He frowned. 'Yes.'

'Then why the look? Is it constipation, or indigestion?'

He did not appreciate the jocularity. As he gestured at the house and its surroundings, he said merely, 'More conspicuous consumption.'

She got out of the car. As he did likewise, she asked, 'What is your problem with people having a bit of money?'

'I have nothing against people having a bit of money. It's when they have so much that it bothers me.'

'Why?'

'Because it's immoral.' His tone was flat, spoken with enough passionate certainty to depress her.

'Not if they acquired it morally.'

He almost sneered at this. 'No. Money is immoral. By definition. Give it away or risk damnation.'

She thought about asking him if he gave all his money away but stayed silent, fearful that he did. Instead she advised, 'Well, try to stop your contempt from showing too much while we talk to the witness, OK?'

They walked to the front door. Grover pressed the bell and they waited. After a few minutes, the door opened and a grey woman of medium height and large bone structure gave them an enquiring look. 'Yes?'

'Mrs Dreifus?'

'Yes.'

'I'm Inspector Wharton, this is DS Grover.' Grover was holding his identification for inspection, as per regulations, but Beverley could not be bothered. 'We were wondering if you could spare us a couple of minutes to answer a few questions.'

'What about?'

'If we could come in?'

She was more hospitable than Janet Lennox had been and complied without hesitation, although she was clearly discomforted. She led them through to a large kitchen, where they sat around a circular pine kitchen table and looked out on to a rather nice golf course. She even asked them if they would like coffee, which they assured her they would not.

'I expect your husband has told you about the death of Anita Delorme.'

'What of it?'

'She died on the night of the twenty-second.'

'Yes?'

'Can you remember what you were doing that night?'

Her look was a questioning one, but she answered, 'Well, if I remember correctly, I was chairing a meeting of the governors of Thomas Cromwell School.'

'Where?'

'Here. In this very room.' At which Grover looked around, his face radiating his low opinion of such opulence.

'About when did it start and when did it end?'

'Seven sharp, lasting until nine-fifteen.'

'Who was at the meeting?'

The questioning look became positively interrogative, but still she did not demand the purpose of this inquisition. Beverley wondered if this, in itself, was significant. She gave them a list of six names and Grover duly noted them down.

Beverley asked, 'When did your husband come home?'

She was not aware that there had been anything in her voice to mark this out as a question of significance, but Ruth Dreifus seemed to find something there. 'About ten, I think.' A pause. 'Yes, it was just after ten.'

'You're certain?'

For the first time she did not meekly accept her part in the script. 'May I enquire why you're asking?'

To which Beverley said simply, 'Anita Delorme was defrauding Atopia to the extent that it is nearly bankrupt.' She watched the reaction.

'What?' Then before Beverley could repeat her assertion, 'No! No, she wasn't!' Mrs Dreifus had the look of a woman who had just learned that her newly dead son had been a pederast.

'I'm afraid she was,' Beverley said. 'And I don't know for certain that she wasn't murdered, so I would like to know the whereabouts of your husband at about the time she died.'

Mrs Dreifus looked confused and it took her a moment to react. 'You surely can't believe that Adam had anything to do with it?'

'I don't believe anything yet, Mrs Dreifus. If you could answer my question. Are you certain about the time he came home?'

She collected herself, took a breath, then replied, 'Yes.'

Beverley believed her. 'Did you ever meet Anita Delorme?'

'Once, I think. At a Christmas party.'

'May I ask what you thought of her?'

She was clearly taken aback by the question. 'Oh . . . Well, I don't know . . . '

Which meant that she very much did. Beverley waited; Grover's pen did likewise. 'As far as I can remember, she was very chatty. Sociable.'

'Did you like her?'

'Oh . . . ' Deep consideration before the lie. 'Yes, I think so.'

'She was quite attractive,' suggested Beverley.

'Was she? Yes, I suppose she was.'

'I don't suppose you know about boyfriends, that kind of thing?'

'Good grief! Why on earth would I be able to tell you anything about that?' She laughed and Beverley smiled; only Grover failed to register amusement.

Beverley stood up. 'I didn't think so, but one has to ask, Mrs Dreifus. I'm sorry for disturbing you.'

She showed them out, charming and effusive, demonstrating a degree of cooperation that more than made up for Janet Lennox. Grover barely waited for the door to close before proclaiming, 'That means he could have done it! If he didn't get home until ten, he might have been out of the clinic by nine-fifteen, gone to Anita Delorme's house, shot her, then come home.'

Beverley walked on without replying, which made Grover even more animated. He hurried after her and repeated his assertion. Only when they were at the car did Beverley say, 'I know he could have done it, Grover, but did he?'

'Why not? He had a good reason.'

She ignored him and got into the car, saying to herself, 'She could have lied, but she didn't. I wonder why.'

'She knows more about Anita Delorme and her husband than she's telling.'

'Maybe.'

'It's obvious.'

Even if it had been obvious to Beverley, she was in no mood to continue the debate with Grover. Anyway, she had other things to consider. 'Back to the station, Grover. I've got to be somewhere in half an hour.'

'Where?'

'Don't worry, Grover. It's nothing to do with this case.'

Thirty-Five

B everley's job frequently brought her into contact with people and places that, had she not been a policewoman, she would have gone to almost all legal lengths to avoid. Rose Melnick and Rose Melnick's flat were high on that list. As she sat before a nervous, clearly stressed widow, she tried to put from her mind the decrepitude of the furniture, the slightly distasteful odour that came from somewhere in the vicinity, the cockroach traps she had glimpsed in the hallway. The irony of Mrs Melnick's forename was all too evident, given the state of her home.

This was not the shabby gentility of age.

'I don't understand why you want to talk to me.'

'Edward Melnick used to be a policeman, I understand.'

'So what?'

'He'd become a private investigator.'

In truth, Beverley did not care doodly-squat about this. She considered the fact that Edward Melnick had harboured romantic but seriously mistaken notions of sleuthing his way to fame and fortune to be worthy only of contemptible laughter, but she wanted an excuse to talk to his widow and thereby gauge her without alarming her. To stride in and accuse her of killing her husband would, she judged, not help the cause.

'Yes.'

'Successful?'

As the conversation began to meander away from anything threatening, Mrs Melnick became more relaxed. 'You must be joking! Most of his cases involved missing pets, or debt collection.'

'So he wasn't busy?'

'Not so I ever noticed.'

'What was he working on at the time of his death?'

She did not know.

'Did he have an office?'

She found the idea laughable. 'Him? He couldn't afford a filing cabinet, let alone an office.'

'So he worked from home? From here?'

'The box room.'

'Perhaps later I could have a look at his records.'

'If you like.' She did not care.

All of this was of little interest to Beverley, but it was serving a purpose. She said, 'You see, there's a possibility he might have been killed.'

Mrs Melnick jumped visibly. Having achieved this un-accustomed feat of exercise, she stared. Then, having stared for a while, she moistened her lips with her tongue.

All this in the silence that Beverley let fall upon the room. A baby was crying somewhere; loud rap music was thumping through the ether.

'What do you say to that?' Beverley asked eventually.

But, at first, Mrs Melnick didn't know what to say. Eventually, 'That doctor!'

'Which one?'

But Mrs Melnick had forgotten Eisenmenger's name and

all she could do was tell Beverley how he had come to her flat and suggested that her beloved Ted had died because he'd taken her tablets. 'It's him!' she finished. 'It's him what's saying I killed Ted.'

'Nobody's accused you.'

'If he died with my tablets inside of him, then it was an accident. *I* never did him in.'

'Just what tablets do you take, Mrs Melnick?'

She knew them only as colours, sizes and shapes, was not bothered by their names. 'I'll have to go and get them.' She did not appear enthusiastic but Beverley's nod and polite, 'Please,' forced her into lethargic action. Beverley followed her into the kitchenette.

There was just enough room for a small table, squeezed into a corner and surrounded by a small gas cooker, a low fridge, a stainless steel sink that was, despite the name, seriously stained, and various cupboards that were covered in cheap, chipped laminate. The remains of a sandwich on a plate lay discarded in the sink.

Mrs Melnick went to a cupboard, got out a large, crumpled paper bag and thrust it at Beverley without a word. Beverley upended the contents on the kitchen table, covering the brown rings that told of tea and coffee drunk, perhaps in happier times for Rose Melnick. She carefully noted each name, the dose prescribed, and the number of tablets remaining in each packet.

'Where do you keep things like aspirin and paracetamol?'

'I can't take aspirin – the doctor said.'

'Then where do you keep the paracetamol?'

She turned again to the cupboard, and came back this time with two supermarket brand packets of paracetamol.

So it was conceivable that Edward Melnick had, while drunk, taken what he had thought was a painkiller, but had in reality swallowed his wife's medication, but . . .

Metformin didn't look like paracetamol, for a start. It was a smaller tablet, and clearly marked with an 'M'. And it was in a plain white cardboard packet, not at all like the rather garish home of the paracetamol.

Mrs Melnick decided that a bit more protestation would not go amiss.

'I didn't have anything to do with it, Inspector. I loved my Ted. He was good to me, on the whole.'

Beverley tried to make something of these last three words but her heart was not for the battle. She could not find it within herself to think Mrs Melnick guilty of murder, whatever her stepson might wish to believe and whatever feelings John Eisenmenger had in his water or elsewhere.

Mrs Melnick's speech for the defence was continuing without sign of abatement. 'He must have had a headache when he was drunk and then taken my pills instead of paracetamol . . . '

Beverley wasn't listening. 'I understand that your husband was given some tablets by Dr Dreifus shortly before he died.'

'Yes. I showed them to the other doctor, the one who called . . . '

'Could you show them to me?'

She tutted, but did as she was asked. The white paper bag was produced exactly as it had been for Eisenmenger, except that it was slightly grubbier and the top was screwed up rather than folded over. Beverley unconsciously mimicked Eisenmenger as she examined the tablets, differing only in noting down the name of the tablets and the instructions on the label.

But then she went one step further: she opened the box and pulled out the foil-backed bubble pack.

Metformin.

She looked up at Rose Melnick and saw on the old woman's face what appeared to be a look of complete innocence; she wasn't even paying much attention.

'These are Metformin tablets,' Beverley pointed out gently.

'Eh?' She began slowly, but quickly built up a head of steam. 'No! They can't be!'

'They are.' Beverley showed them to her.

She grabbed them and held them tightly, examining what was written on the foil with minute attention, all the while her mouth working as she read the unfamiliar words. When she looked back up at Beverley, there was a look of terror on her face, and tears in her eyes. 'I never did it,' she whispered. 'I never put them in there.'

'Perhaps by accident . . . ?'

'I didn't put them in there. It wasn't me . . . It wasn't . . . '

Beverley had no desire to listen to this near-incoherent torrent of denial. 'Mrs Melnick.'

'I didn't kill him. Not at all. I loved him, I really did . . . '

She raised her voice. 'Rose!' She managed to induce a pause, in which she said quickly, 'Are these all the tablets in the flat?'

A frightened nod.

'You're quite sure of that? It's important, you see.'

An equally frightened but more definite nod.

Which left Beverley with a problem. If those tablets had got into the wrong packet by mistake, then where were the originals?

But she found it hard to believe that the terrified, distraught thing before her had maliciously fed her husband the wrong tablets. She said gently, 'Don't worry, Rose. Nobody's accusing you of doing anything wrong.'

'I didn't . . . '

'I know, I know.' She managed to convey to Rose Melnick that she was for the moment safe from arrest and in the space of calm she went through the options. *If* it was deliberate and it wasn't Rose Melnick, then who? Who would have a motive for killing Edward Melnick? Surely, it couldn't be anything to do with his work, could it?

It was a possibility, albeit a pretty far-fetched one.

Beverley stood up. 'This is what we're going to do, Rose. We're going to go through this flat millimetre by millimetre, and if those tablets are here, we're going to find them. Then, you're going to give me all of Edward's investigation files.'

Thirty-Six

E isenmenger had taken to coming into work early, allowing himself an hour or two of working undisturbed by technical staff bringing in slides, the indefatigable organizer of the multidisciplinary meetings taking them out again, secretaries telling him things that were wrong or that he did not need to know, and colleagues.

If he was honest with himself, one colleague in particular.

He told himself that he did not actually *dislike* Dr Throckmorton, merely that he found him in every way unimpressive. When he looked at the man and his deeds he could come up with only one word.

Mediocrity.

The term might have been invented, considered, refined and then finally placed in the lexicon just so that it was there when Dr Throckmorton was born into this sad and ailing world.

His was not the kind of mediocrity that did not matter, though. It was not something that could be allowed because there was nothing of too much consequence in it. He bluffed his way through and covered up, but he was almost certainly harming people as he did so. He lied, too: if not to himself, then to others. Eisenmenger did not like liars and this alone would have induced him to take an interest in Dr Throckmorton, but there was also the question of the attitude of the others towards the man. They were clearly not unaware of the man's deficiencies, yet had done nothing about it.

A conspiracy. It was probably not one that had been formally agreed, had probably not even been discussed, but it was a conspiracy nonetheless.

He had some sympathy for their predicament. The problem of failing colleagues had been with the medical profession for a long time and had never been satisfactorily solved. Everyone made mistakes and to condemn a doctor because of a single error – unless it was a catastrophic one – would be a terrible crime in itself; and if a pattern of minor errors suggested that remedial action was required, those to whom the unpleasant task of taking action fell invariably felt petty and vindictive. Unless, therefore, something awful happened, situations such as this tended to drift.

And he was guiltily pondering this conundrum – and what he ought do about it – instead of working as he should have been, when there was a knock on the door of his room. It was a thing of such awe-inspiring timidity that it was as characteristic as a voice might have been and he was sorely tried not to add Chloe's name as he called out, 'Come in.'

The door opened and Chloe, radiating diffidence every bit as brightly as her knock had done, stepped into the room.

He had expected her to be carrying a tray of slides but she was empty-handed.

'Can I have a word?'

She did not stutter but he heard one in her voice nonetheless.

'Sure.'

She closed the door. The deliberation with which she did this told him that something far from the ordinary was coming. When she turned, her facial expression – anxious, serious, pasty – only reinforced this impression. 'About what happened,' she said quickly, the words clearly rehearsed. 'In the library, last week . . . ' It was at this point, however, that she stalled, either because she had not rehearsed enough or because of stage fright. Perhaps, mused Eisenmenger, she was even *over*-rehearsed.

Had he not liked Chloe, with her myriad mannerisms, Eisenmenger would have perhaps feigned ignorance, played a game, tested her. As it was, he admitted at once that he knew the subject she wished to discuss. Raising his eyebrows, he said, 'Yes? What about it?'

She looked, he judged, at once relieved to have boarded the topic and alarmed that he should guess so easily what was bothering her. She coloured, and not subtly either. Her curly hair formed an ill-matched mousy adornment to the roseate glow that the skin now produced.

'It wasn't what it appeared to be.'

He had difficulty in finding a response to this announcement. What exactly had it appeared to be? They hadn't been in each other's arms, nor were they kissing. They were not even looking into each other's eyes, he seemed to recall. He pondered what to say and decided to be vague. 'Wasn't it?'

'Arnold and I were just checking that our answers matched. You know, that neither of us had made a silly error.'

Answers? Eisenmenger was momentarily unsure what she meant, but then he knew. An EQA, the bane of the histopathologist's life. External quality assessment made sure that pathologists were competent and tried to identify poor performance before it became a problem. Persistently low marks in an EQA meant that the pathologist would be required to undertake some retraining.

'I see.'

'I know we shouldn't, but it's just a silly test, isn't it?'

She almost pleaded with him to agree. He might well have done, had the situation been different. 'It looked to me,' he said slowly but not unkindly, 'that it was more a question of you giving Arnold the answers.'

'Oh, no! No, not at all.'

She did not lie well, the rose hue of her face a perfect meter of the mendacity of her words.

He thought about arguing, then decided he wouldn't. 'Are you entirely happy with Arnold's recent work?'

She nodded vigorously. 'Yes.' Too vigorously, he thought.

'Only I've noticed a few errors.'

She shrugged, but her eyes had slid away from his gaze and when she spoke it was with a tone that was noticeably unenthusiastic. 'We all make those.'

'Of course . . .'

She interrupted him. 'And Arnold's been having a few problems at home . . .'

He could have forced the issue, but he had not been there long enough to press what effectively was a button that launched a nuclear missile. To impugn the competence of a colleague was a major step and required abundant evidence, preferably in writing and stretching back months. He was, moreover, just a locum, and locums had been fed to the ravening wolves before now for such audacity.

'OK,' he said.

Her face relaxed, as did her entire body, the tension ebbing as she saw that he believed her. 'Good. I knew you'd understand . . .'

He didn't, but he opted not to contradict her assumption. Instead, he said with just a hint of warning, 'I hope things sort themselves out in his home life soon.'

'I'm sure they will.'

'Good.'

The silence that followed was brief but painful for both of them. Then Chloe said quite abruptly, 'I really must be getting on. I've got to go through the cases for the head and neck meeting . . .'

With which she turned and walked – very quickly – from his office.

Eisenmenger did not move. He fervently hoped he would

not find himself in the position of having to be the one who decided that Arnold Throckmorton was not fit to practice.

'What background information do you have on the Water Lane practice?'

Grover felt sure he would be able to please his superior. 'Of the three doctors, Adam Dreifus has been there the longest – thirty-one years next March. Donald Lennox joined the practice seventeen years ago and Lynette Parker started only four years ago. She replaced Derek Worringer when he retired.'

'What about ancillary staff – receptionists, nurses, that kind of thing?'

'Four reception staff, one nurse and two people in the dispensary.'

'Have you checked them all out?'

Grover's reaction heralded the answer before his words. 'No . . . I didn't think . . . '

'Didn't you?' Beverley pretended faint surprise. 'I thought that's what we paid you to do.'

'But why? What possible relevance could it have?'

'I don't know, Sergeant. That's the point. Until I find something, I don't know if it's relevant.'

Grover looked less than convinced of this line of reasoning but Beverley considered that the time for education was gone, the time for leadership beckoning. 'Do it now. Nothing too deep. Just make sure that none of them have any secrets.'

'Yes, Sir.'

Beverley stood up. 'I'm going to have a coffee while you get going on that.'

'Yes, Sir.'

She did not see Grover's expression as she shut the door behind her and perhaps it was best that she did not, for it was not one of eternal love or admiration; indeed, it was in possession of no qualities at all that could be described as in any way positive.

Thirty-Seven

'What's going on?'

To say that Lambert's tone was abrasive would be like describing molten lead as 'warm to the touch'.

Beverley, who had a hide made of asbestos when it came to Lambert's fury, asked, 'What do you mean?'

Her uncertainty was genuine – he could have been referring to rumours regarding her social life, progress in a case or the fact that no one ever told him anything. Unfortunately, her attitude came across to him as impertinent and his temperature in consequence increased yet further. 'The Delorme death, of course,' he snapped.

Beverley was acutely aware that Grover was a witness to this. They were seated in Lambert's office, having been summoned there by a peremptory phone call. In order to stop her own countdown to detonation she stared fixedly at a point just above Lambert's head; at, in fact, the *Mare Imbrium* on the map of the moon that, for reasons that were completely obscure to her, he had on his office wall.

'Well, at this moment . . . ' she began, but Lambert cut across her.

'Is it murder, or isn't it?'

She had, in fact, divined that this was the single datum that interested him, but that presented a problem, hence the decision to approach her answer with some circumspection. She therefore hesitated. 'I'm not sure we're . . . '

'I see.' He was triumphant. She had been about to say that she was not sure she was in a position to decide, but Lambert had pounced and pounced well. He turned to Grover. 'Are you sure?'

Grover must have been surprised to find himself in the rifle sights, but he responded well. 'Yes, Sir. I am.'

Lambert turned briefly to Beverley, providing her with a

satisfied smile that she could have happily removed with a shotgun blast, then back to Grover. 'Are you really? I'm so pleased that someone knows his own mind. And what do you think, Constable?'

Grover ignored his sudden demotion. 'I think she was murdered by Dr Lennox.'

Beverley wanted to laugh, but remained carefully composed and inert.

'What evidence do you have?'

'He has admitted he was her lover. It was his gun that was used. He's a keen shot.'

'Motive?'

'His wife was becoming suspicious. He admits he had tried to end it, but Anita Delorme hadn't wanted to. She wanted him to leave his wife, but he wouldn't.'

'Could he have done it?'

'His wife gives him an alibi for the night she died, for what that's worth.'

Lambert grunted softly and looked down at his desk, where a pad of paper was covered in notes and scribbles and doodles, then back up to Grover's face. He slowly panned around to Beverley and then back to Grover, before saying softly, 'You think she's protecting him?'

Grover nodded smartly and Lambert turned to Beverley.

Her first thought was first to laugh scornfully, her second was to explode with anger, her third was to murmur in a considered tone. 'It's one possible scenario.'

'It's more than that. It sounds quite a likely one.'

She felt calmer now that she and Lambert were back in the sparring ring: left jabs, right upper cuts, the odd blow a long way below the belt. 'Is it? There's nothing that places him at the scene at the time she died.'

'If he had a key, there wouldn't necessarily be.'

'He says he didn't. Also, so far we haven't found anyone who saw him or his car. It's a green Jaguar and quite noticeable.'

'He arrived on foot at night.'

She thought it likely that Lambert would have pointed out the flaws in the case against Judas if she had been trying for an arrest warrant.

Grover interjected, 'Anyway, we haven't finished the house-to-house.'

She pointed out, 'No fingerprints implicate him. In fact, no forensics at all would put him anywhere near the scene.'

'He was careful. He wiped the gun down, went home, showered and then destroyed his clothes.' Having parried her thrusts, Lambert then moved into offensive mode. 'How do you explain her possession of his gun? Was she interested in shooting?'

'He says he'd taken her on a few shoots and had lent her the gun for the purpose.'

'Not very convincing.'

Which, to Beverley's mind, depended on one's point of view. She decided to pull the perspective out a bit. 'Are we saying that all this was to stop Anita Delorme making a nuisance of herself over a bit of hanky-panky with some sad middle-aged Lothario? It's a bit over the top, isn't it? This isn't the nineteenth century, where social disgrace was worse than the pox.'

Lambert saw an opportunity to score couple of points and went for it with glee. 'Not everyone has your promiscuous attitude, Inspector.'

'I just can't see that he had so much to lose that he would go to such extremes.'

Lambert's face settled into an expression of indigestion. 'So you think it was suicide?'

'That's still a distinct possibility, yes. Sydenham can't exclude it and, as we've discussed, there is no evidence specifically suggesting a second party's involvement.'

Grover thought to add his usual psychological dimension. 'It would be a very odd way for a woman to commit suicide.'

'But not out of the question. There's nothing either physically or mentally that prevents a woman putting a shotgun in her mouth.' At this juncture Grover leaned forward, mouth opening for a counter-argument, so Beverley went smoothly on, 'To accept the case for murder, one also has to explain how the murderer enticed her to put her lips around the ends of the barrels while he had his finger on the trigger.'

Lambert, God bless him, turned to Grover and showed just how reliable he was as a friend by enquiring of him, 'Well, Sergeant? How do you explain that?'

Grover panicked. After a pause that was relieved only by a drawn-out noise from the back of his throat he said, 'Perhaps she was hypnotized.'

Beverley's heart sang within her breast. Lambert's expression would have caused milk to curdle and fragile birds to fall lifeless from the skies. He dropped Grover with an inaudible but nonetheless painful thud and said to Beverley, 'He could have knocked her out first. The gun blast would obliterate all evidence of that.'

Beverley, old stager that she was, accepted this with an affirming nod, then used it to her advantage. 'If we're after motive for murder, how about revenge?'

'For what?'

'She was defrauding Dreifus, her employer, to fund her lifestyle. He's on the verge of bankruptcy, partly because of it.'

Lambert did not want to show interest, but he had no other choice. 'Did he know what she was doing?'

'He claims not, but I wonder if he had his suspicions.'

'And I take it that again there is no forensic evidence to link him to the scene in the correct time frame?'

'No.'

'Does he have an alibi?'

'No. He arrived home at ten that evening, claiming he had worked at the clinic until nine-fifteen or so. Trouble is, no one can verify his presence there after nine, which, if Sydenham is to be believed, gives him enough time to have done it.'

'Any witness-based evidence that might place him near the scene?'

Grover tried to reintegrate himself into polite society by saying here, 'Nobody's ever seen Dr Dreifus anywhere near Anita Delorme's house.'

Lambert may have thought he was about to score another point by denouncing her theory but Beverley dodged neatly by saying, 'All of which brings me back to suicide.'

There was a pause before Lambert said, 'Yes.'

'An audit of the accounts by the Charity Commission was due. She was about to be exposed. I would rate that as the strongest motive of all.'

A longer pause.

'Yes,' he repeated. His voice now had a deeper tone, one that seemed somehow sadder to the listener.

Silence, during which a helicopter flew overhead, probably on its way to land at the nearby aerodrome.

Lambert nodded slowly, giving the appearance of a balanced consideration of all that he had been told. If Beverley thought she had won by a knockout, she quickly found out it had merely been a standing count, following which he was back and ready to punch. 'If you're sure it's suicide, why are you still wasting time on the case? I can't afford to have my detectives farting around when there's important work piling up.'

She knew by his use of the vulgarism that he was rattled and hoped it would tarnish him in Grover's eyes. 'There's a single, small problem,' she said.

'What's that?'

'It's still entirely possible that she was murdered.'

She enjoyed the reaction this induced in Lambert. After a second's worth of staring – possibly to allow him to review the text and make sure he had it right – he said in a tone that seemed to indicate passions of geological magnitude, 'I'll give you until the end of the week. If you can't make a case against someone by then, you'd better drop it.'

Beverley was happy to rise from her seat and leave the office. Lambert called after her, 'But you'd better get it right.'

Thirty-Eight

E isenmenger knew instinctively that the elderly woman wanted to speak to him, even when she was more than 20 metres away, on the opposite side of the entrance hall to the clinic.

'Dr Eisenmenger?'

He acknowledged this with a smile and a small nod.

'My name's Harriet Worringer. I'm Helena's therapist.'

'She's mentioned you.'

'Has she? Oh, good. I wondered if we could talk?'

She turned without waiting for his agreement, walking away, sure that he would follow. She led him past the reception and up the stairs to the administrative offices. Hers was cramped but tidy: three pot plants on the windowsill, a picture of a couple, another of a small girl of no more than ten.

'It's not very big, but I don't spend much time in here. Please, sit down.' As he did so she went on, 'I would offer you tea or coffee but there's only a ghastly machine that makes everything taste like washing up water.'

He did not argue. It occurred to him that here was a woman who was supremely confident: confident that he would follow when she led, confident that he would accept her judgement regarding the refreshments, confident that she was in control of every situation she met. She had a long but not unattractive face, must once have been something of a prize for an eligible bachelor; he suspected, though, that it would have to have been the most eligible of eligible bachelors. Her clothes were simple but, as far as was able to judge, well matched; they were also, he assessed, expensive.

This key-worker had money as well as breeding.

'What can I do for you?'

'It's not so much what you can do for me, as what you can do for Helena.'

'Anything I can, I hope.'

She nodded. 'You see, it's your input that's going to make all the difference to Helena's recovery. I can only do so much, but she has to feel that you're with her all the way.'

'I would hope she knows that.'

She smiled. 'That's my point, Dr Eisenmenger. You can't assume that she knows anything. She's lost confidence – in her own body, in the future, in everything – and that includes you. You have to reassure her that you're just as constant, just as loving as you ever were.'

'Of course, I will.'

'She has great respect for you, you know. You're more than a partner to her, I think; I would say that you're also something of a symbol for her. Something for her to look up to.'

'Really? I only hope I haven't got feet of clay.'

She smiled. 'I'm sure you haven't.'

'Is there anything else I can do? I feel slightly redundant.'

Shaking her head, she said, 'Just keep coming, keep talking to her, and above all, keeping *loving* her. That's what she needs. A bit of good, old-fashioned TLC.'

As he got up to go, he recognized the male half of the

couple in the photograph on her desk: a young Adam Dreifus posing beside a woman he did not know. When he remarked on it, Harriet Worringer said, 'My daughter and her husband.'

'Your Adam Dreifus's mother-in-law?'

'You know him?'

'Vaguely.'

'I'm very lucky. Not every woman gets on so well with her son-in-law.'

She smiled as she said this and Eisenmenger heard contentment in her voice.

'I did the checks on the staff at the surgery.'

Beverley had a headache and the tablets had yet to touch it. She was standing at the window looking at Fisher being bollocked by Lambert on the pavement outside the station. 'And?'

'They're all clean. No convictions. No criminal connections. Nothing.'

She was wondering what Fisher had done to deserve it, other than existing, but she put this weighty matter to one side at Grover's declaration. 'Nothing at all?' Nobody was that good, not in modern society where the government invented at least one new crime a day.

'Well . . . '

She turned. 'Yes?'

'Charlotte Pelger had a bit of trouble when she was a student nurse.'

'"Bit of trouble"?'

'There was some fuss at a party. She and another student nurse got into a bit of rough and tumble over a boy.'

She held out her hand. 'Let me see.'

Her flicker of interest faded as she read the details. A dispute over a male student colleague, nothing more. A few scratches and bruises; the police had been called but no further action taken. She lingered over the name of the other nurse involved in the fracas. Sue Willard.

Was that name familiar?

She dug around in her memory, came back with nothing, and handed the file back to Grover. 'OK. Thanks.'

Adam Dreifus rarely returned home before ten o'clock, sometimes not until eleven or even later. Whenever he made it back to the house, he was invariably tired and bad-tempered. Frequently Ruth was in bed by the time he came home and he was used, therefore, to returning to a dark, unwelcoming house.

Which was why he was surprised to return that night to a house that was brightly lit, that suggested occupancy, even perhaps vivacity.

'Ruth?' he called as he entered the hall, before he had even closed the front door and shut out the night.

He moved into the deeper part of the hall and put his brief-case down by the table on which sat the telephone and his post. He picked this up and looked through the six items: two pieces of junk, one from the BMA, one from American Express, two from banks. With these still in hand he looked up and called again, 'Ruth?'

He heard a radio playing somewhere, but nothing else. He knew it was the radio because Ruth never watched television, claiming that it was puerile, a destroyer of intelligence. It was typical of Ruth who, he had come to appreciate, was a snob not just when it came to breeding and manners but in every aspect of life, including intellect.

For the first time he noticed an odour in the air.

Something's burning.

He moved deeper into the house, his face bearing a look of perplexity. At the end of the hall, with the stairs rising to his right, there were two doors, one to the left and one straight ahead. He opened the one on the left but was met by dark-ness. In contrast, the lights were on in the kitchen ahead.

Ruth had insisted on a large kitchen, claiming that if she was expected to spend most of her life in a place, she should at least be allowed to ensure that it was spacious and to her taste. He had indulged her, even though now he would have to point out that she was not quite the prisoner in the room that she had claimed she would be.

Here the smell was far stronger; indeed there was a smoky haze in the air.

On the far side of the room was the large stainless steel cooker and he could see that a pan of milk had boiled over on to the hotplate. Smoke was still rising from it, suggesting that the hotplate was still on. He hurried forward around the central island to turn it off.

And almost stumbled over Ruth's body, stretched out on the floor.

'What the . . . ?'

For a second he just stared down at her. Then he dropped suddenly to his haunches and put out a hand to her cheek. As he said, 'Ruth?' he felt that it was cold.

'Oh, God,' he breathed.

She was on her side but her body was slightly twisted so that her head and chest were facing down. He pulled her shoulder back to expose her face. Her skin had the sheen of greased dough; from bluing lips the tip of her tongue appeared dark and dry. He found no pulse when he put two fingers to the side of her neck, nor when he grasped her wrist.

He stood up slowly, his head bowed, his eyes not leaving his wife.

He stayed like that for a long time.

Thirty-Nine

Clive rang Eisenmenger just as he was looking at a frozen section. One of the lower gastrointestinal surgeons had planned to perform a low anterior resection of a rectal tumour but, on preliminary examination, had discovered a suspicious nodule in the liver; if it proved to be secondary from the cancer, the operation would be abandoned and the therapeutic options would concentrate on local radiotherapy and chemotherapy. He had therefore excised the nodule and sent it to the lab for analysis; the only way this could be done with any speed was to freeze it to minus seventy degrees, then cut and stain thin sections for a pathologist to examine. It was far from ideal material from which to come to an important clinical decision, but it was the best available.

'Sorry to bother you, Doc, but Gee-gee was wondering if you could spare him ten minutes in the mortuary.'

'Gee-gee?' enquired Eisenmenger, with heavy irony.

'Dr Throckmorton.' Clive was completely unabashed.

'Is there a problem?'

'He'd just like your opinion. Chloe's at a meeting with some clinicians and Peter Rabbit's gone to the dentist.'

Eisenmenger was his last resort, then. 'I'll be down in ten minutes.'

There was a knock at the door that heralded the arrival of the stained sections. It was unfortunately carcinoma, a result that upstaged the tumour and significantly worsened the patient's prognosis. He phoned the bad news to the surgeon who, he knew, would now abandon the operation. Then he went down to the mortuary.

Arnold Throckmorton in scrubs and plastic apron, topped by a disposable blue hat, cut an arresting, not to say cardiac arresting, figure. He stood with his back to the door, apparently hard at work on the bench in front of him. When the door behind Eisenmenger closed with a slight rattle, he turned and peered at the newcomer over his glasses. He was not wearing a mask, which was a transgression of the safety policy of the mortuary.

'Ah, John. Come and look at this.'

'What's the problem?'

'No problem. I thought you'd like to see this.'

He was standing by the corpse of a middle-aged woman. Eisenmenger suspected that she had once been extremely attractive, with a broad face and greyed hair that had been expensively styled. 'This woman was found dead in her home yesterday evening. She was forty-nine years old, with a past medical history of mild hypertension and mild reactive depression. The house was secure and there were no suspicious circumstances.'

'What have you found?' He asked this as he was bending down, examining the skin minutely for any marks that might tell a story different from the one they had been given. He saw nothing that evoked concern – no bruising that might have been made by fingers grabbing her, no ligature marks, no scratches. There were no transverse scars on her wrists to suggest previous suicide attempts, a possibility he briefly considered because of the history of depression.

'She died of coronary atheroma – but that's not why I called you down here.'

'Coronary atheroma?' Eisenmenger was surprised because it was relatively rare for a woman in her late forties to suffer such a death and it might, therefore, have implications for the blood relatives.

'That's right.'

'How much stenosis of the coronary arteries?'

'About forty per cent.'

'No thrombosis?'

'No.' Throckmorton's voice was taking on a recognizable defensive tone.

'No other significant findings?'

Testily, Throckmorton said, 'That's why I called you down here. She had this.'

He turned to the carnage on the steel workbench. Like a demon from hell stirring a pot of human offal, he rummaged in a deep metal bowl and emerged with a collapsed, pale grey cyst. When it was intact, it had probably measured 12 centimetres across. It was covered with diluted blood mixed with a hint of bile, and when Throckmorton exposed its interior, there was a nauseating mass of thick orange grease and coarse black hair.

Surely he was not excited by a dermoid cyst? Such lesions – occurring in the ovary and usually entirely benign – were common fare.

Arnold Throckmorton burrowed into the depths. 'Look,' he said, moving to one side so that Eisenmenger could share in his delight.

At the base of the cyst, protruding into the cavity, was a tooth, bearing a faint resemblance to a jewel set in a brooch. 'I haven't seen one of those for thirty years.'

Except presumably, Eisenmenger reflected, in people's heads.

He said, 'Oh, yes. How interesting,' but he failed to sound thrilled and Throckmorton once more became cool towards him. 'It's very unusual,' Throckmorton said.

'But it didn't kill her, did it?'

'No, her heart did that.'

'Are you sure of that?'

'Absolutely.'

'What did the heart weigh?'

It was Clive who supplied the answer. 'Three hundred and sixty-five grams.'

Barely enlarged, then.

It was still possible that she had died of ischaemic heart disease, the condition that arose from narrowing of the coronary arteries by atheroma, because different hearts showed different sensitivities to the resultant reduction in blood supply.

'Was there visible fibrosis in the heart muscle?'

'I think so.'

Eisenmenger wondered how hard he had looked. 'May I see?'

Throckmorton was now quite clearly angry; he was being directly challenged as to his abilities. 'No, you may not.'

Eisenmenger looked into the slightly flushed face and saw that beneath the ageing skin there was a man who was clinging on with desperate determination to his self-esteem, who was probably ready to enter into physical combat in order to stop anyone evoking insight within him. 'I'll have to take your word for it then, won't I?' He said this blandly, almost lightly.

'Yes, you will.'

Eisenmenger nodded, then turned and walked away. As he passed Clive they exchanged glances: on Clive's side it was commiseration, on Eisenmenger's it was dark amusement. Clive followed him out. 'Tea?' he asked.

Eisenmenger sighed. 'Won't Arnold be out soon? It would be best if I were gone, I think.'

'Nah. He's got to dictate a report first, and that takes at least a quarter of an hour. Then he'll have a shower.'

Eisenmenger reconsidered. He was feeling slightly reckless and that was the only way to approach Clive's tea. 'Why not?'

As Clive busied himself with a kettle and teapot, Eisenmenger sat in the office and tried to work out what he could do. 'I see what you mean about Arnold,' he said.

Clive laughed. 'I reckon if you were going to murder someone, you'd want him doing the post-mortem.'

'Why, though? Why is he like that?'

Clive shrugged. 'He's old, isn't he? He's been doing this job for forty years and I think he just wants an easy life. Trouble is, he can't stop himself thinking that just because he's been doing it since Adam was a nipper, he must be the best there is.'

As usual, it seemed to Eisenmenger that Clive had just about got it right. Clive brought a mug of tea over to him. It was ochrous and smelled bitter. Eisenmenger began to wonder if he had made a wise decision.

'What do you think I should do, Clive? About that case in there, I mean.'

Clive shrugged. 'Leave it. You'll regret it if you don't.'

'But I just want to make sure he's right . . . '

'Ah, yes, but what if he isn't? What are you going to do then?'

It was a good question. He supposed that if it wasn't her heart but it was still a natural death, he would leave it. If it was in some way unnatural, though . . .

But it wasn't going to be unnatural. It was sudden death and there was no evidence of external trauma; in which case, he might just as well leave it. Except that then he discovered from the coroner's information supplied by fax to the mortuary the name of the body in the dissection room.

Ruth Dreifus. Next of kin: Dr Adam Dreifus.

And that made him think again. Think long and deep and hard.

He became unaccountably intrigued; so much so that he finished the tea without once wincing at the flavour.

They only spoke to Dr Lynette Parker out of completeness. Her name had not cropped up anywhere, but Beverley was well aware that if she only looked where the lights shone down, then she would only see what was not afraid of being seen; that if most shadows held nothing, occasionally they harboured secrets.

Her first impression was one of breezy jollity. Lynette Parker was overweight but from this there seemed to radiate cheeriness and a sense that they were in the presence of a matron, a mother for everyone who would make everything right, on whom they could rely without any fear of disappointment. She had long black hair framing a rounded face that bore circular glasses with golden rims; the light kept catching the lenses so that, as she moved in her chair, flashes of light shone back at her interviewers to accompany the weak creaking of the furniture beneath her. The moments when her eyes became nothing more than bright sparks turned her briefly from homely doctor into megalomaniac, instantaneously evaporating her soul and leaving only an unknowable android, unconcerned by the pathetic antics of the constabulary.

'I don't know why you're bothering with me. I had nothing

to do with the girl.' Her voice was high and slightly wheezy. 'After all, she worked at Adam's clinic, not here.'

'Did you know her at all?'

'Hardly. I might have met her a couple of times, but no more.' Apparently she found the idea absurd.

'When you met her, did you like her?'

Her face registered surprise. 'Good grief! What a question! Why?'

'I'd like to know what she was like. I never got to meet her, you see.'

'I don't think you've missed much.'

'Really? Why?'

She had lost her smile, or at least she had chosen to blend it with disdain. 'A rather *obvious* young lady, if you know what I mean.'

'No, I don't.'

She looked sharply at Beverley, did not like the answer. 'She was quite pretty, I suppose, but she spoiled it by too much make-up.'

'A man-hunter?'

'That was the impression I got.'

'And did she bag her prize?'

A slow, serpiginous smile spread over her face. The glasses flashed as her head tipped backwards in her mirth. 'Oh, yes!'

'Tell me.'

'Don't you know?' she asked mockingly. 'Haven't you discovered yet?'

'Donald Lennox.'

'You do know.' She seemed slightly disappointed that the police had failed to live down to her expectations. 'Yes, poor Donald. A middle-aged man who needs to prove his manhood by serial adultery. Not even a very good general practitioner.'

'Does he have an equally high opinion of you?'

She seemed surprised by the sarcasm, as if what she had said was a matter of public record. 'I don't know,' she admitted. 'I've never asked him.'

'Who might have wanted to kill her?'

'Kill her? Is that what happened?'

'I don't know yet. If someone had killed her, who might it have been?'

She frowned in consideration, although her glances at

Beverley suggested that it was not a thing of great depth. 'I can't think.'

'What about Adam Dreifus?'

Her head jerked up at the mention of his name. 'Adam? I don't think so.' The idea clearly seemed to her to be absurd.

'Why not? She worked for him. He was with her every day.'

'No, not Adam.' She paused, but then began again suddenly. 'Adam? The idea is absurd . . . '

Beverley waited for more but did so in vain. She said eventually, 'Well, as I said, maybe no one did.'

For a moment, Lynette Parker seemed caught up in her own certainties, unable to release herself from them, then, 'No, perhaps not.'

'As far as you know, had Anita Delorme ever had an affair with anyone else?'

She laughed a wheezy laugh. 'As far as I know, she could have been having the whole of the Household Cavalry on a weekly basis, and I would have been none the wiser.'

Forty

B everley phoned Eisenmenger from her flat, found him in. She experienced a feeling of mild disappointment that Helena had not picked up the phone as she had half-expected her to; she would have enjoyed hearing the cold anger and the curt words as she asked to speak to 'John'. The anguished uncertainty that would have been engendered in Helena's mind would have been a delicious thing to create. As it was, Eisenmenger picked up the phone and spoke without guardedness or consternation, leading Beverley to conclude that he was alone.

She told him what she had found and finished with, 'I'd say it was an unfortunate accident, except that Rose Melnick can't find the other tablets, the ones that should have been in the packet.'

'So you think they were deliberately put in the wrong box?'

'That remains a possibility.' One thing had been bothering her. 'I assume you don't give Metformin for gout . . . ?'

'Not if you want to stay on the medical register.'

'I thought not, but I had to check.'

'But wouldn't he have noticed if they were the wrong pills?'

'I'm not sure he would. I don't think he was too bright, and that's if he actually bothered reading any of the litera-ture. And don't forget, frequently tablets have more than one name – Valium and diazepam, for instance. Maybe he thought they were just two different names for the same medicine.'

'And he might well have been drunk, anyway.'

'Exactly.'

Eisenmenger ran through the implications. 'If they were put in the wrong box, then are we saying it was an attempt to murder him?'

'Presumably.'

'But why?'

'I haven't got that far yet.'

'Well, who, then?'

'I haven't even got as far as that one.'

Eisenmenger took the phone over to the window, looked out into the darkness of a warm evening. 'It can't have been Rose. She wouldn't have the necessary technical know-how, and if it had been her, she would have kept the real tablets to show anyone who came asking questions.'

'Which leaves someone at the doctor's surgery.'

'More than that – someone in the dispensary.'

'Couldn't it have been Dreifus or one of the other doctors?'

'Well, usually the GP writes the prescription, but if the tablets were deliberately put in the wrong box, that would have to be a physical act, and that's usually done in the pharmacy. I'm sure occasionally a doctor dishes out a drug himself, so you can't discount it completely . . . ' He tailed off. 'But why, though? Who at the surgery is going to have a motive to kill him?'

'It does seem unlikely,' she admitted.

'So maybe we're just seeing phantoms in the mist. Maybe there *is* no murder.'

'I couldn't find any other tablets.'

'Perhaps he lost them. Perhaps he kept them at the pub. Perhaps . . . '

Beverley cut him short. 'Point taken, John.'

'But you see what I'm getting at, don't you? If Melnick was murdered, it was a beautiful, subtle thing and we have no motive for anyone to do it. It's far likelier that this is nothing but my imaginings.'

Beverley eyed the four box files she had brought away from Melnick's flat. They were bulging with papers that, as far as she could see, were in no particular order. The prospect of trawling her way through them was a distinctly gloomy one. She said, 'I may find something amongst his case notes, but I don't hold out much hope.'

'I'm going to be coming under pressure soon to give the coroner a cause of death, Beverley.'

'I'll be as quick as I can.'

And that was that for the time being, except that Eisenmenger said, almost in passing, 'By the way, this is probably nothing to do with anything, but the wife of Melnick's GP – Adam Dreifus – died suddenly yesterday.'

It was trivial, should not have tweaked her curiosity to any degree at all . . .

Yet it did and, she could tell from his tone, it had tweaked his as well. 'What of?'

'She had some heart disease, possibly enough to have been fatal . . . Certainly nothing one hundred per cent guaranteed to carry her off, though.'

'I see. Are you implying anything from this?'

The pause this time was of Olympian standards; so long, in fact that she wondered if he had gone off for a walk to think about his answer.

'What is there to imply?'

He wanted her to say it, to name the devil and perhaps summon him.

'We can't go about accusing Dr Dreifus of murder just because of a probable suicide and two probably natural deaths. Most of the GPs in the country would end up in chokey.'

'Absolutely . . . ' For a meaningful moment, neither of them said anything. Then he said, 'Fair enough. When I've come up with a natural cause of death, I'll let you know.'

Clive was just preparing to leave when Eisenmenger came down to the mortuary. His preparations for this consisted of rinsing out his tea cup, stretching and switching off the computer. Like all mortuary technicians, his working world was an ante-meridian thing, the afternoon meant for consideration of weightier matters such as the mammary glands on display in the red-top papers, the search for those elusive winners at forty-to-one, the disposal of certain unprovenanced items that were illuminating his lock-up garage with a fiery-red glow.

'Have you got a moment?'

Clive considered. 'I suppose.'

'When's the body of Ruth Dreifus being shipped out?'

'Tomorrow morning. I tried to put them off, but the body's wanted quickly.'

'Can you get it out of the fridge?'

'What, now?' He spoke as if this demand had been made upon a man who had not a minute in the day. It was an arresting image but one that was difficult to square with experience.

'If you wouldn't mind.'

Clive's sigh was a thing of greatness. He did as he had been asked, however. As Ruth Dreifus lay before them on her metal tray that was supported by an adjustable trolley, he asked, 'What are you going to do?'

Eisenmenger sighed; he had bad news to impart. 'I'm afraid I'm going to open her up again. I think we need to finish the post-mortem.'

'It's finished already. Gee-gee's faxed the Coroner's Office with the cause of death.'

Eisenmenger had spent most of the night wondering if this was a wise thing to do and he still did not know the answer. 'No, Clive. Arnold Throckmorton has faxed the Coroner's Office with *a* cause of death. I'm not sure it's necessarily the right one.'

'But I've sown her up. It was a nice, neat job, too.'

'I know, Clive, and I'm sorry, but I need to take samples of the heart muscle, as well as blood and urine.' He looked down at the pale greyness of the corpse. Her eyes were not quite closed. He was wondering if there was anything else he would need. Probably not, but he would only have one chance at this . . .

He added, 'And we may as well take some vitreous humour. Both eyes.'

Clive went to put on a plastic apron and some gloves. When he returned he had in his hands a scalpel. As he began unpicking the stitches, he suddenly looked up at Eisenmenger. 'Isn't this illegal . . . ?'

'Yes.'

Clive's eyes were wide. 'Now, look . . . '

'Don't worry, Clive. I'll make sure you don't have to add this crime to your CV.'

Forty-One

G rover came into the office looking gloomy. 'The house-to-house around Anita Delorme's residence has turned up nothing. No one could identify either Dreifus or Lennox as having been around the house close to the estimated time of her death, and no one could recall having seen any other strangers calling there.'

Beverley had not really expected success with this strategy. If Anita Delorme had been murdered, the perpetrator was hardly going to turn up in a fire engine and dressed as a circus clown, just so that the odd nosy neighbour might see him.

'Still think it's murder?' she asked.

Grover could only shrug. 'I don't know any more.'

Beverley laughed sourly. 'Join the club. I never knew. I still don't.'

Indeed, all the evidence suggested that it wasn't and there was only one thin thread that she could find that made her wonder. The name of Adam Dreifus kept cropping up, wherever she looked. What did it mean, though? There was no evidence that he had murdered Anita Delorme, although he had a potential motive and had the opportunity. There was no evidence that he had murdered Edward Melnick – there was no real evidence that *anyone* had murdered him – and again there was not a whiff of a motive. It was just that people around him kept dying.

Why wouldn't they? He was a doctor, after all.

And there was Lambert's deadline to think about. She had nothing concrete to work on and all the leads had proved weak, useless things. Other cases were piling up and could not be ignored for much longer. She had accordingly decided that Grover would be better employed on other things. Grover, though, was aghast when she voiced this decision. 'But you can't do that!'

Beverley did not even bother to contest this; she merely shrugged, which provoked Grover into further development of his arguments against this proposal. 'I want to keep on with this case, see it to an end.'

'Why?'

'Because I'm involved. It's important to me.'

'Tell me, Grover. Is it the potential murder that's important to you, or is it the adultery?

'Both . . . Either . . . They're both sins.'

'But they're not both crimes. Just remember that. My decision is final.'

The charge nurse called Terry came to Helena when she returned to her room. It was the second day that she had taken breakfast in the dining hall, something which had signified to Harriet a step-change, a huge improvement. Her genuine show of delight when Helena had told her had probably been the most therapeutic thing that had happened to Helena since she had arrived.

'That's wonderful. Really positive. Well done,' she had said.

Helena felt that her face was strangely stretched and discovered it was a smile. 'It was hardly climbing Everest.'

Harriet had teeth that were perfectly white and completely regular and she liked to show them. Everything about Harriet seemed to Helena to be something to which she herself should aspire. 'Don't you believe it. I think to someone as private as you, it was a greater achievement.'

She saw something that made her afraid as Terry closed the door and came and sat down in front of her. 'I'm afraid Harriet won't be coming in for a few days,' he said.

'Is she ill?'

He seemed too grave for this to be the reason but she could think of no other explanation. 'No.'

'Then what?'

He lowered his gaze, looking at the light blue of the bedspread. 'A family bereavement.'

Helena could tell he wasn't talking about some great aunt or third cousin thrice removed. 'Who?'

He hesitated, as if he really would rather that she didn't ask for detail, then said softly, 'Her daughter.'

Helena gasped, genuinely shocked. 'No!'

He shrugged; this was not a gesture of indifference, more one of impotence, as his expression indicated. 'It was quite sudden . . . '

'But how?'

'They don't know . . . there's been a post-mortem but I don't know the results.'

Helena was working through the ramifications of this shocking piece of news. She was profoundly moved, discovering in this how close in such a short time she had come to the dignified, kind and wise old woman. 'First her grand-daughter, now this . . . '

'She told you about Annabelle, then?'

Helena sniffed back a moistness that was turning to tears, and nodded.

Terry said, 'Deirdre will be coming to talk to you for the next few days.' He turned to go after a pause, then turned back almost at once. 'Harriet's an admirable person, Helena. She'll cope, I'm sure.'

With that, he left.

Harriet's words came back to her . . .

I've come to rely on them. My greatest nightmare is that one day, when I need one of them, they might not be there.

Helena felt almost as low now as when she had first come.

Forty-Two

Eisenmenger had noticed the improvement in Helena, had been elated by it, but as he came in that night he was quickly accosted by Terry.

'Helena's had some bad news today and it's knocked her back slightly.'

'What's happened?'

'You know that she'd built up a strong relationship with Harriet, her counsellor?'

'I've met her. I was impressed.'

'Well, unfortunately, last night Harriet had some bad news. Her daughter died unexpectedly.'

Of course. Eisenmenger had not until then made the connection.

Terry said, 'Helena's taken it quite badly . . . it's one of the disadvantages of this kind of therapy. The patient becomes very involved with the therapist.'

'Is there anything I can do?'

'Just be supportive. I'm sure it won't be long before she's back on track.'

Eisenmenger nodded and continued on his way to Helena's room. He found her reading and dressed, which he was pleased to see as it seemed to him to indicate that she had not reverted completely to her former, almost catatonic state. She looked up at him and smiled briefly. 'Hello.'

'How are you, Helena? I heard the bad news.'

She put the book down as grief flooded her face, as if a fragile dam had been breached. 'Harriet's daughter has died.' She began to weep and he knelt beside her and held her. Into his shoulder she said, 'She was only forty-nine.'

'I know, I know.'

'I feel so awful, John, so wretched.'

'Why? It's not your fault.'

'But look at me, John. Here I am, being pathetic, and poor Harriet is having to cope with something far, far worse.'

'You're not being pathetic, Helena. You've lost a child, too.'

'I had a miscarriage, just like a thousand women every day. They don't all end up feeling sorry for themselves.'

'You've had severe reactive depression. That's more than "feeling sorry for yourself".'

But all his reassurances were as nothing and she continued to cry and he held her and waited.

As she became less agitated, less eager to chastise herself for the weakness she seemed to think she was displaying, he released her and gave her tissues to dry her eyes and blow her nose. She said then, 'Poor Harriet's had so much tragedy in her life, yet she's come to terms with it, moved on.'

'Your life hasn't exactly been uneventful, Helena.'

'But I haven't come to terms with it. I thought I had, but I haven't. The infection was still there, an abscess, sitting within my mind, becoming ever more toxic.'

'And now?'

'Now I hope it's gone . . . or going at least.'

'That's good, then.'

There was silence between them, mainly because Eisenmenger did not wish to disturb this plateau of tranquillity by saying the wrong thing. She said eventually, 'You know that she lost a granddaughter?'

No, he did not.

'It was a long time ago, about twenty years. She was only nine years old. She had anaphylactic shock, apparently.'

'It must have been awful.'

'And they never managed to have any more.'

He did not want her dwelling on this and asked immediately, 'Do you know what caused the anaphylaxis?'

With a shake of her head she admitted, 'I don't really know what it is.'

'It's an over-reaction of part of the immune system. Instead of protecting the body from foreign material, the body releases all sorts of chemicals and proteins that do huge amounts of tissue damage. The resulting explosion is out of all proportion to the threat and quite likely to be lethal to the victim.'

'Why does it happen?'

'No one knows.'

'Is it treatable?'

'Sometimes. The problem is that if you don't realize you have the tendency, the odds are stacked against you. If you do know, you can carry adrenaline for immediate intramuscular injection.'

'It must have been horrible.'

'Of course . . . '

'And now this.'

He could feel her sinking into despair and was desperate to haul her out of it. 'Look, Helena, you've got to think about yourself. That's what Harriet would want. She's working to get you better and she'd be horrified to think you're just sitting here dwelling on her misfortune, as terrible as it is.'

She said nothing for a while and he thought he had succeeded, but suddenly she announced, 'I want to go to the funeral.'

'Now, Helena . . . '

'I want to go. I want Harriet to know she's got a friend.'

'I don't think . . . '

'I'm going, John. You can't stop me, and neither can anyone else. I'm not a prisoner here.'

'It's not a question of imprisonment. I'm just not sure it's in your best interests to go to something like that. Not at the moment.'

'I'm feeling better.'

'But you're far from well.'

'John, I am going to go.'

He tried to squeeze comfort from this determination, seeing in it that she was like her old self, but this still did not mean he was happy.

'How? How will you go?'

'You'll drive me.'

'You don't know when it is, or where it is.'

'Of course I don't. I don't suppose it's been arranged yet. When it is, you'll take me.'

He tried several more times during the course of the visit to dissuade her, but without any success whatsoever.

Lynette Parker's face bore its habitual smile as she parked her car at the rear of Donnington Manor, where she had an apartment. It widened as she spotted one of her neighbours taking his dog out for a walk and they stopped and chatted for a short time while she petted the spaniel. Then she walked through the rear entrance and waited for the ornate, art deco lift to take her up to the top floor where her flat was situated. She had to share the lift with an extremely elderly man who was one of her patients and who told her, without being asked, all about his health, or rather, lack of it. She nodded understandingly and exuded sympathy, the smile fading and waxing appropriately all the time. She promised to get him an early appointment and left him at her front door slightly happier than when he had first met her.

Only inside her flat did her face change.

The smile vanished and her whole body sagged slightly, as if the hydraulic system had lost pressure. She went first to a drawer in an antique tallboy from which she took a photograph album, then to the bathroom to begin running a bath and then to the kitchen where she poured a large glass of Chablis. A sip of this before she took it back to the bathroom. She stripped off her clothes, then lay back in the hot water that she had perfumed with oils.

Afterwards, she topped up her glass and then, in a pale cream silk gown, she went straight to the door of the small second bedroom. She took the key from her pocket and unlocked it; once inside, she locked it again. A luxurious bed filled much of the available space. Beside it was a small cabinet on which she put her glass. She pulled the curtains closed, switched on a bedside light and sat on the bed.

A long, deep but excited sigh.

She pulled the cord of the gown, undoing the knot: a slow and sensuous movement. The smile on her face might have been supposed to be unchanged, yet it was now somehow infinitely more pleasured. Her hand went to her breast, began to rub.

Her breathing became faster, her mouth opening, her tongue lying inertly and languidly just behind her lips. She opened the photograph album and began to flick through the photos.

And all the while she rubbed her breast with her hand, enjoying the sensation and beginning to moan.

Photograph after photograph.

Every one of them of Adam Dreifus.

Eisenmenger could not avoid the feeling that there was a degree of perfunctoriness about the cremation service for Ruth Dreifus. The priest who took it spoke in a bored monotone as if the magic of the words was long gone, dissipated by repetition and perhaps by dilution of his faith; the choice of hymns – although they were melodic – was trite; the widower's tribute was maudlin to the point of dreariness. Adam Dreifus struck Eisenmenger as a man who was not so much grieving as withdrawn.

They were there against his better judgement, because he had not wanted to argue with Helena, but he was honest enough and had sufficient insight into his own motives to admit that he was also there because he wanted to see Adam Dreifus. Why, he could not find within himself, but that did not mean it was not somehow important . . .

It was as well-attended as one might expect the funeral of

a respected local resident to be, a woman who was the wife of an important general practitioner, who had been prominent in charity work and who had been a governor of two schools. Eisenmenger and Helena sat at the back, he with one eye on her, the other on Dreifus. At the front, seated next to Dreifus, was Harriet Worringer. She held herself with a dignity that could only be found to be impressive; from a distance she seemed to Eisenmenger to contrast in a near tragi-comic manner with her son-in-law, who seemed crushed by events.

As the service progressed, Eisenmenger's fears that Helena would be adversely affected receded. He saw that she was clearly saddened by what she saw and heard, but then so was he – so was everyone there. Part of his original concern had been the issue of Helena's dependence on the older woman; it sounded to him to be an unhealthy thing, one that could so easily turn to obsession. However, although he saw Helena glance occasionally at the older woman, and she was clearly feeling for her, he saw no evidence of anything stronger.

Afterwards, Helena was keen on getting out quickly, not wishing to be seen, but they were held up in the crush of people streaming out through the chapel doors and Harriet Worringer had sharp eyes. They were walking hurriedly to Eisenmenger's car when she called out, 'Helena!'

They stopped and turned. Harriet had broken away from a group of five ladies of a certain age and was walking determinedly towards them across the gravelled semicircle in front of the chapel. A cold wind rippled the purple and white heads of the bedding plants. Eisenmenger felt unaccountably guilty, as if he had been caught picking his nose and eating it. He felt Helena stiffen beside him and could guess that she, too, was feeling slightly embarrassed at being discovered.

Harriet, though, expressed only delight and gratitude that they had come. 'You really shouldn't have,' she said, her tone scolding but not angry. 'You should be thinking of yourself.'

And, typically, Helena murmured, 'I think I've been doing a little too much of that.'

There was the briefest of brief pauses – one that seemed to draw the universe around them in – and then Harriet said, 'Well, thank you very much, anyway.' She turned to Eisenmenger and gave him a genuinely warm smile. 'And I'm grateful to you, as well, John.'

'My deepest condolences,' he murmured.

Despite the fact that they were standing in a crematorium, surrounded by mourners and having just emerged from a funeral service, this remark served to emphasize that for a little while they had moved slightly away from the death of Harriet's daughter, and it brought them abruptly back to reality.

Harriet dropped her face, possibly to conceal tears, although when she spoke he could not hear them. 'It's Adam who is most affected.' Looking up and searching the crowds for him, she said, 'I worry about him.' He was talking to the priest, or rather, the priest was talking to him. Perhaps it was an uplifting talk about heaven and everlasting life, although if that were the case, it seemed to be singularly lacking in potency: Adam Dreifus wore a deep frown that almost hooded his features as the priest chattered on. His hands were in his pockets, and from what Eisenmenger could see, they were balled into fists.

Turning back to them, Harriet said, 'I think if it weren't for his work, he'd have fallen to pieces already.'

Helena said, 'It means that much to him?'

Harriet was watching Dreifus, who had been abandoned by the vicar and was now being assaulted by the sympathy of an elderly man with a luxurious moustache. 'It always has. In my view, if he hadn't set up the clinic after Annabelle died, he would probably have committed suicide. It's been his whole life for a long time now. I sometimes think he'd do anything to keep it going. Anything at all.'

Eisenmenger was intrigued by this and it was an involuntarily impulse that led him to point out rather tactlessly, 'It can't have been easy to have two jobs and still find time for his marriage.'

Helena glanced sharply at him but said nothing. Harriet, too, turned to him and was clearly surprised by his insensitivity. She smiled in a faint, slightly distant way and said, 'Well, yes, I think it was.'

To quell the awkwardness, Helena said, 'We've made a donation to the clinic.'

Harriet took the cue and smiled. 'That's very kind of you both.' Then, 'You will come back to the house, won't you? We're just having a few drinks and snacks.'

This was addressed mainly to Helena, perhaps as a punishment for Eisenmenger's indiscretion. He watched Helena and saw that she was delighted, so of course she said at once, 'Oh, no. We couldn't.'

'Oh, please do. It would mean so much to me.'

'Well, if you're sure . . . '

And Eisenmenger was left once more to marvel at his dislocation from a world in which such duologues could be considered to contain in any way a logical thread.

Forty-Three

The canapés were delightful and the wine was smooth and without the bitter bite of cheapness. There were the accompaniments of a delightful party and the only problem was that it was a wake. Not for the first time, Eisenmenger was struck by the incongruity of occasions such as this, of being caught by uncertainty as to whether to be happy or sad. Whatever he did seemed wrong.

For the most part he and Helena stayed out of the way, in a corner of the nicely furnished and suitably sparse sitting room. They were unbothered by most of the other mourners – presumably the upper echelons of Donnington society – and so could appreciate that here was the simplicity of expensiveness, that elegance could only be achieved without effort. Occasionally they would interact with the mostly middle-aged and elderly people around them, but these were perfunctory encounters that indicated nothing more than a superficial level of politeness.

Adam Dreifus – they had watched him walking between groups of solemn people for over an hour – eventually found them. He smiled and tried to give the appearance of genuine pleasure that he was talking to them.

'I'm so touched that you came.'

They played the game, of course. Helena said, 'I know we didn't know your wife, but I do know Harriet and . . . '

'I know, I know. I'm very lucky to have a mother-in-law like her.'

Eisenmenger said, 'She's worried about you.'

Dreifus laughed. It was a genuine, almost delighted sound. 'She thinks I'm incapable.'

Before Eisenmenger could shut down mental operations he heard himself asking, 'And are you?'

Just a momentary pause before Dreifus smiled and said, 'Very probably.'

Helena told herself that even for a man who sometimes displayed the social skills of a drunken rhinoceros with diarrhoea, her paramour was excelling himself. She said, 'Harriet said you're getting straight back to work.'

He nodded. 'There doesn't seem to be much else to do.'

'Perhaps a short break, though. Get away from it.'

Dreifus shook his head. 'I never get away from work. There's so much still to do, you see.'

'Have you made much progress?' This from Eisenmenger, ever the scientist.

'There are a few promising lines of research. We're collaborating with an American group, looking at some new molecules that down-regulate certain cytokines – TGF-alpha, that kind of thing.' Talking about this subject, Dreifus found some animation, some signs that his life was not nearing an end.

'Anywhere near clinical trials?'

'Oh, no. We're a long way from that.'

'But it's hopeful?'

He shrugged. 'There's always hope, isn't there? I mean, if I didn't have hope, I wouldn't be able to carry on.'

There was a silence because with that last sentiment Dreifus had slipped down a slope and was back in melancholy. He said suddenly, 'Well, I'd better circulate. Thank you very much for coming.'

He left them, their good wishes following limply after him. Eisenmenger tried to work out if it was at all conceivable that this man was a murderer, and could only conclude that it was not.

It followed that the relationship between Beverley and her sergeant, never an easy-going or tensionless thing, became so taut that it might well have done service as the top E string in a piano. Glover remained polite, but it was a thing entirely devoid of humanity and thus it was as offensive as profanity.

He did as he was told, neither questioning nor asking for elucidation; he usually did it with reasonable efficiency (if without any flair or imagination) and thus Beverley did not have cause to indulge in much verbal intercourse with him. They occupied the same office but it was as if within that office there were two worlds, each only a half-seen and half-heard ghost to one other.

In most ways this suited Beverley, but she was also very aware that this frosted surface might well be hiding something of considerably higher temperature and pressure. Glover had not liked her decision to divert him from the Delorme case and this continuing disgruntlement suggested he had yet to move on from this. It was likely that he had gone whimpering and whining to Lambert. If so, and if Beverley were to be shown to be wrong, Grover would become the hero and once again Beverley's career would be in jeopardy.

She could not afford that.

She had worked very hard to stop her career tumbling into free-fall following the Nikki Exner murder, and had only just succeeded in clinging on to a rocky outcrop before terra oh-so-firma had done blunt dissection on her offal. The climb back up had been proving thrice as hard as she had feared it would be – one more stumble and that would be it. There would be no redemption then, nothing to do but accept the invitation for a quiet chat with the Chief Superintendent and begin working out how far her pension was going to carry her.

But she was not wrong. She was certain of that, not because of any evidence but because detection was as much an art as sculpture was, and she reckoned herself a good sculptress. She could not be certain that Anita Delorme had not been murdered, but she was 100 per cent positive that Donald Lennox was not a killer. Dreifus, though, was a different prospect. Where Lennox delighted in philandering, Dreifus delighted in nothing, except perhaps dedication. Anita Delorme had endangered the clinic to which he had devoted his life; she could not help but think that for one such as Dreifus, this would prove a powerful motive.

Unfortunately, motive was not enough. If it were, then she could probably reasonably arrest every human being in the country on suspicion of some crime or another. True, too, there was something distasteful about both Lennox and

Dreifus, but this again did not seem of sufficient gravitas to allow her to arrest either or both of them.

Beverley was abruptly and almost overwhelmingly seized by panic.

She paused, thinking again of Grover and his certainty. Was it really just the naive conviction of a beginner who had no more experience of police work than what he had seen on television, in film and from the periphery of reality?

Beverley made a decision, then. She was not proud of it, but then pride was one of the few sins to which she had not fallen prey.

She would have to keep a close watch on Grover. If necessary, she would do something about him.

Forty-Four

The forensic report on the samples taken from Ruth Dreifus came back with admirable alacrity.

Eisenmenger could only hope that he had not wasted his money, especially as, technically speaking, he had just broken the law. He was painfully au fait with the strictures of the Human Tissue Act, the flouting of which was potentially rewarded by a hefty fine and three years in prison. He would only be spared that fate if his instincts were correct and there was a whole lot more to the death of Ruth Dreifus than appearance suggested.

Unfortunately, as he read the report, his confidence began to wither like a delicate bloom in the hot midday sun. They had, as usual, screened the blood and urine for all common drugs of abuse, as well as prescription drugs and other medicines; they had found only therapeutic levels of Lisinopril, a not uncommon anti-hypertensive drug. The only other positive result was a trace of caffeine.

No poisons, no overdoses, nothing that would ever justify his actions in a court of law.

Ruth Dreifus had died naturally, or at least not by toxico-logical means.

He sat back in his chair by the microscope and looked out of the window, feeling numb. He felt extremely vulnerable now, fearful that he had just made a serious tactical error. Arnold Throckmorton's attitude to him since their conversation in the mortuary had been noticeably colder but also appreciably warier. He had without doubt turned Throckmorton into an enemy and one, moreover, who was running out of escape routes. It was now entirely possible that he had given Throckmorton a gun with which not only to shoot his way out, but also to execute *him* in the process.

He was idly running through strategies to mini-mize the damage – paramount was to protect Clive by explaining to the police how the mortuary technician had had no knowledge of his actions – when he felt a sudden shaft of aggression.

Maybe his instincts were not wrong. Maybe he was being rash by looking only for the obvious. *If* Edward Melnick had been murdered, then it had been by the subtlest of means; perhaps he should think a little more deeply about Ruth Dreifus, take a little more time . . .

Well, it was clear she had not died by a combination of Metformin and a high level of alcohol, but what else . . . ?

A therapeutic level of Lisinopril.

No other drugs, other than caffeine. Surely Lisinopril did not interact with caffeine? He went to his copy of the *British National Formulary* and looked it up, but did not see caffeine listed with those substances that should not be combined with it.

But there had been nothing else.

He had been wrong, and in being wrong he had broken the law.

Except . . . Lisinopril was an anti-hypertensive, designed to reduce blood pressure. It, along with the majority of similar drugs, tended to alter the level of certain electrolytes in the blood. Could that help? Blood and urine would be useless, the results meaningless . . .

But there was still hope.

He turned back to the front page of the report to find the phone number of the laboratory.

* * *

'What are these?'

Paul, dressed in jeans and bare-chested, was flicking through a file on the coffee table as he sat on the sofa. As Beverley came forward while drying her hair, he turned a rather grubby and distressed box file so that she could read the contents. It was the encapsulation of Edward Melnick's career as a private detective. She had put them under the coffee table. He must have been nosing around.

This was typical of Paul. He was hyperactive, almost patho-logically so: forever moving, searching, reading, fixing, repairing, unpicking, picking. Thin, almost emaciated, with long fingers that he could not stop moving, a forever unshaven face, eyes that were bright. He was beguiling, which was a plus, because Beverley found him useful, as she did most of her lovers.

He was also extremely criminal. He not only moved, searched, read, fixed, repaired, unpicked and picked, he also hacked.

Or, to be precise, he picked and then hacked.

Only for lots of money, though.

Paul had developed his own path through crime: he picked locks on offices, then hacked into various financial institu-tions, transferring money into a labyrinthine network of accounts that he had set up. Providing he broke in without leaving a trace, even if someone found out what had happened, his presence was still hidden.

She moved back to the bathroom, calling over her shoulder, 'It's nothing. Just some poor bastard's legacy to the world.'

Paul had become engrossed by the time she returned, hair now dried. She was dressed in a simple cream cotton dress. He had made coffee – he made good coffee and good love and, un-usually, was even capable of doing both tidily – which he was sipping from a white, gold-rimmed Doulton mug. She went to the kitchen and poured herself some, then came and sat beside him.

'Some sort of private eye,' he said.

'"Sort" is about the right word. Not much of a success at it. Missing dogs and suspicious wives. Not a lot of money in that.'

'Yeah, I noticed.' Paul was not a cockney but he had most of the mannerisms and a few more besides, including an accent that was either delightful or aggravating, depending on her mood.

'He died.'

'So I gathered from what you said.'

'There was a question of whether someone might have polished him off.'

Paul had been flicking through the papers idly, just picking them out at random, almost listless or distracted in his actions, but he suddenly became more intense, more involved as she said this.

'Really?' he said in a tone of voice that suggested only one hemisphere was processing auditory data, while the other was more interested in deeper matters.

She noticed, wondered what he had spotted. 'It's a pretty far-fetched story.'

He said nothing for a short while and she asked, 'What is it?'

'This case. A bit more juicy than the usual.'

'In what way?'

He read on. 'He's made lots of notes. Someone called Dreifus . . . '

The feeling that bit into Beverley then, she had experienced before. It was a canker: a living, slithering thing that fed on her, sickened her, whispered to her of her own demise. Her heart rate went up, her mouth dried. Slowly and with careful enunciation she asked, 'What about him?'

'Her. Ruth Dreifus. She wanted your man to investigate her suspicions that hubby was having an affair.'

'Does it say who with?'

There was a pause while he turned back through some of the papers. 'Delorme. Anita Delorme.'

Beverley found her head rotating slowly but surely, as if the coffee contained more than oils and caffeine.

'And was he?'

Paul shrugged. 'I don't know.'

Relief. A small one, but real nonetheless. 'So what's so interesting?'

More riffling through the papers. 'He'd kept notes of how his investigation was going. And he's kept these.' He held up squashed drug packcts.

'So?'

'According to this he broke in to somewhere called Benhall Grange, as well as a doctor's surgery – apparently Dreifus was a doctor – and got hold of some pharmacy records.'

She almost laughed. Breaking in had never bothered the

eager policeman. 'Sounds fascinating.' She couched this in boredom, feeling almost hysterical within.

'Yeah, but the really fascinating thing is that Melnick reckoned that drugs were going missing. All sorts of discrepancies . . . someone was fiddling the books. Stealing opiates, he reckoned.'

She took a deep breath; she did not know what this meant precisely, but she didn't need to see the small print beneath the price label to know that this was a piece of trouble. 'Can I see?'

He handed the box file over to her. With it on her knees, she picked up where he had left off. Melnick seemed to have come across a drug scam: usually morphine and other opiates, but sometimes steroids, and occasionally amphetamines.

The rotation of the room had returned, worse than ever.

She sat back, so shocked that Paul – never the most observant of individuals – asked, 'Are you all right, Bev?'

She hated being called that, yet somehow it was part of his charm. In any case, he had put his hand to her cheek. She had known him for two years and this, she suddenly realized, was the first real sign of affection he had shown her. Plenty of signs of desire, but none of affection. To a certain extent, it brought her round.

'Fine. Things to think about, that's all.'

'More coffee?'

'Please.'

She was back at the box file while he went for it. It gave her space, which she used feverishly. She had a question that needed – screamed for – an answer.

Who?

But either Edward Melnick had not known, or he had not been inclined to say.

Paul returned with the coffee and sat beside her. 'How could he have got hold of these computer records?' she asked.

'Easy. Give me ten minutes, I'll do it for you now. Do you want me to try?'

He enjoyed nothing – except sex, she was glad to say – more than tapping away at a keyboard and insinuating his virtual self into someone else's life. She shook her head. 'I don't think so. Not now, anyway.'

Disappointed but not surprised, he explained, 'It's easy. My cat's fleas could do it.'

'They can do it on someone else's computer. I don't want anything traced to here.'

He laughed. 'Wuss.'

'Seriously, though. Is it really that easy? Could I do it? Could a retired ex-copper who was playing at being a private detective do it?'

'With help.'

'How difficult would it be to find the help?'

'Not difficult at all. There are thousands of kids out there doing things like this just for kicks. If he'd promised one of them a few bob, I should think they'd have the job done inside an hour.'

She looked again at the printouts. Melnick had discovered something illegal going on at the surgery and had died shortly afterwards. Apparently, it had been an accidental death, but John Eisenmenger had wondered otherwise. Was it all connected? If so, then Eisenmenger had been right once again and someone, somehow, had induced Melnick to take a drug that had killed him. What was more, it seemed a reasonable conclusion that whoever was altering the prescriptions was also the killer. Dreifus had to be the likeliest – and Melnick's visit to Dreifus seemed suddenly very significant to her – but she wanted more evidence before proceeding.

'If we find another computer, I think I'll take you up on your offer,' she said.

He drained his coffee cup, then put his hand on her knee and slipped his fingers between her thighs, moving them up and down slowly. 'I didn't tell you what my fee was,' he said with a sly grin.

Forty-Five

The toxicology laboratory rang Eisenmenger back after two hours, during which he had examined under the microscope the heart samples he had taken; these had also shown nothing untoward.

He scribbled down what they told him, thanked them fervently, then put the phone down. Having stared at the figures for a while, he rang the Coroner's Office.

'Have you got a precise time of death for Ruth Dreifus?'

The pause that followed this enquiry did not surprise Eisenmenger. 'I'm sorry, Doctor, but I didn't realize this was your case.'

'Dr Throckmorton has consulted me on it.' He was fairly convinced that when it came to judgement day, this statement would not be placed on the favourable side.

This time the pause was abbreviated, as his interlocutor was becoming practised. 'But he's already given us a cause of death.'

'Be that as it may . . . ' Eisenmenger loved this phrase, because it teetered on the edge of obscurity and therefore bamboozled the enemy. ' . . . We would like to know the answer.'

'But . . . '

'Surely you know?' It was not so much that attack was the best form of defence, it was his *only* one. He felt that he was on sure ground, though. Those who toiled in the sweatshop that was the Coroner's Office rarely had much of a grasp of the details concerning the deaths with which they dealt.

'Well . . . '

'You mean you don't?'

Back to the pause again. He rushed to improve upon his position. 'If you could ring me back in an hour with an estimated time of death, we'd be very grateful.'

And he put the phone down.

He occupied the next eighty minutes with the standard fare of histopathology – seborrhoeic keratoses, viral warts and oddly behaving moles – before the phone rang again.

'Dr Dreifus phoned the ambulance service at nine forty-three p.m. The paramedics can't be certain, but they say that when they arrived at nine fifty-eight, the body was still warm. Does that help?'

This in a tone that suggested that the last hour and twenty minutes had, as far as he was concerned, been wasted.

Eisenmenger excavated some gratitude. 'To a degree. Thanks.'

He put down the phone and considered the information he had just been given.

Was it just possible?

After an hour of ignoring the pile of gynaecological cytology to be reported, he finally decided to call Beverley Wharton.

'I think I need to talk with you.'

And she said at once, 'What a coincidence. I was rather hoping I might be able to have a chat with you.'

He was immediately suspicious. He knew Beverley well, knew that to have contact with her was similar to having contact with something from the fairy world – beautiful but dangerous. 'Really? Why?'

But Beverley was not ready to divulge and said only, 'Something's come up. Something you might be interested in.'

'Funny you should say that.'

'Where shall we meet?'

It was perhaps a sign of his own state of mind that he said only, 'I don't mind. Why don't you come to the house?'

It was most certainly a sign of her own that as she arranged to get there in two hours' time, she did not wonder about Helena or about why he was happy to entertain her on territory that was decidedly Helena's home ground.

Forty-Six

When Beverley arrived, the door was opened by a man who was undoubtedly the John Eisenmenger she knew but who also carried with him something that she did not normally associate with him – nervousness. He ushered her into the living room and she looked around covertly, seeing no sign of the saintly Helena. Despite her own concerns, she began to wonder . . .

She sat in a deep, leather armchair and he sat at one end of a sofa, forward, almost crouched, without relaxation. Seeing this, it was almost automatic for her to play the situation, use his patent agitation to her advantage, subsume her own emotions.

'Nice house,' she remarked.

'Thanks.' His reply was perfunctory.

'You look a little out of sorts, John.'

He smiled but at the same time his eyebrows rose on his forehead and the effect was one of admission to this charge. 'I think I've got something.'

'Really? Is it catching?' Her voice was low and amused, while her eyes laughed softly.

He tried to join in with it, sustained it for only a moment. 'I told you that Ruth Dreifus was dead.'

'You did.'

'I did a few toxicology tests.'

'You found something?'

He had clenched his left hand and was cradling it in his right, rotating it back and forth with steady determination. 'Ruth Dreifus was on Lisinopril for high blood pressure. That's documented.'

'An overdose?'

'Nothing so simple. Nothing so obvious.'

She waited. She sometimes felt that she was the world's best at patience: she waited for suspects, waited for promotion, waited for a decent man to come along. She wondered how much waiting she had left inside her.

He continued, 'Lisinopril is what is known as an angiotensin-converting enzyme inhibitor, or ACE inhibitor.'

She wondered if he might offer her a drink, decided not to ask for one yet and said only, 'Really? You amaze me.'

The smile reappeared but was no stronger than before, dying almost at once. 'Technical stuff, I know, but there's one important thing to bear in mind. You have to watch the level of potassium in the blood. It's important because the drug may interact with it.

'What happens if it does?'

'Your heart starts misbehaving big time. You might well die.'

'Fair enough.'

'It's standard practice for anyone on anti-hypertensives to have their potassium levels checked at regular – usually annual – intervals.'

'Was Ruth Dreifus having such regular checks?'

'According to the hospital records, she last had a blood test three months ago.'

'Was her potassium level abnormal?'

'No.'

She frowned but said nothing. Eisenmenger suddenly stood up. 'Do you want a drink? White wine?'

'Sure.'

While she wondered where this was going, he fetched two glasses and a bottle of chilled Frascati. As he uncorked it, he continued, 'There's a big problem with detecting things like potassium at post-mortem. Death undoes cells just as effectively as it undoes the soul: within minutes of the cessation of circulation, they begin to leak molecules and ions, among them potassium. Within a very short time after death, the level of potassium in the blood starts to rise and before an hour has passed any comparison with the level when the person was living is meaningless.'

He poured wine into her glass and spilled a small drop on the table top, which she wiped with the tip of a finger that she licked as she asked, 'What's all this about, John? You think she was killed by potassium? As far as I can see you have no proof that it happened and no way of ever finding any.'

But he ignored her. 'Vitreous humour is the jelly in the centre of the eye.'

'Oh, charming.'

'To a pathologist, it's useful stuff. The change in levels of potassium happens there, but it happens far more slowly.'

She began to pay more attention. 'So you *can* tell if she had an abnormal potassium level?'

But, of course, it was not that simple. 'There's a lot of controversy. The level doesn't remain static; it does rise and therefore it depends on the time interval between death and when the sample is taken. For some reason, the two eyes sometimes give different results, probably because of technical problems in making the measurement caused by the viscosity of vitreous humour. Also, not everyone agrees on the precise rate at which levels rise with time . . . '

It was good wine, she decided. She could easily have spent all evening drinking it, but she wanted a little more certainty than Eisenmenger seemed to be willing to provide. She saw, moreover, that he was downing the wine in an uncharacteristically rash manner; her recollection of him was of a man with a more refined palate. 'Did she die of an abnormal potassium level?'

Predictably, his answer was slightly more ornate than a single syllable. 'Adam Dreifus reported her death at nine forty-three in the evening. When the police and paramedics arrived at nine fifty-eight, she was still warm and without rigor. It's impossible to be certain but that would suggest that she died no earlier than six o'clock.

'The samples of vitreous humour were taken at ten o'clock the next morning and she had been refrigerated overnight, which would slow the release of potassium down. That gives us a time period of sixteen hours. Several studies have been done giving the levels of potassium found in vitreous humour at different times after death; they differ to a certain degree but the results here are fairly convincing. Backtracking from my results, I would say that Ruth Dreifus had a potassium level of between 7.0 and 8.5 when she died. I've had vitreous from both eyes measured as a check; the results are in approximate agreement.'

To Beverley it was hardly a bloodstained knife found in a suspect's pocket but she guessed that this was significant. The trouble was, she didn't know what he was talking about. His reply when she asked for clarification was interesting but did not make her leap with joy. 'Anything over seven and you're liable to drop dead at any moment; anything over eight and you're as good as a walking corpse.'

She found the wine quite invigorating and decided that she would like some more but, before she could make her desires known, he had drained his own and was already filling the glasses. As he did so, she asked, 'So why is this murder? You said yourself that it's one of the side effects of these drugs. Perhaps it was just bad luck.' She could see that he was still tense and she guessed that he had more to tell her.

'Except that three months before she died her potassium level was in the normal range – low normal, in fact. Less than four. There's no way that it could have nearly doubled in so short a time, not unless she was actually eating – or being given – potassium.'

'How?'

'Potassium is available either as a tablet or a liquid. There are several pharmaceutical preparations available.'

'Why? What are they used for?'

'Because a low level of potassium is as dangerous as a high one.'

'Could she have got it any other way? Don't bananas contain a lot?'

He laughed gently. 'I suppose she might have received a high enough dose of potassium if she'd eaten them continuously for the whole three months,' he admitted. 'But otherwise – no.'

He was nearing the end of his second glass of wine. He appeared to be a man with something either large or noisome on his mind. She wondered what it was that had burrowed inside him, had changed him, and decided that she knew.

Helena's absence from the house was as imposing a presence as a giant squid in the corner would have been.

Something's happened between them. Perhaps they've broken up.

She tried to catch him up in the drinking race; she had nowhere else to go that night. 'So you're suggesting that someone knew she was on this anti-hypertensive and that this person killed her by giving her extra potassium?'

He nodded.

She finished her glass and put it down casually. 'It's a pretty theory, John, but I don't see what use it is.'

He had clearly hoped for a more positive reaction. 'Don't you? Why not?'

'Because it's unprovable. Even if we discovered he was in possession of tons of this potassium supplement – I assume that you're saying her husband is the guilty party – it wouldn't help. For a start, he could probably make some sort of reasonable excuse about why he might have it. Also, we'd have to try to obtain evidence that he gave her potassium supplements knowing the effect that it would have.' There was a deep frown on his face but she hadn't finished. 'Even then, from what you've said, I get the impression that your forensic evidence might be open to some debate in court.'

He did not say anything directly but instead rose and went to the kitchen; when he returned she was pleased to see that he was the bearer of another bottle of wine. As he opened it, she could see that the frown on his face had become intensified. 'Problem?' she asked, as he poured her some more wine.

'I was afraid you'd be sceptical.'

'Better to be sceptical now rather than sorry after a lot of hard work.'

He nodded, but it was an admission of sadness rather than concordance. Over the rim of her glass she asked, 'You seem troubled. May I ask why?'

His glass was already beyond half empty when he said, 'I've been somewhat rash.'

She allowed her right eyebrow to ascend her forehead but kept her mouth in check, retaining a sumptuous symmetry around it. 'That's not like you, John.'

He looked down at the table and then directly at her. 'She was murdered, Beverley. I *know* it.'

'I'm not saying she wasn't, John. Problem is, that's not enough. I've learned that the hard way.'

His next words came after a long pause. 'It was going to be overlooked, put down as natural, and all because of everyone covering up.'

Which tweaked her interest. 'Covering up what?'

To Eisenmenger this was an irrelevance but at least it meant he could delay facing up to his stupidity. 'Incompetence.'

'Nothing criminal?'

'It depends on your point of view.'

She digested what he had told her while he put himself outside a bit more of the wine. She began to see what might have been distressing him. 'Would I be right in assuming that Ruth Dreifus already has a lawful – and natural – cause of death?'

Once more he looked directly across at her, this time with a slow nod. His eyes did not leave her as she said, 'So you took samples taken at her post-mortem and had them analysed forensically?'

'Yes.'

'I'd have to check,' she said slowly, 'but I think that such a course of action is now specifically prohibited by law.'

'That was my understanding,' he admitted. His voice was soft, his mouth sad, as if he had tears for a lost time of inno-cence somewhere within him.

She sat back in the chair, crossed her legs and sighed, 'Oh, dear.'

He remained silent and she remained solemn, considering

what to do. After several minutes in which he hardly ceased staring at her, she said, 'In that case, we'd better try our damnedest to prove she was murdered, hadn't we?'

'Maybe she wasn't,' he pointed out. 'Maybe I'm wrong.'

'Well, let's put this in context, shall we? If we assume this is murder, there are certain aspects we have to examine. First, does it have to be Adam Dreifus?' She asked this as much for her own benefit as for Eisenmenger's. If she could prove that Adam Dreifus was a killer, then maybe she could prove he had despatched Edward Melnick and Anita Delorme. A triple hit. One that would look very good on her CV.

Eisenmenger said, 'I don't see who else would have had the opportunity. We're not talking about a single dose of something. It would require the constant intake of potassium over several days or weeks.'

'So we come to motive. If Dreifus was the only one who *could* have done it, why would he want to?'

'I was rather hoping that you'd tell me.'

She could think of two very good reasons. 'He's short of money for his clinic; in fact, practically bankrupt. Was his wife rich?'

He shrugged. 'How would I know?'

'I'll have to check, then.'

'Failing that, though . . . what? I suppose the marriage could have been in trouble, but surely a few rows aren't going to drive someone to murder.'

She said, 'I can think of another possibility; quite a strong one.'

'What?'

'Someone in that practice was stealing opiates. Presumably to sell.'

This news actually stopped the wine on its way to his opening lips. 'Bloody hell! Who? Was it Dreifus?'

'I've spent the afternoon trying to find out,' she replied. Paul had taken her to an internet cafe some kilometres from her flat. From there he had within fifteen minutes found his way into the supposedly secure network of Doctors Dreifus, Lennox and Parker. He had required a further twenty minutes to navigate his way through their confusing and seemingly illogical intranet system to reach the prescription and dispensary pages. Much of the content in this was completely meaningless and the rest only yielded anything comprehensible after nearly two hours of scrutiny and guesswork, but that small fraction was high grade, top-notch material.

Prescriptions for opiates had been written and apparently dispensed properly; any audit would have suggested nothing untoward. Only if a comparison were made between the computer records and the prescription forms would any discrepancy come to light. Every time opiates were prescribed, the amount actually given to the patient was less than the amount taken from stock.

Beverley told Eisenmenger all this as he listened with growing interest and perplexity. 'I don't see how it could work,' he decided at the end.

'I think what's happening is that someone has put in a change to the software, so that when a doctor prescribes a certain dose of morphine on his consulting room terminal, a script with that amount is printed off, but a higher amount is recorded in the files as having been dispensed.'

'But there's still the hard copy of the prescription, the one that is taken to the counter for the opiates to be handed over. And it's signed by both the prescribing doctor and the patient.'

'And then it is stored in file,' she agreed. 'But what if a copy were to be made, one with the higher dose?'

'What about the signatures?'

'Signatures are easy to forge; ask any con man.' He was still doubtful and she added, 'Unless you specifically compared the prescriptions with the patient's notes, you'd never detect the change.'

He thought of another objection. 'There must be a controlled drugs book, detailing exactly who gave what to whom, the dose and the duration of the treatment. That's filled in by the dispensing pharmacist at the time the drugs are handed to the patient. It would immediately highlight a difference between the prescriptions and what should have been given.'

She agreed. 'It would, but unfortunately the surgery has gone over completely to a paperless office. That "book" no longer exists except as a computer file with password access only by the dispensing staff . . . '

He understood. 'And the same software fix has been applied to that?' he guessed.

She nodded and Eisenmenger was forced to admit that it

might work. The only real danger would be if someone actually got hold of the drug packets dispensed. They might then see from the labelling that there was a discrepancy, but even then if the drugs were dispensed in weekly amounts, it would not necessarily be damning.

'But it would take some computer know-how to do it . . . '

She shook her head. 'My . . . informant . . . tells me that such expertise is readily available and can be purchased for a relatively small amount. There's no point in looking to see which of them has a university degree in computer hacking.'

'But it could be Dreifus,' he mused. He had lost the nervousness, as if the thrill of the intellectual chase was proving a potent antidote to anxiety.

'It is him.'

Her certainty surprised him. 'Do you know for definite?'

Beverley sighed silently. Time to admit her own failings. 'I know all this because it was first found by Edward Melnick.' He looked up at that, but said nothing. 'When I went to see his widow, she gave me a file containing notes on his cases. This was the last one he'd been working on.'

When he drank the wine this time, it was with calm deliberation. 'Quite a coincidence.'

'Not really.'

He waited.

'He was working for Ruth Dreifus at the time. She suspected her husband of having an affair with Anita Delorme.'

He said at once, 'An affair? But that could be motive . . . '

'He wasn't, John.' She said this with enough certainty to have caused Heisenberg second thoughts. Just for good measure and before he could argue, she added, 'I've looked into it, and I'm perfectly satisfied that Adam Dreifus was not having an affair with anyone.'

This was not, in strict Socratic terms, true, since she was only sure in her own mind that he was not having an affair with Anita Delorme. She felt herself justified in such a statement, possibly in a slightly optimistic fashion, by the fact that Edward Melnick had been unable to find evidence of adultery.

'How did Melnick find out about this opiate business?'

'As far as I can make out from his notes, he trailed Dreifus and did some unofficial – and, I suspect, illegal – checks, but came up with nothing very interesting, other than his parlous financial situation. Then he broke into both Benhall Grange and the surgery to look for evidence of the affair, and found a stash of drugs. His notes aren't clear where he found them, precisely. Melnick wasn't quite the intellectual equal of Sherlock Holmes, but he was a cut above Dr Watson. He figured out that the likeliest source was the surgery pharmacy, so he used a bit of his police nous and followed a few standard procedures. He checked to make sure there had been no recorded break-ins, then he hung around the surgery on various pretexts and discovered who was on opiates, got to know them and found out what doses they were taking. He hit pay dirt by employing someone to hack into the surgery computer system.'

Eisenmenger had thought of something else. 'Surely the pharmacy staff would have to be in on this.'

'I don't think so. As long as Dreifus knows where the prescriptions are filed, he could perform the whole operation himself.'

'And now Melnick's dead.'

'As is Ruth Dreifus. Both apparently by natural means, both potentially by clever use of pharmaceutical agents.'

'Why kill Melnick?'

She shrugged. 'My impression of Melnick is that he wouldn't have been above a little bit of blackmail. Maybe he saw this less as a moral quest, more a fiscal one.'

Eisenmenger returned to his wine quite suddenly and finished the glass. Beverley wondered if he was becoming drunk. She had slowed her own consumption.

'So Dreifus kills Melnick to stop him blackmailing him about his sideline in opiates. Why kill his wife soon afterwards?'

She, too, had wondered about that, and thought she had a possible answer. 'Melnick was working for Ruth Dreifus. He couldn't take the chance that she didn't know something of what he had discovered.'

Eisenmenger had to admit that it was not inconceivable, but nor was he convinced. Not that it mattered. Whatever the motive, the evidence suggested that Dreifus had killed both Edward Melnick and Ruth Dreifus. The only remaining problem was proving it, if only to pre-empt his own arrest for breaking the Human Tissue Act.

Their conversation lapsed into silence. He looked idly at his glass and she looked at him as she sipped some of her own wine. She had slipped off her shoes and now she curled her legs under in the chair. She knew that he was watching and could see the tautness of her skirt around her thighs. The quiet between them became almost somnolent and this somnolence brought with it an intimacy that perhaps Eisenmenger was not aware of, that Beverley sensed with well-practised antennae.

She asked, 'Where's Helena?'

He pushed his way through his thoughts, looked at her and said, 'Oh, she's out.'

Beverley's watch said that it was close to ten. 'She's late.'

There was a telltale hesitation before he explained, 'She's away for a few days.'

'Staying with friends?'

' . . . Yes.'

She paused, showed no sign of her disbelief, then asked in a silky voice, 'Is there any more wine?'

He came to and she reflected that perhaps John Eisenmenger's antennae were fairly well-attuned as well. 'Well . . . '

She didn't say anything but pushed her glass forward.

'It's getting rather late.'

Time for some education in the ways of the world; her world, at least.

'John, what we've discussed tonight has been very interesting but the bottom line is that it's all theory and hot air. Without a lot more groundwork, Dr Adam Dreifus carries on as he's always done, collects his pension and maybe kills a few more people. I'm the one who's going to do that groundwork. Not you . . . me. Don't I deserve a little more wine before I go?'

She saw him reconsider his position, saw that he had exposed his oh-so-soft underbelly, and moved in for the kill.

Slowly untwining her legs, she leaned forward. She was not wearing a particularly revealing blouse, but her demeanour made up for it as she said, 'You've got to keep me on side, John. You've broken the law, and I'm the only one who can save you. I think it would be in your best interests to keep me happy, don't you?'

Forty-Seven

Helena's days had turned to a turgid crawl, the slowest of waltzes, a funereal procession of tasks that seemed to her to do nothing more than to prop up the waking hours and separate the hours of darkness. She felt isolated once again, a thing not only without anchor to the world around, but also without interest. She was an observer, not a participant; someone passing through, untouched and untouchable. She tried to engage but found herself acting the part, and acting it badly. Her therapy sessions had become exercises in toleration, periods to be endured, and she found herself beginning to give up even trying to play the game, retreating into listlessness and silence. The only time she now made any effort to engage was when John came to visit, but this was achieved with almost complete emotional exhaustion. After his visits, she would retreat to her room, where she would take to her bed until the morning and be seen only by those staff making their rounds.

Eisenmenger found Helena in bed, curled into a foetal ball but with her eyes wide open, staring at ghosts, at spirits, at memories and thoughts, but staring at nothing real. His heart withered within him as he beheld her. She was, if anything, worse than when she had first arrived and he felt as if he had not just a mountain to climb but one that was growing taller and steeper as he gazed upon it.

He came and sat on the bed beside her. Her eyes flicked towards him but then reverted to their initial position, no expression animating her impassive, almost doll-like face. 'Hello, Helena. How are you?'

He put out his hand to touch her shoulder beneath the duvet and found the shape of her upper arm intensely, almost painfully, moving. She said, 'Fine.' She said it listlessly, emphasizing the patent untruth of the assertion.

'Are you tired?'

'A bit.'

'What have you been doing today?'

'The usual.'

'Have you had a therapy session?'

Nothing.

'Helena?'

Nothing.

'Helena?' He squeezed her shoulder gently.

She reacted. 'Yes! Yes, I have. All right?' But it was a re-action in voice only, unaccompanied by movement.

He felt as if he could do only harm, that whatever he said would only serve to bury her further in her despond. The idea of discussing their one and only holiday or amusing anec-dotes from their life together seemed farcical, the idiot concept of an outsider to their lives together, of someone who thought he knew best because he knew *something*.

He felt the silence between them not only lengthening but also deepening, becoming solid, a barrier that grew taller and broader with each second. In desperation he said, 'Tell me about Harriet.'

He was at once afraid that he had spoken crassly, that in attempting to reach for her he had pushed her even further away, perhaps beyond his reach. Yet his heart thrilled as, after a pause of two seconds, she turned her head to him, her gaze no longer on things outside the room but actually on him. 'Harriet?' she asked.

'Yes.' He did not go on because he felt that he was in a mire, that his first footstep might not have brought about calamity, but that that did not mean the danger was extin-guished. At any moment he might find himself sinking to disaster. 'She's important to you, isn't she?'

He saw Helena think about this, actually engage with some-thing other than her own decay, and he was glad. 'Yes,' she admitted, but it was in a guilty voice. Then she uncurled some more and actually came up to support herself on one hand so that she could put out the other to his arm and say,

'So are you, John . . . But, about this, you can't help . . . I know you can't . . . '

'But Harriet can?'

She nodded, and even as she did so she began to cry. 'And now she's gone,' she said through tears. 'She's got troubles far worse than mine. I have no right to expect her to help me . . . '

He saw the weeping and was afraid, once more, panicking that he was opening half-healed wounds rather than closing them. 'I'm sure she won't forget you, Helena.' This lie hurt him but, he thought, better to hurt himself than hurt Helena. 'She's not the kind of person just to abandon you.'

'I'm sure she wouldn't, if she could, but I'm afraid that all this will prove too much for her. You saw her at the funeral.'

'She'll recover. She's resilient.'

'She's lost everything. Perhaps she's not resilient enough. Perhaps no one is.'

She was sinking back down, both physically as she lay her head on the pillow, and mentally as he watched her face lost once more its imitation of animation. He said urgently, 'You've got to believe in her, Helena.'

She was back in the foetal position. For a long time she did not reply and when she did, he heard the saddest words he thought it possible to hear.

'I believe in her . . . but does she believe in me?'

The next morning Eisenmenger felt so low that he thought seriously about phoning the department and claiming illness, something he had never before considered. The temptation to do this stretched his sense of morality to near invisible thinness, but it held and he sat now in his office, unable to motivate himself to do anything useful.

There was a knock on the door but he was spared the inconvenience of inviting the person in, because the door was opened and Dr Throckmorton entered. Eisenmenger knew at once why he was there and did not need to wait for long for confirmation that he was correct in this assumption.

'John, I have something very serious to discuss with you.'

'Have you?' Eisenmenger was in no state to mount any form of defence; in fact could think of none anyway. It was one of those occasions when he just had to stand and take it.

Throckmorton brandished some papers; they were half-folded and stapled at one corner. Eisenmenger did not need to read them to know what they represented. 'What is the meaning of this?'

'I would say it's a toxicology report.'

'Yes, yes, it is.' Eisenmenger was not to be rewarded for getting the first one right, however. 'It is on Ruth Dreifus.'

Eisenmenger had already divined that this was the case and so wasted no effort on mock surprise. 'Where did you get hold of that?'

'Never mind where I got hold of it. It should not exist. It was not required; it was not even your case.'

Eisenmenger did not trust himself to say anything. Throckmorton mistook this for shame. 'Was it?' He advanced, giving an air of being a man who was triumphant and remorseless. 'Was it?'

It was his attitude that irritated Eisenmenger the most. 'I did the toxicology because you hadn't, and you should have done.' He stood up as he said this, which forced his adversary to make a tactical withdrawal. 'Rubbish!'

'Ruth Dreifus did not die of heart disease. If you were in any way conscientious, you would admit that to yourself.'

Throckmorton's face was flushed, his breaths rushing to chase each other; as Eisenmenger said this, he became triumphant. 'That's your opinion. Mine is that she did. And I have been doing this job a lot longer than you.' He moved forward and unsheathed his rather podgy index finger to close in for the fatal wound. 'I would also point out that you, my friend, have broken the law.'

Eisenmenger was trying to remain calm but atavistic instincts were strong within him. He was being attacked, threatened not just physically but also professionally and, what was more, his opponent he considered to be a fat, rather mediocre buffoon. Unfortunately, he had nothing much with which to counter this attack, except wishful thinking. 'Maybe,' he said, 'But I've found another cause of death. An *un*natural one.'

Throckmorton went from incomprehension, to shock, to anxiety within a single breath. His face did a dance, his expression running around a bit and ending up pale and frowning. 'What do you mean?'

'If you'd read the report . . . and if you were a halfway decent pathologist . . . instead of just charging in here and making a fool of yourself, you'd see that she had abnormally high levels of potassium in her vitreous humour. Quite high enough to have killed her.'

He saw Throckmorton evaluate this, saw uncertainty fight with dignity, and quite enjoyed the spectacle. 'But how could this have happened?'

Eisenmenger was not about to engage in the kind of speculation that last night he and Beverley had let run free. He said only, 'I don't know, but I think it's worthy of a bit more investigation, don't you?'

Throckmorton frowned, still unsure, then clearly decided he still had some ammunition left in the locker. 'But you still broke the law, and the law is very strict these days.'

Eisenmenger shrugged and smiled, a sign to Throckmorton that he thought he had the better hand. 'Let's see which of us ends up the worse after this, shall we?'

Throckmorton stared at him for an instant and might have been on the point of saying something, but then turned and strode from the office. Eisenmenger sank back into his chair. His head was hurting more than ever and his heart was now just a dead weight in his chest.

Forty-Eight

There had recently been some complaints concerning a nursing home, with the matron of the home suspected of defrauding those in her care by illegally drawing money from their bank accounts using their credit and debit cards. Beverley had given Grover the task of looking into this, more or less telling him exactly what to do. It was useful for Beverley to give Grover this task, as it meant effectively that she did not have to interact with him. Grover was too proud to ask Beverley for day-to-day help and they therefore passed their working hours in parallel but non-communicating lines. As far as Beverley was concerned, if Grover succeeded she could claim the credit as having masterminded the arrest, and if he failed she could quite legitimately point out that Grover had not consulted her sufficiently.

All in all, it seemed to Beverley to be going fairly well.

That is, it was, until late one evening, when she returned to her desk after a long and ultimately fruitless interrogation of one of seven suspects in a rape case, to find Grover sitting at his desk. This was not of itself something that she would normally find in any way worthy of note, but Grover's demeanour was distinctly odd. He was flushed, almost as if in the grip of some ague: clearly agitated but also apparently angry.

She sat down and saw at once a report on her desk. It detailed the financial aspects of the lives of Doctors Dreifus, Lennox and Parker, and all their relatives. Her eyes glanced up to see Grover looking at her; fixated on her, to be more accurate.

Beverley returned to the report.

Adam Dreifus was in deep doo-doo, worse even than she had previously suspected. His overdraft, which he had extended six times in the past two years, now stood at £57,623, which was unfortunate as his agreed limit was only £52,000. He had remortgaged the house in which he lived twice, using up all the equity. He had credit card bills totalling another £22,000.

Lennox was far better off, with only minor credit card bills, no overdraft and a manageable mortgage on the house. He had several medium-term and long-term savings accounts and, moreover, his wife was independently wealthy.

The surprise in the package was Lynette Parker. Unmarried but living an expensive lifestyle that included large re-payments on an Italian sports car, heavy rent on a large flat in a converted country house and a penchant, according to the credit card company, for extremely expensive shoes. She had no savings and ran a small overdraft, despite moonlighting as the medical officer at the local racecourse, a role that Beverley judged was something of a well-paid sinecure.

But this was not, as far as she could see, of any interest to her.

She was disappointed to see that although Adam Dreifus had taken out life assurance on both himself and his wife some twenty years before, he had cancelled the policy on his wife just eighteen months ago, presumably because the premiums were proving prohibitive. It did seem poor plan-ning if he were intending to kill her. Ruth Dreifus was not, unlike Mrs Lennox, wealthy, and it seemed as if they would have to look elsewhere for a motive when a small footnote in the report caught her eye.

Ruth Dreifus was not wealthy but her mother, Harriet, was. Indeed, from the figures in the report, 'wealthy' was a somewhat mealy-mouthed description of her worth. Dr Derek Worringer's family had been in shipping and they had not been deckhands.

She sat back, momentarily stunned but then, catching sight of Grover's baleful glare, Beverley smiled at him as sweetly as she could. 'Something wrong, Sergeant?'

'I would like to tell you formally that I think your decision to sideline me from the ongoing investigation into Dr Dreifus and his colleagues is despicable.'

She stared at him. Was he joking? Was she really listening to a subordinate giving her his opinions on her decisions? The lunatics had not only taken over the asylum, it seemed they were now also drafting the mental health laws.

'Despicable?' she said.

He nodded. It was a staccato display and he dropped his gaze at once. She said nothing for three heartbeats, would have liked to have sprayed him with napalm, but controlled her emotions. She said merely, 'Thank you, Grover. Your opinion is, of course, noted. Ignored, but most definitely noted.'

He was persistent. It might have proved endearing, had the circumstances been different. 'Fisher's mentioned something about drugs going missing.'

'What of it?'

'Is it Dreifus? Or Lennox?'

She sighed. 'I don't know, Sergeant.'

'This could be big. Very big.' He sounded eager.

'Perhaps.'

'It must be.'

'Must it?' She decided that she had kept her temper for long enough.

'I want you to take me off the nursing home case. I should be . . . '

At which she snapped. His pig-headed self-righteousness would have been more than a stoic could bear, and was most definitely well beyond Beverley's limit for safe stowage. 'I don't give a finger's worth of fucking whether you agree or not, Sergeant. You've got your work to do, now go and do it.'

Without a further word, Grover got up from his desk and walked from the room. Beverley watched him go, fairly certain that he was heading for Lambert's office, if not immediately, then certainly in the not-too-distant future, and hoping, for his own sake, that she was wrong.

She shrugged. Grover's future was in his own hands; she had things to think about.

Depending on the will, here was a potential motive for murder. Assuming Harriet was not eccentric enough to leave all her money to the local cat refuge or the man who had once saved her life on safari in Kenya, then she had probably bequeathed all her estate to Ruth Dreifus. If the terms of the will were favourable to him, when Harriet died, Adam Dreifus was going to come into an awful lot of money.

Eisenmenger's joy when he saw Helena that evening, saw that she was miraculously changed from the thing of drear negation back into a semblance of humanity, did not last long.

'John!'

She was dressed in her nightclothes and dressing gown, but she sat out of the bed, her face joy-filled, her eyes bright.

'Hello, Helena.' He could not stop his mouth from forming a smile. 'You look better.'

'I feel better. Much better.'

'That's good.'

'Harriet phoned me.'

He kept the smile, but as face paint only. Inside he felt partly dismay that a single phone call from this relative stranger should act as such a potent tonic when his own charms were seemingly so ineffective, and partly dread at what he now suspected about Harriet Worringer's tenuous hold on life. He and Beverley had spent half an hour discussing the report on Adam Dreifus's money situation.

'Is she well?' He asked this as small talk, but found that it was almost a Freudian indication of his own thinking.

'She's still fairly low, but she's getting better.'

'Good.'

'John, I was so touched that she thought to phone me.'

'Of course you were.'

'It's bucked me right up.'

'So I see.'

And then Helena frowned. 'What's wrong?'

He widened the smile, said, 'Nothing. Why?' And found in widening the smile that he had only deepened its artificiality.

'Aren't you pleased?'

Then he found how brittle her joy was. She began to descend with startling, almost sickening velocity into distress. It was like watching a space rocket that had been soaring into the upper atmosphere begin to come apart, explode and disintegrate in terrible beauty.

'I thought you'd be pleased.'

There was nothing about her that suggested artifice in this reaction, only genuine despair.

He said quickly and without thinking it through, 'It's just that we're a bit worried about her.'

It arrested the fall with a jerk. 'Worried? What do you mean?'

At the same time as he regretted saying anything, he was elated by her reaction, feeling as if he had reached over and caught her wrist as she fell past him to the ground.

He was wary, though. 'Has she ever talked about her son-in-law?'

'No, I don't think so.' Helena's tone was questioning as she replied.

'Does she take tablets?'

'I don't know.' This time the tone was not just questioning, it was taking on puzzlement.

'She's healthy, right?'

'John, what the hell are you talking about?' She had reached for, and embraced, consternation.

But he was suddenly very afraid of what he had done. 'Nothing. It doesn't matter.' He was thinking as he spoke, *That's pathetic.*

Unfortunately, Helena seemed to agree with him. 'What does that mean? You said you were worried about her. What did you mean?'

He was having the most rewarding conversation he had had with her for what seemed liked weeks and wishing he were somewhere else. 'Please, Helena, it doesn't matter. I shouldn't have said anything.'

'But you did,' she pointed out and he heard the lawyer in her as she said it.

'I know, but . . . ' His search for suitable words was rushed and consequently unsuccessful. ' . . . It might be dangerous.'

Which, of course, only worsened his situation. 'Dangerous? You mean Harriet might be in danger?'

'Not for certain . . . '

'But she could be?'

'Well . . . '

'How?'

He tried to sidestep this onrushing leviathan by undertaking deep inhalation and edging in another direction. 'It's just a possibility, that's all, Helena. There's no proof, no real evidence.'

He watched as she weighed this, saw a woman whom he had been missing for too long, found himself back in love with her.

She asked, 'Who?'

He hesitated, completely balanced between encouraging her in this recrudescence and trying to shield her from involvement. He made the decision blindly, hoped that it was the right one.

It wasn't.

'Adam Dreifus.'

If she was surprised by this information, she did not show it, asking only, 'How? Why?'

And he told her what he suspected. He framed his words carefully, though, avoiding mention of Beverley Wharton. When he had finished, Helena had been transformed from a near-moribund basket case to someone who had discovered a world she had previously forgotten. 'We must warn her,' she announced.

'Not yet.'

'Why not?'

'Because it's entirely conceivable that all I'm doing is fantasizing. Maybe Melnick did take the Metformin accidentally.'

'But what about the potassium levels you found in the samples from Ruth Dreifus?'

'Open to interpretation, I'm afraid. I'd bet a lot of money a defence team could find a very eminent forensic pathologist who would rubbish my conclusions. I'm half inclined to rubbish them myself.'

'What about the inheritance?'

'We don't know for certain that he stands to inherit anything. It's not automatic, it depends on her will.'

'Ask her.'

He smiled. This was more like it; working with Helena was sometimes like trying to stay on a panicked horse. 'She might want to know why we're asking.'

'Is that really so important?'

'Yes, it is.'

'But . . . '

He took her hands in his. 'Look, Helena, I'm as keen as you are to make sure Harriet doesn't come to any harm, but at the moment she's a very vulnerable old woman. Adam Dreifus is her only living relative and she's probably relying on him just to cope. The last thing we want to do is take that away from her unnecessarily.'

'No, John. The last thing we want is for Harriet to die,' she pointed out.

'Yes, of course, but it's just a question of finding something more concrete than we've got at the moment. I'm sure it won't take long.'

She did not like it but his words made her pause.

'How?' she demanded. 'What kind of evidence can you find?'

He had not told her about Beverley's part in the investigation, had implied that he had been the one who had had possession of Melnick's notes and that it was from these that he had gleaned much of the information. Before he could introduce the idea that they might need to include the police – more specifically, could introduce the concept that they might need to include Beverley Wharton – she said, 'You said, "we".' The voice was thoughtful, coming from the near past.

'What?'

'You said, "We're a bit worried about her."'

'Yes, well . . . '

'Who did you mean by "we"?'

He was marvelling at her sharpness and at the same time wondering at her paranoia as he explained, 'We – you and I – are going to have to get help with this.'

She gazed at him – she actually gazed into him – for a longer time than he found comfortable, then looked down into

her lap. He was foolish enough to think he had passed through
some sort of proving ground.

'Helena?' This gently, because he had bad news to impart.
When she looked back up at him, control of the situation was
lost from him as she enquired with a cold, aggressive hiss,
'Beverley Wharton?'

He began to feel that somewhere along the line she had
been blessed with an extra sense. 'I asked for her help,' he
admitted. As he spoke, he was a small child admitting to
unmentionable deeds in the lavatory.

And any thought he might have had that she had lost the
ability for incandescence was forever gone as she exploded.
'What the fuck did you do that for?' This was screamed but
at the same time surprisingly breathless.

'As I said, Helena . . . '

'But why her?' Her volume remained in the red. She had
moved forward and was confronting him. Somewhere in his
head a voice was debating whether this was very good or very
bad for her therapy.

'Because she is the police officer we know best.' It had
seemed obvious when he had first rung Beverley, but now
that he was being asked – forced at the point of an acid-
tipped blade – to justify it, he found his motives less easily
justifiable.

'But she's a two-faced, conniving bitch! She killed my stepbrother!'

It was a story that lived with them, that had defined Helena.
Without Beverley Wharton, Helena would have been a very
different person. 'But, Helena,' he said in a voice that he kept
as calm as he could. In the corridor outside, he heard movement. 'I couldn't think of anyone else to turn to. Certainly,
no one who would treat what I said with any seriousness.' His
next words followed on without pause, as easily as oil flowing
over bare skin. 'At the time, I thought it best.'

He wondered whether it was a lie, but knew at the same
time that it was very close to the truth. Yet what exactly were
his motives?

While this doubt arose within him, he saw that his words
appeared to have had the effect of mollifying her, certainly
of making her think. There was a knock on the door of her
room and Terry put his head in. 'Everything all right?'

Eisenmenger said nothing, watching as Helena's head jerked around and she snapped, 'Fine.'

Perhaps he thought about further enquiry but, if he did, her expression whispered wise advice to the contrary and he withdrew.

When she returned her attention to Eisenmenger, he saw that he had made progress, that she was a long way from happy but that she had seen some sense in what he had said. 'Did it really have to be her, John?'

What could he say to that?

He dropped his head and wondered why he did it. Was it shame, guilt, or the desire to hide his features? While he was searching everywhere for some words, Helena said suddenly and with a sigh, 'I'm sorry, John.'

When he looked up, he saw her tears in her eyes and she was reaching out to him.

He took her in a hug that lasted a long, long time.

Forty-Nine

When Beverley was summoned to Lambert's office, she knew that Grover was responsible. Lambert stood before her and, even before he spoke, he was performing a perfect but unconscious mime of a man who was being powered by superheated steam with the safety valve stuck on closed. 'What is it with you, Inspector?'

Beverley had fixed rules concerning dealing with fellow officers and one of these was always to show complete disregard for a superior officer's temper. 'Sir?'

He did not immediately respond, possibly because he was so angry his nervous system was misbehaving. Then, 'Not only are you deliberately pushing a very able officer to the sidelines without a proper reason, but then you compound the offence by using profane and disgusting language to him.'

Which news caused her to forget insouciance. 'What?'

'You heard. Sergeant Grover has come to me concerning your behaviour. He has accused you of bullying him and of sexual harassment.'

She fought to contain her emotions. 'That's absolute . . . poppycock, Sir.'

He noted her use of the word, perhaps even extracted some savage amusement from it; he certainly grinned. 'Is it? You're quite well known for your colourful language, aren't you? And he's told you that he doesn't agree with swearing, hasn't he?'

'Yes, but . . . '

'So he believes that by your use of the expression . . . ' he paused, looked down askance at a piece of paper on his desk, ' . . . "A finger's worth of fucking", you were deliberately trying to upset and goad him.'

'Don't you think that his reaction's a little bit over the top, Sir?'

'No, I don't. And why isn't he helping you with the Dreifus case?'

'I told you, Sir . . . '

'You told me a lot of . . . "poppycock", Inspector. Now get him involved with the case, or I'll be forced to accept what he says as true and take formal action.'

Helena was aware that things had changed, but at the same time she was aware that she had swapped one daemon for another. If the profound depression caused by her miscarriage had been banished, she found that it had been replaced by a multitude of worries, harpies that tormented her just as much.

Harriet was in danger. John thought so and that was as good as certainty as far as she was concerned, no matter what the courts might say. She occasionally – almost continually – considered him the most irritating entity in God's hallowed creation, but she recognized that he was only irritating because he was usually right. If he had goofed up quite as often as other people did, he would have been far easier to live with.

And far less interesting.

But she knew he was also interesting to Beverley Wharton. Which would not have been a problem, except that there was within her a small place, but an intensely painful place, that half-suspected that Beverley Wharton was also interesting to him. Beverley Wharton was interesting to all heterosexual men. It was one of the many aspects of her universe that she hated – that was as painful as red-hot embers dropping on her eyeballs – but that she had to endure. There had been many times when in the alcoves of her mind she had stopped to speculate about a world in which the woman who had destroyed her life had been ugly. Would it have been less painful?

She rather thought that it would.

The reasons he had given for involving Beverley Wharton were plausible, but that did not mean they were not just excuses. An implausible excuse was of no use to anyone and John Eisenmenger was not stupid enough to present to her anything that was useless.

But even recognizing her limitations did not mean that she could climb over them, that they were no longer extant. She could not just make a decision and then change her life as easily as she might change her hair colour. Trust was like virginity: once lost, never regained.

A worthy sentiment, except that John Eisenmenger had never done, or said, or given her indication of, anything that suggested he was not worthy of her utmost confidence.

And still she could not allow herself to dare to hope that he did not desire Beverley Wharton.

She had been lying in her bed, but suddenly rose into a sitting position. She had not slept well since she had arrived, the mattress being too soft and the bed too narrow. Anyway, it was not *her* bed, and that was what mattered the most.

She felt sick.

Deep breathing.

Gradually the nausea passed and slowly she lay back, looking at the ceiling. It was nothing special – no different from most other ceilings she had stared at in the darknesses of her life – but she hated it and wanted desperately to see her own, to all intents and purposes identical, ceiling.

This optimistic thought proved to be a foundation on which she climbed into something approaching calm objectivity.

She had to be professional about this, professional and self-less. Whatever there may or may not be between John and

Beverley Wharton, the important thing was to make sure that Harriet was safe.

John had asked her not to get involved, but surely it would do no harm to find out the truth about the will? If Adam Dreifus was not a beneficiary, then no one had to worry about her safety.

Surely Harriet's safety was paramount?

She did not realize she was drifting into sleep as this thought, smudged at the edges, was her last for the night.

Fifty

'OK, Grover. I understand that you want to be more involved.'

'I just want a fair chance, Sir.'

'Fancy yourself as Hercule Poirot, do you?'

'No, but I want to be treated like everyone else. I appreciate that you think I'm a bit of a . . . waste of space, but if I could just be given an opportunity to show what I can do, I'm sure you'd change your opinion.'

Beverley found her jaws almost tetanically clamped together and therefore her diction was less than perfect. 'I haven't got much option, have I?'

He made a mistake: he smirked. It was probably then that his fate became irrevocable. Beverley took note but made no outward sign. Having sighed, she said, 'OK. This is what's happening.'

She went on to explain about the missing drugs at the surgery.

'How is this connected to Anita Delorme?'

'It probably isn't.'

'Are you certain of that? It's a bit of a coincidence, isn't it? All this being discovered just after a suspicious death.'

Beverley snapped. 'Look, Grover, I'm not sure, OK? In actual fact, I haven't the faintest fucking idea what's going on, all right? All I know is that I don't want you jumping from theory to theory every time a new piece of evidence presents itself. I want you to do your job, which is to do as I tell you to do.'

He did not like this advice, but he took it. 'So what do you want me to do?'

'Where are those background reports you prepared on the surgery staff? We need to go through them again. Then I want similar checks made on everyone working at Benhall Grange. Also, we're going to have to search both of them. Melnick found some evidence, we might strike lucky as well. I want you to lead at the Grange and I'll take the surgery, OK?'

Grover failed to hide that he was very 'OK' with this arrangement.

'What now?'

Perhaps Adam Dreifus had a bedside manner that was second to none but, if so, he was strict about its application, for as Beverley approached him in the surgery he sounded like a very angry general practitioner indeed. There were no patients to view this display of ire and so presumably he felt that his public persona was relatively safe, although they were in view of two receptionists, a cleaner and Daksha, all paying rapt attention – albeit with varying degrees of covertness – to the exchange.

Beverley did not mind an audience, not when it was someone else's dirty undergarments being held up for perusal. 'Another matter has come to our attention, Dr Dreifus.'

'*Another* matter? You mean, this is nothing at all to do with Anita?'

Beverley was not about to go that far. She used anodyne language, partly because she thought to save him from embarrassment, but very much mainly because she had her own reasons for being vague. 'We think you may have a problem with some of your procedures.'

As a collection of words, it could have had at least five interpretations, but her tone eliminated most of them. Dreifus might have been angry but he was sufficiently streetwise to see that it was probably going to be in his best interests to usher them towards some privacy. Accordingly, he swallowed his irritation and said in a more measured tone, 'Come with me.'

With a stare around the reception area, not exactly picking out individuals in the audience but sending out a general message that they had better get on with some work, he walked away and Beverley followed.

His office was at first sight unchanged, but then Beverley noticed a photograph of Ruth Dreifus, which she was sure had not been on the desk before. She did not remark on it, although she wondered at its significance.

'No assistant?' asked Dreifus.

Beverley smiled. 'Not this time.' She said, 'If you don't mind me saying so, you're back at work very quickly, Dr Dreifus.'

As it turned out, he apparently did not mind. Indeed, he agreed. 'I know, but I couldn't think to do anything else.' He stopped, brooded. 'Haven't spent much time at home over the past few years, what with work here and the clinic . . . suddenly felt that I didn't belong. The house was Ruth's territory. I was a guest, a part-time resident. It didn't seem right to change that.' There was another pause, but he had not finished. 'I never knew what people meant by "ghosts" in a house, but I was starting to. Even when Annabelle died, it wasn't like that . . . '

Could this man be the killer of his wife? Part of her believed in him completely as an innocent widower, and part of her knew from hard experience that a killer was *exactly* what he could be. It just meant that he was little bit madder than she at present believed.

'Had you expected her to die?'

He clearly found the question odd. 'Of course not.'

'I mean, there had been no signs, nothing that in retrospect you think now could have been her heart . . . ?'

'Nothing . . . ' But then he paused before saying from this thoughts, 'Mind you, she had complained of indigestion a couple of times . . . '

'Indigestion?'

'The differential diagnosis of central chest discomfort includes both cardiac pain and acid reflux into the gullet.'

'Oh. Did she mention this to anyone else?'

'I don't know.'

'She had high blood pressure, I think.'

'You've been doing your homework.'

'I read the autopsy report.' Her face was blank. He clearly wondered where this was going but he let it ride and said, 'Yes, she did. Nothing serious, but we thought it best to get it treated.'

'ACE inhibitors. Is that right?'

'Yes.'

'Did she take anything else?'

'No. Not regularly.'

'But occasionally?'

'Why are you asking these questions?'

In order to keep him on the end of her line, she risked letting him a little closer to the truth of her suspicions. 'Tell me, Dr Dreifus, in your opinion, is there any possibility that your wife could have died as the result of an accidental drug interaction?'

His reaction was sudden, a slight jump. It could have been genuine surprise or genuine guilt. 'Drug reaction?'

'Was she taking anything else at the time?'

He seemed to have been dazed by this revelation. When he said that, no, he was sure she was not, it was with distraction as the most recognizable thing about him.

And then he contradicted himself. 'She had had a cough, and sore throat. She was taking some cough medicine.'

'Did she buy it?'

Once again he did not immediately respond.

'Doctor Dreifus?'

He focused on her and then admittedly slowly. 'I got it from the dispensary for her.'

'Was it a proprietary brand?'

He became strangely thoughtful. 'A generic one, I think. Nothing special.'

'When did you give it to her?'

He considered. 'I suppose about two or three days before . . . ' A pause, in which he apparently found a bit of indignation. 'Look, what's all this about? My wife died of heart disease. The pathologist thinks so, and so do I.'

'Nobody's suggesting . . . '

'Is this what you spend your time doing? Taking perfectly natural deaths and trying to turn them into something they're not? Isn't there enough crime already? You don't do too well clearing up the real ones without inventing them.'

The clichés came at regular intervals, tired barbs that every police officer in the country heard at least once a week and probably far more often. Like blades gone blunt they had little effect on someone as thick-skinned as Inspector Beverley Wharton. 'No. I actually came here concerning another matter. As I told you, I believe there may be certain irregularities in your procedures.'

'What does that mean? Procedures regarding what?'

'Controlled drugs.'

Part of Beverley's interviewing – or, indeed, interrogation – technique was to lob grenades into the cosy world of the person before her, to see what fell from the trees and to see, more especially, how they reacted when they heard the thump.

Adam Dreifus did not do well. There was surprise and that, she thought, was most probably genuine, but it could have been surprise that she knew about it, rather than surprise that it was happening. He followed it up, however, with nervousness and she could think of no good reason why he should have chosen that particular emotion. 'Controlled drugs?' he asked, presumably just to exclude the possibility that his hearing had misled him.

She did not respond, pointing out instead, 'And this isn't a crime that I'm making up.'

He fretted; it was not a pretty sight. 'What kind?' he asked eventually.

'Opiates, mostly. Steroids.'

If anything, his nerves were getting worse. 'How do you know?'

'Here.' She gave him the drug packets from Melnick's box files.

'What are these?'

'As I said, mostly opiates. They were prescribed and dispensed here.'

'So?'

'We also have access to your computer records regarding those same prescriptions.' As she said this, she handed him printouts of the records that Paul had accessed. After a pause, she said, 'They are different – in each case the amount recorded is greater. That suggests that someone is syphoning them off.'

He held up the printouts. 'How did you get hold of these?'

'That's not really relevant, is it? Do you agree there are discrepancies?'

He did. He did not want to, but could not do otherwise.

'And you didn't know about this?'

'No.' Superficially this answer was constructed out of certainty, but Beverley had heard answers such as this many times before. Anger could sound remarkably like conviction and anger was an easy cover for a lie.

'Edward Melnick didn't mention it?'

Now that *did* surprise him. 'Melnick?'

'He came to see you. He'd found out about this little scam and he decided you ought to know about it.'

'No, you're wrong.'

But she heard a lie in that reply. It was too pat, too quick. 'Am I? His records suggest otherwise.'

'They're wrong. He came to see me about his gout, nothing more. A purely medical consultation.'

'I see.'

She saw no point in arguing; there would be time later. 'Who has access to the computer?'

He was staring at the photocopies as he said distractedly, 'Everyone.'

'Everyone? Surely not.'

He took notice of her. 'Oh, you mean for prescribing. Everyone has access rights for viewing, but as far as prescribing is concerned, only the medical and nursing staff.'

'No one else? What about the dispensary staff?'

'No one. Why should they? They don't prescribe.'

'Those who do have prescribing rights, their access is by password?'

'That's right.'

'Known only to them?'

'Yes.' He was looking at her as he spoke, staring at her with a question in his eyes. She wondered what that question was, not entirely sure that it was one for her.

With a smile she said, 'Well, it shouldn't be too difficult to find out who's doing the stealing, should it?'

'Someone might have hacked into the system from outside.' He did not sound confident in the idea; rather the opposite actually.

'I don't think so, Dr Dreifus. Whoever it is has to destroy the original script and then replace it with a forgery in order to keep the records straight. No one on the outside could do that.'

'Sounds very far-fetched,' he opined sniffily.

She ignored his scepticism. 'When it comes to crime, it's the far-fetched that sometimes produces spectacular results,' she pointed out. 'If the idea's not far-fetched – if it's mundane – then the chances are we're going to cotton on pretty quickly.'

'That doesn't mean that every lunatic scheme is going to work.'

She smiled. 'This one appears to have done, don't you think? After all, just considering the drugs represented by those prescriptions,' she indicated the printouts as she said this, 'we're looking at morphine going missing that could be sold for over five hundred pounds, and this is over a period of only three weeks. When did you have this computer system installed?'

'Six, maybe seven years ago.'

As he said this, she saw a man who was deflated, who apparently could not even defend himself any more. He asked tiredly, 'What do you want me to do?'

'I'm going to have to interview the staff. Meanwhile, my colleagues are going to have to search the premises.'

'Is that absolutely necessary?'

'Yes.' She thought it a stupid question and she let her tone tell him so. Had he swallowed a dung beetle he would have looked less distressed. What she said next proved to be no cure for his indigestion. 'And we will also be searching Benhall Grange.'

'Oh, come on, now. That is completely out of the question. This has nothing to do with the clinic.'

'Yes, it does.' She rather enjoyed contradicting people like Dreifus. 'Some of the stolen drugs were found there.'

He did not argue, expressed no surprise, asked no questions, and this intrigued her. She wondered what he was hiding. 'But you can start by showing me the computer system. Then I'll need to speak to all those with prescribing rights. Also, I'll need to see where the scripts are filed after they've been dispensed. I'm going to have to get some specialists in forensic IT in here to take your system to bits. Perhaps they'll be able to tell us who's been helping themselves to the Smarties.'

The improvement in Helena's demeanour was noted by everyone who came into contact with her the next morning, and remarked on by more than a few. She was scheduled for a therapy session at ten and this she attended, dressed in her day clothes, exuding self-confidence and unspoken optimism; all questions regarding the reasons for her changed affect were met with consternation. She did not know why she felt different, she claimed, she just did.

And then she disappeared.

Fifty-One

'You do realize how much disruption you're causing to us and our patients?'

'Believe me, Dr Parker, I wouldn't be doing it if it wasn't a matter of the utmost seriousness.'

'This time it's something about missing drugs, I understand.' Her tone was supercilious, bored.

'Opiates.'

'First it's that Delorme girl, and now you're here about drug dealing, or trafficking or whatever you call it.'

That Delorme girl. She might have been talking about a fallen woman.

Perhaps she was.

'Life's like that. Rest assured, Dr Parker, it's not by choice that I'm back here.'

'Well, just as Anita Delorme died without my help, so this also has nothing to do with me.'

'I'm sure.'

'It's probably just an accounting error, or something.'

'I don't think so.'

Lynette Parker held up her hand and waved her rather podgy fingers. 'Whatever.'

'It is quite important,' Beverley pointed out.

'Of course.' This was said as though she actually thought exactly the opposite.

Beverley counted to ten, decided that ten more might help,

then discovered that it did not. In a voice that showed the strain of remaining polite she said, 'Have you ever had any inkling at all that this was happening?'

'None at all.'

'As far as you're aware, no one who works here has ever had any drug problem?'

'Good grief, no.'

'Ever hear of anyone at the surgery with money problems?'

'We've all got money problems, Inspector.'

'But nothing out of the ordinary?'

'No.'

'Adam Dreifus has quite serious money problems.'

This unsettled her, which gave Beverley some relief from her irritation.

'Well . . . yes, he has *commitments* . . . '

'So perhaps he's found a way of making an extra couple of bob.'

'I really don't think he'd stoop to pinching morphine and selling it on the black market.'

'Not a "professional" thing to do, you mean?'

'Absolutely.'

'So you're saying it must have been the practice nurse?'

She teetered on the brink of the trap, then pulled back. 'No, of course not . . . ' A moment's thought followed this, then, 'I don't know *who* it was.'

'It was somebody, though, wasn't it? It didn't just steal away from the dispensary on its own.'

'If we accept that there is a discrepancy.' Her body language was one of discomfort and, since she was so portly, it was shouting at Beverley.

'Oh, don't worry, Dr Parker, there's a discrepancy all right.'

With a frown that was deep enough to have hidden a pencil in, she suddenly seemed to decide to take offence that she was being interviewed and, by implication, suspected. 'Well, it's absolutely nothing to do with me.'

'Not all of the missing drugs are opiates.' This shift in the direction of the conversation, one that was not signalled, seemingly surprised her.

'No?'

'Some steroids have gone missing, too.'

'Oh?'

'You have an expensive lifestyle.'

'Do I?'

'A nice flat. A very nice car.'

'And? What of it?'

'I understand that you also work as the medical officer at the racecourse.'

Lynette Parker's face darkened and her voice became low, almost guttural. 'So?'

'I was just wondering if anyone ever approached you for help with their performance.'

She stood up at that. Considering the inertial task she had set her musculature, she did so impressively quickly. 'How dare you? That is a completely baseless allegation.'

Beverley's voice was bland. 'It wasn't an allegation. It was a question.'

Realizing her error, Lynette Parker could only mutter, 'Yes . . . well . . . '

'I take it the answer's no.'

She nodded stiffly. 'That's right.'

'Good.' Abruptly Beverley took her turn to get to her feet. 'Thank you for your time. I'll let you get back to your medical duties.'

'Is that all?' This question almost suggested disappointment.

'Unless you have something else to tell me.'

'No. I can't think of anything.'

'Good.' Beverley left the room.

The taxi fare was colossal but Helena thought it worthwhile because she would have had to have taken a train and a bus after a long walk if she had relied on public transport. Even then, despite the feeling that time's winged chariot was not just hurrying near but in sight and bearing down on her, she hung back outside Harriet's house, sitting on a garden wall some 50 metres away, wondering if she was doing the right thing.

As she debated the wisdom of her actions, several people – a harassed woman with two small children, a postman, three elderly couples and a young Asian woman – walked past her, some casting vaguely curious glances at the sight of a well-dressed young woman sitting idly on a wall in the middle of the day.

But she knew that she would not bow out; it was not in her nature, not when someone was relying on her, even if they did not know it. Accordingly, after perhaps an hour, she rose from her wall and walked towards the house.

It was a house with memory. The front door was unpainted wood, intricately carved, grimy and yet not unpleasant; the doorbell was a white enamel button set in a large wooden plate; the windows, ivy-clad, were bleary yet not menacing.

What if she's not in?

She had come all this way and yet only now did this situation present itself for discussion.

The door opened while her mind entered the suspension of uncertainty.

'Helena?'

Harriet looked awful, but delight was overlaid on this foundation. Helena's smile was partly due to relief. 'Hello, Harriet.'

'What are you doing here?'

Which was as good a question as she had been asked for quite a few months. What, in detail, was she doing there? 'I . . . I wanted to see you. After your phone call . . . '

There were bags under Harriet's eyes, a new feature not hidden by cosmesis. 'Oh, goodness! How kind!' She stepped forward and embraced Helena. It was so comforting, so perfect, that it was almost as if Helena's mother had returned.

In the low-ceilinged sitting room, where the scent of furniture polish was like a warm security blanket, they sat and sipped coffee poured from a cafetière. 'You've crept out under the wire, have you?' Harriet's question was playful and gossipy and yet Helena could hear how sad she was.

'There was a power cut and the electric fence went down.'

'Didn't Terry spot you?'

'He was oiling the rack.'

Helena heard something in the laugh that she was certain was genuine delight. 'You're being naughty, I think.' Harriet looked at her severely.

Helena smiled. 'How are you, Harriet?'

'Better for seeing you.'

'Likewise.'

But suddenly, Harriet abandoned the pleasantries, her eyes narrowing above the smile as she asked, 'Are you really better, Helena?'

It was the question of a therapist rather than a friend and it turned Helena from a visiting friend into a patient. Helena, already feeling keenly that she was being deceitful to someone she both liked and admired, found herself skewered on the question. She was sure she was colouring as she replied uncertainly, 'Yes.'

And then she heard herself add, ' . . . for now.'

The environment was distinctly improved, but they might just as well have been back in the hospital, back in the soulless rooms of the unit. Harriet's coffee was excellent – vintage Dom Pérignon compared with the acrid sparkling wine dispensed by the vending machine outside Helena's room – but Helena found herself playing the patient role with disturbing ease.

Harriet had infinite subtlety. '"For now?" What does that mean?'

Something in Helena's head was calculating a way forward, a route through her problem. 'I've found a purpose again.'

'That's good.' No one could have doubted that Harriet was genuine in this sentiment, but she would have been beyond human if she had not then asked, 'What purpose is that?'

Helena suppressed the shame that was generated by her manipulation of the encounter, as she took the opportunity Harriet was giving her. She took it obliquely, however. 'Do you mind if I ask you something?'

Whatever surprise Harriet felt at this question, she was too well-trained to allow it to show. 'Of course not.'

'This may seem to be an odd question, but I need to ask you about your will.'

Perhaps Harriet was now regretting her rush to accommodate Helena's curiosity. Certainly she was frowning as she responded, 'My will? But why?'

Helena's face began to misbehave, the muscles doing their own thing, the blood washing into her skin to warm it, swell it, blush it. She tried to ignore this, tried to ignore the question too, and said, 'Who are your heirs?' She followed this with an assurance. 'It *is* important.'

'Well . . . ' Harriet was still frowning but Helena could see that she had made progress, that Harriet was considering the request. Then, after a brief but penetrating stare at Helena, she took a breath and said, 'Had she lived, Ruth would have inherited . . . '

'But now?'

Perhaps this sounded too eager, for Harriet looked at her again, and hesitated before saying, 'The provisions in the will allow Adam to inherit if Ruth should predecease him.'

Predecease. Helena found this snippet of legal jargon comforting at exactly the same time as she felt panic at the rest of the sentence. Once again, John Eisenmenger's predictions were proving unnervingly spot on.

'Would you tell me why you're asking, Helena?' Harriet's tone was a clear sign that she wanted an answer.

Helena could not lie to Harriet, and she did not have the invention or desire to prevaricate. Even so, she had difficulty framing her reply, was aware that what she was about to say would prove a shock. 'John has suggested that . . . ' She did not exactly pause but she did have to elide a couple of words. ' . . . Ruth's death may not have been entirely natural.'

'What?' Despite this question, it was obvious that Harriet had heard every word of Helena's announcement, a fact that was proved when she went on, 'Not natural? What does that mean?' The coffee was forgotten. 'Suicide? Is that what you're saying?'

Helena felt almost suffocated by her embarrassment. Harriet was reacting badly and she felt as if she were endangering their friendship. All she could do was shake her head and search for words . . .

Meanwhile, Harriet moved swiftly on in her cerebration. Her face told Helena that she had guessed what they suspected. 'Murder?' This was said incredulously.

'It's possible . . . '

'But the post-mortem said it was natural . . . Her heart . . . '

Helena felt miserable, rushed along by events that she herself had forced into a stampede. 'I understand there's some doubt about that.'

Harriet looked at Helena as if she had lately discovered that her visitor was, in fact, Venusian and prone to eating children. 'Doubt?' Harriet sounded affronted that there should be such a thing as doubt about her daughter's death. 'What do you mean?' And then, 'Who? Who are you saying murdered Ruth?'

'We're not certain of anything, Harriet. It's just that John thinks it's a possibility.'

Harriet's eyes had always been pale and clear but now they were *shining*, almost flashing.

But not with joy.

Obviously close to tears, but still thinking furiously, she said after a pause, 'Adam? You think Adam killed Ruth?'

'We don't think anything, Harriet,' said Helena, desperately trying to regain the situation. 'We're just exploring possibilities.'

Her reward for this platitude was a grimace, one that signalled worse to come, despite Harriet's silent and calm contemplation of her.

Helena had once been caught by her father smoking behind the wooden garage beside their house, the one she still dreamed about, the one that had housed his dark green Humber Super Snipe saloon car. Her emotions now were a perfect facsimile of what she had felt then.

Fittingly, Harriet's reaction was much as Helena's father's had been. She did not show her anger, which made it all the worse in Helena's mind. She merely thinned her lips, gave her head the smallest and slowest of shakes, and then stood up. 'I think you should go.'

'No . . . You don't understand . . . '

This time when she shook her head there was no margin for doubt. 'Please, Helena. Do as I ask.' She might have been tired, exhausted by a day's exertion, perhaps sad also because she had discovered that a favoured niece had let her down.

Helena wanted to say something to defend herself, to explain, to cry out, perhaps just to scream her innocence, but she was confined by her own convictions, by the bonds of her illness and its therapy, by sheer, bloody convention. All she found herself allowed to say by these bonds was, 'I'm sorry.'

To little effect, and she saw tears in Harriet's eyes, which made matters worse. She stood up, hesitated because in a dream world she might have said something more, but found that reality was an altogether harsher place to live, and walked out of the room. She was followed by Harriet, who said, as they approached the door, 'I know you mean well, Helena, but you're wrong. Completely wrong.'

Helena turned; if it was to argue, Harriet's expression proved a potent antidote to the desire. She said only, 'I was worried about you.'

There was a small paradigm shift in Harriet's perspective and the sternness left her. She paused, nodded first, then smiled a sad smile. 'I know you were, Helena. But I have lost my grandchild and my husband, and now I have lost my daughter. All I have left is a son-in-law, and I do not wish to lose him.'

'I know . . . '

' . . . *And* I know that Adam is not a killer. I would stake my life on that.'

Helena could only nod, apologize again. Harriet held out her hands – a sign of forgiveness – and Helena took them gratefully. 'I'll be back, soon, Helena. Look after yourself.'

Helena left the house feeling chastened.

It did not stop her wondering if Harriet spoke more truth than she knew when she had offered to stake her life on her certainty of the innocence of Adam Dreifus.

Fifty-Two

The next interview was with Charlotte Pelger. With a smile, she said, 'We meet again.'

She had her hair down and this transformed her face from potentially attractive to something almost luminous. Gamely ignoring this, Beverley said, 'You can't have much spare time, what with a job here as well as at the Grange.'

Charlotte replied somewhat primly, as if Beverley had implied something scurrilous. 'It's not illegal, is it? And I'm not the only one. Daksha does as well.'

Beverley was forced to concede that, no, it was not illegal to have two jobs. 'You have prescribing rights here, I understand.'

'*Limited* prescribing rights.'

Before, Beverley had thought her maternal, probably to a suffocating degree; now she seemed defensive, perhaps unnecessarily so. 'But you have password access to the computer system.'

'Yes.' Before Beverley could ask another question, Charlotte said, 'Dr Dreifus said there were some discrepancies in the drug record.'

'That's right.'

'What sort?'

'It looks as if some morphine and other controlled drugs have gone missing.'

'Well, it can't have been me. I can't prescribe those.'

'I'm afraid that's no alibi.'

'No? Why not?'

'Because the system's been tampered with. Whoever is doing this doesn't need to have full prescribing rights.'

In response, her shrug was theatrical, meant to tell this nosey policewoman that she was entirely innocent. Beverley asked, apparently a propos of nothing, 'Are you married?'

'What's that got to with anything?'

'I don't know. Are you?'

'No.' As if this were a defect, she said it in a defensive tone and then had to explain. 'I'm an only child, you see. My mother developed Parkinson's disease and, of course, I had to help out with the nursing, didn't I?'

Beverley heard a lot of bitterness in that rhetorical enquiry. 'I see.'

'Dad wasn't much use, and then he got cancer of the pancreas.'

What an irritating man her father must have been. 'So you had to nurse both of them?'

She nodded. 'We didn't have the money, you see.'

'Are they still alive?'

A brisk shake of the head. 'No. Dad died two years ago, Mum six months later.' Maybe there was sadness there, but she could not keep the relief away and Beverley found that she could not blame her. The thought of being in such a situation herself made her feel ill.

But she had an investigation to prosecute. 'Did they leave you much money?'

Consternation met indignation and decided to cooperate. 'I beg your pardon?'

'Were you left much when they died?'

'What the hell . . . ?'

'I only ask, because you have two jobs. Presumably, not for fun.'

Beverley had seen happier people with dislocated jaws. 'No. It's not for fun.' She sighed. 'They rented the house and Dad was a hospital porter. Mum, of course, hadn't worked for years.'

'And nursing's not that well paid, is it?'

'You can say that again.'

'So a bit of extra cash would come in handy?'

Consternation had left the room but indignation had its feet under the table and was feeding hungrily. 'What in hell does that mean?'

'Nothing. Nothing at all.'

'I'm not a thief.'

'No? Well, if not you, then who? Someone is.'

'I really couldn't say.' But there had been the briefest of hesitations and there was something about her voice that suggested otherwise.

'No suspicions at all? This is in strict confidence.'

She was definite. 'None.'

'No? Well, fair enough.'

'Sorry.' She did not sound sorry, but in Beverley's experience people rarely did.

'Tell me about Dr Lennox.'

'What about him?'

Beverley smiled in what she hoped was a conspiratorial manner. 'You mentioned the last time we spoke that he was having an affair with Anita Delorme.'

It took a moment, but Charlotte Pelger snapped at the bait with relish. 'Well, it was obvious to everyone, really. I mean, they thought no one knew, but Daksha saw them snogging in a lay-by once, and there was one occasion when I overheard him on the phone to her, and what he was saying to her would have made a rugby player blush . . . '

'Really?'

'Oh, yes.' She was well into her stride now, eating up the ground as she marched effortlessly into the land of scuttlebutt. 'Of course, he recently cooled it.'

This was news. 'Oh?'

'On a couple of occasions I found her crying in the office first thing in the morning. And a couple of days before her death, I saw her cut him dead: she treated him like a dead rat floating in the tomato soup. That made me wonder . . . ' She seemed to have a penchant for ellipsis, and she exuded the scent of prurience like body odour.

Beverley frowned. 'When I talked to you in Anita's office about why she had been unhappy, you said you didn't know.'

She was momentarily nonplussed, then explained airily, 'I was in shock, not thinking straight.' She added, 'I'm sorry.'

'What other gossip have you just remembered?'

Which gave Charlotte Pelger the perfect chance to go off down a different branch of memory lane. 'She wasn't the first one Donald Lennox treated badly. I mean, look at poor Dr Parker.'

Somewhat startled, Beverley suddenly found herself forgetting about Anita Delorme. 'Lynette Parker? You don't mean . . . ?'

A slow and very deliberate nod. 'Oh, yes.' This excited her. 'Mind you,' she added, leaning forward, 'I'm fairly sure it was rather more on her side than his. I don't think Dr Parker's really his *type*, if you know what I mean.' Beverley could guess but she had no need. 'He prefers younger, more aerodynamic models, if you get my meaning.'

It was a colourful description that fitted Anita Delorme well and, as she was neither visually handicapped nor profoundly deaf, Beverley did get her meaning.

'Mind you,' continued the nurse, now enjoying herself so much she had no need of verbal prompts, 'poor Lynette's desperate for anything. Anything at all. Why, there's even been a rumour that she has her sights set on Dr Dreifus. I suppose now he's a widower, she'll really be gunning for him.'

Beverley noted the verb and wondered what it signified: at the very least thoughtlessness, if not a very poor sense of humour. She said, 'When you were younger, you got into a spot of bother, I understand.'

A look of concern and anger passed briefly across Charlotte Pelger's face. 'What do you mean?'

'Some sort of bust-up at a party when you were a student.'

She snorted. 'Oh, that.'

'Yes, that.'

'That was nothing.'

'The police were called.'

'Some silly little tart tried to steal my boyfriend. I objected. She backed off.'

'And by "objected", you mean what?'

'I showed her I wasn't going to be ignored, ridden over.'

'Did you hurt her much?'

'Hardly at all. You must know that the police took no further action against either of us.'

Beverley nodded. 'Her name was Sue Willard, wasn't it?'

'Possibly. It was a long time ago.'

'Do you know what happened to her?'

'Haven't the foggiest.'

Beverley left it at that, but once again the name Sue Willard seemed to be familiar.

The dispensary smelt clean in a way that was unique to industrialized society – in a way that was unnatural – and the air, bereft of anything unpleasant, seemed bereft of life, while the order that was around her only worsened Beverley's impression that she had entered a place that could never be comfortable. Yet the packets and tubs, the varied colours and the sheer order of the place sent her messages that hinted at sweet shops from her past.

Dreifus did not bother to introduce her to the staff: the tall and austere-looking grey-haired woman with half-moon glasses who had been dealing with an awkward patient a few days before, and Daksha Singh.

'Jeanette? Could you show the Inspector where we keep the scripts?'

Jeanette smiled a nervous twitch of the lips. 'Over here.'

Under the counter was a stack of filing cabinets.

'Are these kept locked?'

'Not during the working day, but I lock them every night.'

'Who has a key?'

'I do, and Daksha, of course. And each of the doctors.'

'What about Charlotte Pelger?'

It was Dreifus who answered. 'No.'

Beverley examined the lock. There were faint scratches, but these could be found around all locks. She saw nothing that convinced her that someone had been trying to force it, but it was hardly high security. She reckoned she could have unlocked it in two minutes with a bent paper clip.

Of Jeanette she asked, 'Have you ever noticed anything amiss with the prescriptions?'

'In what way?'

'Out of order, or perhaps something about one of them that you thought odd.'

'No,' she said uncertainly, before adding, 'No, I'm sure . . . '

Beverley turned to Daksha. 'What about you?'

'No, nothing.'

She was punting these questions purely in hope and wasted no time in regret that they failed to produce results. 'Show me where you keep the controlled drugs.'

They were in a heavy steel cupboard that was bolted both to the floor and the outside wall behind; the lock was considerably beefier than the one on the filing cabinet. Beverley could find nothing to criticize there, had not expected to.

'Could you show me the register for controlled drugs?'

Jeanette said proudly, 'We don't have a book, as such. It's all on computer.'

Beverley merely replied, 'Perhaps you could show me that, then.'

Ostensibly, it was perfect. The information was all there and up to date; the last entry had only been twenty-five minutes before.

She announced tiredly, 'I'll need to speak to each of you alone.'

Fifty-Three

J eanette proved to be a good, reliable witness, and completely unhelpful. She had worked at the surgery for sixteen years, and before that for a big chain of high street pharmacies. She was precise and eager to oblige, but she had noticed nothing untoward.

But then, why should she? The beauty of the scam was that no one would.

She did not even, it appeared, indulge in gossip, and Beverley was finished with her in the space of ten minutes.

Daksha was, if anything, even worse. Not only had she
not noticed anything of use, she seemed to have failed to
notice anything at all. She chewed gum constantly (a habit
she had not displayed at Benhall Grange, presumably because
Dreifus had forbidden it) and she gave answers that did not
really inform, that barely filled the gaps in the conversation.

Beverley moved on to more general matters. The dynamics
of life in the surgery were beginning to prove of great interest.
'How long have you worked here?'

'Um . . . a year.' She did not seem to be sure.

'A year?'

'Yep.'

'And what about at Atopia?'

'What?'

'Atopia. Benhall Grange.'

'Oh, the clinic. Um . . . about six months, I guess.'

Beverley did not want guesses, but she made a tactical decision not to pin her witness down. 'Do you enjoy it?'

'I guess.' Daksha, it seemed, guessed a lot.

'Do you get on with Jeanette?'

A shrug.

'She's your superior, isn't she?'

'Yeah.'

'And what about the doctors?'

'What about them?'

'Do you get on with them?'

She paused over this one. 'I don't have much to do with
them.'

'No?' Beverley gave up on subtlety and adopted a more
direct style of questioning. 'What about Dr Lennox? Has he
ever tried to chat you up?

She smiled at this. A thing of slyness. 'Oh, yeah. He tried
it on.'

'And?'

She made a face. 'Do you know how old he is?'

'Older men aren't for you?'

'You must be joking! All that drooping flesh and heavy
breathing? I don't think so.'

'Do you use drugs?'

'No.' For emphasis, she swung her jet black hair in a math-
ematically exact and rather beautiful arc.

'Have you ever used drugs?'

'Never.'

'What, never at all? Not even cannabis, or ecstasy?'

'Well . . . ' She looked sheepish.

'Yes?'

'A bit of E, perhaps.'

'But nothing heavier?'

'No.'

'Do you live on your own?'

A nod.

'What about your parents?'

'What about them?'

'Where do they live?'

'In Hounslow.'

'Any brothers or sisters?'

'One brother.'

'What does he do?'

She shrugged. 'He's a scaffolder.'

'Is he a good boy?'

'Yes.'

Beverley stared hard at her. Only after a while did she say, 'Unless there's anything you want to say to me, I think that'll be all for now.'

It seemed that Daksha Singh had nothing more to add.

The letter to Eisenmenger had been faxed to the general histology office, so that by the time he came to read it, almost everyone else in the department knew its contents. It was from the coroner and it stated in the cold, and therefore menacing, language of the law that an official complaint had been made concerning his behaviour in the case of Ruth Dreifus. As a consequence, the coroner would no longer be making use of his services in the foreseeable future, at least until he had provided a satisfactory explanation of his conduct, and the concerns raised had been dealt with. Just reading the paragraph left him feeling slightly breathless.

The next one was shorter but its punch was even harder.

The coroner had felt compelled to report his behaviour to the police as a possible breach of the Human Tissue Act.

Feeling a little numb and extremely light-headed, he made his way to his office. He had only felt like this once before, when he had been playing open-side flanker in a rugby match at school and had collided head first with the base of the post. When the pain had eventually subsided, the world had seemed that little bit more removed than usual.

He had known, of course, that this was a possibility, but this foreknowledge gave him little balm. It was entirely correct that he had, technically speaking, broken the law but it had been done for a higher good. He was dependent now on Beverley Wharton to come through for him, and there was no balm from this either.

Somewhere inside his head a voice said that things could not get much worse.

It lied.

An hour later, when he had tried but failed to perform some work, the telephone was the first intimation of the fickleness of small voices between the ears. 'Dr Eisenmenger? The medical director would like to see you as soon as possible.' A surprisingly young voice, but one that sounded as if it had quickly learned to enjoy the glory that accompanied the position of PA to the medical director of the Trust.

Eisenmenger did not wish to see the medical director but that did not seem to be amongst the available options. 'Why?'

He knew he would not get a meaningful answer . . .

'He wishes to discuss an important matter with you.'

. . . not that it mattered. He had an unsettling premonition concerning the subject about which he was to be required to discourse. The young voice informed him, 'Dr Montgomery will be available at noon.'

She did not ask if Eisenmenger would be as fortunate and her tone signalled that it did not matter anyway. His debate about whether to disappoint the medical director was not a serious one. What would be the point? He was not about to go on the run, and in deferring the appointment he would only be delaying things. 'OK,' he said. 'Is the meeting to be in his office?'

It was.

She caught Donald Lennox on his way out of the surgery, calling him back politely but commandingly. As he turned, she saw his expression turn from annoyance to wolfish charm. 'Inspector Wharton! I had heard you were on the prowl again.'

'I need to talk to you, Dr Lennox.'

'And that will be a delight, but I have calls to make, I'm afraid. Perhaps later this afternoon.'

'Perhaps now. It won't take long.'

She could see that the no-doubt novel experience of being countermanded produced a degree of dyspepsia, but he showed good grace and said merely, 'Very well. If it can't wait.'

Back in his office, she went through the questions she had asked everyone else, and received the same answers. Donald Lennox had held no suspicions that anything was amiss and was most definitely not the responsible party. He had noticed nothing odd and was stunned to discover that drugs had been going missing. His was a performance to convince that he was an innocent, but his roving eyes that kept snatching glances at her legs gave away the lie of all this.

'Tell me about your last few days with Anita,' she suggested.

Which brought his eyes back to her face. 'I thought this was about drugs, or something.'

'It's about what I want it to be about.' Having pointed this out, she repeated her suggestion.

'What about them?'

'You've given me the idea that everything was just hunky-dory.'

'What of it?'

'Other people have a different idea. They've suggested you were dumping her and she didn't like it.'

His answer was one of evasion. 'I'm not sure I know what you're talking about.'

But he did. She could see it in his eyes. Why, she wondered, did people bother? She put it succinctly. 'You told me it was the perfect relationship, but it wasn't, was it? You were trying to dump her, weren't you?'

He shook his head, but none too convincingly.

'No?'

'We'd had a row. I said some unfortunate things, that's all.'

'And the day she died? Were some unfortunate things said then?'

'I was making it up to her. I had thought it best to let things be, but she was so upset. Distraught, really. I realized then that I had made a mistake.'

'How did you "make it up to her"?'

He raised his eyebrows and asked sarcastically, 'Do I really have to go into the details?'

She snorted. 'Maybe not.' Her perception of the relationship had altered drastically in the last hour; perhaps it had also altered significantly. 'And you "made it up to her" in the woods?'

'Yes.'

She pointed out, 'But you told me that neither of you saw this as anything other than a bit of fun. Now the story seems to be that poor Anita Delorme was rather in love with you.'

'Well . . . '

'Which, I would imagine, would present a bit of a problem for you, what with your devoted wife and all her money.'

'Anita didn't want to marry. That is the truth.'

'So *you* say. I only have your word for that. If she had wanted you all to herself, if she had proved to be a bit more possessive than you had previously imagined, that would present quite a dilemma for you, wouldn't it?'

He was flushed, partly due to anger, partly due to discomfort. 'It didn't happen like that.'

She affected not to hear. 'It might have tempted you to take drastic action.'

'Look, let me say this once and for all. I did not kill Anita.'

Beverley almost believed him, but she was not about to let him see that. 'No? Are you sure about that? Even if you didn't pull the trigger, perhaps you pulled the strings, Dr Lennox. Perhaps you gave her no other option.'

When she left the room, she was well aware that the wolfish charm had gone from his features, replaced by deep anxiety, and she felt good because of it.

She went in search of Adam Dreifus and found him in his office, the door open. She had not expected him to be in a good mood and her prediction was amply fulfilled. He was on the phone, just finishing the call, and she heard through the partly opened doorway, 'OK, Harriet. Thanks for telling me.'

She knocked on the door frame and was invited, in a voice that might have been used by God on judgement day, to, 'Come in.'

His face matched the tone.

'I've finished for now.'

He was distracted; angry, as well. When he asked, 'For

now? What do you mean by that?' it was only after a fight to find enough attention.

'Depending on what the analysis of the computer system tells us.'

'When will that happen?'

'We'll be taking them away as soon as possible.'

That brought him to the present time and present location with quite astonishing speed. 'What? Take them away?'

'We'll have to examine the server to look at the source code for the prescribing system. From that we may be able to tell who altered it. We may also have to look at the hard drives of every computer in the building.'

'You can do that here, can't you?'

'I'm afraid not. The equipment will be taken away.'

'No.' He was shaking his head but this was superimposed upon a general trembling that had taken hold. His voice, though, was quite firm. 'No, you can't do that.'

People were forever saying that to her and she was forever having to correct them. 'I'm sorry, but I can, and I will.'

'I won't allow it. We can't operate without the computers.'

'What happened thirty years ago? Doctors didn't have computers then.'

'You're just being infantile. I tell you, we can't suddenly lose the use of the computers and still function.'

'This isn't a debate, Dr Dreifus. I need to see what's been done to this system, and I will.'

'And what are we supposed to do?'

She thought about his predicament for a few seconds. 'Close the surgery for a couple of days.'

'For God's sake! We can't do that!'

But Beverley wasn't interested. 'What would happen if this place burned down overnight?'

He stared at her, his eyes wide. He did not wish to answer because to do so would be to admit that his protestations were in vain. She left the room, politely assuring him that a team of technicians would be along shortly.

Fifty-Four

In the event, it was not a cosy talk between professionals, a chat about how bloody awful life in the new NHS was. If Harold Montgomery's rather uncomfortable attitude had not told Eisenmenger that there was to be more to the duologue than mutual moaning, then the presence of Simon Bueger, the director of human resources, was a clue he could not miss. It was another bad sign that, having been introduced, Mr Bueger said nothing and did nothing, except make notes.

'I'm afraid we've had a complaint.'

'You don't surprise me.'

Montgomery looked disappointed and faintly disapproving that there was so little contrition on display. Bueger took a note. 'Do you know what about?'

'Probably it concerns the case of Ruth Dreifus.'

'Yes,' he admitted, although it was a reluctant admission, perhaps disappointed that the initiative was not his.

'I did what I did because the cause of death was wrong.'

'Dr Throckmorton thinks otherwise.'

'We'll see, shall we?'

'And there are procedures for this kind of thing. If you think a colleague has made a mistake, you should discus it with him . . . '

'I did.'

' . . . And if there's still a dispute, you should get another opinion.' He had ridden over Eisenmenger's interjection and raced to the end.

'I deemed it a little late for that, given that the coroner had been informed and the body was due to be released for cremation.'

The medical director was a dermatologist, an esteemed body of professionals who, no doubt thankfully, had little contact with the ancient art of morbid anatomy. 'Yes, well . . . ' The unspeaking presence in the corner – almost spectral in the way he remained inert – said nothing and said it very clearly. 'There's also the matter of your conduct in other cases.'

'Is there really?'

A nod. 'Dr Throckmorton is very unhappy about your autopsy practice in general.'

'Snap.'

This time there was a frown. 'I don't think you should be so flippant. These are serious matters.'

'Which is why I did what I did. You surely don't think I would have risked prosecution under the Human Tissue Act if I was having a laugh, do you?'

But Harold Montgomery did not know and was not willing to comment. 'I'm afraid, under the circumstances, that we will have to terminate your locum contract.'

Eisenmenger almost laughed. He asked scornfully, 'Am I supposed to care? That department has serious problems, Dr Montgomery, and sacking me will only make matters worse.'

He stood up, nodded politely but coldly at the still silent but attentive personnel apparatchik, and walked out of the room, his mind almost literally buzzing with anger, anxiety, indignation and, in contrast with all else, relief. He had found his time in the department to be dull, demoralizing and dismaying. Pathology had changed in the years since he had last held a permanent consultant post, and not for the better. It had become formulaic and robotic, a pressurized enslavement, totally bereft of creativity or the spirit of intellectual enquiry. Although considerably better paid than most jobs on a production line, it was in essence now identical to them: life was ruled by targets to be met, by as many sick people to be turned into well people in as short a time as possible.

He returned to the department to pick up his few personal possessions from his office, only to bump into Chloe Branham and Barry Schwartz. Both of them looked across at him and both of them showed embarrassment, she by colouring, he by looking down at the floor. He sailed past them, refusing to mirror their awkwardness, making a point of greeting them by saying in as normal a tone as possible, 'Good afternoon.'

When he was safely in his office, he breathed out long and hard, paused and would have begun collecting his things, except that there came a knock on the door.

It was Adam Dreifus.

'Dr Eisenmenger?'

He was white and trembling. He might have been septic, except that his tone gave away the real reason for his appearance.

Fury.

'Yes, of course. Come in, Dr Dreifus.'

He did so and Eisenmenger, ever the good host, would then have invited him to take a seat, perhaps offered him a cup of coffee, except that Dreifus had something on his chest that he wanted to share.

'Who the hell do you think you are? How dare you go around saying that I killed my wife? Do you know how upset my mother-in-law is? Do you know how upset *I* am?'

Well, yes, Eisenmenger did know, because the evidence was standing before him, steaming metaphorically, and very nearly in reality. But as for the rest of what Dreifus had had to say, he was completely baffled. He had not said anything to anyone . . .

'How?' Dreifus demanded. 'How am I supposed to have killed her?'

Called upon to reiterate his theory, Eisenmenger found that it was not a particularly convincing thing. 'I found a high level of potassium in one of the post-mortem samples . . . '

Dreifus brandished some paper. 'It says nothing about this in the autopsy report. Arnold Throckmorton states quite clearly that it was a natural death.'

'When he wrote that, he didn't know that result.'

'So he agrees with you? He also thinks I'm a murderer?'

Tiredly, Eisenmenger admitted, 'No.'

'That does not surprise me. Arnold Throckmorton is twice – ten times, even – the pathologist you'll ever be. I could not believe that he would be a party to this.'

'Oh, don't worry. He is of a completely different opinion.'

'Well, that's lucky for him, because that means I will be suing only you for defamation.'

Eisenmenger was beginning to feel almost concussed by the day's events, a feeling not helped by his own doubts about the affair, which were resurgent. He felt crushed by circumstances, unable to fight back.

'Look, I don't know where you got this idea from, but I have never said categorically that you murdered your wife.'

'Your girlfriend did.' To which he then added, 'And the police seem to think that her death was not all that it seemed, either.'

Apparently Beverley had been busy. He said in feeble defence, 'All I'm saying is that there may be some issues about the death that require further investigation.'

'Does the coroner think this?'

'No.'

'Well, then, what you believe is not germane, is it?'

Technically speaking, he was absolutely right, but Eisenmenger had gone beyond technicalities. He had to prove that Ruth Dreifus's death was not what Throckmorton said it was, because if he did not, he was liable to go to prison.

But Dreifus had calmed down, at least to the point where curiosity got a look in. 'How?' he demanded.

'How what?' responded Eisenmenger inelegantly.

'How am I supposed to have overdosed her on potassium? Do you think I injected her? Is that it?'

'I don't know how it came about,' Eisenmenger admitted, careful not to give Dreifus ammunition for any lawsuit. 'She was on ACE inhibitors, so there would be a tendency to accumulate potassium. If she somehow came to imbibe a concentrated source of the stuff . . . '

'You think I gave her Slo-K tablets? Don't you think she might wonder why I was asking her to take them?'

'There are lots of ways to give potassium. Not just tablets, but also powders, or sweetened syrups, or even adhesive patches.'

Dreifus looked disgusted. 'So now I waited for her to fall asleep and covered her with sticky dressings?'

'I didn't say that.'

'Is that all you can come up with? What about bananas? They're a good source of the stuff. Perhaps I force-fed her thirty ripe bananas.'

In some desperation, Eisenmenger added, 'There are also issues, I believe, with the death of Edward Melnick.'

At the sound of the name, Dreifus raised his eyes to the fluorescent lights. 'Melnick again?'

'We still haven't satisfactorily explained how he came to take Metformin.'

Dreifus was mocking. 'You think I force-fed him some of those, do you?'

'I'm not saying anything like that.'

'And why? Why should I want to kill him?'

Eisenmenger considered it wise not to go into details. He said only, 'I'm not saying you did.'

This was not supposed to happen. He was a pathologist, a thinker, a boy from the backroom. If he had abstracted – perhaps in more senses than one – the theory that someone had murdered Ruth Dreifus and that Adam Dreifus was the only logical suspect, then he ought to be insulated from situations such as this.

'You're a forensic pathologist, aren't you?'

'Yes.'

'Think you're something special, I understand.'

'I wouldn't . . . '

'Quite the detective.'

'No, not really.'

'No? From what I've heard about you, you regard yourself as some sort of super sleuth.'

'No . . . '

Dreifus advanced towards him, his demeanour suggesting that it was not to shake him warmly by the hand; the throat, perhaps, but not the hand. 'You are going to regret ever even thinking I had something to do with my wife's death. I will be consulting a solicitor and I will take action against you.'

'Look, Dr Dreifus.'

'No, you look, Dr Eisenmenger. You and your girlfriend have caused enough grief already. For your own sake, I suggest you shut up from now on.'

Eisenmenger could not resist asking, 'Is that a threat?'

Dreifus looked murderous for a moment, then turned and walked from the room.

'John?'

'Hello, Helena.'

'Will you come and pick me up?'

He did not understand what she meant. 'Pick you up? Why?'

'I'm coming home.'

'Is that a good idea?'

'It's one of the best ideas I've ever had.'

With which she cut the connection.

Fifty-Five

Grover had something to prove and he was the kind of man who welcomed a hard task. The harder the better; impossible was best of all. What he found during the course of his search of Benhall Grange, he reckoned Fisher would never have found if he had kept looking until the second coming. He would have thought it was rubbish, a small piece of litter, the kind of thing that can be found at the bottom of a million clothes lockers. Just a small silver chad, a tiny circle of foil, nothing significant in the least.

In actuality, Grover almost missed it.

He picked it up, looked at it briefly, screwed it up, then stopped. Two letters had caught his eye, the only two on it. He flattened it out, examined it again. Then, he opened an evidence bag and popped it in, sealing the top carefully.

He might be wrong, but he thought not.

He felt a swelling sense of pride, thought perhaps to contact Beverley at once, then decided not to. He would make absolutely certain of his facts first, then he would tell her in a straightforward and modest manner that he had just cracked the case.

He did not stop to wonder at his desire to please Beverley Wharton, a woman that every cell in his body ought to have detested.

She was waiting in her room, bags packed, dressed neatly, fully made-up. After they had kissed, she said, before he could ask any questions, 'If you take that bag, I'll bring the rest.'

They were in the car before he summoned the courage to ask what was going on.

'I told you, I'm coming home.'

'Against medical advice?'

'Almost certainly.'

'Oh.' He had more to say but could see that it would either be useless, or unwise, or quite possibly both, to proffer it.

There was silence as he pulled away from the parking space and drove out on to the road that meandered around the hospital site. Only when they were on the public highway did she speak again. 'I'm sorry.'

'What for?'

'I went to see Harriet. I expect you know by now.' She went on, 'She couldn't accept it.'

'Maybe she's right.'

She looked sharply at him. 'Do you know something I don't?'

He wanted to tell her his predicament, wondered how she would take it. He did not want to put strain on her . . .

Then again, she *seemed* to be back to normal . . .

Her whole attitude appeared to have reverted to the one he knew, loved and despaired of . . .

'I can't prove it, Helena. Big problem when it comes to murder.'

'He inherits, John. If she dies, he gets the squillions.'

He saw a glowing and growing spark in her, and began to be reassured. It was still with some tentativeness, however, that he told her, 'Beverley's taking the surgery to bits to try to get to the bottom of this drug thing.'

But even the name of her nemesis did not seem to affect her. If anything, she seemed to be pleased that they were being helped. 'Well, I hope she's quick. We don't know how long it'll be before he moves on Harriet.'

He waited until they were back at the house and Helena was unpacked and settled in before telling her of his difficulties. He scrutinized her carefully, analysing her reaction. She was horrified and expressed regret that she had caused some of them. They were on the sofa together, drinking tea.

'I'm not particularly worried about Dreifus – it was just the final thing, coming so soon after being sacked and told that I may have broken the law. He's huffing and puffing, but he'll have difficulty proving his case and will have to spend a lot of money to do it.'

'He might have a lot of money soon,' she pointed out.

'He'd have to be mad to try anything too quickly in that direction.'

'Maybe he is,' she replied bleakly.

'Adam Dreifus may be obsessed, but I don't think he's mad.'

'Well, that's one good thing. I'm fed up with chasing after mad people.'

Helena had gone shopping, displaying great shock at the state not only of the flat's cleanliness but also of household supplies. Inevitably, he fell to rumination on his predicament.

And what a predicament.

He was, after all, fairly certain to be investigated by the police, a new and wholly unwelcome experience for him. Even if he were able to achieve the required standard of proof that Ruth Dreifus had died unnaturally, it might not be enough for him to escape censure at best, a fine and imprisonment at worst.

He was completely dependent on Beverley finding something in the background of either Adam Dreifus or someone else at the surgery, because they were dealing with what was effectively very close to the perfect murder. He had a horrible feeling that the best he would be able to achieve would be circumstantial evidence, and accompanying that fear was the fear that it would not be enough. And then there was the drug anomaly at the surgery. Was that connected? If Edward Melnick had been murdered, then it almost certainly was, but he was not in possession of proof about that death either.

It really was a most slippery case, faint and nebulous, murders done at a distance and seemingly almost by magic, perhaps not even murders. There were no facts, only motives and opportunities, apparently nothing to grab hold of, nothing even to stand on.

Nothing except his own instinct.

He tried to stop all the facts, all the suppositions about the case, from whirling around inside his mind, tried to slow them down so that he could look at them and analyse his feelings towards these curiously disparate, almost mundane entities. He wanted to hear what the voice in his head had to say about each one when it was isolated from its brethren, when it was defenceless against scrutiny.

Firstly, there were the deaths, those of Edward Melnick and Ruth Dreifus: were they murders? That was easy. He had to assume they were, it was *sine qua non*.

Therefore, the questions were, *why* were they done, and *how* were they done?

The *why* was apparently easy. Adam Dreifus was connected to both victims. He had killed his wife because he would then be the heir to Harriet Worringer's will, and he had killed Melnick because Melnick had discovered his illegal drug racket.

But, once the murders were divorced from each other and from their suppositions, the connections seemed to become friable, unable to hold. Dreifus only had a motive for killing Melnick if he were connected to the missing opiates; if he were not, then he had no motive. As for the death of Ruth Dreifus, it was of course conceivable that Dreifus was playing the longest of games, killing his victims in reverse order so that no one would suspect what was happening. If so, it was a fairly pathetic ruse; it was not as if there were sixteen people between Dreifus and the money. Reversing the order of just two killings was hardly the action of a Professor Moriarty.

In any case, Adam Dreifus did not need to play convoluted games with the order of his murders, because he had a way to murder people that was almost undetectable.

Perhaps, then, Adam Dreifus was not the killer.

Which seemed to lead him back to his starting point, because he had just argued himself out of any motive at all. Who else had a motive for killing Melnick and Ruth Dreifus? And, just as importantly, how could they have done it?

If these were murders, and Adam Dreifus were not the killer, then who was, and by what means were the drugs administered? Dreifus was the only one who had opportunity to carry out the deaths . . . surely?

No matter how many times Eisenmenger tried to fight his way out of the thicket in which he found himself, he failed.

Beverley was on her way to the offices of ITD – Information Technology Diagnostics – the company subcontracted by the county constabulary to undertake forensic examination of computer hardware and software, when Grover called her. It was not the first law she had broken when she answered his call on her mobile without the use of a hands-free kit.

'What is it?'

'I've found something at Benhall Grange.'

'Amaze me.'

'A silver foil chad.'

'A what?'

'When you pop a tablet out of its blister pack it's the thing that gets ripped off.'

'So?'

'It came from a pack of pethidine tablets.'

That made her pay attention. The traffic around her became a secondary consideration. 'Are you certain?'

'I've checked with an independent pharmacy. There's no doubt.'

'Where was it?'

'In one of the staff lockers.'

He was teasing her, giving her titbits but keeping her waiting for the one thing he knew she wanted. She played by his rules and kept her temper, but only because as far as she was concerned he was just a dead man wanking. 'Whose locker?'

'Daksha Singh.'

At that moment she nearly knocked over a motorcyclist who had cut in suddenly as the traffic was slowing at a red light. He turned a helmeted head towards her, completely anonymous, almost android and alien, but still able to communicate anger; perhaps it was the only emotion that was left to him to express.

'Are you all right?' Grover sounded almost amused as she swore softly into the phone, so she ignored him.

'Does she know?'

'She doesn't start until four today.'

'OK. I'll be back in an hour or two.'

'Shall I pull her in?'

'No, not yet.'

'But ... '

'Not yet,' she repeated, this time with considerably more emphasis. 'You can spend the time running your checks on her again. Make absolutely sure that she really is as clean as you said she was.'

There was silence, which somehow managed to sound offended and aggrieved, before he said, 'By the way, there's something else.'

'What?'

'Apparently the coroner has lodged a complaint regarding your friend, John Eisenmenger.'

How did he know that John Eisenmenger meant anything to her? She replied mildly, 'He's an acquaintance, Grover.'

'Well, anyway, apparently he may have contravened the Human Tissue Act.'

'Who's handling it?'

'CI Lambert wants us to.'

A bonus. 'Contact the coroner. Get the details.'

Grover was apparently mollified by being given something slightly substantial to do, unaware that she was merely pushing him away with trivia. 'Right.'

She cut the connection and spent the next ten minutes battling with the driver of a white van who had confused driving with stock car rallying. Had she had the time she would have had the greatest of pleasure in pulling him over, examining his van and finding at least ten contraventions of the road safety laws.

ITD occupied a low-rise building on the road that led out of the city and towards Wales. It did not look like much and fitted in well with its neighbours: a small newsagent on one side, a special effects company on the other. Beverley's previous contacts with them had surprised her, because she had expected them to be archetypal computer nerds, and discovered them to be surprisingly sociable, normal and professional. They worked quickly and they worked efficiently. She was confident that they would uncover useful information from the surgery's computer and she was not disappointed.

'It's quite elegant, really.'

These words were spoken by a dark-haired woman of about twenty-five. The accent was soft and liltingly Irish, and she wore thick-rimmed spectacles that somehow did not make her look unattractive.

'In what way?'

'It's just a few lines of code inserted here, here and here.' With a pencil she pointed at a computer printout that, had it been unrolled, would probably have been 20 metres long. What she was pointing at was as meaningful to Beverley as higher dimensional mathematics written in ancient Sumerian.

'And that's enough?'

This was answered with a nod.

'Can you tell who did it?'

'The record of the logon has been erased.'

Beverley sighed. 'Damn.' She should have known that it was never that easy.

'But, yes, I can.'

Which caught Beverley by surprise. 'How?'

'Simple erasure doesn't remove the data, only the address of the data. Even if you actually go to the trouble of wiping the information, there are still traces that, with the right equipment, you can detect.'

'So who did it?'

'The username and password were those of someone called Adam Dreifus.'

Fifty-Six

B everley learned of Grover's second breakthrough as soon as she entered her office. He did not bother to pretend cool insouciance this time; he was excited and he showed it.

'Daksha Singh's brother, Sanjit, has a record of drug dealing.'

She had not even taken off her leather jacket and this news made her forget to do so. She sat in her chair, staring at Grover, trying to assess the significance of this.

'Don't you see what this means?' asked Grover. 'It completes the case against her.'

Still Beverley refused to join in the elation.

'Inspector?'

She said slowly, 'Yes?'

'Shouldn't we pull her in? And her brother?'

Beverley at last reacted: she rose from her desk, slipped off her jacket and hung it up by the door, then turned around to Grover. 'It doesn't make sense.'

Grover was outraged. 'What do you mean?'

'Why should Adam Dreifus be stealing drugs and then giving them to Daksha Singh?'

'Maybe it wasn't him, maybe she stole his password.'

'And how would she do that?'

This obstacle proved a difficult one and he had no immediate answer. Beverley suggested doubtfully, 'Maybe they
were having an affair.'

'What?' It was difficult to tell whether Grover was shocked
merely at the idea of yet more adultery or shocked at the age
difference between Dreifus and Daksha.

'That would explain matters quite nicely.'

It might explain a few other things of which Grover was
ignorant, but she kept her counsel on those.

'But she's so young . . . '

'Old enough to steal narcotics and pass them to her brother,
but too young to have an affair?'

'Dreifus is twice her age. More, actually. I just don't see it.'

He had a point, but it would have required the threat of a
red-hot needle in her eye to get her to admit it. 'Maybe you
don't Grover, but that doesn't mean I'm going to discount it
as a possibility.'

'I just . . . '

'*You* just do as you're told, Grover. I have noted your opinions, so now you can shut up.'

His mouth was opening, so she unholstered the Gatling gun.
'And while we're about it, why didn't you pick this up the
first time you ran checks?'

It proved an effective thrust. Grover could only drop his
head and mumble something that might have been an apology.

To which she said, 'So, when you can function slightly
above the level of the cockroaches in the canteen, I'll listen
to what you have to say. Until then, you will do what I tell
you to do.'

His face became momentarily twisted, assuming something
of the gargoyle about the mouth, but he did not argue, asking
instead in a surly voice, 'What do you want me to do?'

'I think you can call on Miss Singh. Ask her to come in to
the station for a chat.'

'What happens if she refuses?'

'Arrest her on suspicion of theft and dealing in controlled
substances. That should make her cooperative.'

'What about her brother?'

'Have we got an address for him?'

'He was on parole but he's been missing for the past three months.'

'Maybe his sister can shed some light on his whereabouts. I suggest you add that to the list of questions.'

'What about you?'

'I'm going to have a chat with Dr Eisenmenger about what he's been up to.'

'Is that top of the list of priorities?'

She heard sarcasm and reacted badly. 'What the hell does it have to do with you?'

'I don't mean to be impertinent . . . ' She noted that he had at least learned a degree of diplomacy. ' . . . But can't it wait?'

But Beverley knew things that Grover didn't. 'No, it can't.'

She turned away from him, went to the door, then paused. 'One more thing. Find out what you can about a woman called Sue Willard. She was the nurse who had that spat with Charlotte Pelger.'

She left before he could moan at her.

When the door opened and Helena stood there, it was one of those moments that the universe delights in concocting. Beverley had been confidently expecting to see Eisenmenger; Helena had certainly not been expecting to see her least favourite person in the world. Something happened that for the two of them was slowed to the point of congealment, frozen to absolute zero, as shocking as sudden bereavement.

'Oh . . . ' For once, Beverley betrayed her surprise and it gave Helena the chance to recover and, with a frown of distaste, ask imperiously, 'What do you want?' The personal pronoun word was emphasized, much as Lady Bracknell might have done; *better* than Lady Bracknell would have done.

But Beverley had officialdom to fall back on. 'I'm here to talk to Dr John Eisenmenger about a complaint we've received concerning a possible breach of the Human Tissue Act, 2006.'

She even managed to pull herself together enough to show her warrant card.

Helena examined it, presumably just to make sure that Beverley had not been sacked from the police while she wasn't looking, then stood aside, allowing entry.

Eisenmenger was unpacking the shopping. He looked up

as Beverley came in, and was unable to change the expression of surprised guilt before Helena saw it. 'Beverley.'

Helena spoke first. 'Inspector Wharton is here in connection with something about a breach of the Human Tissue Act.' Her tone of voice was faintly disbelieving, almost mocking.

Whether Eisenmenger was going to join in with this pretence was not to be known to mortal mind because Beverley said at once, 'I already know that John broke the HTA and I don't give a toss.'

'So why are you here?'

In a way that was inevitably – calculatedly – going to annoy the lady of the house, Beverley sat down in an armchair. 'Because I need your help.'

Fifty-Seven

C *ough medicine.*
  These two words would not stop intruding on his thoughts, had been doing so for a long time before Adam Dreifus realized they were there. He only noticed them when he hit his thumb with the hammer and swore and sucked it hard. He had been putting up the mirror in the sitting room, a whole marriage too late . . .

He sat down, his thumb throbbing.

Eisenmenger had pointed out to him that potassium supplements could come in many forms, including as a sweet syrup.

Yet that was absurd. Completely absurd. This man, Eisenmenger, was completely and totally wrong. That was all there was to it. Ruth had had a cough. He had always told her that cough mixtures were little more than placebos, a way of making money for the chemists, as useful as chocolate teapots and toy poodles, but she had insisted. She had said they soothed her throat, if nothing else, and would he get her some from the dispensary? What, Ruth had asked, was the point of being married to a doctor if you couldn't get free medicines?

Only he hadn't got Ruth the medicine . . .

She had.

She had volunteered to get him some. She had said it would be no trouble.

What if Eisenmenger were right, though? What if Ruth had died because her potassium had been high, exacerbating the effects of her anti-hypertensive medicine? How could she have ingested so much potassium so quickly? What if the medicine had been somehow laced with the stuff?

The affair was a diversion, nothing more. It had never meant anything, really. Nothing at all. She had had some silly idea a few weeks ago that they should make more of it, of course. But what had she thought? That he was going to divorce his wife and move in with her? It was a bit of fun and, after the tantrums and shouting and crying, he had thought she had accepted that. Had shown a bit of maturity.

Yet he could not stop thinking that perhaps he ought to check the medicine . . .

He found that he was still holding the hammer. He put it down on the floor and went upstairs, searching for the bottle. He remembered it well. Brown glass, full of a viscous liquid. He had never actually looked at the contents.

He found it easily enough. On top of Ruth's bedside cabinet, a plastic measuring spoon beside it. He took it to the bathroom, unscrewed the cap and smelled the contents. It was a sweet odour, faintly fruity.

Then he poured some of the contents out on to the pale cream – 'champagne', he thought it was called – of the basin.

Bright red.

The throbbing in his thumb was getting worse.

He knew at once what was in the bottle.

Kay-Cee-L.

A liquid potassium supplement.

Beverley told them what Grover had uncovered as they sat before her on the sofa. Helena said, 'But that would suggest that Daksha Singh murdered Melnick.'

'That would seem to follow.'

'And if she murdered Melnick, then she also murdered Ruth Dreifus.'

'Logically, yes.'

Eisenmenger was saying nothing.

'Except we can't prove it.'

Beverley shook her head. 'No.'

'Which means that it doesn't help John.' Helena said this in a slightly accusatory tone, as if Beverley had let them down. 'No.'

Had Eisenmenger not been lost in a private place, he might have been astonished to witness unanimity between Helena and Beverley. As it was, he apparently failed to spot this rare and wondrous miracle. Helena said thoughtfully, 'But was she acting on her own, or with Adam Dreifus?'

'The likeliest thing is that it was a conspiracy between them. Lovers clearing the way for future happiness, that kind of thing.'

Eisenmenger said suddenly and from deep concentration, 'It's not as simple as that.'

They both looked at him. It was Helena who asked, 'What do you mean?'

He was still thinking, even as he spoke. 'If we're going to get anywhere with this, we're going to have to make a lot of assumptions and hope to God they're the right ones.'

Since Beverley considered this nothing more than a rather trite truism, she said nothing. Helena asked, 'And?'

Eisenmenger took a while to consider his words. 'It's not just that we have to assume certain things, but we have to move on from those to yet other assumptions.'

This sounded to Helena suspiciously like sophistry, but she knew him too well not to hold her tongue. Beverley asked, 'Like what?'

Eisenmenger suddenly stood up, as if cramp had affected his legs and he wanted to stretch them. He said, 'We have to assume that both Edward Melnick and Ruth Dreifus were murdered. We know how and we think we know why, but perhaps our assumption of who is incorrect.'

Since Beverley had only been assuming that these two had been murdered because Eisenmenger had told her so, she felt slightly annoyed that he was suddenly demoting the thesis from a fact to an assumption. 'What are you talking about?'

'There are several possibilities. Firstly, it does not necessarily have to have been both Adam Dreifus and Daksha Singh. It might have been just one of them.'

Beverley pointed out, 'But the evidence points strongly to Daksha Singh being involved. And it's difficult to see how she could have murdered Edward Melnick and Ruth Dreifus without Adam Dreifus's knowledge.'

He nodded, but it was not a particularly supportive nod and in response he said obstinately, 'Not necessarily. It's quite amazing how good people can be at denying the reality that's kicking them in the testicles.'

'But even so . . . '

He shrugged. 'I don't know for certain, Beverley. I don't know *anything* for certain; I only have assumptions. It's my assumption that he's innocent of this. I have no proof of it.'

'But we know that Dreifus prescribed Melnick tablets for gout – tablets that, it turns out, were for Metformin. And Ruth Dreifus wasn't prescribed any medication at all. It must have been her husband slipping her something.'

But Eisenmenger shook his head. 'Dreifus wrote a prescription. Quite possibly he didn't physically touch the drugs at all.'

'No, but that doesn't exclude the possibly that he took the tablets from the dispensary himself and personally handed them to Melnick.'

'And maybe Adam Dreifus did exactly what he said he did. Maybe someone else gave Melnick the Metformin. Melnick wasn't a bright man, he wouldn't have read the information leaflet. He would have done what he was told to do.'

'Daksha Singh,' said Helena.

Beverley asked, 'What about Ruth Dreifus? How was she given the potassium if not by Dreifus?'

'Potassium supplements come in all sorts of preparations: effervescent and slow release tablets, effervescent powders, even highly flavoured liquids like cough mixtures. Perhaps she was given one of those.'

Beverley said suddenly, 'She'd been under the weather. Dreifus said she had had a cold. He said he had got her some cough mixture.'

'Perhaps he asked Daksha Singh to supply it. In which case, he might not have known what was in it.' Helena's tone as she said this ran from wonder to excitement.

'Maybe. Certainly, we need to get hold of that cough medicine. There may still be some in the house.'

'Suddenly, everything comes back to Daksha Singh, whose brother has a drug connection.'

'And in her locker', added Eisenmenger distractedly, 'you've just found evidence that she was handling pethidine.'

'So, you're now suggesting that Dreifus is innocent and that Daksha Singh did all this – stealing the drugs, murdering two people – completely on her own?'

'It's a possibility that can't be excluded.'

Beverley said in an irritated voice, 'It seems to me that we can't exclude anything.'

Eisenmenger begged to differ. 'The cough medicine may be the key you're looking for. If Dreifus hasn't destroyed it, that's good not only for him, but also for me, because if it contains a lot of potassium it might get me off the hook. Also, it would be very interesting to know who supplied it.'

Beverley looked at her watch. 'We'll hopefully have Daksha Singh in for questioning by now, but she can wait a while. I think a chat with Adam Dreifus might be of value first.'

Eisenmenger walked her to the door, while Helena remained seated. As he let her out, Beverley said, 'Of course, this could be a load of bollocks, couldn't it?'

Eisenmenger smiled. 'Oh, definitely. Complete bollocks.'

'Thanks.'

He laughed. 'Pleasure.'

Fifty-Eight

Adam Dreifus had not felt tension like it for a long, long time – not since his medical finals. And dread, he told himself. Don't forget the dread. That reminded him of the day his daughter had died.

There had been a lot of deaths recently, he now came to realize.

Too many.

Had she killed Ruth? Why, for God's sake? Was it revenge,

or something? To get back at him for refusing to leave her? Had she even, as Eisenmenger claimed, killed Melnick?

That was even more far-fetched . . .

When Melnick had come to see him, oily and disreputable and smelling strongly of last night's alcohol and last month's sweat, he had sent him packing, telling him that what he was suggesting was rubbish . . .

He knew now that it wasn't, though, and she had been most interested to hear what had happened, what had been said . . .

Why on earth would she be stealing opiates?

The doorbell rang and he got up from the sofa almost explosively, trembling slightly. He had to talk to her, find out what, if anything, was the truth of these fears.

Beverley called in at the surgery and was told that Adam Dreifus was at home, studying. Reflecting that she would have rather liked some time at home 'studying', she got back in the car and drove to his house. She did not tell the station what she was doing

It was a minor matter.

Eisenmenger could not stop thinking about the case. He was wrong. He knew that he was wrong but not how he was wrong; nor did he know why he knew it, except that what Beverley had said had made him think again, reassess some of the assumptions he had been making.

For half an hour he tried to spot which assumption was slightly wrong, which one did not quite interlock with the others and then, quite suddenly, he saw what it was.

The murders had been a thing of beauty, of subtlety and lightness. Was it really likely that someone of the age of Daksha Singh had done them? He had never met her – and perhaps he was therefore wrong – but he could not see these crimes being carried out by someone so callow.

What, then, of the evidence against her?

A single speck of silver foil. Something that might easily have been missed, but something that also pointed straight at a likely suspect, one with a brother who had a record of drug dealing.

What if it were planted evidence? If so, it was a thing of supreme subtlety and lightness of touch.

Something, indeed, exactly like the murders.

He knew then that Daksha Singh was innocent.

But there was more. Suddenly there was so much more.

Involuntarily he said, 'Suppose I was right. Suppose he doesn't know?'

This was quite sudden. Helena had her eyes closed, had been almost asleep. 'What?' She thought Eisenmenger sounded a little agitated.

'Supposing Dreifus doesn't know.'

She brought her head forward off the back of the chair. 'What are you getting at?'

She had been wrong. Eisenmenger was *very* agitated. 'If Dreifus didn't know, what does that suggest to you?'

Of course, she did not really know what he was talking about; she rarely did. 'That he's innocent.'

'But what about the murderer?'

She tried, but failed, had to shrug. 'I still don't see, John.'

'If I'm not deluded, if I'm anywhere near the truth, Daksha Singh is innocent and someone else killed two people, one of them the wife of her lover, and she hasn't told him. You don't do that for someone you quite like, someone you think of as an acquaintance.'

Helena began to see what he might be trying to say. 'She's obsessed with him?'

He looked at her, his face grim, almost terrified. 'More than that,' he said simply. 'She's mad.'

Fifty-Nine

The doorbell's ring was not answered.

Beverley looked around the large front garden. There were three cars in front of the garage, one of which she recognized as belonging to Adam Dreifus. She did not recognize either of the others. One was presumably his wife's, and she idly wondered whose was the other. She turned her attention back to the house.

Perhaps he got fed up with studying and went for a walk.
She tried the doorbell option again, with identical results.
He could be in the back garden, out of earshot.
She walked to the left, where there was a path that curved around the side of the house.

The back garden was wide but not long. It was reasonably tidy, although the lawn needed mowing, and it was also empty. The back door, though, was open.

She looked at it for a moment, then decided that even if Adam Dreifus were not at home, she should investigate to ensure that burglars were not busying themselves inside, and walked towards it.

She poked her head inside and heard a phone ringing deeper within the house.

If not Daksha, then who?

From what Beverley had said, there were two other, more or less likely suspects. Charlotte Pelger and Lynette Parker. Neither had an obvious motive for stealing drugs, but both had opportunity and both could conceivably have become obsessed with Dreifus.

Was there anything he had missed that might tell them who was the murderer? He sensed that time was running short, but he sensed also that he had missed a thing of great importance.

Suddenly something Rose Melnick had said came back to him. As the words formed again in his head, he realized that a tiny part of him had thought at the time that here was an oddity, but he had ignored it.

Yet within a second it blossomed into a hugely significant thing. Perhaps into the answer they had been seeking. He thought about phoning, decided to drive.

He said to Helena, 'Come on.'

'What now?'

He was already walking out of the flat. 'I'll explain in the car.'

Sixty

The phone stops ringing, but not because it has been answered. Beverley knows she should call out but she is spooked and does not want to. Why she is spooked is difficult for her to say and she does not waste time analysing it; she is spooked, and that is enough to go on. She knows that police officers, like soldiers, who rationalize their fears away have an unfortunate habit of going to meet their maker. It is probably just an empty house and she will have to face Adam Dreifus and his anger when he returns from posting his letter to discover an uninvited police inspector poking around in his sock drawer and leaving dirty footprints on his shag pile.

There is a groan from deep within the house.

And still she does not call out.

She does, however, increase her pace. Into the hallway, briefly into the downstairs cloakroom, before the groan again; it is clearly from a doorway to her right. She debates for a second whether to open the door slowly or suddenly, then takes a deep breath and flings it open.

It crashes against a heavy piece of furniture but Beverley does not turn her head, is not even aware of the noise, for the scene in front of her demands all her of attention, every thought, every sense.

There has been a bloodbath. Litres of bright, viscous red on the carpet, splashed on the walls, on the mirror; the dainty three-piece suite with its rather chintzy fussiness has been soaked.

Yet that is not the most arresting thing, for sitting on the sofa is a couple.

Sitting side by side, upright and for all the world as if they were discussing the tribulations of the Conservative Party or the woeful performance of the England cricket team, are Adam Dreifus and Charlotte Pelger.

Both of them are blood-drenched, but Dreifus is stilled,

whereas Charlotte Pelger is moving slowly. A quick survey of the room to ensure that they are alone, then Beverley strides across to them, and kneels down. Dreifus is dead, a conclusion made obvious by the number of cuts she can see and by the four depressed fractures on the top of his head; a carving knife projecting from his neck and a hammer on his lap are an unneeded confirmation of his physical state.

Charlotte Pelger is only half-conscious. There is too much blood on her for Beverley to see any cuts or stab wounds. Her head is lolling. 'Charlotte?'

The eyes open slowly.

'Who did this, Charlotte?'

She does not hear at once and Beverley asks, 'Was it Daksha Singh?'

A slight widening of the eyes as she nods almost imperceptibly.

'Where are you hurt?'

But in response to this, nothing. There is nothing.

'OK. Stay there. I'll call for help.'

She stands up and turns away as she reaches for her mobile phone.

The same lift, the same drear surroundings, the same atmosphere of cold, aggressive uninterest. If it had seemed to take a long time to reach Rose Melnick's flat before, this time it seemed to Eisenmenger to take an aeon. They rang the doorbell and stood side by side before the battered door, the boarded window.

It seemed for a few seconds that she wasn't in and Eisenmenger was already calculating where they might find her, had opted for the nearest public house, when the chains were rattled, bolts and locks released.

'Yes?' She was drunk, peering out at them, seeing first Helena, then Eisenmenger. Her expression became fearful and angry when she recognized him. 'What do you want?' she demanded.

'One question, Mrs Melnick. Then I'll go.'

'You said I killed my Eddy . . . '

'You didn't, Mrs Melnick. I know that now.'

'I had the police round.' As if the neighbourhood had never seen such a thing.

'I'm sorry, Mrs Melnick. Really, really sorry.'

Helena watched this contrition with silent interest. She was fearful it would not be long before he went down on his knees. She said, 'My name's Helena, Mrs Melnick.'

The Melnick eyes were turned upon her and seemed to like what they saw. She smiled. 'Hello, dear.'

'We're really sorry to be bothering you at this time, and we fully appreciate what you must have been going through, but we have to ask you just a few more questions.'

Rose Melnick stole a glance at Eisenmenger. 'What about?'

'About the time shortly after Mr Melnick died.'

'What about it?'

It was cold and very draughty on the concrete balcony but neither of them suggested that this was a conversation better conducted indoors. Helena asked, 'You mentioned that someone came from the surgery, with bereavement leaflets.'

'That's right. I was touched, I was. I reckon a lot of doctors wouldn't be so caring.' Another glance at Eisenmenger, as if to suggest she wasn't so far from one such as she spoke.

'Who was it who came?'

Mrs Melnick then held her breath; indeed, she held it for so long they began to fear for her welfare, until she let it out with an explosive sigh and shook her head. 'Do you know? It's gone.'

'You can't remember?'

'Not at the moment. I remember how nice she was, though. She . . . '

It was Helena who got the interruption in first. 'She?'

A nod in reply. 'She made me a nice cup of tea.'

Eisenmenger asked, 'So whoever it was went into the kitchen?'

'That's right . . . Oh, I wish I could remember her name. It's on the tip of my tongue.'

'Was she in there alone?'

'Yes. She insisted that I sit down while she made it for me.'

Eisenmenger and Helena exchanged looks. Mrs Melnick went on happily. 'She couldn't find the sugar. I heard her opening the cupboards and went out to find it for her.'

'And you can't remember her name?' Helena almost begged this.

'Mmm . . . ' Less effort was likely to be expended in a

breech birth but, it seemed, with more result. She began to shake her head again . . .

Then, 'You know . . . It was a nurse . . . '

'Pelger? Charlotte Pelger?'

Rose Melnick broke into a wide grin, all the better for displaying her unclean false teeth.

'That's her!'

Sixty-One

B everley dials 999 on speed dial and has the phone to her ear when she hears the slightest creak from behind her. She turns just as Charlotte Pelger is bringing down the hammer in a short, sharp arc, aiming at the top of her head. She drops the phone, twists, feels the crunching thud as the hammer crashes into her scalp and skull. She feels the shudder through the bones of her head, her facial bones rippling. She hears the crunch of her cranium as it fractures. Just before darkness sucks her in, she thinks she hears a near ultrasonic ringing in her ears, and she knows there is a berserking pain that wants to eat her alive.

She falls to her knees and it is only a low-level instinct that makes her try to rise again, but her legs have gone, are now merely appendages. She is helpless and Charlotte Pelger, her eyes curiously bright as she peers from a blood-covered face, stamps down on the mobile, then raises the hammer again.

Grover had located Daksha Singh when she came home from the gymnasium. She was shocked to be confronted by a policeman, and astonished to be arrested on suspicion of stealing controlled drugs from the surgery. She was so astonished that she did not protest and Grover noted this, drawing conclusions as to her guilt. When he had returned to the police station and had deposited the suspect in one of the cheerless interrogation rooms, he looked around for Beverley but without success.

He asked Fisher, who was doing the crossword, if she had phoned in.

'Nope.'

He looked at his watch. She had been gone for three hours; a long time but not unduly long. He then phoned her mobile.

No answer.

From directory enquiries, he found a number for John Eisenmenger, then rang that with an identical response. He then rang the surgery and discovered that she had called in earlier, asking about Adam Dreifus. Upon learning that Dreifus was at home, he duly called him. He listened to the unanswered ring for a few minutes, then put the phone down.

Fisher said, 'You know you asked me to find out what I could about Sue Willard?'

'Yes.'

'Here.' He held out a single sheet of paper for Grover to take. While Grover read it, Fisher said, 'She was knocked down not long after that business with Charlotte Pelger. Hit and run.'

The phone rang again and Fisher picked up the receiver, then waved at him and held it out. 'It's a call.'

'For me?'

'For the lovely Beverley,' said Fisher with a leer.

'Who is it?'

'A lawyer. Helena Flemming.'

The name meant nothing to him. He took the receiver impatiently. 'Yes?'

'Can I speak to Inspector Wharton?'

'She's not here. I'm Sergeant Grover. Can I help?'

'I need to get a message to her.'

'I can take it.'

'It's very urgent.'

Grover was becoming exasperated. Would this woman never reach the point? 'What is it?'

'Tell her, we were wrong. Tell her, it's not Daksha Singh. The one she wants is Charlotte Pelger.'

Grover was completely mystified. 'Not Daksha Singh?'

'No.'

'Who are you?'

Helena could have done without this. 'I'm a lawyer.'

'What do you know about Daksha Singh?'

She ignored him, said, 'It's very important. Could you tell her that?'

Grover was shaking his head but he said tiredly, 'I don't know where she is at the moment, but when she makes contact, I'll tell her.'

He cut the connection, wondering what was going on, convinced that he had been kept in the dark yet again.

'They don't know where she is.'

Eisenmenger did not like that; did not like it at all. He drove in thoughtful silence. It was Helena who said, 'She said she was going to see Adam Dreifus.'

'That was some time ago.'

There was a short pause before Eisenmenger glanced across at her and she said, 'Do you know his address?'

'He's a doctor. He'll be in the phone book.'

'I'll ring directory enquiries.'

Sixty-Two

'Sarge?'

'What is it?'

'Something funny's going on.'

Grover did not have much of a sense of humour at the best of times and this was not the best of times. Daksha Singh was proving a vociferous detainee who, having initially come voluntarily to the station, had now decided she wanted to leave. In order to keep her there, he had therefore had to formally arrest her. The consequence of this was that Daksha – displaying an unexpectedly profound knowledge of the laws of the land – had demanded the presence of a solicitor. He had thus far refused, but the pressure was telling on him.

Where was Beverley Wharton?

'What is it?'

'Ambulance control report a call twelve minutes ago. It was from Inspector Wharton's mobile.'

Grover jumped. 'What did she want?'

'They don't know. The line went dead before anything was said.'

He began to panic. What should he do? What could he do?

Fisher said helpfully, 'Would you like me to run a trace on the signal?'

'Isn't that Beverley's car?' Helena points at a blue coupe.

Eisenmenger murmurs, 'Well, she's clearly still here.' His voice, though, is questioning.

The drive is large but it is starting to look crowded. Besides Beverley's car, there is a smart and expensive looking German saloon that Helena recognizes as belonging to Adam Dreifus, a smaller but new hatchback, and a beaten up Mini Metro. It is beginning to rain, a fine drizzle that is almost unnoticeable yet oddly uncomfortable.

Helena says, 'Presumably she won't want to be disturbed. Perhaps Dreifus has confessed.' This facetiously.

There is a pause before Eisenmenger replies thoughtfully, 'Perhaps.'

But then there is an interval in which they both just look at the house, and the drive, and the garden, and the cars . . .

Helena says thoughtfully, 'I wonder why she hasn't answered her mobile?'

'Bad signal, perhaps. Or maybe her battery's flat.'

She looks across at Beverley's car. 'She's been here a long time, hasn't she? If she came here straight after leaving us.'

Eisenmenger, who is getting out of the car, says, 'We should tell her about Charlotte Pelger.'

Helena calls him back before he shuts the car door. 'John?'

'What is it?'

But she does not know exactly what she means to say and therefore cannot properly articulate her fears, murmurs only, 'Is this wise?

He replies, 'Is what wise?'

'Interrupting them.'

'What harm can it do? If he's confessed, I don't suppose he'll suddenly recant just because the doorbell rings.'

He turns and crunches gravel as he goes to the front door. She wonders why she is so worried.

Eisenmenger rings the bell, waits for five seconds, then knocks loudly.

He rings the bell again. She gets out and stands on the gravel drive, looking around.

He looks across at her, calls, 'It's a big house. Maybe they're round the back.'

Eisenmenger begins to walk around to the back of the house.

Helena finds herself walking over towards the garage as Eisenmenger turns the corner.

She looks at her watch to see that it is five twenty.

The beaten-up car is a hideous shade of yellow, not helped by splashes of rust on the paint of the bonnet and wings, and wheel arches that have turned the corner and are now splashes of paint on rust. The tax disc tells her that it should have been renewed two months before. She peers in through the glass and sees that the interior is a mess: crisp packets, sweet wrappers, pens and old magazines cover the front passenger and rear seats. Idly she looks over the titles: *Puzzler, Coffee Break, Heat* . . .

'I love him so much.' Charlotte Pelger is looking at Adam Dreifus over her right shoulder as she speaks. She displays sorrow and devotion and regret. 'We were a perfect couple.'

Beverley hears noises, little more. Charlotte Pelger does not care. Her audience is in her head, a far more appreciative audience than any she might encounter in the real world.

She turns back to Beverley. 'He wasn't good enough, though.' This is delivered through a hiss.

All Beverley can do is watch, but it is from the bottom of a dark well, and there is a mist all around her.

'He betrayed me. He betrayed us both.'

Beverley is aware that blood is coursing – not dripping, not trickling, but *coursing* – down her neck. She opens her mouth, discovers though that it remains closed, that her body is no longer hers to command.

'I only killed them for him.'

The doorbell rings and Charlotte Pelger freezes. She does not look round, just stares at Beverley, as if she were responsible. Then there is a knocking on the door. Still she does not react, just waits; waits and stares at Beverley, hammer in hand. There is another ring.

When nothing more happens after a few moments, she relaxes and she smiles. It is not a smile one would like to meet down a small alley at night. Continuing exactly as if nothing had interrupted her, she says, 'I thought that after I had freed him from his wife, he would rejoice.' She laughs. 'Rejoice! Nothing to stop us now. His burden gone forever!'

With shocking suddenness the smile vanishes, a frown takes its place. 'But he let me down. I did it for him, for us . . . I'm not a murderer, you know. I don't go around killing people for fun. Melnick was a danger to us, he had to die. Adam's wife was just a frump. I know, he told me so.'

She crouches down in front of Beverley, who is on her knees, fighting unconsciousness, barely winning. With an earnestness that only the insane can conjure, she says, 'They weren't in love any more. He'd said that ever since the first time, when we realized what we meant to each other. How could we be together while she was still around?'

A deep sigh, the kind that a misunderstood philanthropist might produce. 'It was supposed to be a surprise.' She looks back to the corpse.

'Such a wonderful surprise,' she says sadly.

Eisenmenger has reached the back of the house, surveys the garden and decides it unlikely that Beverley and Dreifus are taking tea under the spreading chestnut tree, as the drizzle has become distinctly heavier. The kitchen door is open and he walks towards it.

He steps inside.

Beverley does not hear the footfall that sounds at the back of the house, but Charlotte Pelger does. She walks to the door at once, pauses merely to glance back at Beverley, her face bearing no expression whatsoever, then passes into the hallway.

The hammer is in her hand.

. . . Nursing Times.

Helena turns, looks back towards the house and, as she begins to run, calls out, 'John!'

Sixty-Three

Eisenmenger has looked around the kitchen and is just starting to wonder if the entire house is empty. Standing at the door from the kitchen to the hallway, he is completely unaware that, hidden from view behind the open door, there is a figure. He is just filling his lungs to call out for Dreifus when Helena's call, faint but full of urgency and fear and dread, comes to him. He turns and thus the hammer catches him only a glancing blow, half ripping his right ear off, slamming then down into his shoulder, cracking on to his collarbone.

Helena runs around the side of the house, hears Eisenmenger cry out, tries to accelerate and almost slides to the ground on the loose gravel. She bursts through the kitchen door just in time to see a middle-aged woman, covered in blood, standing in the hallway and raising a hammer over the kneeling form of Eisenmenger. His head is down and there is blood flowing with enthusiastic abandon from the side of his head as he clutches his shoulder. He is facing the carpet, almost as if he is concerned that it is going to be ruined by so much haemoglobin, and he is seemingly unaware of what is about to happen.

'No!'

Helena rushes forward, arms outstretched, and charges over Eisenmenger into Charlotte, sends her staggering back to collide with the side of the stairs that lead up to the first floor.

But having done this, Helena does not know what to do now. Surprise was her best weapon and now it is gone; and then there is John, clearly badly hurt and in need of attention.

Charlotte has no such quandary to wrestle with. She has not dropped the hammer and has not been seriously injured by the fall. She therefore rises to her feet, on her face an expression that has gone beyond determination and reached fixation. She has the hammer in both hands, a club, and she moves forward, eyes only for Helena.

There is little room in the hall and John Eisenmenger is effectively blocking, both physically and morally, her escape to the kitchen. To Helena's right there is another doorway, the door ajar, and Helena moves towards it, but Charlotte is closer and moves at once to block this escape. She even smiles.

Then she stands there for a moment, eyes first on Helena and then on Eisenmenger, who is trying to stand up but is so stunned that he is only partially sensate.

'You won't make it,' she assures them. 'Not the both of you.'

Helena says, 'Neither will you.'

This is ignored. 'Which is it to be? You, him or both of you?'

Which, of course, is no question at all.

Helena wants to run, feels she is certain to die, but has always been a person who believes in 'doing the right thing'.

She steps forward, her gaze upon the hammer, saying nothing.

Charlotte begins to swing the hammer in front of her, her arms outstretched. The arc brings the head of the hammer crashing into the wall on her left, tearing the nice wallpaper. with its small pink and green flower motif, leaving perfectly circular depressions in the dusty white plaster beneath. The noise is loud and booming.

Charlotte moves forward, one small step at a time.

Helena, eyes still on that hammer, waits for it once more to be partially embedded in the wall, then rushes forward and tries to grab both the hammer and her assailant's hands, but Charlotte, with insolent ease, lashes out towards her with the hammer and catches her hand a bone-splintering blow against the wall that causes Helena to screech and jerk it back.

Charlotte just carries on, swinging the hammer lazily.

Helena has little room left. She is only 2 metres or so in front of Eisenmenger, who has collapsed into a semi-sitting position.

In desperation, Helena tries again to grab the hammer again, but has to do so now with her other hand. Her clumsy attempt is easily avoided by Charlotte, who grabs her wrist, holds it for a second and then squeezes it, her nails breaking Helena's skin.

All the while Charlotte is silent and Helena is panting and making small squeals.

Helena begins to kick out, but Charlotte does not seem to mind. It is as though the place where Charlotte is living is not affected by anything that Helena can do, as though it is physically elsewhere. The blows may land but they mean nothing, merely striking flesh that does not feel. Her eyes in that blood-covered face do not leave Helena's face, have about them an enquiring look as if she would quite like to know what Helena is thinking but is far too polite to ask.

Abruptly, Charlotte twists Helena's hand and arm, forcing Helena down to the floor. Once she is down far enough, Charlotte uses all her weight to push Helena further down so that she is on her knees and Charlotte is standing above her. She is only small but then so is Helena, and Charlotte has the advantage of being insane.

Helena knows what is coming next and is frantically trying to free herself, but her arm is almost breaking and her other hand is useless. She is almost bent double so that she can see the skirting board and, at the periphery of her vision, John.

'John!'

She can surely only have a moment or two left. John is heavily concussed and there are prodigious quantities of blood on the carpet around him.

'John! Please!' As if he were just being recalcitrant, having a tantrum.

She feels Charlotte's position shift slightly as she lifts the hammer.

The grip on her wrist loosens just a fraction.

Maybe she can wrench her hand free.

She does not wait for the optimum moment, fearing that it will never come. She jerks her hand as much as she dares, tries to twist her body to lessen the pain . . .

And fails.

Charlotte's grip reasserts itself and Helena is not free.

The scream is an eruption, assaulting her ears, high and horrible and rising, yet even as it does so, dying.

Helena even hears that at the end of it, as it fades, there is the faintest syncopation of a gurgle.

When the hammer falls, it strikes her painfully on the small of the back, but it is a pain that she welcomes. The grip on her wrist is loosened and her arm is allowed relief, just before Charlotte falls both forward and slightly to her right, landing heavily on the backs of Helena's legs.

Helena looks up to see Beverley leaning on the door frame, a confection in blood, on her face a look that displays a battle between concentration, bleariness and suffering. When she looks down at Charlotte, she sees a long knife, perhaps a carving knife, protruding at an acute angle from her right flank, pointing upsides towards the middle of the chest.

Then Beverley, without a word, begins to vomit.

Sixty-Four

Beverley came out of it the worst. She had a depressed fracture of the skull with some consequent intracranial haemorrhage; she required neurosurgery and several weeks of convalescence and recuperation. Eisenmenger was severely concussed and had lost a considerable amount of blood; he also required plastic surgery to reattach his ear. Helena told him that they were no longer quite equal in appearance – the right was higher than the left – but he could not see it. She herself had compound fractures of three long bones in her hand, which was painful and inconvenient but she counted herself fortunate; the orthopaedic surgeon warned her of the possibility of arthritis in later life.

They went to see Beverley in the convalescent unit. Helena went not without mixed feelings, but aware that she could not ignore what had happened, what Beverley had done. Eisenmenger kept his feelings to himself.

They found her fully dressed, her hair cut far shorter than usual. She also sported a large, rectangular dressing on the side of her head, held in place by an elasticated bandage.

'The bastards shaved my head and now they've given me this fashionable headgear,' she said drily, without being asked. 'Still, you should have seen me a couple of weeks ago.'

'Suits you,' murmured Eisenmenger, although his tone was ambiguous.

Helena said, 'How much longer will you be in here?'

'They say another two weeks, provided there are no problems.'

'Then what?'

'I'll be off work for several months, apparently. Seems they're afraid I might start having fits and disgracing myself in public.'

'Best to be safe.'

Which platitude brought the conversation to a juddering halt, as platitudes often do. They were in an atrium, with grey light filtering in between trees and shrubs; there was even a pond with a fountain. Beverley asked Eisenmenger, 'How did you know?'

'Know what?'

'That she was bonkers.'

'Oh . . . '

'After all, she covered it up spectacularly well.'

'Well, I began to wonder what, if all my assumptions were right, someone like Charlotte might be like, what her frame of mind might be. The more I thought about it, the more it seemed to me that here was someone fixated on Adam Dreifus. For her to kill two people without telling him what she was up to seemed the act of someone who has lost normal values.'

'You can say that again. According to Lambert, her house was a shrine to him.'

Helena asked, 'Were they lovers?'

'They'd had an affair, but it had been going nowhere for months and was gradually petering out. I would guess that as far as Dreifus was concerned, it was a little light relief. Presumably Charlotte never got over it, though.'

'So why did she kill him? And in such a manner, too.'

Eisenmenger said, 'Because I truly think that Dreifus was ignorant of what she had done. His was a masterpiece of self-deceit. When, though, he discovered the cough medicine was in fact potassium supplement, he could no longer pretend to himself that things were all right. I assume Charlotte had provided him with it; Ruth Dreifus had probably asked him to get some from the dispensary – why should she pay for it? – and he had asked Charlotte. Charlotte knew exactly what medications Ruth was already on, saw that a little extra potassium might do the trick, and handed it over. It was in a brown glass bottle so Adam Dreifus never saw its colour, but even if he had, he still might not have guessed.'

He turned to Beverley. 'I'm still not sure how she managed to get Melnick to take the Metformin.'

'It seems that Mrs Melnick had forgotten a few essential details. When she was shown a picture of Charlotte Pelger, she recognized her as the nice girl who had come round from the dispensary with her husband's tablets. When Adam Dreifus had seen Melnick the first time, it had been to discuss the drug discrepancies, probably Melnick suggesting that he might quite like to make a contribution to his retirement fund. In the meantime, Dreifus tells Charlotte about the conversation . . . '

'Did Dreifus know about the irregularities already?'

'We don't know. If he did, we can find no evidence that he was involved directly. Perhaps he indulged Charlotte. Who knows?'

'What happened after that initial conversation?'

'Melnick had a repeat prescription for anti-inflammatories for gout. He gets this filled out but Charlotte tells him that one of his usual tablets isn't in stock. She promises to get him a substitute, even offers to bring it round to his flat. "It's on her way home." What she gives him is Metformin, without a prescribing leaflet. I don't supposed Edward Melnick ever read one of those in his life.'

'And she just waits,' said Eisenmenger thoughtfully. 'She knows from Dreifus that Melnick is a very heavy drinker. Sooner or later, he'll have a couple of those tablets while he's got a sky-high alcohol level, and . . . '

'But if she loved him so much – enough to murder two people – what happened?'

Beverley knew, had seen it before. 'Dreifus led her to believe it was love between them, probably as part of his seduction technique, but love is a two-way thing and I don't suppose he was ever serious about it. A bit of recreation. Unfortunately for him, Charlotte had different ideas. She fell in love. She fell so in love that she fell out of the bottom of it and into obsession. Stalker territory.

'So she killed. Even killing Melnick I would guess was

rationalized in her mind as having been done for Dreifus, saving him from the disgrace, or some such. Certainly the murder of Ruth Dreifus was to release him from his prison.'

Eisenmenger interrupted. 'Melnick was employed because Ruth Dreifus suspected her husband was having an affair, and he was, only not with Anita Delorme as she thought. Perhaps Melnick said something in his conversation with Dreifus about that, or perhaps Charlotte was afraid that Ruth might have been given hints about the drugs.'

'Maybe. But what I think is certain is that Dreifus, having discovered his squeeze had been going around getting rid of people, got rather upset. He remonstrated with her, which, were he now around to look through the retrospectoscope, he would have been able to see was not a wise move.'

'She went berserk,' concluded Helena.

'And then some,' agreed Eisenmenger. 'She broke. She had expected, I would say, gratitude, if not congratulation. Instead she got the realization that he was a shit.'

'She had a history, I think,' said Beverley thoughtfully, which surprised both of them. She explained about Sue Willard. 'There's no evidence that Charlotte Pelger had anything to do with the hit and run, but I'd put money that either she was driving or she paid for it to be done.'

Helena remarked drily, 'Not a woman to cross, then.'

Eisenmenger frowned. 'How does this tie up with the other case you were investigating? Anita Delorme's death?'

'It doesn't. There's no evidence that anyone else was involved in her death. She killed herself, probably because Lennox was dumping her and because her little scam was about to be exposed.'

They left her after an hour because Beverley was tired and, despite herself, Helena felt a bond with Beverley that she did not like but could not deny. It was with something approaching genuine gratitude that she said, 'Thanks for what you did.'

Beverley's face was stony as she said tersely, 'No problem, It's what I'm paid for.'

'Well, anyway, as I said . . . Thanks.'

'If you'd do me a favour in return, it would be much appreciated.'

'What's that?'

'I killed someone. In this wonderful world we live in, that makes me a bad person unless I can prove otherwise.'

'But she'd already sliced one man like a cucumber, hit you on the head with a hammer, almost done the same to John, and was about to batter me to raspberry puree.'

Beverley shrugged. 'Doesn't matter. The Police Complaints Gestapo have already been in contact. I'll need you to stick up for me. They'd like to make sure there was nothing else I could have done.'

It was Eisenmenger who pointed out, possibly somewhat unkindly, 'It's the law, Helena.'

She did not trust herself to reply for a moment. Then she said simply, 'Don't worry, Beverley. I'll tell them.'

And just to prove that bygones were not completely bygones, she added with a tight smile, 'I believe in making sure the truth is told. I'm the last person to pervert the course of justice.'

Left alone, Beverley sighed. 'Touché, Helena. Touché.'

And without any irony at all, she reached for the phone and dialled a number. After a short pause, she said, 'Paul? It's Beverley.'

A pause. 'No, don't worry, I'm fine.'

Another pause. 'I've been thinking about what we were discussing.'

Again. 'I want you to do it.'

Once more. 'Paul, the shit was told that I might be in danger, and couldn't be fucked to do anything about it, and that's just the last in a long line of things he's done to me. He deserves it. He deserves everything that happens to him.'

She listened some more. 'I'll be very grateful, Paul.' She did not use any emphasis at all, did not need to.

The pause this time was quite short but it started with a sigh in her ear. 'Thanks, Paul.'

She put the phone down and smiled a secret smile.

Epilogue

When Grover was summoned to Lambert's office, he did not know what to expect and had he been given a thousand years to come up with possibilities, he would still not have guessed what was about to happen to him.

Operation Ore had come across his name. He was accused of downloading pornographic images of children, and the gentlemen who sat in Lambert's office wanted him to take them to his house where they would confiscate his computer and go through every inch of his house looking for incriminating material.

Grover was outraged, was sure it was a mistake.

Grover was about to be a very astonished man.